When Canaries Die

Books by Luis Figueredo

When Canaries Die
Breaking Arrows
Dime

For more information
visit: www.SpeakingVolumes.us

When Canaries Die

Luis Figueredo

SPEAKING VOLUMES, LLC
NAPLES, FLORIDA
2025

When Canaries Die

ISBN 979-8-89022-226-8

For Sully, the world's greatest Newfie, whose constant warmth and companionship I could not repay even with a lifetime of dog treats and belly rubs. But I'll try anyway.

Acknowledgments

My first manuscript, *Dime*, gathered dust in the den, until my daughter Jordan put me on the path of waking up at four in the morning to write about Pierce Evangelista and his next legal challenge. She took it upon herself to publish it, and stoked my desire to keep writing.

I want to thank the loves of my life, my awesome wife Maria and my children, Erik, Toni, Jordan and Maddox who fill my heart with joy every day.

To my mother, who gave me the gift of dreams and the opportunity to realize them. To my sister, my biggest fan. Your courage and perseverance has been an inspiration to all of us.

To my publishers Kurt and Erica Mueller, and the team at Speaking Volumes, once again thank you for doing a great job. To my editor for your superb advice which made sure my story was the best it could possibly be. To Patricia and Amy and the entire team at AME for all your hard work.

Last but not least, my friends, Hernan Organvidez for answering my sophomoric questions about police procedures and investigations and Yami Pereyra Diaz for our enlightening conversations about the challenges her parents faced when they crossed the Rio Grande with an infant dreaming of a better life on American soil. To J.C. Canabal for your boundless energy, insight and being a great sounding board. And of course, Connie Diaz for your exuberance and humor.

"The single biggest threat to man's continued dominance on the planet is the virus."

—*Dr. Joshua Lederberg - Nobel Laureate*

Prelude

Kayapo Indian Village, Brazil

Doctor Sophia Wild, a major in the U.S. Army, and a senior physician, watched helplessly as the young girl curled up on the cot convulsed. Her tiny arms and legs riddled with lesions oozing pus spasmed, and her head lurched as another seizure swept over her body. Blood mingled with pink froth sprayed out of her mouth each time the virus planted its death kiss, and her lungs struggled to expel the buildup of fluid that was overwhelming them.

The girl's coughing fit and the sound of choking was muffled by the hazmat suit Wild was wearing. The respiratory disease swept over the isolated Indian village situated on the edge of the Amazon Rainforest like a tidal wave gathering power and size, killing more than three-quarters of the tribal members who displayed flu symptoms in less than two weeks. From a sneeze, a cough, or by speaking, airborne particles containing the virus floated unseen in search of new hosts.

The makeshift clinic was the largest hut in the village. It had been used as a meeting place for village men to discuss community issues. Now it contained twenty hospital beds, all filled with people awake but far from lucid and in various stages of the illness. Their ultimate fate was unknown.

Sophia stood by the young girl's bedside as the girl started to cough again, staring down at the girl's blood now spattered on her gloves. The virus took healthy adults at about the same rate as children and the elderly. Very soon, the girl would be added to that reckoning. Beyond keeping victims as comfortable as possible and treating secondary infections, there wasn't much the doctor could do but let the virus run its course.

When the girl's coughing fit subsided, Sophia left the gloom of the clinic to make a call. The number of people contracting the respiratory virus was doubling each day, and she desperately needed medical supplies and more doctors and nurses.

She walked for twenty minutes, about a hundred yards up a steep hill until she was safely outside of the village before taking off her respirator and dialing her boss on the satellite phone.

It took her several minutes before she could reach him at the U.S. Army Medical Research Institute of Infectious Diseases. Colonel Bernard Cone, the commander in charge of Medical Research, struggled to hear her.

"How's it going down there, major?"

No one was watching, so Sophia allowed herself a frustrated frown. "I've never seen anything like this. This virus is just as contagious as COVID-19, but far more deadly. The mortality rate is about ninety percent. We lost seven patients yesterday, and eleven today."

Before sitting behind a desk, Bernard had been at ground zero for the West African Ebola outbreak, the 2009 swine flu pandemic, and the Haiti cholera epidemic. The memories of those experiences still clung to his mind and still came to him in his nightmares.

"This is hell and we're losing," Sophia added.

"Is it contained?"

Sophia let out a long-exasperated breath as she surveyed the village below her. It wasn't much to look at. About fifty huts resembling beach sheds made from mud walls and tightly thatched rooms made from the leaves of palm trees that extended to the horizon in every direction. The huts formed a giant circle. Just beyond the village was the Xingu River. "We have no way of knowing for sure."

Bernard continued to hold the phone to his ear but stopped listening. Instead, he played out worst-case scenarios in his mind.

"What are you doing to keep the virus contained?"

Sophia snapped. "Everything I can think of, but it's not enough. We've got the identified victims quarantined. But their numbers are increasing every day and we have nowhere to put them."

Bernard tried to maintain an air of calm. "So, what you're saying is what you're doing is not working."

"I have no way of knowing if we've isolated the virus. Many of those that aren't sick leave every day to gather food. Some of the villagers travel along the river to the other villages. I can't convince them to stay put."

The idea of the virus spreading made her stomach roll over. "If they've come in contact with the virus, they could have traveled to other villages and infected others before becoming symptomatic. I have no way of knowing."

"We can't risk another pandemic," he said in obvious reference to the COVID-19 outbreak that crippled the world.

"This would be much worse," Sophia interjected before falling silent.

Sophia took a moment as she thought about her experience combating the virus over the last few days. Based on the number of people exhibiting flu-like symptoms, vomiting and diarrhea after exposure, she guessed that the incubation period was about two-to-three days. Patients developed lesions all over their bodies only hours after exhibiting flu-like symptoms. Their bodies rapidly deteriorated and by the second day after becoming symptomatic, their eyes hemorrhaged. And after a few days, their internal organs shut down. "This virus is not like anything I've seen in my lifetime."

"If this virus is as contagious and as deadly as you say, we can't risk letting anyone leave the village. We have to keep it contained," Bernard insisted.

"I don't know if we can," she admitted. "I'm almost out of supplies and I'm here with one nurse and one kid fresh out of med school. I'm not even sure where this disease came from or if it's already spread to the other villages."

"Major—"

"I'm not done, Bernard. This virus is extremely aggressive. I don't have the resources to be sure, but from what I can tell, it attacks the lungs and the kidneys first. The kidneys are shutting down within hours of the patient showing symptoms."

Bernard fell silent, trying to think the situation through. It wasn't hard. He'd faced similar situations and prayed that the dense jungle served as an adequate buffer between the village and the rest of the world.

"Gather samples and get your team ready for extraction," he said.

"Extraction?" Sophia felt her mouth go dry. "What the fuck are you talking about, Bernard?"

Even from three thousand miles away, she could feel his deep sigh. "You're describing a virus that could wipe out a billion people. Standard operating procedure is to incinerate the village. The operation has been endorsed by POTUS. I'm sending a chopper. Have your team ready to leave in three hours."

"Bernard, there are people in the village that haven't been infected."

The line went dead, and Sophia dropped the phone.

Suddenly, she felt utterly defeated and unsettled. Sophia kept her mask off as she started the one-mile trek back to the village, stopping several times to throw up. When she reached the outskirts of the village,

Sophia wiped the sweat and vomit from her face and put her mask back on.

She opened the door to the clinic and waved her team over.

"Pack up the blood samples. We're leaving in two hours," she ordered with more than a hint of distaste.

Doctor Petersen tried to discern whether she was joking. The nurse was too stunned to react other than just stare.

The young doctor's expression went from confused to defiant when he realized that Sophia was serious.

"No way in hell we're leaving these patients," he snapped.

"Stand down, captain, these orders came down from the president himself, so move your ass and be ready to rendezvous with the chopper in two hours." Sophia's face had become a dead mask. The only thing she couldn't hide was her own disgust.

* * *

The outside roar of the chopper intensified as it touched down just outside of the village perimeter. The loud thumping sound of the rotors brought the curious villagers out of their huts.

Sophia and her medical team jogged, heads down towards the chopper with their medical equipment in tow. When they were all safely inside, Sophia motioned to the pilot to start climbing. Seconds later, the helicopter was airborne. Captain Petersen's eyes seemed full of hate.

Shaking with fear, Sophia looked through the window at the tiny village as it grew smaller by the second. In a few hours, all the men, women, and children, those infected by the virus and the uninfected, were going to die. No one would survive. There was no plausible way that she could ever come to terms with her government's decision. She prayed silently, asking for forgiveness for the innocent lives that were about to be forfeited.

Chapter One

Washington D.C.

When the plane began to descend, Pierce Evangelista turned to Moses Black, sleeping next to him in the window seat and gave him a nudge.

"Wake up. We're about to land."

Mo's eyes fluttered, straining to focus. Pierce glared at his friend and mentor with inquisitor's eyes. He stared into Mo's eyes that once struck fear into his adversaries. They were missing the confident glint bordering on insolence that made people turn away, uneasy if they looked at them too long. Mo had grown visibly older since the last time Pierce had seen him. His cheeks had hollowed and as he struggled to unfasten his seatbelt, his right hand trembled.

"Are you sure you're up for this?" Pierce asked him.

It had been two years since Mo and Pierce had worked together. After beating the Department of Justice and securing the Kialegee Tribal Town's rights to their Oklahoma reservation, Mo retired to his house on Hutchinson Island, and a life of flowered shirts, loafers and 9 A.M. tee times.

The eighty-three-year-old gave a frustrated shake of the head. An old warrior, desperate for one last fight. "What are you talking about? Mo asked. "Of course, I am. I've had a two-year sabbatical, and I'm ready to get back in the game," Mo declared, anxious to get a bit of chalk on his cleats.

Pierce nodded subtly. A gesture that said he wasn't convinced.

During his fifty-plus-year career, Moses Black had been one of the shrewdest and most successful lawyers. A tough as nails trial attorney that left no stone unturned and took no prisoners. Unlike Mo, Pierce deployed a different strategy towards resolving conflicts. His touch was deft and tactical, almost ninja-like, leaving no evidence that he was responsible for pulling the strings behind the scenes. Mo's approach was more like carpet or saturation bombing, scorched-earth warfare. Mo likened trials to combat, and he reasoned that the most effective way to win was to destroy the enemy's ability to wage war. He was the grand master of the mind game. His tactics were deliberate and relentless, psychologically weakening the will of opposing counsel.

Pierce preferred an intellectual approach. He believed in mastering his opponent's position. He zeroed in on their motivation, objectives, and their legal argument. He would absorb every possible detail, no matter how seemingly mundane. When he was finished, Pierce used his superb intellect, unusual powers of observation, and mastery of the law to systematically whittle it down until there was nothing left but a nub.

When Pierce was a first-year associate at the law firm, Mo recognized that he was better than everyone else. The most experienced and prodigious lawyers at the firm could not match the quickness of his mind. The young litigators in the firm were brought along slowly and deliberately. They were trained how to build a case and pound the other side into submission. An approach Mo excelled at. Mo, however, recognized Pierce's analytical mind and talents were rare. Instead of bringing him along slowly, he made him his second chair at trial and nurtured Pierce's creativity and versatility instead of disregarding it. Mo's decision to trust a first-year lawyer with the responsibility reserved for a junior partner was unprecedented and ruffled more than a few feathers. When questioned by the firm's leadership committee, Mo pushed back and said, "You don't make Da Vinci or Michelangelo go to art school. You put a brush in their hands and let them fucking paint."

Mo and Pierce were more than a formidable duo. They were unbeatable. Something U.S. Congresswoman Ana Rodriguez recognized, and the reason she had asked them to fly up to Washington.

They stayed seated as the other passengers prepared to disembark. Once the plane was almost empty, Pierce grabbed his bag from the overhead compartment, and Mo followed suit. They kept a leisurely pace towards the baggage claim area. There they were met by an impeccably dressed young man.

"I trust your flight was a good one." He smiled, shaking Pierce's hand and then Mo's.

"It was fine. Good to see you, J.C. How's your mom transitioning to Washington politics?" Pierce asked.

A condescending smile played at J.C.'s lips. "Stepmom," J.C. corrected him. "Going from mayor of Miami-Dade to one out of four hundred and thirty-five members of the House of Representatives is not an easy transition. The congresswoman is learning to adjust to being a smaller fish in a much bigger pond."

They followed J.C. to a black Escalade parked in the loading zone. About forty-five minutes later, the driver pulled into the underground parking of the Rayburn House Office Building and stopped in front of the elevator.

"This is us," J.C. said.

They rode the elevator to the third floor. Pierce wondered why the congresswoman declined to discuss the matter on the phone and insisted on a face-to-face meeting.

After exchanging a quick greeting with the congresswoman's assistants, J.C. led Mo and Pierce to Ana Rodriguez's office.

"Thanks for coming," she said, striding across the carpet to give Pierce a quick kiss on the cheek.

"It's our pleasure, congresswoman," Pierce smiled.

"Ana, please. No need for formalities," she shrugged and turned to Mo. "Pierce has been helping me since I first got into politics as a councilwoman in Doral."

"Yes," Mo smiled in a way that suggested he remembered and shook the congresswoman's hand.

"And how are you Mo?" she asked in a tone that suggested that she wasn't dispensing with normal pleasantries.

"Well, now that I'm retired, I'm switching from drinking coffee to alcohol much earlier in the day," he said.

The remark elicited a flicker of a smile from the congresswoman.

"Something to look forward to," she said. "I'm hoping that I can talk you into putting your retirement on hold. I could really use your's and Pierce's help."

Mo's face perked up at that.

"If there's nothing else, congresswoman," J.C. said. His body language suggested that his involvement in the meeting was done.

"I believe I have everything we need. Thank you."

J.C. smiled vaguely and swatted Pierce on the arm as he brushed by him and disappeared through the door.

Pierce's eyes took in the empty space on the wall and a similar sized portrait of the president on the floor leaning against a bookcase, as he took a seat on the sofa. Mo poured himself a cup of coffee from the carafe sitting on the table and took a seat in the chair across from Pierce and next to Ana.

Ana wasted no time launching into the reason she needed their help.

"The Department of Homeland Security and the Executive Office for Immigration Review are making it impossible for migrants to be granted asylum. Meanwhile, parents and children are living in a sea of tents on land contaminated with feces because there are no public toilets." Ana's jaw tightened. "The camps are an outgrowth of the president's

Remain in Mexico policy, which has caused the encampments to swell to 15,000 migrants."

After years of working with Ana Rodriguez, Pierce had come to know her body language. She was pissed as hell but was maintaining a calm exterior.

"Senator, Amanda Cortez from Texas has taken up the mantle in the Senate and a group of us in Congress have condemned the administration's harmful policies that have dismantled the asylum system."

Ana explained that their efforts at introducing legislation that expedited hearings and treated asylum seekers like human beings were being met with fierce opposition from an endless parade of senators and representatives who blocked the vote by extending the debate on the measure.

"The situation on the border is deteriorating before our eyes . . ." Ana's voice faded for a moment. "The conditions in the makeshift tent encampments are deplorable and our government turns a blind eye." A familiar sense of fury and helplessness rose in her.

Pierce nodded thoughtfully, but didn't immediately speak. The description played in his mind like a homemade movie. He'd seen similar conditions in the refugee camps of several countries when he volunteered with the International Relief Teams after graduating from college. He had gotten his hands dirty in more countries than anyone could count.

"We're pushing as hard as we can in the Senate and the House, but the president's minions don't let us get any traction. I'm afraid that without your help we won't have any chance," Ana said with utter finality.

Pierce could see that Ana had learned the hard way that the weight of the game at this level was much different. Despite her good intentions, a political solution without a lawsuit challenging the legalities of the government's actions had little chance of success.

Mo put his coffee cup down on the table. The calculations started behind his eyes, but they took longer than they used to.

"We can look into filing a lawsuit against the Department of Homeland Security, and Citizenship and Immigration Services for injunctive relief," Pierce began.

Mo nodded and turned his head, so he was looking directly at Ana, "If we can convince a court that the United States' immigration practices violate U.S. law, you might have the leverage you need to force a vote on your legislative reforms."

The congresswoman leaned back in her chair, suggesting that she wanted them to lay out their strategy further.

Pierce obliged. "We are going to have to dive into the details. The objective will be to prove that the United States is guilty of violating both U.S. law *and* international human rights laws by carrying out policies that undermine our non-refoulement obligation."

Mo added to Pierce's thought. "To be successful, we'll need to document the living conditions in one of the encampments."

Ana considered that for a moment. "Senator Cortez's office works closely with the National Immigrant Justice Center and the American Civil Liberties Union. We might be able to use her contacts to get you access to someone with knowledge of the camps."

"We're also going to need to interview people that were forced to return to their countries," Mo stressed. "We need to present a complete picture. Not just how the current rules are responsible for untenable conditions, but we also have to establish that those conditions are directly responsible for refugees returning to countries where they face torture, inhuman or degrading treatment, punishment and other irreparable harm."

"The senator should be able to help us with that as well," Ana said with more optimism than she actually felt. Ana's left eyebrow arched in a curious expression. "Okay, but realistically, how long will it take before we can get in front of the judge?"

Pierce thought about it for a few seconds while Ana observed him. "We don't know exactly," he said. "It's going to depend on what we find when we get down there, and how cooperative the people at the camps are."

Ana exhaled a tired sigh. "Meanwhile, the numbers in the camps continue to grow and the lack of clean water and functioning toilets is a perfect recipe for the spread of disease."

"Best-worst-case scenario," Pierce interjected. "While it's a long shot, with any luck, you may not need to wait until we go to trial."

Ana's mood shifted from frustration to cautious optimism. "Well, that's clearly best case. What's the worst case?"

"We lose," Mo said.

Pierce's mind ran through a half-a-dozen possibilities. "There are ways to ratchet up the pressure on the Hill before we step into a courtroom."

Ana had a pretty good idea what Pierce meant. "Are you talking about using the media?"

Pierce nodded. "After we file the lawsuit that details the conditions in the camps and the human rights violations, we'll circulate it to the leadership on both sides while simultaneously leaking it to the media. We start our media blitz with a press conference with you and Senator Cortez. Then we launch a full-frontal assault on social media."

Mo agreed with Pierce's strategy. "Voters are increasingly getting their news and information from social media platforms. Elected officials and their staff constantly review posts on Facebook and Twitter. If the vast majority of tweets, Facebook posts, pins, or other content on these sites express strong opinions condemning the government on this issue, word will spread on the Hill. I suspect that Democrats and Republicans on both sides of the issue will look to the Department of Justice for guidance. If our lawsuit has the scale and precision we're planning on, justice won't be able to guarantee them a win and you may be able to cut a deal before we ever get to trial."

Ana nodded. "This is more political than legal. The president won't like the optics of losing and having a court condemning his administration and throwing out his asylum policies. He'll look to congressional action to mitigate the risk by not letting that happen on his watch."

Mo glanced at Pierce, whose expression said differently. "That should put the Democrats in a position to exact meaningful concessions, and if Republicans aren't willing to go along with it, the president will suffer the consequences if he loses," Mo said to Ana.

"This could work," Ana replied, suddenly hopeful.

Pierce nodded as well, but internally he wasn't as confident as they were. The president did not always yield ground, even when it was smart to do so. He didn't care about public opinion. All he cared about was guaranteeing himself attention and adulation with his base.

One option was for his supporters in the Senate to negotiate a settlement prior to a court ruling and salvage as many inequitable policies as possible; or they could roll-the-dice and go on the offensive by doubling down on the exclusionary practices. In Pierce's experience dealing with narcissists with power, the second option was definitely in play.

Chapter Two

Belo Monte hydroelectric dam site near Kayapó Indian Village

On the thirteen-hour bus ride home, Claudio Sousa felt like he was coming down with something. One minute he was sweating, the next minute he was freezing. Over the last couple of days, he noticed several of the workers at the construction site had dry coughs and runny noses. He was careful to stay away from them, but the worker housing at the job site consisted of very cramped conditions, part barracks, part locker room with terrible ventilation.

He was glad his three-week shift was over. He'd been on the road nearly nine hours, with four hours to go before the bus pulled into Belem. Claudio was feeling general discomfort all over. He had promised his little brother that he would make it back in time to take him to the Clube de Remo futbol game against their biggest rival, Paysandu. The winner qualified for the championship round of the *Campeonato Brasileiro Série C.*

For the past week, life in Brazil's largest city in the region revolved around the match against Paysandu. The game dominated every topic of conversation around the city. News and politics took a back seat. It didn't matter that crime, unemployment and corruption were climbing and Brazilians were all feeling the pain; what mattered was that the Remo futbol club was one win away from going to the championship round.

Claudio took a sip of water and mopped his brow with his shirt-sleeve. He was sweating again. He shook it off and told himself he'd be fine after a few hours' sleep. With a little rest, he'd be good to go for the game. He was almost as excited as his little brother. The road sign told him that Belem was just under two hundred kilometers away.

He had just under three hours to go. He reclined the seat as far as it could go, closed his eyes, and passed out. The changing engine noises, corners and frequent stops and turns as the bus navigated the city's streets woke Claudio and told him they were close.

Claudio stepped off the bus, his brow and neck glistening with sweat. The stink of the hot dumpster garbage produced a wave of nausea. As the shadow of the bus pulled away, Claudio summoned the strength for the long ten-block walk home, which seemed more daunting with each passing minute. The streets were lined with shops and merchants busy preparing for the morning flurry of activity. About half of the shops which would normally be open were closed, signs prominently displayed in their windows, *"Fechado para o jogo,"* ("Closed for the game.")

He willed himself forward, repeatedly telling himself to tough it out. All his little brother had talked about for the past two weeks was the game against the Remo futbol club's hated rival, and Claudio wasn't going to disappoint him by letting a bug he caught at work stop him.

Claudio turned up a narrow street and navigated the wooden walkway made from rotting planks. His progress was slow, like a man in the ocean being pummeled by the incoming tide. The cold sweat penetrated his shirt like it wasn't there, but he ignored it. Another twenty yards to go before he was home.

The pink door to the turquoise shack Claudio called home flew open the moment they spotted him. His twelve-year-old brother, Rafa (short for Rafael), intuitively picked his way, landing on the sturdiest planks as he hurried to greet him. A solitary gasp slipped out of his mother's lips when she first laid eyes on her eldest son's pale face and red-rimmed eyes.

"*Filho, voce esta horrivel*," she said, unable to mask her concern.

Claudio managed a weak smile, careful not to get too close to his mother. He didn't want to risk her catching whatever it was he caught at work. "Eu vou ficar bem. Vou me lavar e estarei bem para ir ao jogo," he said, reassuring her that he would be fine and just needed to wash up before leaving for the game.

Shivering, Claudio stepped into the bathroom and looked at himself in the mirror. He grew slightly concerned at the sight of the red blotchy rash all over his face and neck. The thought occurred to him that he should go see a doctor, since whatever he caught could be more serious than a simple flu bug. He could hear his mother talking to him through the bathroom door. Telling him to forget about the game and go to bed. A few hours wouldn't make a difference. He'd take his little brother to the game and see a doctor first thing in the morning after a good night's sleep.

Claudio splashed water on his face. He was relieved that the nausea had passed. He covered his mouth and nose with a bandana, and made his brother do the same before leaving for the stadium.

Outside the stadium, Claudio and Rafa passed endless rows of hospitality tents, sponsored by Sony, Samsung, Michelin, Gillette, and many others with their corporate logos branded on them. There were live cooking stations, DJs playing samba music, and bars throughout the tents. They came across lots of fans wearing blue and white soccer jerseys with the home team's emblem; and a sprinkling of the rival team's color-schemes. The atmosphere was loud, boisterous, and decadent, like that of Brazil's legendary *Carnival*. The feeling of being a part of a 40,000-people-strong-party gave Claudio a surge of adrenaline that flooded his body with enough energy to give him a temporary reprieve and the strength to navigate the waves of screaming and sing-ing fans, some headed to the game and others there just for the party.

Claudio finagled decent seats on the side of the field where Belem would eventually score the winning goal. He had paid a month's salary for them, but he knew it would be a once in a lifetime experience.

Midway through the second half, Claudio felt a wave of nausea building that he didn't feel would pass. He told Rafa to stay put while he went to the bathroom. Rafa nodded, never taking his eyes off the action on the pitch. Claudio put one hand on the handrail to steady him-self and staggered up the stairs towards the bathroom. The sickness rose up like a big, unstoppable wave. A spasm gripped his body, and he projectile vomited onto spectators seated to his left. He could tell he wasn't done and dropped to his knees with his head down to avoid splattering anyone else. He tried desperately to make it to the bathroom, but he told himself that this was good. His body was trying to get rid of whatever he had caught. He felt two security officers trying to help him to his feet as the crowd gathered around him. Claudio heaved two more times. He knew something was horribly wrong when he saw blood on the ground. Before losing consciousness, he handed his ticket to one of the security guards and pleaded with him to find his brother.

Chapter Three

Matamoros Camp – on the U.S.-Mexico border

Maggie Malone, an attorney in the Houston office of the American Civil Liberties Union, was assigned to pick up Pierce and Moses in Brownsville and take them to the Matamoros Camp. She eased the Ford Explorer through the clogged checkpoint at the U.S.-Mexico border.

"That's the camp just up ahead," she said, pointing to the thousands of makeshift shelters made up of tarps and trash bags clustered at the edge of the Rio Grande River. Each tent, on average, was home to four or five people. The camp was massive, tarpaulins stretching out as far as the eye could see.

Mo wrinkled his nose at the sour, musky smell that permeated the SUV as they drew closer, while Pierce listened to the hum of the wipers as they worked to clear the droplets of rain from the windshield. The large numbers of people milling around with forlorn faces and broken eyes rivaled those of the raindrops.

"How many people are living in the camp?" Pierce asked.

"We're up to 17,000. Primarily from the Northern Triangle countries, Nicaragua, Guatemala, El Salvador, Honduras, and Mexico." There was a sigh, and then Maggie added, "Between fifty-to-a-hundred more every day, most victims of unimaginable trauma."

Mo pinched his nose. The stink was overpowering. "Why does it smell so bad? Don't they have bathrooms?" He nodded with a hint of disgust.

A thunderstorm had flooded the encampment, turning the beaten-down grass into mud. Pierce visually scanned the squalid conditions and shot Mo a quizzical look that said, '*Really?*'

Maggie didn't appear to mind the question. "There're 10 portable toilets for 17,000 people. They use a wooded area nearby as a makeshift bathroom. When it rains, it smells particularly bad, and it's been raining all morning."

Mo looked out the window and watched a small crowd move, never stopping for obstacles but swirling around them as they made their way to the river. His nostrils flared. "It smells like a petting zoo mixed with hot wet garbage, topped off with a large helping of shit and piss."

Surprise registered on both Pierce's and Maggie's faces. "That's oddly specific," she laughed.

The rain slowed to a light mist. They all got out and waded in about fifty feet. The unholy mix of thousands of unwashed bodies, rotted food, and human waste assaulted Mo's senses like tear gas. Mo tried not to swallow.

People were gaunt and moving as if on autopilot. Pierce noticed a small group huddled together, taking turns charging their cellphones from the extension cords that ran down from a light post.

Mo stopped to look at children on the side of the muddy path: some sitting, left to watch over their families' meager personal possessions; others sleeping on wet blankets in the middle of brackish water. Since, his retirement, Mo's mind didn't fire on all cylinders until much later in the day and at least four cups of coffee. But as he stared at the garbage bags held together with sticks, stones and metal rods, and children clearly suffering from lack of food, he was uncomfortably awake.

Pierce squinted at the swell of humanity crammed into an unsustainable situation. He wanted to remember every detail.

Maggie continued the tour, walking them down near the river's edge. "Because there's no running water, people have to wash in the river, putting them at risk of drowning or getting sick from being exposed to the sewage from the camp."

Maggie kept walking. "Women are especially at risk of sexual violence, given the lack of toilets and lighting in the camp. Foot soldiers of the drug cartels patrol the camp looking for women and girls to kidnap and sell to brothels on both sides of the border."

Over the last week, while waiting to make the trip down to visit the camps, Mo had given up golf in favor of his new obsession with learning everything he could about the camps. He had read every article he could find surfing the internet. But nothing he read prepared him for what he was seeing. Mo looked stunned. "How long have most of them been here?"

A frustrated expression fell across Maggie's face. "Some have been here for weeks, up to a few months waiting for asylum. They're put in illegal limbo. Some stick it out, and others give up hope and leave."

A frown creased Pierce's brow. He was accustomed to bad behavior in politicians, but this had to be the worst in his career.

They walked another thirty feet, and Pierce caught sight of a young woman and her baby angling toward Maggie from the right. Maggie smiled and hugged the young woman.

Her hair was tangled, framing a gaunt face and eyes that had witnessed more atrocities than any human should suffer. It was an expression Pierce was familiar with from the refugee camps where he had volunteered in Bangladesh and Syria.

"This is Yamilet," Maggie said. "She and her young son arrived from El Salvador a month ago. They fled the horrific violence from the gang war between MS-13 and Barrio 18. Yamilet and her son arrived upriver at Reynosa, where they asked for asylum and were told by U.S. officials to wait in Matamoros. She was assured that there would be a shelter for her and her child. Now she begs every day for a tent while she waits for her asylum interview."

Yamilet didn't understand English but could tell that Maggie was telling them her story. She kept her eyes lowered and said in a low voice, "Nadie esta seguro, cualuier calle puede llenarse de cuerpos masacrados, cualquiera puede desparecer."

Pierce glanced at Mo and translated. "She says that she had to flee her home because nobody is safe. The streets are filled with butchered bodies, and anybody can disappear."

Mo's face seemed to lose all expression.

Maggie took the baby in her arms. "Yamilet lines up in the hot sun at 11 a.m. in hopes of getting one of the few plates of food provided by Mexican immigration officials at 1 p.m., then she gets in line again by 2 p.m. for the 5 p.m. serving—most days only 40 or 50 people get food before it runs out."

Mo shook his head. "So how are these people getting basic necessities like food and water?"

Maggie looked across the camp and sighed. "They mostly rely on religious organizations, immigration activists and individual donors who regularly arrive with food, water, blankets and other basic necessities."

The sick feeling in Mo's stomach grew. After a moment, he said, "At the rate the camp is growing, the food and supplies being donated won't be enough."

Maggie gave Mo an uneasy look. "We don't have enough as it is." Her resigned frustration seemed to hide a little fear. "Violence has been on the uptick. Just last week, two inhabitants were shot."

"Desperation does things to people. Even good ones," Pierce said.

Pierce continued to look around the camp for almost thirty more minutes. When he had seen enough, he asked about the possibility of speaking with some of the migrants.

"I'm still working on that," Maggie said as she nodded.

Pierce could tell she wasn't sold on the idea.

Maggie frowned. "Most are afraid to talk. They're scared that if they cooperate, it will hurt their chances at getting asylum."

"Then, I guess we're done for today." Pierce put his hand on Mo's back prompting him to move forward again. "Let us know if you can find some people that are willing to talk to us and we'll come back out."

They started to walk back in the direction of Maggie's car when a group of kids ran across their path, forcing them to stop for a moment. Once they got into the SUV, Mo stared at them in the rearview mirror as they waved good-bye. It took over an hour for them to travel the last one hundred yards to cross the border and just thirty minutes to drive the remaining twenty-eight miles to the airport.

Pierce and Mo thanked Maggie and said their good-byes. When Pierce had first met Maggie, he instantly got a feeling that she was tough, street smart and knew how to take care of herself. Nevertheless, he wanted to mention to her that she should exercise caution when visiting the camps. When they had first arrived, Pierce noticed several men keeping track of their movements.

"I saw them too," Maggie's face hardened as she pulled a Glock 19 from her bag. "I'm a Black woman and an American. I know when I stick out. About two weeks ago, I started to notice some interested looks, and I'm not talking the kind that want to buy you a drink, so I began to carry this baby with me," she said before sliding the gun back inside her bag.

Pierce studied her. He was pleasantly surprised by her candidness. Maggie was a beauty, almost six feet tall with perfect features and a husky voice. Her dark skin, with a touch of cream, green eyes, and perfect teeth, revealed a battle-tested and confident smile. She could use a little softening around the edges, but her appeal was undeniable.

Pierce nodded. "Stay safe and let me know if you can get some interviews set up."

Maggie smiled. "Will do. Safe travels," she said, and pulled out into the airport traffic.

* * *

With the name Maggie Malone, she liked to tell people that she was Black Irish. She insisted that one of her ancestors in her family tree had to be Irish because Black people weren't named Malone.

Maggie grew up in a tough neighborhood in Yonkers, New York. When she was 14 years old, Maggie chose to be homeless rather than suffer her stepfather's lurid looks and duplicitous advances. She was smart, analytical with an eidetic memory that allowed her to remember almost everything she read, and a quick-witted debater who frequently challenged her teachers - questioning everything she was told.

Maggie blitzed through Queens College in three years and got a full scholarship to Fordham Law School. She turned down offers to work at several New York law firms. Maggie never forgot what it felt like to be homeless and hungry; and picked the ACLU instead. It didn't take her long to establish herself as a talented litigator with a promising future. When the opportunity to move to Houston, Texas, and work on the Border Litigation Project presented itself, her friends and colleagues told her to turn it down, that it was an undesirable assignment. Maggie didn't listen. She closed her eyes and jumped.

Chapter Four

The Centers for Disease Control and Prevention (CDC) – Atlanta

Doctor George Shepherd's office looked like the command bunker of an army in fighting retreat. Next to him was a wastebasket, with the half-eaten remnants of the prior evening's carryout meal; and a cold cup of coffee balanced precariously on a stack of unopened mail. His face was haggard and unshaven. He had slept very little since receiving the news of an outbreak in Miami. He focused on his next task: a consultation with the head of Infectious Diseases at the University of Miami Health System in Florida.

There were now seventeen cases in Miami, Florida. Eleven were passengers on the same flight that originated in Sao Paulo, Brazil. Approximately ten days earlier, the U.S. Army had sent the CDC the blood samples that Doctor Sophia Wild had collected from the Kayapo Indian village in Brazil. Her field notes accompanied the samples, describing symptoms similar to the Zaire Ebola virus that had a human mortality rate of 90 percent.

The data on his three computer monitors confirmed what Shepherd had already suspected. The mystery disease was viral. In response to the outbreak in Miami, Doctor Shepherd's office organized a virtual meeting with Doctor Rotenberg from the University of Miami, and Major Wild.

"I've asked Doctor Wild to join our meeting this morning," Doctor Shepherd started. "She recently returned from Brazil, where she treated patients with symptoms that sound like what you're dealing with down there."

Doctor Rotenberg was thankful for any help he could get. "We now have nineteen cases of an undiagnosed, but severe, febrile illness characterized by prostration and multi-system failure."

Doctor Shepherd suspected that diseases such as influenza had been considered, but he had to ask the question as he went down his mental checklist.

He asked, "Have you run serological tests for influenza?"

Rotenberg was hovering in no-man's-land. He stared blankly and nodded. "All the patients tested negative for influenza. Everything we've tested, blood cultures, stool cultures, urine cultures, even cerebrospinal fluid cultures, has been negative."

Sophia made a mental picture. It was pretty much the same as what she encountered in Brazil.

Rotenberg's tone was decidedly desperate, as he was running out of options. "Despite the negative cultures, we've treated the patients for malaria, leptospirosis and dengue fever, but. . ."

"There has been no effect. The patients are all deteriorating, no matter what you do," Sophia said, finishing his sentence for him.

Rotenberg frowned. "Precisely."

Rotenberg put several of the patients' laboratory records on the screen. Sophia nodded as she glanced at the values, and noted the low levels of healthy blood cells, and liver and kidney malfunction in every patient.

"The red and white blood cell, and platelet levels are well below acceptable ranges. These levels suggest the patients may have severe aplastic anemia," Sophia said.

Both doctors agreed. Then Rotenberg said, "We biopsied the bone marrow in all the patients and are waiting to confirm our diagnosis."

Doctor Shepherd chewed his lower lip for a moment, thinking. "I wouldn't wait. Start on the blood transfusions to raise the blood cell counts and control the bleeding. I suggest incorporating dialysis as part of the supportive care regimen since the kidneys aren't functioning."

Doctor Rotenberg shot him a look that said he would immediately start the treatments.

Sophia studied the charts on the monitor. Her expression radiated concern. Clinically, the patients' symptoms resembled the Kayapo Indians she had treated to a horrifying degree. She had seen enough. "Looks like you're dealing with the same pathogenic viral infection my team ran into in the Amazon," Sophia said. "I suggest completely isolating the patients. Put them in a totally isolated wing and implement strict barrier nursing if you haven't already done so. This disease is highly contagious and every bit as deadly as the Ebola virus."

Rotenberg accepted Sophia's comments with a nod. "We've taken every step possible to establish a barrier between the inside and outside of the ward. Staff wear protective gear, remove outer clothing, and shower before going off duty. Everything that is taken into the rooms where the patients are situated is disinfected or destroyed," he said with a slight edge to his voice.

"As an additional measure, stop all lab work and sterilize the lab. Send all samples by overnight to the CDC," Shepherd instructed. "Quarantine anyone that handled or came in contact with the samples that wasn't wearing protective clothing."

The other thought that made Sophia sick to her stomach was the fact that wiping out the Kayapo village did not contain the virus. It had already spread to Sao Paulo and Miami.

"Were the other passengers on the flight isolated?" Sophia asked, not expecting a positive answer. That would have been too easy.

Shepherd sank into his chair, his face contorted at the logistical impossibility. "We've quarantine the pilots and crew; and are tracking down all the passengers on the airline's manifest. About a third of them took connecting flights. Most to other cities here in the U.S. However, five left the country: three passengers boarded a flight to Amsterdam; and two flew to Paris. We've contacted the Health Departments and instructed them to locate, isolate, and monitor everyone who came in contact with the passengers."

Sophia's mind whirled at the horror of four hundred infected people transferring the virus throughout the United States and Europe. It could take as little as one sneeze to spread the disease in a community.

"In Brazil, there's already three hundred and eighteen cases reported; and one hundred and eighty deaths. It's spreading like a wildfire down there," Shepherd added.

A shiver ran down Sophia's spine at the thought that the flight from Sao Paulo may not have been the only one carrying infected passengers.

Doctor Shepherd stared through stinging eyes at his computer. "Major, when your team was in the Amazon, did you develop any theories on the source of the virus?"

Sophia let out a long breath but didn't immediately respond. "None, really. We assumed that the origin is zoonotic. The thought crossed my mind that this disease could be connected to the cutting down of the rain forests. We're changing the ecosystem down there and exposing different species of bats, for example, to livestock and humans that had previously been living in isolation. The Kayapo Indians were the first to be infected. I'm guessing that the construction workers working on the Belo Monte hydroelectric dam site located on the fringe of the rainforest must have also come into contact with the virus."

Shepherd was more intrigued by Sophia's theory than Rotenberg. Rotenberg listened, but just barely. He clenched his jaw. What he really wanted was to get help with the rising number of patients infected with the virus in his hospital under control.

"When can I expect a team from the CDC to get here?" Rotenberg asked.

Shepherd took a deep breath. "I'm deploying a member of my staff today to do some advance work before the team arrives. The rest of the Rapid Response Team will be there in two days."

Rotenberg's eyes practically popped out of his head. Two days amid the panic and chaos engulfing the hospital sounded like an eternity to him.

Organizing his thoughts, Shepherd momentarily focused on Sophia. "Major, would you have any objection to assisting? I would like to ask your Commanding Officer to send your team to Miami, since you have experience with this virus."

Sophia's mouth felt dry with fear. "No objection. We're here to help in any way we can."

Turning his attention to Dr. Rotenberg, Shepherd said, "I will get in touch with my counterpart at FEMA and ask him to send down as many dialysis machines and supplies as they can spare. Get started on the blood transfusions as soon as possible."

Rotenberg mumbled something unintelligible and nodded. He looked as anxious as Sophia felt. "Thank you, Doctor."

When Sophia logged off the call, her mind was in turmoil. Her worries of exposure to the disease came back in a rush. This virus was the most contagious and deadly she had ever encountered. When she was in Brazil, she had been constantly on edge, wondering whether every headache, ache, and pain she felt meant she had contracted the virus. She had dodged a bullet and now she was jumping back into the middle of a deadly outbreak.

Chapter Five

Offices of ACLU – Houston, Texas

At five-thirty sharp on Fridays, the work week ended. The coffee pot was emptied, the office door locked, and the phone ignored. Maggie switched from coffee to a bottle of bourbon she kept in her bottom desk drawer and continued to toil over the draft of the lawsuit against the United States that Pierce and Moses had sent over.

When she finished reading the Complaint, Maggie took a deep breath, stood, and walked around the office. Up to this point, she didn't give the lawsuit more than a puncher's chance at success: not impossible, but unlikely. She nodded her head in admiration and decided that Pierce's and Moses' reputations as formidable and skilled practitioners was well deserved. They didn't waste precious pages focusing on the litany of human rights violations that were occurring every day in the camps. The courts had read and heard those arguments before, to no avail. Instead, they took a different approach. They shook the tree that needed shaking and waited for the poisonous fruit to fall into their hands, for not even Washington could operate with impunity. Maggie felt the early rumblings of excitement, poured herself another drink and read the Complaint again.

Halfway down the hall, Bobby Moore, the Executive Director, closed his laptop decisively and entertained thoughts of the weekend ahead. Catching the light coming from Maggie's office, he wandered over to have a look. Bobby sauntered down the narrow corridor, past the empty desks and mismatched chairs that looked like flea market furniture and poked his head into the tight room. It looked more like a closet than an office. The walls were sparsely decorated with reproductions of iconic images that captured the hope and struggle of the Civil Rights Movement. The scent of burned charcoal, from a time when people smoked in their offices, swaddled the walls and furniture.

"So, what's keeping you here so late?"

Maggie took a deep breath as a sense of dread hit her in the gut. There was a checklist of issues and approvals that had to be covered before the ACLU took on a case or worked as co-counsel. Maggie had cleared all but one of those hurdles. Despite her doggedness and cajoling, the Executive Director would not agree to sign off. It wasn't until Senator Cortez's office applied considerable pressure that Bobby Moore relented.

"I received the final draft of the Matamoros Complaint against the U.S. this morning. The lawyers working with Senator Cortez and Congresswoman Rodriguez want to file it on Monday, so I only have the weekend to review it."

Bobby took his jacket off and sat down opposite Maggie, unfastening the top button on the white shirt that his wife ironed for him every morning.

"What do you think?"

Maggie took a sip of bourbon as if she needed fuel and rattled off a short version of the legal arguments contained in the Complaint. Bobby offered unsolicited advice at every turn, maintaining the constant cynicism of losing an unwinnable case.

"They've made credible arguments. One, in fact, that may be hard for the Department of Justice to sidestep."

Bobby feigned intrigue. "Tell me about it," he said and pointed towards the empty glass next to the bottle of bourbon.

Maggie nodded and filled Bobby's glass. "They did a nice job showing how the United States' current asylum policy violates Federal laws, such as the *Immigration and Nationality Act* and the *1951 United Nations Convention Relating to the Status of Refugees*," she said.

Bobby seemed to absorb and consider every word and shook his head gravely. "But to apply for asylum, a person needs to be physically present in the United States. The refugees in the camps are in Mexico and aren't protected by our country's asylum laws. By keeping them on the Mexican side of the border, the Immigration Regulations that require us to give asylum to refugees don't apply."

Maggie tapped the keyboard as she contemplated the legal arguments on her computer screen and, with an indifferent movement of her head, implied that she disagreed.

Bobby fancied himself a trial lawyer, a hard-charging courtroom brawler with no fear, but after thirty years in the trenches, gutter fighting for indigents, he had started to settle for small wins and stopped swinging for the fences. "The U.S. now has Safe Third Country Agreements with Guatemala and El Salvador. By scheduling the hearings in those countries, the Department of Homeland Security has legally navigated around our safe haven policies."

Maggie reminded herself to be patient. "Maybe not." She kept it vague but sounded confident. "The Complaint alleges that the government violated the rule-making process. If the government failed to adhere to the strict notice requirements for proposed rules and changes in policy, the whole thing comes crumbling down. That's pretty black and white."

Bobby took a sip of bourbon, narrowed his eyes. He looked at things differently. Maggie was a fine trial lawyer in her own right. If this was a jury trial, their prospects might be slightly better. He could think of at least two occasions where Maggie's face and legs added a dimension that helped sway a juror or two that was on the fence. He saw this case going only one way. "The Department of Justice usually gets an extremely wide berth. If they can assert a good cause exception, the judge will give them a pass."

"Good cause?" Maggie snickered, looking up from her laptop. "There's no imminent threat. The asylum seekers in the camps are not in the United States. As you pointed out, the non-refoulement policy doesn't apply, therefore our government doesn't get a pass," Maggie insisted.

Bobby nodded slightly and frowned with great suspicion while Maggie continued to refute his point.

"The Department of Homeland Security violated the *Administrative Procedure Act* which governs the process which federal agencies must follow. The Department promulgated a rule that allows for asylum seekers who are at our border to be sent to El Salvador, Guatemala, and Honduras without following the rules governing notice and public comment. This not only violates our laws regarding rulemaking, it also violates international law regarding Safe Country Agreements."

Bobby sipped his bourbon slowly. He still wasn't sold, so he poked and prodded Maggie. "Section 553(b)(B) authorizes federal agencies to dispense with the APA's requirements for notice-and-comment for good cause. You can bet the farm that the Department will provide supporting reasons for invoking the good cause exception," he said with total confidence. "Besides, the court will not rule against the Department on a human rights issue where the U.S. is complying with the safe third country provision."

Maggie gave a short laugh, trivializing the point. "There are grave risks in moving asylum seekers to those countries. Gangs like MS-13 and Mara 18 have tens of thousands of members throughout the so-called safe third countries. They're the primary reason people flee El Salvador, Guatemala, and Honduras."

While Bobby took a moment to absorb Maggie's argument, she pressed on. "Just last month, 140 asylum seekers were sent to Guatemala. When they arrived, each was only given 72 hours to decide whether to stay in Guatemala or return to their home countries . . . Basically, would you like to be killed here in Guatemala or would you prefer to die closer to home? Not much of a choice," she said sarcastically.

The severity of the comment caught Bobby off guard. Deep wrinkles broke across his forehead. After three years of give-and-take, Maggie had learned to anticipate his arguments.

Bobby took a long sip and looked past Maggie through the dirty window as he contemplated locking horns with the Department of Justice. He had already concluded that convincing a judge to throw out immigration policies aimed at national security over a technicality would be an impossible undertaking. In his vast experience fighting for indigent's rights, this case was unwinnable; and his subordinate's opinion should fall in line with his. She was book smart but experience poor.

"It took me almost thirty years of practicing law before I learned that it's never black and white when you're suing the government," Bobby said, and waited for a response, but got none.

Maggie swallowed and maintained her poker face, but just under the surface, she fumed. It was clear to her that too much time in the trenches and two heart attacks had taken their toll on Bobby Moore; and he no longer had the physical and emotional stamina or appetite for challenging cases.

He gave her an uneasy look, followed by a phony smile. He was getting nowhere with Maggie and remembered that he had promised his wife he would be home in time for dinner. He drained his glass and gave a noncommittal shrug. "Gotta go. Don't work too late." Bobby managed a tight grin, and, out of a sense of obligation but bereft of any sincerity, said, "Don't hesitate to call me over the weekend if you need help."

Maggie immediately recognized the hypocritical tinge in his voice. "I will," she said without hesitation.

After Bobby left her office, Maggie emptied the last of the bourbon into her glass and grimaced at the question that rattled noisily in her brain. *When exactly did Bobby check out and start to just punch the clock?*

An hour later, Maggie took her last sip. Alert but pleasantly inebriated, she used her mobile phone to arrange for a car to drive her home. A quote from one of her favorite books, '*To Kill a Mockingbird*' that she always turned to during challenging times, echoed in her thoughts:

"*Real courage is when you know you're licked before you begin, but you begin anyway and see it through, no matter what.*"

Chapter Six

Miami

Three months later, the deadly virus owned the front page of the Miami Herald and every newspaper in the United States:

"World Health Organization declares the Kayapo virus world's worst outbreak as death toll surges."

Pierce read the story on his laptop early Saturday morning. He sipped coffee and surfed the internet for related stories. The media painted a picture of despair as governments declared national emergencies. The virus named after the village where it was first discovered spread worldwide within months. It took less than ninety days for the blood supplies in hospitals and blood banks to run dangerously low. The World Health Organization declared a pandemic in March, and by the end of that month, the world saw more than a two-and-a-half million people infected and nearly two million deaths. Conspiracy theorists and white supremacist groups were proliferating stories over the internet that the virus was created artificially and spread on purpose as a bioweapon.

Individuals and organizations exploited the social media platforms to spread misinformation and perpetuate fear-mongering theories, triggering mass hysteria and panic among millions of viewers. With the country's healthcare system on the brink of collapsing and the virus spreading faster than a California wildfire, countries across the world declared mandatory shelter-at-home measures, closing schools, businesses, and public places. Dozens of companies and many more independent researchers began working on tests, treatments, and vaccines. However, at the outset of the virus, uninfected blood was the only known treatment for slowing down the death rate. The push for the human race to survive the pandemic became the only concern, and blood became the most valuable commodity. Homicide rates worldwide skyrocketed as the demand for human blood dwarfed the world's supply. Criminal groups preyed on underprivileged and vulnerable men and women in developing countries as a major source of trafficked blood. The U.S.-Mexico border towns of Tijuana, Juarez, and Matamoros became among the world's deadliest.

Pierce surfed the internet and clicked on news stories about the surging body count on the U.S. – Mexico border. One that particularly interested him contained videotaped images from the TV news choppers showing a pile of shredded bras, underwear, T-shirts, jeans and sneakers, and parts of mangled bodies spread out over 20 meters. A news reporter at the scene described each pair of shoes as a captured and murdered body.

A spokesperson for the Mexican government speculated that "the brutal executions appear to be related to the worldwide demand for blood." A police officer at the scene estimated that they recovered parts of 53 different bodies.

Social media accounts displayed footage of vultures playing tug of war with intestines and coyotes carrying off body parts. Pierce suspected that the first responders or persons driving on the desolate road used their smartphones to record and upload the disturbing footage.

"It only takes a couple of hours for the turkey vultures to smell decaying flesh. Bodies in the desert disappear quickly. There could have been twice the number of the police's original estimate of 53 bodies," Jose Ramos, a forensic scientist, posted, fanning the flames of the conspiracy theories on social media.

Another Instagram account appeared to have firsthand knowledge of the crime scene: "The screaming sun was so intense that it baked the flesh off what was left of the dead bodies and mummified them. I saw the gray holes and no blood pooling at all. They had drained the bodies of all their blood."

The bloodless corpses looked like broken dolls. Pierce zeroed in on the images of the scattered and torn clothing. A silent reminder that they once belonged to individuals. People who made the same daily decisions about what to wear and what to eat. Men, women, and children who, in the not-too-distant past, were hunted and murdered for their blood.

At least one Mexican cartel expanded its criminal oligopoly and set up laboratory operations to siphon, test and distribute blood. To the cartels, blood was just another black-market commodity to traffic. Migrants from Central American countries streaming to the U.S.-Mexico border seeking asylum became easy targets for the cartel's sicarios responsible for carrying out assassinations and kidnappings. With both Mexico and the United States in the grips of a pandemic, the cartel's men targeted and murdered migrants with no interference from law enforcement. The Food and Drug Administration and the *Center for Biologics Evaluation and Research,* responsible for regulatory oversight of the U.S. blood supply, overnight instituted a "No questions asked" policy.

* * *

In Miami, the bustling streets transformed to empty asphalt. Humans had vanished except for the occasional police car patrolling the streets. Yellow crime scene tape closed off beach entrances. Gone were the sights of people swimming in the ocean or engaging in different activities on Miami Beach's white sands. There was no one left. No music, no sounds. Pierce could almost hear the little waves from his South Beach apartment. Silence fell over Miami Beach for the first time since it became a city in 1917.

Pierce was grateful for his balcony. From there, through his binoculars, he could see the cruise ships at anchor, each with its own quarantined crew. Now and then a medical transport vehicle would pull up, and personnel in full hazmat suits would remove the latest patients stricken by the virus, and retreat towards the Miami Marlin's baseball stadium, which had been converted into a field hospital. States across America converted field houses, stadiums, arenas, and parking lots. Facilities normally used for basketball, hockey, baseball, and tennis all had new functions now, as the death toll surpassed two million.

The transport whirled past the cruise ships, where Disney's theme songs and classic pop hits once wafted across Biscayne Bay. Only now, the panorama was brilliant in color and silent in nature.

The last sixty days were a bit dreamlike to Pierce. In the heat of Miami, everything melts, but Pierce never fathomed that it could include the legal system. During the COVID-19 pandemic, the government never ceased to function.

The Kayapo virus, however, was much more devastating. It overwhelmed major cities and spread through countries with millions of infections and almost as many dead. This time, the justice system did not pivot to online operations immediately. The speed with which this deadly wave battered the country had had a paralyzing effect on governments worldwide. Pierce checked the U.S. District Court's website several times a day for any sign that they would soon resume operations.

He didn't want to think about what would happen over the next thirty days. The raging death tolls of people stricken by the virus and people murdered for their blood would change the face of the planet.

Media outlets speculated that about a million people worldwide - most of them from poorer countries—had been reported missing and were presumed dead. The New York Times reported that the U.N., humanitarian groups, and governments stopped keeping track of those reported missing and presumed dead soon after the initial outbreak of violence.

The death toll in the migrant camps and in the poorer areas - where the targeted violence frequently occurred - was accepted as a necessary and unfortunate evil to prolong the survival of the infected population. Those who forfeited their lives performed a public service, as the genocide spread with shocking speed and brutality.

Pierce, like the rest of the world, was at the mercy of the pharmaceutical and biotechnology companies working on a vaccine. By filing the lawsuit challenging the U.S.'s decision to close the border, he hoped to save the lives of the migrants in the camps. The cartel's death squads routinely patrolled the streets, hunting for life-giving blood. The men, women, and children crammed into the overcrowded migrant camps were vulnerable and easy targets.

There was only one plausible way Pierce could think of to reduce the numbers of migrants openly hunted and murdered by the cartel. What he needed was for the U.S. District Court to resume operations. He hoped to convince the judge that the country's blood shortage did not justify genocide. By opening the border and moving the people in the camps to the U.S. side of the river, Pierce hoped to slow down the violence and save lives.

Chapter Seven

University of Miami Hospital

Doctor Wild's eyes were red and weary as she stared at the Intensive Care Unit, which had double the number of patients than standard critical care beds. While it reminded her of the war zones the army deployed her to during her twenty-year career, what she was dealing with was much worse. She wore the face of someone in the middle of an unspeakable nightmare. The Kayapo virus had killed over 92 percent of the people infected.

"It feels like we're sleepwalking, just going through the motions, trying to keep them alive this hour, so we can deal with the next one," a Physician Assistant standing a few feet away complained as she struggled to control her emotions, each word laden with grief.

Exhausted and defeated, Sophia stopped to offer words of encouragement, but all she could do was nod, unable to think of anything thoughtful or reassuring. Patients were lined up on gurneys in the hallways.

"I hear that at other hospitals in the area, ambulances are sitting in parking lots, waiting for eight-to-twelve hours to move patients into beds," the Physician Assistant added.

Sophia had heard the same, as bad news always spread quickly. Most of those people were infected and dying and that, along with the sudden scarcity of toilet paper, was all people were talking about.

The governor issued a "Shelter-at-Home-Order" requiring people to remain in their homes and travel only if absolutely necessary.

Near-hysteria engulfed the hospital. People wearing masks, rubber gloves and face shields just kept coming, and coming, only to be told to wait outside by hospital staff. Their infuriated shouts and screams demanding answers and treatment echoed through the lobby whenever the front door, guarded by Miami-Dade police officers wearing hazmat suits, opened.

Nurses, doctors, and hospital administrators were stretched beyond their limits, working 36-hour shifts to care for as many patients as possible. The University of Miami Hospital cancelled all but lifesaving surgeries, choosing instead to deploy all its resources towards treating virus-stricken patients.

Ten days. Without a new steady supply of blood, that was the latest projection before the hospital ran dry. The number swirled around in Sophia's head. Ten days. Doctors were rationing blood, treating patients in hallways, and deciding who lives for a while longer and who dies.

What would happen in the next thirty days when the rate of infection and number of deaths tripled or quadrupled? It was the precise question that Sophia asked herself. With a vaccine rumored to still be months away and the country's blood supply almost gone, the thought of standing around helpless while those infected were condemned to die, terrified her.

* * *

Maggie sat at the kitchen table and waited for the coffee to brew. Bright, early morning sunlight streamed through the wooden blinds. Maggie was not a morning person. She hated mornings, hated early morning meetings. One of the positives of the Shelter-at-Home Order was she didn't have to deal with morning traffic on her way to the office, which she absolutely despised. The only thing she liked about mornings was breakfast food, although she rarely ate breakfast. When she did, it was usually a cherry frosted Pop-Tart, later in the day.

Maggie's laptop made a chiming noise; a programmed reminder that she had a virtual meeting with Mo and Pierce in one hour.

At 33, she was barely old enough to remember life without the internet. The first deaths linked to the Kayapo virus barely caught anyone's attention. But soon additional zeros were added to the daily count, and everyone began to look at each other and ask: "what's happening?" News of the Kayapo virus spreading at an uncontrolled rate then dominated the news websites. All but Fox News reported similar facts: millions of infected, world in chaos.

At first, Maggie refused to stop believing that people were not inherently good. She tried to see good in evil and accepted that desperation did things to people, even fundamentally good ones. But what followed once the deadly virus placed the world in its death grip opened her eyes and changed everything. The CDC and WHO kept the rest of the world updated on efforts to develop a vaccine and preached about *herd immunity,* but it felt more like the *End of Days.*

The Latin America News Dispatch reported that large numbers from South America were making the dangerous trek by foot, bus, and car to the U.S. border to escape the violence of the para-military groups and drug cartels' sicarios engaging in blood trafficking. Genocidal groups targeted people living in slum communities and slaughtered them for their blood.

BBC News and Al Jazeera both produced stories that reported on the aftermath of the virus and the global blood shortage. No sooner was the news that the world was running out of blood made public than a manhunt got under way aimed at capitalizing on the desperately needed resource. One hundred days is all it took for the organized carnage to account for one million deaths. In countless villages, hundreds and thousands of civilians, men, women, and children, were rounded up like cattle and slaughtered. Governments and the media increasingly looked away as the systemic annihilation conducted primarily in African and South American countries increased. Public attention and sympathy were riveted on the millions stricken by the Kayapo virus and the genocide of the poorest and marginalized communities accepted by many as necessary for survival. The world was blind to the violence, and deaf to the screams. Debates condemning the murder of innocents versus utilitarian rationalizations that a few deaths to prolong countless lives were an acceptable cost raged on social media sites.

"One hundred thousand refugees flood the U.S. Mexican border" was the lead story in the Houston Chronicle. With the border closed under Pandemic related authority, desperate asylum-seeking migrants sought other ways to cross the Rio Grande River. As they crossed, some carried boxes on their heads filled with food. Some removed their pants before getting into the river and carried them. Others plunged in, leaving their possessions behind desperate to evade the two terrifying predators preying on the camps: disease and the death squads.

Maggie slipped out of her robe and expertly applied some foundation, eyeliner and lipliner before joining the virtual meeting.

She poured herself a second mugful of coffee, adding milk and a tablespoon of honey before clicking on the Microsoft Team's meeting link. Pierce instantly appeared positioned in front of his monitor.

"Good morning, counselor," she said.

Pierce smiled. "Good morning, Maggie. Mo should be signing in any minute."

Maggie gave a shrug. "No worries, we're basically on house arrest, so it's not like I have anywhere to be."

Pierce nodded, taking the government ordered lock-down in stride.

"Damn it," Mo said in frustration as he struggled to get his webcam to work.

"Mo, we can hear you," Pierce chimed in.

"What?' I'm connected? Why can't I see you?"

Maggie sighed. "Move your mouse to the top right-hand corner and click on the icon that looks like a camera."

They watched the arrow move to the top of his screen and, after a click of his mouse, Mo's cherubic face suddenly appeared on both of their monitors.

"There you are," Mo smiled, because it was impossible not to smile at Maggie. "Pretty as ever." Over the last few months, he had grown very fond of Maggie as he learned about all the challenges she overcame as a homeless child surviving on the streets of New York City.

Mo lowered his chin and peered disapprovingly at Pierce. "Why are you wearing that Jets shirt? They are the perennial doormat of the NFL. They lose every year. Hell, they haven't won the Super Bowl since way before you were born."

Pierce stirred his coffee. His initial thought was to let Mo's remark pass since it wasn't the best time to delve into his allegiance to his favorite professional football team, but Pierce couldn't let Mo's blatant disrespect of the team he had cheered for since he was in diapers go without a retort. "I grew up in New York rooting for the Jets, win or lose. I admit, mostly lose. But the Jets to me are like donuts for you, Mo. You know that in the end they're no good for you, but come Sunday morning, that's all you think about."

The smug look drained from Mo's face. He tried to adjust his camera, giving off the impression that he was trying to cover up a felonious act.

"I see the half-eaten éclair, Mo. No need to hide it," Pierce laughed.

Mo scowled, as if Pierce had uttered a heresy. "It's a cronut from Bomboloni's Bakery. Big difference," he said incredulously.

Maggie smiled. "Now, now, boys. Having grown up in New York, I still root for the Jets, the Mets and the Knicks. And as for donuts. . ."

Maggie giggled. "Let's just say Voodoo Doughnut's Bourbon Maple Pecan is sinful on Sunday and every other day. So, you go for it, Mo."

Mo bristled. "Let's get started," his tone was brusque and business-like.

Pierce resisted the urge to smile. "Yes, we should get started. We have a lot of ground to cover." Pierce moved the conversation to their lawsuit against the United States. He explained that the U.S. District Court expected to resume operations. "The clerk of the court doesn't have an exact date yet, but she indicated that she thinks most of the judges will begin holding virtual hearings by the end of the month," Pierce said.

Maggie grimaced as images of dead bodies flashed through her mind. Between the surging numbers of infected people, and human husks of people murdered and drained of their blood, the border resembled an apocalyptic wasteland. "The situation on the border is spiraling. If we don't get in front of a judge soon, there may be no one left to save." Maggie imagined Yamilet and her baby caught between the cartel and the infected. "We need to schedule a special hearing before the judge as soon as possible. The situation in Matamoros is a time bomb."

Mo nodded. "I hear that the U.S. deployed 10,000 National Guard troops. . ."

"They weren't sent there to help," Maggie cut him off. "They're only there to prevent refugees from crossing the border. That's only making matters worse."

Pierce, Maggie, and Mo all agreed that the number of refugees trying to escape the virus and the cartel was growing too big to control.

Maggie was visibly irritated. "The cartel is rounding up everyone in the camps and killing them so they can sell their blood. Neither the U.S. nor the Mexican government are doing anything to prevent it."

Mo shook his head in disgust. "From what I read, in the past two weeks alone, more than 40,000 refugees were intercepted trying to cross. All were denied political asylum and sent back to Mexico."

"We are going to have to convince the judge that not only is the emergency law closing the border and cancelling immigration hearings illegal, but it is also putting the lives of all those refugees in danger. The people in the camps are sitting ducks out there," Maggie declared in a tone suggesting that, despite the impossible task, they would have to figure out a way.

Pierce regarded Maggie's point thoughtfully. He knew the political realities and suspected that a strong legal argument wouldn't be enough to persuade a federal judge to strike a law that the government would argue was helping to protect people from the epidemic. Panic had the people firmly in its grip and shrewd politicians exploited that fear. Pierce's only hope was to convince the judge that the U.S. interests of controlling the spread of the virus were better served by setting up camps on the U.S. side of the border. Keeping the refugees in a controlled environment improved their chances of minimizing the spread of the virus. The rising death toll in the overcrowded camps and lack of clean water and food was like lighting a match after turning on the gas. Despite the heightened efforts to guard the U.S.-Mexico border, it was only a matter of time before the horde became too large and desperate to control and overran the Border Patrol.

Pierce heard rumors that a small group of politicians in the Capitol were urging more aggressive shoot-to-kill policies aimed at targeting illegal border crossers, but most lawmakers did not support the use of force and firearms.

"I've asked Senator Cortez to schedule several virtual meetings for us. The first is with the Texas governor and attorney general."

Maggie's face transformed into something that was between a frown and a wince. "To what end?" She asked.

"To ask them and several other governments affected by the new rule to join the lawsuit." Pierce said. "Despite the border closure measures, migrants desperate to escape the camps are risking their lives every day. Those that successfully evade the Border Patrol and make it to the U.S. could be infected by the virus. This is a very dangerous development for communities along the border."

Mo was familiar with Pierce's objective and nodded in agreement. "The Department of Justice may be able to dance around the violation of the *Administrative Procedure Act*. These are difficult times, and the U.S. will argue a compelling governmental interest exists. By closing the border, they are protecting the public and minimizing the threat of the infection," Mo said in a lecturing tone.

Maggie put her teeth together and hissed contemptuously. "They enacted the rule before the pandemic."

Mo made a show of deliberation. "That doesn't matter anymore."

"That's rather extreme, don't you think?" She snapped with a defensive nod.

Mo seemed to sense her unease. "Maggie, the U.S. will argue that this is now a matter of national security."

Maggie didn't care for Mo's opinion. She glanced at Pierce. "What do you think?"

Pierce didn't believe that they needed to abandon the procedural argument regarding the government's failure to comply with the law. But he didn't want to live or die by it. "If our strongest argument is that the U.S. violated the *Administrative Procedure Act* by failing to properly notice the rule, I think a court will deny our motion for summary judgement and rule in favor of the Department of Justice," he said.

Mo nodded in agreement. "We need to be smarter. This virus is very contagious and presents a legitimate reason for closing the border. The DOJ will argue to the court that the people seeking asylum could already be infected. They're living in the camps where people are dying from the virus."

Maggie clung to the image of Yamilet and her baby and felt helpless and ashamed. In a moment of brutal honesty, she wanted to scream, *those motherfuckers are turning a blind eye to innocent people being butchered,* but she exercised practiced restraint.

Mo eyed Maggie warily. "Are you okay?"

Very good question, Maggie thought to herself.

Pierce gave her a reassuring nod. "The people in the camps are desperate and risking their lives to cross the border at any cost. The grim reality is every day some of them slip by Border Patrol. Their numbers are growing, and conditions in the camp are rapidly deteriorating."

Maggie listened to Pierce's point of view without showing any emotion. Inside, however, her stomach was churning.

"It only takes one person carrying the virus to infect an entire town. If we can convince the court that the camps are powder kegs ready to explode and the administration's "Remain in Mexico" policy actually puts American citizens at greater risk, we can use the government's argument against them," Pierce said.

When they finished discussing the strategic plan, Maggie said that she wanted to personally assess the situation in the Matamoros camp and check in on Yamilet.

"That's out of the question," Mo glared at Maggie, predictably appalled by the audacity of her pronouncement. "The border is closed, and it's not safe. . ."

Maggie didn't let Mo finish his sentence. "I'm sure Senator Cortez can pull some strings and get me permission to cross the border." She gave Pierce a slight nod and said, "Having firsthand knowledge of the camp's conditions when we make our case before the judge can only help. What do you say, Pierce? Can you help me?" Maggie asked in a solicitous voice.

Pierce glanced at Mo, whose expression had soured. He bit his tongue to keep from telling Maggie that he thought it was a bad idea. Instead, he considered her request. Her mind was already made up; and she would go with or without his help.

Chapter Eight

New Orleans

"We at Lighthouse are innovators and are saving lives." Ben Bowman, the Chief Executive Officer of Lighthouse Blood Centers, a network and trade organization specializing in supplying blood to hospitals during this crisis, was quoted on an internet newsfeed. What started as an uptick in global commodity prices for blood skyrocketed overnight. And Lighthouse Blood Centers, an independent healthcare organization specializing in diverse testing services to support organ and tissue transplantation and providing life-saving blood supply to hospitals in the southwest, was perfectly positioned to storm the castle. Lighthouse acquired donation centers along the Interstate 35 corridor—from Laredo, Texas, to Duluth, Minnesota and Interstate 10 corridor—from Jacksonville, Florida, to Santa Monica, California. Before Lighthouse, the blood supply chain existed primarily of local donors selling to hospitals within driving distance. Bowman's experience in supply chain management taught him to plan for shortages and to look outside of conventional sources for blood supply. When a Mexican drug cartel offered to supply him with blood, Bowman jumped at the opportunity. Lighthouse's Texas donation centers provided a perfect cover for blood supplied by the cartel.

Lighthouse was an essential governmental service and not subject to the Quarantine Order. Its employees in every office were busy shipping blood to hospitals around the country. The internet was bursting with stories about poor people from undeveloped countries being herded into holding pens and rendered unconscious before being drained of their blood. Human rights organizations worked hard to create a public awareness and shame governments for turning a blind eye.

Bowman was careful not to send all the blood supplied by the cartel from his Texas facilities. He worried that when the FDA finally approved a vaccine for the Kayapo virus, those who looked the other way would suddenly grow a conscience and be the very ones prosecuting him.

Red blood cells have a shelf-life of 42 days, so most of the blood supplied by the cartel was shipped to Lighthouse facilities throughout the country before being distributed to hospitals. This provided Lighthouse with plausible deniability by giving the appearance that the blood supply sold by Lighthouse was being provided from many legitimate sources instead of murder victims.

When word spread that blood transfusions were the only known treatment for slowing the spread of the virus, the average price of a pint of blood quadrupled overnight. Ben Bowman's net worth reached $2 billion, but with a steady supply of blood from the cartel, he was confident he would double that. The Federal government's only mission was to make sure hospitals had a steady supply of blood, so FDA certification of blood bought and sold by Lighthouse to hospitals was almost automatic. Hospitals desperate for blood supplies practiced a "don't ask" policy. All they wanted was a steady delivery of O+, AB and B- blood types.

Bowman read the stories on the internet of the barbaric methods deployed by the cartel to drain its victims. The cartel had no guidelines or screening procedures. They followed only one rule: "Stay away from anyone that looked sick." Lighthouse personnel were instructed to treat all blood received from Mexico as if all clinical protocols had been followed. Lighthouse's Texas facilities processed all the blood supplied by the cartel before sending it to Lighthouse distribution centers across the U.S.

* * *

Ben Bowman was the epitome of money and power. He was a man accustomed to getting everything he wanted; and he bullied, cajoled, and threw enough money around to make sure he always did. Bowman was a man that was rarely ever satisfied. He always wanted more. More profits and more legal protection to insulate his growing empire from liability. He was a domineering savant on good days and a combative tyrant on the other days. Frank Collins, Lighthouse's General Counsel, and two other lawyers took their seats at the conference table in the corner of Bowman's office suite. After weeks of due diligence, Bowman retained a very influential lobbying firm in Washington. Bush & Rinehart was widely regarded as a firm with great access and the ability to exert influence. Every serious corporate player had heard of Carl Rinehart. He was *Mr. Washington*, the ultimate insider, regarded as one of the most aggressive purveyors of influence on the Hill. When wealthy and corporate clients want to pass or block legislation to maintain a favorable status quo, Carl was one of the best at protecting and advancing their interests.

"Gentlemen, we need to double down our efforts on making sure that any proposed legislation that grants companies working on a vaccine for the virus immunity from criminal and civil liability is broad enough to cover companies that provide medical services like Lighthouse," Bowman demanded.

Well, Collins thought to himself and wanted to say, *let's start with the fact that our company is doing business with a criminal organization and knows exactly how they're getting the blood that's being shipped to Lighthouse. The Federal government grants companies immunity that make or distribute critical medical supplies, such as vaccines, unless the company is guilty of willful misconduct. Lighthouse was a knowing and willful participant in acts that led to the loss of countless lives. So, you're pissing up a rope.*

Except that he treasured his job and said without much conviction, "The Bush firm is very close to the Secretary for Health and Human Services. They should be able to convince the Secretary to help our cause."

Bowman's greed put profit ahead of lives. "Willful misconduct needs to be defined at an impossibly high standard so that no plaintiff could ever sue."

Collins thought that pulling his teeth without anesthesia would be easier. Based on his communications with lawmakers and the company's lobbyists, the government knows where and how Lighthouse is getting about 35% of the blood supply they're selling to hospitals. The intel Collins put together showed that the Justice Department wasn't willing to give Lighthouse a complete pass from all legal liability. Lighthouse was making millions from the thousands of migrants murdered.

If lawmakers were ever pushed to investigate the matter, they needed a scapegoat to make an example of. They saw that as a small price to pay for the fortune Lighthouse had made and would continue to make. "The government wants to be able to levy a moderate civil penalty under the willful misconduct standard if it becomes necessary. Nothing criminal, just a fine. It's more about optics than the money," Collins said.

Bowman showed his displeasure with a furrowed brow. "Fuck fines! And fuck optics!" Bowman screamed.

Collins swallowed deeply, causing a hollow feeling to develop in his stomach.

"No civil penalties. Not a fucking dime," Bowman barked at Collins.

Collins sank back in his leather chair. "Understood, sir."

Bowman's eyes opened wide. "Do you?" With a look of utter frustration, he said, "I'm starting to wonder why I hired you."

Collins shifted in his chair uncomfortably and didn't say a word.

"Listen up, numb nuts. A civil penalty opens the door to private lawsuits. Every human rights organization and two-bit ambulance chaser claiming to represent the family of someone who went missing will file lawsuits against us."

Bowman walked to the window and gazed at the view of the sparkling waters of the Mississippi River and reflected for a moment. "This thing has to be properly managed to make sure we're in the bill. With this pandemic, everyone's eyes are off the ball. Senator Littlefield can extend the immunity protections and tweak the willful misconduct definition without anyone noticing."

Bowman walked to the conference table, placed both palms flat on the black Italian marble, glared at Frank Collins and said, "I've given a ton of money to Littlefield's PAC and to lobbyists to spread around the political apparatus, so I don't give a rat's ass about optics. You tell the senator and the Bush firm that I expect results."

* * *

It was dangerous living in the migrant camps during the pandemic. In Matamoros, nearly 2000 people were kidnapped and killed as soon as the camp became the primary target of the Zeta cartel. The Zetas raided the Matamoros camp every night for 11 weeks. The Mexican government made no effort to stop the attacks. Raids and abductions became a daily part of life. The camp's inhabitants warned each other when they spotted the cartel's motorcycles and vans. When people heard the motorcycles in the distance, they stopped what they were doing and hid. Some dove into the swirling waters of the Rio Grande River, hoping to evade the reach of the cartel's men.

The virus and the cartel's traffickers turned hunters; both preyed on the camp's inhabitants with a relentless vengeance. Most of the people living in the camp had a slim hope of survival. Everyday U.S. Customs agents and the National Guard captured hundreds of migrants trying to cross the Rio Grande. Though thousands of migrants died trying to cross the Mexican wilderness, many still chose to take their chances through remote and dangerous routes. The risks were immense for these individuals. Most ended up as skeletal or decomposing corpses by the time they were found, but staying in the camp was a death sentence. Yamilet knew she could not cross the deadly migrant corridor with her infant son. Her only option was to try and find a way to stay alive.

Chapter Nine

Brownsville, Texas

Except for "essential commerce," the United States and Mexico suspended all travel across the border. Only critical services such as food, fuel, healthcare, and life-saving medicines were permitted to cross.

Pierce worked through Senator Cortez's office to secure a diplomatic exemption to the border measures to permit Maggie to visit the Matamoros camp. Mo expressed his displeasure but didn't interfere because he knew Maggie would find a way to visit the camp without Pierce's help.

Mo called Maggie three times on her five-hour drive to the border.

"You're only authorized to visit the camp. You can't travel anywhere else," Mo cautioned Maggie over the cellphone. His tone betrayed his concern. "Mexico is using a QR code-based registration system to enable it to conduct contact tracing."

Maggie inched the car forward towards the *"Bienvenidos A Mexico"* sign and a green arrow identifying an open lane. "Got it, got it, got it, Mo." she said.

"Another thing, your re-entry permit is only good for 24 hours."

She glanced down at her passport and permit on the passenger's seat. "I know. I read it. Stop worrying," Maggie snapped. "I'm going to visit the camp, make sure that Yami is okay, and I'll be back in the U.S. by dinnertime."

Mo changed the subject, pretending to be satisfied, but he wasn't. Visiting the camp was a bad idea. Even before the onslaught of the worst plague in the history of the world, the camp's inhabitants were frequently raped, kidnapped, tortured, and victims of other violent attacks. "Don't forget the meeting with the governor is the day after tomorrow."

"I know. Pierce is going to handle the meeting, but I plan on attending via Zoom. Okay, I gotta go. Later Mo. I'll call you when I'm on my way back." Maggie hung up and continued to inch the car forward.

The bridge was crowded with police cars, official vehicles, and an ambulance, just in case it was needed. State police, Mexican military personnel and immigration officers with automatic rifles were all stationed at the checkpoint to perform temperature screenings; validate health questionnaires for essential commerce; and to expel all others attempting to enter the country. The officer waved at Maggie to pull the car forward. She pulled up slowly until the officer signaled her to stop. She slipped on her blue surgical mask covering her nose and mouth while an officer in head-to-toe hazmat suit came to her window.

The sullen officer glowered at her from behind his mask, keeping his distance. "The border is closed."

"I have a permit," Maggie said, handing the officer the permit and her passport.

The officer reached for the paperwork with his latex-gloved hands and used a handheld device to scan her passport into the system. He handed them back quickly, anxious to be rid of them. Then he took Maggie's temperature reading before asking a series of medical questions.

Maggie kept her face relaxed and answered his questions. When he was finished, the officer glanced at Maggie for a long five seconds before waving her through and turning his attention to the next vehicle.

* * *

The sprawling refugee camp situated on the southern bank of the Rio Grande, directly across from Brownsville, Texas, came into view a few minutes later. The number of makeshift shelters scattered in smaller encampments along the river's edge surprised Maggie. They had more than tripled since the last time she'd been there. Maggie wheeled to a stop in front of the camp and parked just outside where a gate and chain-link fence had existed the last time she visited. Instinctively, she slid back the lid of her console and put her re-entry pass and passport inside and locked it.

The camp had been victimized by continuous and worsening waves of violence. There were abandoned tents everywhere, shattered glass and personal belongings scattered as though a tornado had cut through the camp. The sour musky smell followed her everywhere she walked and looked for Yamilet. The awful smell was human decay, and it was so thick and pungent that Maggie couldn't stop herself from retching and vomiting for a few minutes. She kept to the perimeter of the camp, where the smell of rot wasn't as intense.

The Rio Grande was bristling with migrants bathing, washing clothes and fishing in the same bend of the river where many migrants had drowned trying to swim across. Throughout the dirt alleys of the tent city, she saw children curled up on the floor amid a sea of crushed plastic bottles, old diapers, and chicken bones. Some had a feverish, lifeless look in their eyes. She passed by a couple of sleeping children laying on mats made of cardboard. The low chatter of voices huddled over an unconscious little girl about seven years old told Maggie that it wouldn't be long before the virus took her. Near the woods, she noticed a group of men watching her. The white cotton masks could not hide the fear and desperation in their eyes.

It was almost 4 p.m. and still no sign of Yamilet. After another hour of looking, with no luck, worry began to take over as the thought that

Yamilet was dead took hold. Out of a mixture of curiosity and desperation, Maggie took a detour and walked along the sad and neglected street past smashed and boarded up windows. The smell of death still lingered in the air a hundred yards outside of the camp. How many in camp lay dead? She wondered.

Maggie crossed over scattered debris and garbage to get to the Bible Institute facility, a ministry a short distance from the camp that collected baby formula, diapers, and canned foods for migrants. After passing several abandoned storefronts, Maggie wondered if the ministry was still functioning. Sitting on a piece of cardboard with her back resting against the building with its yellow façade was a young woman cradling a small child. Maggie stared at the young woman and felt her heart drop the moment she recognized Yamilet. She was sitting still, trance-like, staring wide-eyed but seeing nothing. Her eyes were red, *watery, swollen, and* severely blistered.

Maggie kept her distance and eyed Yamilet cautiously. "How long have you been sick?" She asked her in Spanish, choking back tears.

Yamilet stared at Maggie with uncertainty, too startled to say a word. She looked away, fearful tears stinging her eyes. Then finally she took a quivery breath. "Not sick," Yami answered in English.

Afraid she might breathe on her, Maggie instinctively recoiled.

Yamilet closed her eyes tightly and began shaking as if chills were sweeping through her. The tears were instant. "Cartel's men stay away from sick people. I go to junkyard and find gasoline in cars and rub in my eyes. Make look sick," Yami struggled to find the words. *"Es la unica manera de mantenerme viva,"* she said, her voice muffled by her mask, but the pain in her eyes was clear as crystal. At times, Yamilet shared details and at other times she just drifted away.

Sweat broke out all across her forehead, and she mumbled to herself. One moment she was engaged, the next she was frightened and withdrawn. The deeper Maggie dug, the sadder Yamilet's story became, and after an hour she'd had enough. Yamilet was barely hanging on. The gasoline would soon cause permanent damage, eventually blind her, but that was of little consequence. She wouldn't survive much longer without help. Help that Maggie was in no position to give.

Chapter Ten

Miami

Doctor Sophia Wild wasn't sure if she believed in Hell, but if such a place truly existed, she was in it. She had just spent the last two hours playing God, deciding which patients got blood transfusions; and which were to be made as comfortable as possible and left to die. She was only supposed to be in Miami for a week, but with each ominous wave of newly infected patients, her stay was indefinitely extended.

Doctor Wild made a mental note to go to the bathroom right before the start of her shift because she knew that once she put on all the layers of protective gear, it would be at least ten hours before she would be able to eat, drink or relieve herself.

With the death toll and numbers of infected patients surging, hospitals in almost every city were being pushed to the brink; and morgues were filled beyond capacity, with bodies stacked on top of one another. Newspapers listed the names and ages of the people who had died and been left unclaimed. Sophia saw older and younger patient's mouths panting under oxygen masks, feet shivering because of high fevers, and lying-in bed alone with teary and fearful eyes.

Public Service Announcements advised everyone to stay home and call special numbers if they were feeling flu-like symptoms. The sense of helplessness among the medical staff was palpable.

With all the hospital beds occupied, hospital staff advised everyone calling for help that there was none to give. Miami's death toll had risen to 946 people in 24 hours with 21,503 new infections. Every day, twice as many people would die as the day before.

* * *

Yamilet focused intently on the distant sound of dirt bikes.

"We have to go!" Yamilet gasped and scrambled to her feet.

Maggie nodded uncomfortably. "What's happening?"

"Los Zetas," she snapped, fighting her own tears and panic.

The sound of the bikes echoed as they got closer.

Yamilet glanced over her shoulder at Maggie, then looked in the direction of the camp. "You're dead if we don't run."

"We can go faster if I carry Giovanny," Maggie said as she took the baby from Yamilet.

Armed men on dirt bikes, followed by two black vans, appeared on the horizon.

Yamilet and Maggie sprinted towards the tent city. There were shouts coming from the camp as several men barked orders at terrorized migrants rushing to find places to hide.

Maggie turned back around and glanced fearfully over her shoulder. The cartel's men were still well behind but closing fast.

Yami and Maggie weaved through the tents at as fast a pace as they could manage. Yami peeked inside a tent with a red circle spray painted on it. "Aqui," Yami called to Maggie and waved at her to hide inside.

Maggie hesitated. The flies buzzing around the exterior of the tent told her there were dead bodies inside. She knew the red mark meant that the people inside were infected.

Yamilet tugged at her arm. "They dead a couple of days. Not catch sick from a dead," Yamilet declared.

Maggie's eyes watered and she gagged as the smell of rotten eggs hit her like a sledgehammer. Everyone inside was dead. A man, woman and infant not much older than Giovanny huddled together in a sleeping bag. Flies buzzed around the eyes of the infant that were wide open and bright red from the sickness. Maggie guessed that he lived for a couple of days after his parents died because the decomposition wasn't as advanced.

The other two bodies were grotesquely bloated, causing their eyes to be pushed out of their sockets and forcing their tongues out of their mouths. There was a silver crucifix hanging around the woman's decaying neck.

The bile rose in Maggie's throat, but she held it together. Maggie sucked breaths through her mask, eyes watering from the intense smell of rot, but that didn't help much. The smell was so strong she could taste it.

The screams and sounds of men and women pleading for their lives while being herded like cattle and thrown into cargo vans echoed all around them. A motorcycle suddenly stopped just outside the tent and revved its engine.

Maggie's heart started to hammer away at her insides. She closed her eyes, pinched her nose, and prayed. Yamilet reached for a small bottle in her bag and splashed her hands with gasoline. She vigorously rubbed the gasoline into her eyes, triggering uncontrollable tearing and redness.

Then she poked her head outside the tent and began coughing uncontrollably.

Startled, the man on the motorcycle reached towards his face to make sure his mask was secure. He spotted two of his companions approaching and waved them off, signaling that whoever was in the tent was infected. They took off in separate directions. Instinctively, he backed the bike away and screamed obscenities at Yamilet as he ordered her back inside the tent.

Maggie and Yamilet stayed inside the tent until the roar of the motorcycle engines felt like a horrible memory.

Chapter Eleven

Hutchinson Island, Florida

As the clock ticked past midnight, Moses Black grew increasingly nervous. He'd been trying to reach Maggie on her cell phone for almost six hours. Mo stared at the view of the darkened beach from his balcony. There were no artificial lights anywhere, just weak moonlight and shadows. It was the middle of the turtle nesting season. The local ordinance required that all lights from houses and condominiums located along the shoreline be dimmed or turned off. Bright lights discouraged females from nesting. They could also draw hatchlings inland since the baby turtles have an innate instinct that leads them in the brightest direction, which is normally the moonlight reflecting off the ocean.

The rustling sound of the ocean breeze sweeping through the palm trees added to the sense of gloom. Mo's instincts were screaming at him that something had gone terribly wrong.

* * *

Over the years, Mo had found that early morning walks on a secluded beach before sunrise, with the rhythmic song of the waves rolling onto the shore, were one of his favorite things to do. He often roamed the beach, barefoot, throwing breadcrumbs at the birds to clear his mind. However, this time, it was the dead of night, and waves breaking on the shore were the only sound. There was no other sound, no human, not a single bird or insect. Mo walked through the darkness, killing time. Living on Hutchinson Island had been his respite. Unfortunately, these past hours, feeling isolated and unable to find and help Maggie, made it feel more like a prison.

After a few hours, the first signs of morning started to show. The sun peeked over the horizon, and the sky filled with soft pink light in the east. It had been a long night, and the morning brought with it more questions than answers. Mo waited until just after seven before he began making calls.

Pierce had gone on a five-mile run around 6:00 a.m. to exercise away the cabin fever. He needed the jog to stay loose, to take the edge off all the coffee he was consuming.

Pierce's cellphone rang, and he picked it up. Mo skipped their usual morning chit chat, which covered sports and politics, and launched into a long diatribe.

When he was almost finished, Mo took a deep breath and sighed into the phone. "We agreed to talk around six after she left the camp. Calls are going straight to her voicemail."

Mo tried to chase the most recent images of the camp he'd seen on the internet from his mind.

"She could have misplaced her phone," Pierce countered.

His voice rose almost in anger. "We shouldn't have let her go." Mo's tone was serious, something in it hinted at fear.

Pierce sighed quietly. "She had her mind made up. She was going with or without our help."

Mo let out an understandably frustrated breath. The confident façade that he kept between him and the rest of the world was showing cracks.

"We'll find her," Pierce said with a practiced calm he didn't feel.

There was a moment of silence. Pierce heard the sound of the waves crashing onto the shore. Mo clutched the cellphone with white knuckles, and his eyes peered ahead, ignoring the golden petals stretching out over the rich blue ocean as his mind searched for answers.

Mo cleared his throat. His mouth was dry. He'd been walking the beach for hours without a drink. "Pierce, Maggie could be in real danger. We need to find her."

Pierce made a mental list of who to call for help and said, "All right. Give me a couple of hours to work on this."

"Call me as soon as you know something."

"Will do," Pierce replied, wishing he could have said something a little more comforting as he hit the red button and ended the call. Even though Mo didn't have any concrete information, Pierce felt a strange nagging at the back of his mind, an uncomfortable feeling that Mo might be right. Maggie was in trouble.

* * *

Pierce spent the next two hours calling Senator Cortez's office, U.S. Representative Rodriguez, his contacts at the Department of Justice and anyone else he could think of to help.

Special Agent Nick Russo at the Federal Bureau of Investigation didn't sound optimistic. He advised Pierce that the border closing made it almost impossible to investigate Maggie's disappearance. The U.S. was only working closely and collaboratively with Canada and Mexico to limit the spread of the virus. They had no official way of searching for missing people outside their jurisdiction.

"We have 8000 troops deployed in Texas for border support. The Mexicans have two battalions stationed at Matamoros. Their orders are to keep the border locked down. The biggest difference is, before the pandemic, the Mexicans didn't care about illegal border crossings. Now, they don't want *anyone* crossing into Mexico. They're calling it '*Operación Bloqueo*'."

Pierce wasn't the slightest bit deterred. "All I need is for you to check and see if Maggie made it back through the checkpoint. If not, send a team to do a sweep of the Matamoros camp."

Nick's eyes shifted from the computer screen to the ceiling and he swore softly.

Nick, who was one of the most unflappable people Pierce ever met, looked like he saw a ghost when Pierce asked him to put together a team to look for Maggie. Nick explained that the surging numbers of people infected with the virus and dropping dead in the camp had everybody spooked. "The higher-ups are scared shitless of this virus, and it's trickled all the way down. There's no cooperation or back door to get this done," Nick said.

Pierce laughed quietly. "There's always a back door."

Nick didn't confirm or deny the statement, so Pierce took it as a yes. "What about doing something off the books?"

Nick felt his face twist into a frown. He wanted to avoid that scenario. With the virus spreading at such an accelerated rate going anywhere near the camp was fraught with risk. "That's too big a lift, Pierce. Even for me."

Nick regretted the comment the instant he uttered it and stayed silent for a second. He knew Pierce too well. There was no such thing as an unsolvable problem or too heavy a lift. Pierce's entire professional life had been centered on solving problems; and taking on and winning unpopular cases other lawyers shied away from.

One of those unpopular cases had included Special Agent Nick Russo. When several agents, including Nick, were the subject of a politically motivated internal probe aimed at making them scapegoats of the Bureau's alleged wrongdoing to repair the FBI's credibility, Pierce went to war with the Justice Department and the FBI. In typical fashion, Pierce was two steps ahead.

He used his contacts in the news media and nimbly changed the narrative. Pierce publicly condemned the FBI for bending to political whims and launching a manhunt against its own agents. He used the public stage to paint the FBI Director into a corner and convinced two senators to demand a formal Congressional inquiry. The FBI Director suspected the inquiry was a well-planned ambush, so he conceded to Pierce's terms, which included reopening the investigation and formally clearing the agents of any wrongdoing.

* * *

Nick owed Pierce. He stewed for a moment as he felt himself walking an impossible tightrope. The police had abandoned the camp, and the cartel had free reign to commit acts of violence. The camp was nothing more than a collection of misplaced humanity waiting to die. The chances of Maggie escaping the violence in the camp unscathed and uninfected were nil.

Nick didn't try to hide his skepticism. "Pierce, we're standing in the eye of the storm. Even if I can get a team into Mexico, they won't be allowed in the camp."

Pierce anticipated this and quickly replied. "Let's start by checking to see if Maggie ever left Mexico. If she made it back, that should be easy enough to confirm."

"And if she didn't?" Nick asked, knowing Pierce wouldn't be satisfied with his search ending there.

Pierce took a sip of cold coffee and looked out his window at the empty street, normally bustling with rush-hour traffic, with the same sense of bleak despair that gripped most of those living in the city. He knew the idea of organizing a search for Maggie was laden with complications, but he had to try. "I'll call Senator Cortez and see what she can do to help convince the Mexican government to let us send a team into Mexico. I understand that the camp is off limits, but you can do a sweep of the perimeter."

Nick didn't want to send any of his men to look for Maggie. It was all too unpredictable, and dangerous. He would not put any of his men's lives at risk. Getting politicians involved would only complicate matters. The Mexican authorities no longer controlled the city. Matamoros was firmly in the grip of the Zeta Cartel, Mexico's most ruthless and violent crime syndicate. In Matamoros, doing business was a delicate balancing act. To safely search for Maggie, Nick had to cut a deal with the devil.

With a battalion of an American-sponsored, SWAT-style unit of police known as GOPES (for *Grupo de Operaciónes Especiales*) stationed less than a mile from the camp, Nick hoped Daniel Gonzalez, the head of the Zeta Cartel was open to cutting a deal. He could arrange for the U.S. Border Patrol to allow a few tanker trucks carrying stolen oil, gas or bricks of cocaine to cross the border into the U.S. in exchange for the cartel allowing GOPES to search for the missing American.

"Hold off on the senator. Let me see what I can work out with my local contacts," Nick said, but without conviction.

"One more thing," Nick said before ending the video call.

"Sure. What is it?" Pierce asked.

"Text me Maggie Malone's cellphone number."

Chapter Twelve

Matamoros, Mexico

It was Yamilet's quick thinking and the gasoline that saved them. The cartel that rounded up and murdered the camp's inhabitants was made up of greedy and violent men. For now, the world's demand for blood surpassed that for recreational drugs and a partnership of sorts had been struck with Lighthouse Blood Centers, an American company.

About an hour after the cartel's men had left the camp, Yamilet stuck her head out of the tent and peered into the darkness. Some of the fear seemed to drain from her face.

"We can go now," Yamilet said.

Maggie willed herself out of the tent. She had lost her cellphone in the melee to escape the cartel's men. Now she needed to get back to her car before they came back. With her American passport, she was sure that the Mexican government would let her through. The expired re-entry permit would only be a problem on the American side of the border, but in the grand scheme of things, she'd rather take her chances with the Americans.

Getting Yamilet and her son into the country was going to be next to impossible. Maggie didn't want to think about leaving them behind, but she had no options. She suggested paying a smuggler known as a *coyote* or *pollero*, to sneak Yamilet and her son across the river into Brownsville, where she would wait for them. But Yamilet explained that they couldn't count on the coyotes. "The U.S. border grows harder and more dangerous to penetrate, and the coyotes make easier money working as spotters and informants for the cartel," Yamilet said in broken English.

Maggie and Yamilet moved through the camp towards where Maggie remembered leaving her car. The sun was falling behind the Rio Grande, but there was still light enough to see a few of the camp's inhabitants covering their noses and mouths with soiled shirts, walking around inspecting the wreckage from the violence. Some sat by the river's edge openly sobbing while others staggered around, calling out names. Maggie initially thought that they were the lucky ones, having escaped the cartel's men. But abandoned with nowhere to go, they would eventually succumb to the virus or be killed by the cartel. The human suffering was hard to ignore; but Maggie had no choice but to push away the guilt and try to maintain her focus as Yamilet led her through the sour smelling encampment.

There was no sign of the SUV at the edge of the camp. Maggie retraced her steps, just to be sure. She scanned her surroundings a second and third time.

"Shiiit," Maggie exhaled, drawing out the word for a full two seconds. It was the only word that kept echoing in her mind. Her car, passport and re-entry permit were gone. Maggie knew that her takeaway from all this should be terror or despair. But it wasn't. She had never been in a situation this dangerous before, but it wasn't completely foreign. Growing up homeless on the streets of New York City, Maggie learned to improvise and figure her way out of whatever dilemma she'd gotten herself into. Once she accepted her new reality, her old survival skills kicked in. Maggie sensed that they didn't have much time before the shit-show they were in got a whole lot worse. She would bet her meager life savings that the cartel's men would be back soon to wreak havoc.

"The junkyard. How far is it from here?" Maggie asked. Her mind was already working on formulating a plan.

"Junkyard?" Yamilet looked surprised. "Not far. Only a few minutes that way," she said, pointing north.

Maggie nodded but didn't otherwise respond and started walking north along the narrow sidewalk. The sidewalk turned to dirt and before long they were standing in front of a dumping ground filled with piles of garbage, scrap metal, and a sprawl of rusted cars and trucks. Someone had ripped the gate at the entrance off its post, and it was lying on the ground. The wood and asphalt shingle structure next to the entry looked like it was in the process of collapse, with no glass in the windows and no door in the frame.

Yamilet explained that the old man that guarded the junkyard caught the sickness. Right after he died, people picked through the piles and ransacked the place. The junkyard had been abandoned ever since.

Maggie surveyed her surroundings before wading in. The waning quarter moon cast faint shadows on the rubble, making it difficult to distinguish one pile from the next. When Maggie reached the top of a ten-foot mound covered with construction debris and broken glass, she thought she spotted what she was looking for, a scrap pile of worn car and truck tires.

Maggie rummaged through the pile until she found two nearly identical car tires. Now it was just a matter of finding a good piece of wood and rope.

Maggie let out a long breath. "This will do," she said, dropping a partially smashed pallet by Yamilet's feet.

"There's better, thicker scrap wood over there," Yami said in Spanish.

"I'm not looking for the best wood. What we need is something that isn't heavy." Maggie kicked the pallet and appeared to be satisfied. "This is sturdy enough," she said. The inflection Maggie gave to the word *sturdy* suggested she meant they would have to make it work.

Ideally, she would have chosen to use four tires and a well-made piece of wood, such as an old door to build a raft, but it came down to what they could carry from the junkyard to the river.

Based on her expression, Yamilet didn't feel the same way.

"Stay here, I'll be back," Maggie said before disappearing to look for something to secure the pallet to the tires. There were only a few points of light emanating from the street, making it almost impossible for Maggie to tell what she was looking at. She searched blindly for rope in the trash piles, which felt like trying to find a needle in a haystack.

It took Maggie forty minutes before she returned, carrying a small coil of tying wire. Not perfect, but the best she could find under the circumstances.

Maggie stared at the tires and wooden pallet for a moment to consider what she wanted to do. Then she worked quickly, running wire through the tire, and weaving it in between the openings in the slats of the pallet and back around to the tire. She used a small, rusted pipe to twist the wire until it broke off. Then she ran a second wire through the same openings and twisted the two ends together. When she finished with the first tire, she fastened the second tire to the pallet the same way.

Maggie stood up to inspect her work. Then she dropped down to a squat, gripped the pallet, and shook it. Satisfied, she looked back at Yamilet and nodded.

Yamilet's eyes narrowed as she studied the makeshift raft. Her face was frozen somewhere between fear and skepticism. Thousands of migrants attempting to cross the Rio Grande died trying to navigate the river's unpredictable currents, deep water, and frigid temperatures. She found herself left with few options. In fact, only one.

Maggie gave a voice to Yamilet's thoughts. "I know that this plan is equal parts crazy and stupid, but it's the only chance we have of getting out of here alive."

Yamilet took a deep breath and said a quick prayer. She conjured up her bravest face.

"My father used to say that life is about accepting the challenges along the way, and choosing to keep moving forward," Yamilet said in Spanish.

Maggie nodded thoughtfully. "Okay then. Let's get going."

Chapter Thirteen

Mexico City

Special Agent Nick Russo leaned back in his chair and massaged the familiar kink in his neck. He spent the last two hours reviewing the footage of border crossings in and out of Mexico over the last twenty-four hours. He was able to confirm that a white Ford Explorer registered to Maggie Malone left the U.S. and entered Mexico. However, the U.S. Custom's database had no record of Maggie Malone reentering the U.S.

His counterpart with the Policía Federal Ministerial, Celerino Sánchez, explained that the camp was a cesspool of disease.

"The snippets of information that we've pieced together are that half of the camp's inhabitants are infected with the virus and dying. The other half are being hunted and butchered. Last night, the cartel's men raided the camp, the same night that your American went missing," Celerino said.

"I get it. Wrong place. Wrong time. But that doesn't answer my question."

"Nick, my officers are sure that Ms. Malone would not have survived last night's raid on the camp." Every description by Officer Sanchez of the futility of the situation fell on deaf ears.

"Cel, I need you to search the camp," Nick insisted. He owed Pierce that much.

"The camp is off limits to my men. We don't police what goes on in there."

It never ceased to amaze Nick how easily Mexicans looked the other way, even when lives hung in the balance, as long as a cash payment was involved. To Nick's dismay, the thought that the Americans were different was nothing more than a carefully crafted illusion. When the country's blood supply began to run out, the U.S. subsidized the kidnappings and mutilation of men, women, and children in third world countries. Mass murders were increasingly meaningless. What mattered was keeping privileged Americans alive at any cost until the pharmaceutical companies could develop a cure or a vaccine.

"How much is it going to cost to send a team in there to look for the American?"

Celerino let out an understandably frustrated breath. "Nick, my men aren't with me on this one. Money doesn't matter to them. What good is it if they catch the virus and aren't around to spend it?"

Nick frowned. "Cel, I've managed to negotiate a window with the cartel for your men to go in and look for the American."

Celerino let out a low breath. "I don't think you understand. My men aren't worried about the cartel. When it comes to the cartel's sicarios, they can handle themselves. It's the virus."

"Your team will be in protective gear," he said in a disbelieving voice. "Don't be a pussy."

Celerino stood his ground. "None of my men are willing to walk into that deathtrap. We still don't know how contagious that son of a bitch is . . . I'm sorry buddy, but I can't help you out."

"All right," Nick let out a huge sigh as he tried to digest the scope of the problem. "Give me thirty minutes and I'll call you back." Nick ended the call and against his better judgment, searched the personnel files on his laptop for volunteers.

* * *

Nick put together a team of six agents. He leaned back and pondered the operation, and then a light dawned. When he got Celerino back on the line, Nick explained that he had a six-man team and two dogs ready to go.

"We need an escort for my men. Send a small, disciplined team and sweep the perimeter and the surrounding area. That's relatively safe."

Celerino thought about it for a second and exhaled sharply.

Nick pressed him. "My men will search the camp. We'll take one of the dogs with us and leave one and the dog's handler with your team."

"To what purpose?"

"If the guns don't keep the migrants away, the dogs will," Nick said. "We'll have a drone in the sky directly over the camp. If she's there, between the two of us, we should be able to spot her."

There was a brief pause over the line.

"Cel?" Nick said in a slightly impatient voice.

Celerino realized he'd been silent too long. "One hundred yards is as close as we're getting."

Nick picked up on the finality of the statement. "Understood. How long for your team to be ready?"

"We'll go at first light."

"Roger that. We'll be at the border at 0600."

* * *

Maggie and Yamilet kept to the deep shadows that clung to the walls, for stealth, while taking turns carrying Giovanny as they slowly dragged the raft from the junkyard to the river. Maggie and Yamilet both froze at the sound of a passing truck, trying to pinpoint its direction and distance. When they reached the edge of the mesquite thicket, they weaved through the dense scrubland, passing small sporadic clusters of tents situated outside of the camp. Some of the camp's inhabitants were trying to get away from those infected by the virus. However, even from a distance, Maggie could still smell rotting flesh in various stages of decomposition. Some haggard migrants watched them with curiosity as they dragged the raft forward towards the riverbank. Others glanced at them with indifference and a few frowned as they passed by their tents. But none dared approach them or look either Maggie or Yamilet in the eye.

The damp, putrid smell assaulted Maggie's nose in waves. Maggie gagged a few times before vomiting what little her stomach still contained.

She wiped the spit and vomit drooling from her mouth. "Fuck me. This smell isn't something you ever get used to."

Giovanny choked out spit and vomit. Yamilet swallowed the excess bile that had worked its way up from her stomach and pressed Maggie to keep moving. They continued heading east, and then parallel to the river far enough to escape the smell of decay before settling in just behind the last line of shrubbery before the riverbank.

The dense mesquite thicket provided a good hiding spot while they waited for the right time to cross. Maggie decided that between 6:30 and 7:00 A.M. would be the best time to attempt the crossing. The sun, beginning to peak over the horizon, would give them some light, so she wouldn't have to swim in complete darkness and the Border Patrol would be getting ready for a shift change making it less likely that agents would be watching the river.

At half past midnight, Maggie and Yamilet watched the border patrol vehicle driving slowly along a dirt road that dipped and curved on the other side of the Rio Grande. The search lights swept along the banks of their side of the Rio Grande and cast ominous shadows on the small trees that disappeared as the truck pulled away.

Around six in the morning, Maggie walked to the riverbank and launched a branch as far as she could into the river. She wanted to gauge the strength of the current.

She had always thought of herself as a strong swimmer. The first pool she ever swam in was a small, heavily chlorinated cement indoor pool at the Bronx Community College. The college created the swimming program to teach inner-city kids how to swim and gave $1.00 to any child that showed up for lessons. So, every day that the college offered lessons, Maggie made it her mission to collect a dollar. Summers she went to the free outdoor pool in Van Cortlandt Park and swam laps in the large Olympic size pool.

Looking at the murky, rushing waters, across the darkness to the distant silhouette of the riverbank, Maggie felt an overwhelming urge to vomit. The distance didn't worry her. The river was about as wide as the length of a football field. There were narrower, safer places to cross, but those were widely trafficked and heavily policed. It was the fast current, and the hidden undertows that scared her. The Mexicans called it the Rio Bravo—treacherous river. She watched the branch, following it as it floated downriver. Maggie expected the force of the water to push them downstream, so she looked for eddies, rocks, changes in water conditions and anything else that could present a danger. It was the strong current, cold-water temperature and the unknowns that she was afraid of. When she had walked about 100 yards, she started back towards where Yamilet and Giovanny were sleeping.

By the time Maggie returned, Yamilet was already awake.

Maggie let out a long, slow exhale. "It's time."

A flash of dread crossed Yamilet's face, but she managed to remain silent. Giving in to her anxiety would only make matters worse.

Maggie opted to take off her shirt, pants and shoes and shoved them into a plastic bag that she fastened to the raft.

Shivering, she told Yamilet to lift the other end of the raft. Yamilet nodded, but her face was an empty mask devoid of any emotion. When they got to the edge of the riverbank, Maggie lowered herself into the river and eased her end of the raft onto the water.

The river's cold temperature caused Maggie to breathe very fast and deep.

"Easy does it. Okay, Yami, now you."

Another nod, another blank expression.

Yamilet approached the raft cautiously, holding Giovanny close to her. When she was firmly on top of the wooden slats, she assumed a fetal position and pressed her son firmly against her bosom.

Maggie looped her left arm through the small opening in the tire that jutted out beyond the wooden platform and waded into the river with the buoyant load in tow. The mud was soft and forgiving beneath her feet. The frigid water, however, chilled her to the bone. Shivering, Maggie continued to wade across the river. Several steps later, she lost contact with the bottom.

Chapter Fourteen

Matamoros Migrant Camp

The Search and Rescue Drone, equipped with both a digital imaging camera and cellular base station fastened to it, flew a precise grid over several square miles, taking pictures. Images of debris, scattered violence, and the dying groping silently for help filled each frame.

At seven sharp, two vehicles carrying six FBI Hostage Rescue Team agents and a team of Mexican Federal Police Officers arrived at the rutted and dusty road leading to the entrance of the migrant camp with very little fanfare. Captain Fernando Lopez walked to the edge and looked out across the vast encampment. When it was light enough to use the binoculars, he swept across the area. Lopez studied what he could see. It was immediately apparent that the shredded tents and scattered personal belongings were the result of the chaos and destruction caused by the cartel's death squads.

Lopez lowered the glasses and reflexively checked to make sure his mask was properly secured. Then he raised them once again and watched as his men in heavy protective gear started on the edge and fanned out.

Captain Lopez's orders called for his men to keep a safe distance and search the camp from the perimeter, but the densely packed tarps and garbage piles made it impossible to separate the proverbial wheat from the chaff.

The commander of the American unit, Captain Richard Boselli, was responsible for extracting the High Value Target, Maggie Malone, if they spotted her in the camp. No one expected to find her alive.

Legs jutted out from most of the tarps. At that distance, it was impossible for Lopez's men to tell if they were sleeping, sick, or dead. "My men will circle the perimeter. Are you ready?" Lopez asked Boselli, though his tone suggested the question was just a formality.

Boselli nodded. "See you on the other side."

Boselli was in contact with Special Agent Russo.

Nick's voice came on over Boselli's radio.

"Captain, the drone has detected a ping from the target's cellphone. I'm sending the coordinates now."

Pressing the switch on his communication device, Boselli let out a low breath, "Roger that, sir. Standing by."

Boselli turned to his team. "It's business time, gents. Lock and load." His voice was calm and professional.

Lopez's men worked the perimeter, scanning the tents despite the fact that from their distance there wasn't much to see.

Boselli always loved the feeling he got just before engaging in a high-risk event. It was a moment of intensity that was impossible to reproduce in civilian life. Even though no one would be firing at them, the search for, and extraction of, Maggie Malone, was just as dangerous. All it would take is a malfunction of a piece of protective equipment or a breach of safety protocols. If one of his men became exposed to the deadly pathogen, it would mean a death sentence for all of them. The brutal reality was that it was impossible to tell apart the uninfected from the newly infected. This made everyone a potential threat. There was something terrifying about the speed with which the virus viciously infected the camp's inhabitants.

Not one of the men that volunteered felt comfortable with the operation. Now moving through the camp, they pushed the distraction from their minds and were solely focused on finding Maggie Malone.

One of the officers entered the GPS coordinates into his smartphone and barked out directions to the team. Boselli went first. Right behind him were Bo Nelson and his Search and Rescue Dog, Magnet. The rest of the team fell in step. Even with their heavy gear, they covered the distance from the edge of the camp to the location in five minutes.

After narrowing the possible location, Boselli said over the comm. "This is the sweet spot."

Two men shouldered their rifles and pointed them as a warning to anyone who came within twenty feet, while the others swept the area for Maggie Malone. The all too familiar stench of death was heavy in the air.

"Anything?" Nick asked over the radio.

"Nothing yet," Boselli spoke into his headset.

After a few minutes of searching with no luck, they started sorting through the rubble in search of the phone.

Stopping at a green tarp with a suspicious red splatter dried across it, an officer poked his head in and took a quick glance around. He stopped to stare at the decomposing body when the moaning of a woman lying next to the body startled him, causing him to fall backwards.

Boselli and one of the other team members moved in the direction of the crashing sound.

"Easy, Mike." Boselli snapped at the officer as he frantically scrambled to his feet.

"God, it stinks in here," one of the men that followed Boselli into the tent blurted out.

Boselli looked at the two bodies. "They don't look like they've been dead long enough to smell like this."

"The woman is still alive," Mike said, pointing down at the puddle close to where they were standing. It was burnt orange in color. "This is feces and urine and I'm pretty sure there's blood in there as well."

Nick's scratchy voice came back on the radio. "We just received another ping. The cellphone is fifty yards north of your present location."

The new coordinates led the team to a small group of four men huddled in a hushed, almost meditative circle around two power-strips bulging with seven or eight chargers. None of the men were wearing masks, despite the highly contagious virus.

Magnet barked at the men. Boselli and one other Special Agent came within fifteen feet of where the men were sitting.

"We're looking for a phone that was lost in the camp," Boselli shouted in Spanish across the short distance separating them. "If you turn over the phone, me and my men will be on our way. If you don't hand it over, my men are going to confiscate all the phones."

One of the migrants looked like he was thinking about running but didn't. The others surveyed the guns pointed at them with lifeless eyes.

One man nervously raised his hand and slowly stood up, careful to avoid any sudden movement that might cause the men pointing guns at him to start shooting or the German Shepherd to attack him. A few curious onlookers filled in behind Boselli and his men. One of the members of the tactical unit turned and pointed his gun, sweeping it across the crowd and ordered them to step back. The temptation to fire into the crowd to avoid getting infected was a strong one. Their numbers grew and a crowd of curious migrants inched closer and surrounded Boselli and his men. Boselli felt Bo and Magnet move past him towards the mob, closing in on his six. Magnet reacted aggressively, snarling, and lunging at them. They started to fall back.

The same man nodded and looked around at the men pointing their weapons at him. "Oficial, encontramos tres celulares. No sabemos cuál quieres."

Boselli's brow furrowed. He tossed a plastic Ziplock bag halfway across towards the man, ordered him to put all three phones they had found in it and back away.

Boselli radioed back to Captain Lopez. Lopez and his officers were standing by just outside the southern end of the camp.

"Captain, we found no sign of the asset. But we believe we have located her phone," Boselli said into the headset.

"My men swept the perimeter. Nothing here. We are standing by at the rendezvous point with the transport." Lopez said over the comm.

"Roger that."

The crowd, many infected and desperate, spread out around Boselli's team. News of Americans in the camp drew the horde to them like moths to a flame.

Boselli's men pointed their guns at the growing swarm. Magnet continued to bark at anyone who got too close.

Boselli turned his attention to his team. Their masks made it impossible to read their reactions. He didn't need to. He knew they were spooked. "Nothing more we can do here," he barked into his headset.

"Bo, take Magnet and lead us out."

"Copy."

Boselli checked his weapon. "I got the rear. Now, let's get the fuck out of this hellhole."

Chapter Fifteen

Rio Grande River, Mexico

The temperature of the water was cold enough for hypothermia, but warm enough to give Maggie time to reach the other side of the Rio Grande. Maggie swam through the morning light with the raft in tow. Ahead, the distant silhouette of the riverbank. She gradually felt the strength of the current and as she swam forward, it became increasingly difficult to stay on course. When they reached the middle, the sheer force of the river was much stronger than Maggie predicted and threatened to rip them apart as it pushed them downstream.

Kicking her legs wildly and holding on to the raft, a powerful wedge of water suddenly sucked Maggie under. Her heart rate soared, and her survival instincts screamed for her to let the raft go. Down became up. Unable to take in air, her lungs screamed. With all her strength, she kicked to the surface and strained to lift her head above the river. She began swallowing water and coughing. Emotions crashed over her with an intensity and swiftness that made it impossible to distinguish between them. The sensation of staying afloat being replaced with the sensation of drowning.

Relax. Don't struggle, she told herself. *If you panic, you'll drown.*

Maggie forced herself to stay calm, rotated onto her back and let the current sweep her far downstream with an unflagging fury. Harnessing the strength that comes from fear, she managed to keep her left arm through the opening in the tire.

Yamilet could see that cold water and exhaustion were beginning to overwhelm Maggie.

"Hold on!"

Yamilet tried to scream words of encouragement, but Maggie couldn't hear her over her own labored breathing and the loud roar of the river.

When they came upon a calmer area, Maggie took a deep breath, flipped over, and fought the urge to swim across the flow and began swimming diagonally with the current toward the shoreline.

Maggie's left shoulder tightened. She thought about switching arms but recognized the sheer impossibility. The current would twist the raft away from her before she could transfer arms.

She looked over at the shoreline. It was only about 100 feet away. *You can do this,* she told herself.

Straining to drag the raft holding Yamilet and Giovanny, Maggie suddenly felt a blinding intense pain like she had been shot.

The pain cut through her, feeling like a razor slicing away at her shoulder joint. The shore was now less than 50 feet away. Maggie rotated her torso to change the angle of her left arm and ease the burning feeling. It felt like she had torn something in her shoulder.

"Kick!" Maggie shrieked, trying to empty her mind of the intense pain she was feeling. Stroke after stroke, her rubbery legs kicking and her right arm lunging and pulling, Maggie willed them to the river's edge.

Stumbling and splashing triumphantly out of the water, Maggie fell onto the ground, where she lay shaking and coughing up water. Her legs were quivering, her left arm numb. And yet, she couldn't help but feel a sense of accomplishment.

Above her, vultures glided and circled, waiting for the end.

Looking up, Maggie suddenly felt a surge of elation. "Fuck you."

Maggie said to Yamilet, teeth chattering, "Toss me the plastic bag with my clothes and push the raft out into the water."

Yamilet wiped the tears from her face, resisting the urge to celebrate. The relief she felt was mixed with anxiety. God only knew when the Border Patrol and the National Guard would show up. Yamilet worried that they were already on their way. She and Giovanny needed to disappear quickly.

Maggie only needed a couple of minutes to catch her breath.

Yamilet still had tears in her eyes. "We go now," she pleaded.

Maggie nodded. Feeling a surge of adrenaline, she lifted her heavy torso off the ground and stripped out of her sodden undergarments. She dressed as quickly as her rubber limbs allowed her. Then Maggie and Yamilet silently vanished into the dense mesquite brush away from the river.

Chapter Sixteen

Austin, Texas

It had been thirty hours since Pierce's last contact with Special Agent Russo, but that wasn't unexpected. Coordinating a search and rescue mission with the Mexican Federal Police and negotiating a window of time with the cartel for them to conduct the operation without interference was no small task. In fact, the more that Pierce thought about it, the more that it seemed like too much to expect.

His laptop pinged, sending him a reminder that his virtual meeting with Senator Cortez and the governor of Texas would start in thirty minutes. Pierce logged on a few minutes early and waited patiently in the virtual lobby to be invited to attend the video conference.

Senator Amanda Cortez logged on and smiled when she saw Pierce. In his few brief dealings with the senator, Pierce quickly realized that Amanda Cortez was a force, politically astute, brilliant, indefatigable, and widely respected. She possessed a remarkable capacity for reading people. Having graduated with a Ph.D. in experimental psychology from Baylor University, she had worked as a licensed clinical psychologist at the Children's Medical Center in Dallas for fourteen years before being elected to the U.S. Senate.

Chronically behind schedule, the governor made a habit of showing up late. On the screen, at the end of the conference room, the governor's chief of staff appeared sitting next to a University of Texas mug and a powdered donut.

"Good morning, senator. The governor will be joining us momentarily," the chief of staff said through a sappy smile.

Governor John Lyndon Johnson looked at the clock on the wall and noted the time before taking his spot at the head of the conference table. Instead of his customary dark suit, he was wearing a pair of khaki pants and a Texas Longhorns sweatshirt. At the opposite end of the room, the large video screen was split into three. The left third showed U.S. Congresswoman Ana Rodriguez from her home in Florida; the middle portion featured Senator Cortez, who was tucked away in her office in Dallas; and Pierce Evangelista was in the last third. In the room with the governor was his Chief of Staff Casey Robinson, Attorney General Vania Smith and the governor's executive assistant, Abby Williams.

"Good morning, everyone. Senator, happy to see you. I hope Liam and Mathew are all in good health during these challenging times," the governor groaned, referring to the senator's husband and son as he lowered himself into his chair.

Pierce picked up on the forced pleasantries, the strained looks, the feeling that the governor could not wait for the meeting to end.

Senator Cortez began in her typical calm and deliberative voice. "They're both well. Thank you for inquiring, governor. And thank you for agreeing to meet with us on a Saturday morning."

As the senator offered some background for the meeting, the governor interrupted her with no desire for a preliminary introduction. His staff had already briefed him on the lawsuit filed by Pierce Evangelista. Notwithstanding his good ole boy friendly demeanor, it was clear that the meeting was only agreed to as a professional courtesy between elected officials from the same State.

"Amanda . . .," the governor said, before catching himself. "Pardon me, senator. You don't have to fill me in on the lawsuit." What the governor was really saying was that he had no intention of getting involved.

Senator Cortez remained the epitome of outward civility but seemed to look right through the governor. "Governor, with all due respect. In this matter, sitting on the sidelines and doing nothing is not an option."

Pierce could almost see the governor frown.

Senator Cortez pressed on. "We're facing a crisis, and the real problem is on *our* doorstep, not Washington's. Our border with Mexico is turning into a war zone."

The governor nodded. "Unfortunately, that's not a problem I can solve."

"Maybe not, but it's not something that we should ignore." The senator's gaze narrowed, and she said, "We need to do the right thing and leave politics out of this. Just two days ago, thousands of refugees tried to cross the border from Reynosa into Texas. Eleven were killed and many more were severely injured."

The governor glanced at the attorney general, who wore a slightly pained expression, and then looked back at the senator. "Under the circumstances, the Texas Rangers and the Border Patrol agents at the scene handled the situation appropriately," Johnson said, noting that the collateral damage in light of the overwhelming numbers attempting to cross at the same time was an acceptable result.

Ana Rodriguez shook her head, disappointed at the callous disregard for human life. "Matilda Menendez, Maria Guadalupe Sanchez, Jose Alvarez. . ."

"I beg your pardon," the attorney general interrupted.

"These are the names of the people murdered two days ago, that Governor Johnson says is acceptable."

Casey Robinson jumped to the governor's defense. "Congresswoman, you misunderstood the governor's comment."

"I don't believe I did," Ana snapped back.

A condescending smile played at Governor Johnson's lips. "Now, now Casey. Nothing wrong with a little straight talk," he said with a healthy Texas twang. He intentionally made his accent a little thicker when he wanted to make a larger point about the large cultural divide between Texas and the rest of the country.

There was some nervous laughter, but it didn't do much to break the tension.

Amanda Cortez knew the governor's slab of aww shucks Texas cowboy accent meant that they could pound sand if they were there to ask him to break ranks with the president.

Pierce sized up Governor Johnson as a consummate politician more concerned with building and preserving alliances. The senator's heartstring tugging hadn't worked, so Pierce shifted strategies. "Governor, if I may, I'd like to offer a different perspective."

Johnson leaned back in his chair, crossed his hands behind his head, smiled and casually said, "Floor's all yours, counselor."

"Thank you, governor. I'd like to begin by stressing that the metrics we have traditionally used to measure success for policing the border no longer apply, and I will explain why," Pierce said.

The governor reached for his mug, took a sip and nodded.

"The past few weeks, the number of arrivals at the southern US border is at a level never seen before. The cause for the historic exodus is the violent attacks sweeping through the poorer communities in Central and South America and the virus."

Everyone shook their heads. Then Casey Robinson volunteered what everyone already knew: the Migrant Protection Protocols closed the border to guard against the spread of the virus.

"However, closing the border doesn't prevent the spread of the virus. It actually increases the risk of exposure to Texas residents," Pierce said.

The governor drummed his fingers on the edge of the conference table. Finally, he let out a long, slow breath. "Counselor . . . in Texas we have a saying when things sound like a whole lot of something but don't add up. And what you're saying sounds like all hat, no cattle to me."

Pierce watched everyone in the room smile and nod their heads. "Right now, the number of people stricken by the virus is relatively low in Texas as compared to other parts of the country, but all it takes is one person carrying the virus slipping through to infect a whole town."

The governor chewed on his lower lip, thinking.

"With the high-tech surveillance equipment and the substantial increase in numbers of law enforcement stationed at the border, the latest modeling developed at Yale and MIT predicts that CBP will apprehend 78% of the illegal immigrants trying to cross the southern border."

The smiles vanished, and the room fell silent, but after a few seconds Pierce spoke up.

"Twenty-two out of every 100 people trying to cross every day are slipping past the CBP and your Rangers and making it to Texas. No one knows how many of those are carrying the virus with them. Chances are that more than a few of them are infected, given how quickly the virus is spreading in the camps."

Pierce purposefully paused, allowing the frightening likelihood to rattle around the room.

All at once, the meeting digressed into a free-for-all with splintered remarks. Governor Johnson pushed his chair a little further away from the table, and for his own part tried to figure out how to get a handle on the situation. If Pierce was right, he was looking at a ticking biological time bomb.

Casey Robinson leaned closer to the governor and stressed the importance of keeping this quiet. "Sir, the last thing we need right now is the press getting wind of this. They'll create a damn panic, and this situation will spin out of control."

As strange and counterintuitive as it seemed, the best course of action at that moment was to do nothing. Governor Johnson looked up at the videoconferencing screen and said, "Senator, I can't thank you and Congresswoman Rodriguez enough for shedding light on this crisis." The governor's gaze shifted and locked on Pierce. "Counselor, you've given us a lot to think about. I am going to huddle up with my staff and come up with a plan of action."

"In the meantime, let's all do our best to keep this out of the press," Robinson interjected, with the same sappy smile.

The senator directed her comments to the governor. "We can give you a few days, governor. The hearing before the court is next week. The heightened risk to citizens living in cities on the southern border is something that we will have to make known to the court."

". . . and the press," Robinson mumbled.

The governor nodded uncomfortably and smiled even though he didn't feel like it. "Thank you, senator," he said and gestured to Abby Williams to exit the meeting.

* * *

The bickering between the Chief of Staff and the attorney general went on for several minutes. Casey Robinson only focused on controlling the narrative in the press. Attorney General Smith, who remained mostly quiet throughout the meeting, was playing a longer game. She'd been doing a lot of thinking about the points raised and what the future might hold. She was a realist, and she knew that trying to dodge this bullet, this late in the game, would be futile. By the time the unbroken reposted chains sped around social media, the governor would need a scapegoat, and she would be it. As the State's chief law enforcement officer, the governor would insist on her resignation for failing to challenge a policy that turned Texas into the epicenter of the virus. With a disaster of this magnitude, it was likely that the governor himself would not survive the wrath of social media.

Vania Smith had endured difficulties before, but none of them compared to what she was now facing. "Governor, the virus is extremely contagious and a death sentence for everyone that gets infected."

Johnson glared at Smith, annoyed by her comment, which failed to add anything of substance and only pointed out the obvious.

Smith quickly added, "governor, my point is merely intended to underscore the fact that if we're on the wrong side of this when the number of Texans infected by the virus escalates, the press as well as the public will blame our administrations for blindly siding with Homeland Security, instead of protecting the citizens of Texas. When that happens, our political careers are over."

"So, are you suggesting we side with the senator against the president's administration?" Johnson asked even though he already knew the answer.

Her expression flared briefly. "We need to put Texans first."

The governor's mouth puckered a bit. "I thought that was what we were doing."

"Right now, optics are important."

Johnson let out a long breath. "What's your point?"

Smith took off her glasses and rubbed her eyes. "We can't afford to sit this one out. Mr. Evangelista doesn't have to win. The court can refuse to overturn the rule closing the border; and we can still lose because his argument sells newspapers and appeals to the conspiracy theorists that monopolize and manipulate the internet."

The governor sat in quiet contemplation. His approval rating had tumbled when he issued the precautionary and widely unpopular shelter-at-home order in hopes of slowing down the spread of the virus.

"The numbers of infected are going to increase; and if we don't choose the right side, we'll get the blame," Smith warned.

A flash of anger crossed the governor's face. "Right side? Texans are going to get sick; and there isn't much we can do about it."

"Yes, and many will die. The only way to get out of the path of this runaway freight train is to file an Amicus brief challenging the administration's border policies. What's happening at the border is endangering the lives of Texans, and we can't be seen as standing by and doing nothing," Smith said, realizing that they were in an impossible position.

Johnson's expression suggested that wasn't the advice he was looking for. But he suspected that Smith was right. So far, he had managed to hang on to his popularity despite the spike in unemployment and struggling economy caused by the pandemic. However, the nightmare scenario painted by the attorney general was worrisome. Every crisis has a moment where things fall into the abyss, or disaster is averted. If the voters believe that he could have done more to protect them, they will turn their backs on him during the next election and his political career would turn into a modern-day Greek tragedy.

Casey Robinson looked daggers at Smith and groaned in frustration. "You can't be serious. We can't break ranks with the president."

Smith stared back with equal intensity. "The president will throw Homeland Security to the wolves. Heck, he's got a bunch of cabinet members he can sacrifice. When this spirals out of control, he'll survive it; but we won't."

Abby Williams continued to take notes. The expression on her face said that she agreed with the attorney general.

After years of working side by side with the governor, Abby Williams had come to know his body language like the back of her hand. When Senator Cortez backed him into a corner, at first, he was pissed as hell, but she also opened his eyes to the chink in his armor - his soft underbelly.

The governor leaned back in his chair, considering what he'd just heard. He didn't want it, but with the storm he saw brewing it looked more and more that he didn't have a choice. The angst that had existed in his expression only a few moments before had completely disappeared. His face projected only icy resolve when he looked at the attorney general.

Finally, he said, "Get the brief ready. I'll call the president."

Chapter Seventeen

Brownsville, Texas

Maggie and Yami stepped out from the shadows of the mesquite thicket into the blinking daylight of Santa Rosalia Cemetery. Chicory forced its way through the cracks in the sidewalks. The streets in the neighborhood were quiet. They headed east past small plots of land choked with tall grass and weed trees and loose pipe railings that had split free from rusted chain-link fences. Two, three and sometimes five trailers squeezed together on a single plot. Liquor and wine bottles, cigarette stubs, and decommissioned cars littered the streets.

Maggie and Yamilet wandered past a small Baptist church, with a blue cross and a sign advertising times for worship. As the morning grew lighter, Yamilet took to reading the signs written in Spanish on the storefronts. On their left was a generic church with a sign *Todos necesitamos a Jesus* in a mostly vacant strip mall. Maggie noted that many of the businesses were closed or appeared to be out of business with soaped over windows.

A couple of miles east of the river, Maggie and Yamilet stopped in front of a Catholic church. Maggie stood there wondering whether to go inside and ask for help. It seemed like a lifetime ago that she'd gone to church.

The old wooden door opened with a deep groan. They entered the church, dipped their fingers in holy water, made the sign of the cross, and treaded slowly across the nave. As they drew closer to the pulpit, from the corner of her eye, Yamilet caught sight of a man dressed in a black clerical suit shuffling towards them.

"Good morning." His voice echoed among the columns. He watched Maggie and Yamilet with inquisitor's eyes as they turned, making their way across the creaky pews towards the sound of his voice.

"I'm Father Santiago," he said, studying their tired faces as they drew closer. "I was just about to drink my morning coffee. May I offer you some?" he asked, raising his thermos.

Maggie managed a smile. Yamilet cast her eyes downward. It was a gesture she had practiced as a child to show respect for members of the clergy.

Father Santiago, a short tubby man with thinning dark hair and a studious face, waddled past the confessional and led them through a narrow corridor to an office.

"Please sit." The priest turned on a portable electric heater to burn the chill from the air and poured them each a cup of coffee. Father Santiago stayed a safe distance away from them as a precautionary measure.

Maggie braced herself at the end of the couch closest to the heater. Her legs bent unreliably as she sat; it was more like a collapse.

Father Santiago bowed his head as he sat down and said a prayer.

Maggie waited for the blessing to be finished, took a quick breath and told Father Santiago their story from the beginning. For his part, Father Santiago remained silent. After thirty minutes, he started checking his watch; sometimes his gaze was focused on his intertwined fingers.

At the end of Maggie's account, Father Santiago sighed heavily. "That is quite a story." His tone was skillfully noncommittal.

Maggie was sitting on the edge of her seat. "We need a place to stay until we can figure out our next steps," she said in a tense voice.

Father Santiago studied them over the rim of his coffee cup. His eyes moved from Maggie to Yamilet and settled briefly on Giovanny, who was sleeping, his head lolling on Yamilet's bosom. He looked as if he wished this entire matter would simply go away.

"The way things work around here, churches in Brownsville are the first places that U.S. Immigration and Customs agents look for undocumented immigrants." He spoke these lines without genuine emotion, as though they had been written for him.

Maggie had a sudden premonition that Father Santiago wouldn't help them. "We just need an hour. That should be enough time to get on the internet and look for a place we can stay and email a colleague for help," she said.

Father Santiago allowed his face to register an expression of grief, then he leaned forward. "I don't think you understand what I'm telling you. I'm afraid that if you stay here much longer, ICE will show up and arrest Yamilet and her son."

There were so many ways to help. But all the Church was willing to provide were reasons not to and a stale cup of coffee.

Maggie thought about it for a second while looking over at Yamilet, who seemed to be understanding every other word. "Fifteen more minutes is all I'm asking. If you point me in the direction of a computer, I'll make some arrangements and we'll be out of your hair," she promised.

Father Santiago made a show of deliberation, but it was clear his mind was made up. "I can't. You've already been here too long. ICE has been keeping a close eye on us, particularly over the last month."

It sounded to Maggie like a well-rehearsed excuse. "Father, we don't have anywhere to go," she pleaded, desperately trying to appeal to his sense of compassion.

His eyes nervously darted between them and his watch. The thought of immigration agents bursting through the church door and arresting them terrified him. Father Santiago shrugged, reached into a bag, and pulled out two blue surgical masks. "Take these," he said. Then added, "If you walk around without them, the police will stop you."

That was all Father Santiago said. He didn't elaborate, and after saying it, he just handed Maggie and Yamilet masks.

Maggie sensed his unease and accepted the mask with a conciliatory smile.

After a moment of stunned silence, Father Santiago opened the door to his office and poked his head around the corner before leading them to a side door for them to exit through. Maggie and Yamilet slipped quietly down the narrow hallway.

"Keep to the side streets. We're in a city-wide lockdown," he warned them.

Maggie held a frown that seemed to run out of room on her face.

When they reached the door, Father Santiago flashed an anxious look. "Okay, it would be for the best if you leave now," he said politely, almost apologetically.

Maggie and Yamilet left the church through the side door.

All at once, Maggie remembered why she stopped going to church. She loathed the circular logic and duplicity that characterized the church's moralities. Confused, Yamilet looked at Maggie with a mixture of disbelief and worry. Maggie tried to smile through it, but there were flames in her eyes and tears in Yamilet's.

"Last time I put money in a fucking collection plate," Maggie muttered with a shake of her head.

* * *

Giovanny fussed and cried.

"We need milk for the baby," Yamilet told Maggie, feeling the emptiness in her own belly.

Maggie nodded, suddenly feeling guilty and worried. Giovanny hadn't had anything to eat since the night before. They were all hungry. Famished, in fact. Maggie wriggled her hand into her pocket and fished out six dollars. She could take care of the food problem, at least for now, but as for the rest of it, it was getting harder and harder not to label their situation with the word "*fucked.*" The last time she felt this lost, she was a homeless fourteen-year-old living on the streets of New York City.

"I left my wallet in the car, but this should be enough to get the baby something to eat," Maggie said.

"I have money," Yamilet said. "I keep it in Giovanny's diaper. The men that tried to rob me at the camp would not stick their hands in a dirty diaper, so I kept my money in a small plastic bag by his bottom," Yamilet said in Spanish.

Maggie's eyes locked on Giovanny's diaper. Suddenly, she had a big smile on her face. "And here I thought the kid was just pooping all the time," she giggled.

Yamilet pulled out a small plastic bag containing forty-seven dollars and two gold wedding bands.

They came upon a mini-mart two blocks from the church. The eroded sign above the store was missing several letters, a couple were burned out, and some looked like they had been the objects of target practice from bullets or BB guns.

A sullen young man sitting behind the counter was busy looking at his phone and paid them no attention. A lock of his slicked back, blacker-than-black hair fell over his forehead. The sleeves of his shirt were rolled up, revealing Aztec symbols and tattoos of women that covered both his arms. Maggie pulled a carton of milk from the refrigerator and slid it across the counter, along with two pre-made sandwiches in clear plastic wrapping.

The young man looked up from his phone. He rang up the items rapidly, peering at Maggie through the hair that had fallen across his eyes rather than brushing it back.

"Any motels close by?" Maggie asked. They needed to get off the streets as soon as possible. Every extra block they traveled increased their chances of getting caught. But what Maggie wanted most was a keyboard and an internet connection. "Nothing too expensive," she added.

The young man made a face at Maggie and then smiled. The brooding persona was gone, as if it had never been there. "¡Jajaja! Ain't no five stars here morenita. The pinche places in this barrio are all cheap."

She thought that over for a second. "Gotcha. Can you point us in the direction of the closest one?"

He shook his head while looking at Yamilet and Giovanny with big-eyed dismay. His eyes shifted back to Maggie. "You don't want the closest," he scoffed at the question. "You want Las Palmas over near Highway 83. They pay off La Migra, so they mostly don't fuck with them."

Maggie gave a nod of mutual understanding, turning over the scenario in her mind. "I hadn't thought of that. Thank you."

"Go three streets down, turn left towards the highway and you'll see it up a ways," he said, handing Maggie the bag with the carton of milk and sandwiches.

Maggie grabbed the bag. "Thanks again."

He whirled back to Yamilet and Giovanny, hair flying, and smiled. His wide grin contrasted sharply with his deep scowl. "¡Órale! Fuck those ICE pendejos. We look out for our carnales."

Chapter Eighteen

University of Miami Hospital

There was a quiet knock on the door. Sophia Wild tried to ignore it and slip back into her nap.

"Doctor Wild," the voice called to her from just outside the door.

Sophia remained motionless on the couch.

A second knock.

Sophia felt her eyebrows rise involuntarily. She opened her eyes and looked at the illuminated clock. The blue numbers told her it was 3:20 in the morning.

"Yes, what is it?" she asked, shaking off the grogginess.

The nurse opened the door slightly and poked her head into the darkened office. "Your telephone calls are transferred to the main desk. There is a Colonel Bernard Cone trying to get through to you."

Sophia sat up and rubbed her burning eyes. "Fine . . . fine, I'll turn off the call forwarding. Please ask the colonel to call back in five minutes."

Sophia didn't turn on the lights. With some effort, she reached over, turned off the call forwarding and picked up the phone on the second ring. The colonel's voice came on.

"Major, why aren't you answering your cellphone?"

"Sir, my shift starts in ninety minutes," Sophia said, her frustration apparent. "I was catching up on some sleep."

Cone noted the sound of exhaustion in her voice. He asked quietly, "How are things going down there?"

Sophia had no interest in talking, so she responded with one word: "Mayhem."

Maybe it was the quiet sense of dread that soaked through the protective medical suit to her core each time she stepped into the hospital's red zone to treat the 440 confirmed cases that quelled her desire to talk, or maybe it was simply exhaustion. The dark truth was that corpses were stacking up all around her like chips at a poker tournament, and she felt helpless to stop it.

Sophia glanced at the clock and frowned. "Colonel, I'm about to pull a sixteen-hour shift. Can whatever it is that you want to talk about wait? I'd like to get some rest before my shift starts."

"I'm afraid it can't."

Sophia let out a long breath. "Well, what is it? You've got me on the edge of my seat," she snapped sarcastically. "Don't keep me waiting."

Cone ignored her tone and focused on his reason for the call. "The president put me in charge of a team of advisors to develop policies for handling the virus."

Sophia considered the comment for a moment. "What does that have to do with me?"

"I want you on the team."

Sophia's mouth seemed to suddenly dry out, and she took a sip from a glass of water on the table next to her. "The CDC has been studying the pathogen for months now. You should cherry pick one of their best."

"Researchers. . .," Cone scoffed. "I want a doctor with field experience."

Sophia started to say something, but Cone cut her off.

"Major, you were the first doctor to encounter the contagion. You not only treated the first patients to contract the virus in Brazil, but you've been on the front-line treating patients in Miami. As far as everyone is concerned, there's no bigger expert than you."

Feeling desperately inadequate against the chaos swirling around her, she let out a frustrated growl. "I'm barely caring for these people. I haven't been a part of any advanced epidemiological *studies*. I'm just a doctor. I'm hardly an expert."

"The president disagrees."

Sophia was completely thrown. "The president?"

"Yes. You have boots on the ground experience fighting this virus. We need that perspective to establish better policies to control the spread of this disease."

Sophia resisted the urge to chew her lower lip. "What do you need me to do?"

"Support the president. The numbers of people infected with the virus are climbing in Texas and Southern California. They're still not as high as Miami and New York, but the Texas governor shared a theory with the president that is troubling. If it proves out, we may have to pivot from how we're dealing with the border situation. We'll need all-hands-on-deck to develop and implement SOPs should that eventuality come to pass."

Sophia settled back on the couch, trying to process all the information. "What's next?"

"Get tested, then go back to your housing and wait. After you get your results, we'll send a car to take you to Homestead Air Force Base and fly you to Washington," Cone said.

"What about my shift?"

"You're done there, major. You're needed in Washington."

Sophia took a deep breath and let it out slowly. "Yes, sir."

"Pack up your gear. You're going to be here a while."

Chapter Nineteen

Brownsville, Texas

The few people on the street stared malevolently at anyone who came within six feet of them. They moved briskly and with purpose, anxious to return to their homes where the illusion of safety existed.

The walk to the Las Palmas Motel took ten minutes. The motel sign was old and rusty. Maggie scanned the motel property and shuddered. It gave the impression that it wasn't meant to be used for more than an hour at a time. There was only one car and an old pickup truck parked in the patchwork of cracked asphalt that served as the motel's parking lot.

Maggie spotted a young woman with her head resting on the counter. She had a skull and rose sleeve tattoo and was wearing a white wife beater with black bra straps showing. She was a plump twenty-something, and her bleached-out hair was every which way. The woman tensed visibly when she spotted Maggie and Yami walking towards her and reached for her N-95 black mask. The designer glasses finished off the ensemble. Kind of ironic, Maggie thought, but that was probably what she was going for. Maggie could never get her head around the whole purposely choosing to be ironic thing. She thought about the fads when she was growing up. But today, social media bullying and pandemics were a lot of adversity for a kid to grow up in. She wondered if there would ever be a time again where a kid could simply eat a meal without having to take ten pictures and post it to the world or hang out with friends without having to first get medical clearances.

Staring with a guarded, wide-eyed expression, the girl grumbled something that sounded like, "Can I help you?"

Hmmm, no fake hostess smile, Maggie thought. Maggie explained that she lost her wallet, which contained her driver's license and credit cards. She asked if she could use the computer in the Business Center.

The girl behind the counter could not have looked more disinterested. She looked like she wanted to stab someone. "The Business Center is for guests only."

Maggie frowned deeply. "Haven't you heard a word I was saying?"

The lingering smirk on her face said it all. "Not my circus. Not my monkeys. If you're not a guest, I can't let you into the Business Center."

Maggie studied the girl for a moment, then tilted her head toward her right shoulder as if she thought there might be some other way to deal with her. She moved her face as close to the girl as the partition separating them would allow. She looked serious, almost fierce. "If I can use the Business Center, I can make a reservation online." She slapped a twenty-dollar bill onto the counter. "Twenty bucks for swiping the magnetic lock. Write down your cellphone number. If I'm lying, you still make twenty bucks. If I'm telling the truth, I'll make a reservation, plus there'll be another twenty bucks sent to you."

The girl's brow actually knitted for a moment as she considered the offer. She reached for the bill. On the back of her hand was a tattoo of an eagle holding a snake in its mouth, perched high on top of letters M.M., and slid it into her bra. "Or I could just keep the twenty bucks and call the cops."

Maggie glanced at her name tag, "Rosa" and shook her head slowly. "Don't be stupid."

Rosa's eyes practically popped out of her head, and her face turned crimson. Maggie instantly knew she'd hit a nerve.

"Stupid? You don't know me." Rosa yelled from behind the desk.

Maggie looked at the girl through squinted eyes. She noticed a healing cut on her swollen lower lip and other marks on her face that suggested unpleasant possibilities. She flashed a thin smile. "You're right, I don't know you," Maggie said. "The young man at the Go Mart said you'd help us. Guess he was wrong."

Rosa made a face like she wanted to throw up, and spit out the words, "That wannabe *cholo* don't know shit."

Maggie shrugged and let a practiced perplexed expression fall across her face. "He said you help your own. Guess he was—"

"Oh, so you believe everything—"

Maggie snapped in a louder than normal voice. "I hate being interrupted!"

Rosa blinked several times and stopped talking, more out of surprise than anything else.

"Like I said," Maggie said through discreetly clenched teeth. This time in a lower, even-tempered voice. "I lost my wallet and am trying to get us home. The young man directed us to this motel, said you'd help my friend and her baby. We need a room for the night which I can pay for," she said, in the sunniest tone she could muster.

Rosa sat there and chewed her bottom lip for a few seconds, hesitating like she was thinking long and hard. She glanced over at Yamilet and her baby. Giovanny was attacking his bottle of milk.

Rosa frowned slightly. Finally, she grumbled, "Fuck it." And bobbed her head for Maggie to follow her.

* * *

Rosa led Maggie to a door across from the elevator and used her magnetic key to unlock it. The darkened business center smelled sour. The cement block construction clung to the stench of cigarettes combined with mold and mildew. Maggie closed the door behind her and sat at a desk and powered up the computer. The familiar pang of the computer and the standard desktop photo of a rainforest gave her a sense of relief.

She opened Google Chrome, paid for one night's stay at Las Palmas, and then accessed her email account.

She weighed her options given her current predicament. Her boss, Bobby Moore, would cover his ass. He would not only refuse to help Yamilet and her baby, but Maggie was also sure he'd insist on turning them in to ICE to avoid being charged with a criminal offense. She had few friends back in Houston she could trust, and those she trusted didn't have the connections and money to help her. She needed an ally. A formidable one. So, it was ride or die with Pierce and Mo; she thought. Maggie took a deep breath, hoped for the best, and started typing.

Pierce and Mo,

I am writing this email because I'm in a tough situation and desperately need your help. Too much to put in an email. I booked a room under my name at Las Palmas motel in Brownsville. I will sit by the phone and await your call and explain everything.

Maggie Malone

Maggie was careful not to put any details in the email that the federal government could use to charge them with a crime. She hit send and stood up to leave when she remembered the piece of paper with Rosa's cellphone number. Accessing her account, Maggie transferred twenty dollars.

Yamilet waited anxiously in the lobby cradling Giovanny, who had fallen asleep after finishing his bottle of milk.

Rosa gave Maggie a brisk nod and slid two room keys across the brown Formica counter. "Room 108. Through the doors in the back, past the pool. Room's the last one on the left."

Not exactly a riveting conversationalist, Maggie thought, as she reached out and scooped up the two plastic keys.

They walked the short distance waving away mosquitos buzzing around the green swimming pool overrun by particles and algae. An empty wine bottle floated along the surface.

Room 108 was next to the ice machine, which was clattering away to itself. Stepping into the room, Maggie took in two double beds with pictures of still life flowers that matched the bedspreads, and cigarette burns in the frayed carpet. "It isn't the Ritz Carlton, but I've seen worse," Maggie mumbled to herself.

Yamilet sat on the edge of the bed while Giovanny slept. She looked tired and scared; and much older than her 23 years of age. They ate the sandwiches they bought at the Go Mart and waited.

* * *

Maggie jumped at the sound of the phone, waking from a bad dream where eight-foot-long alligators surrounded her car, and one was chasing her.

She grabbed the phone and pulled it to her ear. "Hello?"

"Young lady, you certainly have a flair for drama." There was no mistaking the relief in Mo's voice.

Emotionally drained, Maggie sighed and said, "I'm over this drama shit. Let's just say the trip didn't work out the way I'd planned."

"We'll have time for that. Say hi to Pierce," Mo said.

Maggie felt a little jolt of "everything is going to be all right" when she heard Pierce's voice.

"I'm happy to hear you're okay," Pierce started.

"I wouldn't say okay," her voice cracked. "You could say I'm treading water and in need of help, which is why I sent the email."

"You've treaded enough water for one day," Pierce said good-naturedly.

Maggie grew conspicuously quiet and marveled at Pierce's remark. Pierce suspected she was having an internal monologue concerning his last comment.

"The motion cameras on the U.S. side of the border photographed you walking along the edge of the river this morning," Pierce volunteered. "The FBI matched the pictures to the pictures on your cellphone that they recovered at the camp."

"You were gone before the FBI could confirm that the woman in the photographs was you," Mo interrupted.

"FBI?" Why would—"

"Pierce asked them to look for you when you dropped off the face of the earth," Mo answered her question before she could finish it.

Maggie was speechless.

"Customs has no record of you entering the country. You're in Brownsville, so my educated guess is that you swam across the Rio Grande," Pierce said.

Maggie took in a deep breath and said, "Good guess."

"What were you thinking? Do you know how many people drown trying to get across the Rio Grande?" Mo asked acidly.

Mo's tone surprised her. He was not someone prone to outward displays of emotion. "Mo, my car was stolen, along with my passport."

Mo scolded her. "All you had to do was walk up to the Border Patrol on the Mexican side, and U.S customs would have held onto you until they could confirm your story."

Maggie exhaled through her nostrils. "It's a little more complicated," she countered defensively.

"Happy you're a strong swimmer," Pierce interjected, trying to ease the tension.

She appreciated the gesture. Clearing her throat, Maggie said, "I'm going to need help getting out of here. I have no I.D. or credit cards, so renting a car is out of the question."

"I'll make arrangements to fly you home," Pierce replied. "I have a client that will lend me his private jet. We can pick you up first thing in the morning, but you'll need to get tested before you can board."

Maggie let out an exasperated breath. "Pierce, I'm out on an island here. Not sure where I can get tested or how I could pay for it."

"I'll take care of it. Stay put. I'll send someone to your motel to test you this afternoon."

"Make that three tests."

Mo felt his face twist into an irritated frown. The silence over the line lasted probably ten seconds. "Three?"

"I'll explain later, but I couldn't leave Yamilet and her son behind. They're here with me." Maggie kept her tone as relaxed as she could manage, though under the circumstances it took a fair amount of concentration just to keep her voice even.

"Are they the complication you were referring to?" Mo asked.

Maggie glanced over at Yamilet and Giovanny. Yamilet was staring at her with white ringed eyes. "I had no choice," Maggie said, careful not to say too much over the phone.

Given the stockpile of corpses on social media, Pierce understood why Maggie made the decision she did. Infections and abductions were both skyrocketing. It wouldn't be much longer before Yamilet and her baby were either infected by the deadly virus or taken. Either way, Yamilet and her son would have ended up victims of the deadly pandemic and in a ditch along with the other corpses. Maggie was out of her depth, and Yamilet and her son desperately needed help. It seemed most productive to work this problem on the assumption that once Homeland Security discovered their whereabouts, they would seize

Yamilet and Giovanny and send them back to Mexico. There was no easy way out of this. By his silence it became clear Pierce was attacking the problem with characteristic goal minded determination. It only took a few seconds for him to realize there was only one path available.

"Slight change of plans," Pierce finally said. "After we drop you off, we'll fly Yamilet and her son to Florida. We have the resources here to protect her while we sort things out."

"Then I'm coming with you," Maggie said.

Chapter Twenty

Brownsville, Texas

Yamilet turned the television to a channel showing cartoons to keep Giovanny entertained. It was already over two hours past the time Pierce said they would be there to pick them up. Maggie paced back and forth to the degree the cramped motel room would allow. After countless circles, she laid back on the bed and stared up at the ceiling. Yamilet was sitting on her bed dabbing the tears that leaked from the corner of her eyes, giggling at SpongeBob and the goings-on in Bikini Bottom.

At a quarter past ten in the morning, there was a brisk rap on the door. Maggie jumped to her feet. She opened the door and smiled at the sight of Pierce standing there wearing a mask and holding two cups of coffee. The white mask accentuated his intense blue eyes.

"Sorry we're late. We flew into a pretty strong headwind." Pierce glanced over at Yamilet and saw that she was watching him with growing curiosity. Pierce made a point of greeting her in Spanish.

"*Buenos dias*, Yamilet," he smiled benevolently.

Yamilet managed a weak smile. "*Buenos dias.*"

"*Mi nombre es Pierce. Soy amigo de Maggie.*" Pierce said, handing Yamilet a cup of coffee.

There was a flash of recognition in her eyes as she reached for the cup. "*Te recuerdo.*"

Yamilet took a cautious sip. "*Gracias.*"

"We're ready," Maggie announced, anxious to leave the motel. They walked along the narrow walkway past the swimming pool.

Parked next to the lobby was a dark blue passenger van. Pierce climbed into the front passenger seat. Once Maggie, Yamilet and Giovanny were seated, the driver started the engine and headed east towards Brownsville/South Padre Island International Airport.

Thirty minutes later, the van rolled to a stop outside of the terminal designated for private aircraft.

The labored howl of a jumbo jet climbing into the blue-sky startled Yamilet. She'd never seen a commercial jet up close before. Pierce escorted them through the small private lobby.

"That's us," he said, pointing to a Bombardier Challenger parked on the tarmac. The airstrip just ahead rumbled as planes lifted into the sky.

Maggie watched the procession of planes crawling in line at the end of the runway, waiting to take off, and pursed her lips. "That's a lot of planes, considering we're in a lockdown."

"About a quarter the usual number," Pierce said.

Maggie carried Giovanny up the boarding stairs. Once they were settled in the cabin, she placed him on Yamilet's lap and slipped the seatbelt over them.

"*No hay necesidad de estar nerviosa,*" Maggie smiled, trying to calm Yamilet's nerves. Yamilet barely nodded, staring straight ahead as if she had been riveted to the seat.

The plane jerked forward towards the runway. Yamilet's eyes widened, and she hunched forward, bracing herself for the next blow. "*Dios Mio.*"

The growl of the engines turned to a roar as the jet gained speed and bounced slightly down the runway, throwing her back into the seat. The airplane hangars and the world behind them whirled by and suddenly they were slicing through the air, climbing away from Brownsville.

Maggie sipped the last of her coffee. "So, where do we go from here?"

Pierce pulled the elastic straps off his ears and removed the mask. "We have our preliminary injunction hearing in three days. Afterward, I'll file an application for a Withholding of Removal proceeding. After the hearing, Yamilet and her son can stay with Mo. He has plenty of room at his house on Hutchinson Island."

Maggie stared at Pierce with a resigned expression. "The president's Executive Order temporarily blocks new asylum applications."

Pierce didn't disagree. However, he rarely looked at a problem from only one angle. He believed that when presented with a challenge, knowing what to ask was the difference between doing more of the same and doing something extraordinary. Ninety-nine percent of the applications filed were applications asking for asylum. The president's order specifically and *only* blocked new asylum applications. It was the one percent not mentioned in the president's order that got Pierce's attention.

"The president's order doesn't specifically prohibit withholding - only proceedings," Pierce said.

Maggie's dark eyes narrowed, a skeptical brown. "Hmmm, that's interesting. But even if we can get a hearing, winning is a whole different story. Those cases are much harder to win."

Pierce nodded thoughtfully, looking down and swirling the last of his coffee around the cup before taking a sip. A mannerism Maggie didn't know how to read.

"Harder, yes but when we win, it will establish a favorable precedent."

Maggie looked idly out the small round window at 50,000 feet. Pierce's plan was a little too slick for her taste.

"At best, this is a Hail Mary?"

He chuckled. "Don't discount a 'Hail Mary'. It can be a game changer." Pierce grinned as disarmingly as he could. "You wouldn't happen to know how the term 'Hail Mary' became popular?"

Maggie shook her head. "Nope, not a clue."

Pierce laughed and leaned in a little closer. "The Dallas Cowboys were trailing the Minnesota Vikings 14-10 in the NFC Championship. With seconds left on the clock, Dallas quarterback Roger Staubach threw a 50-yard touchdown pass that sent the Cowboys to the Super Bowl. When Staubach described the winning play after the game, he said, "I got knocked down on the play . . . I closed my eyes and said a Hail Mary.""

Maggie nodded thoughtfully. "Cute story, but I'm not drinking the Kool Aid. To win a withholding only case you have to convince the judge that you possess a 'credible fear' of persecution. Sounds easy, but it almost never happens. A lawyer would have to wheel his client into the proceeding on a gurney shot full of bullet holes for a judge to find a 'credible fear' of persecution."

"I get it. The applicant's sworn testimony alone rarely satisfies that threshold."

A look of annoyance rippled over Maggie's face. She'd traveled down this road more times than she cared to remember. "Oh, subjectively speaking, it should. These people are risking everything to run away, leaving behind their homes, lives, and families. All a judge has to do is pull back the curtain to see that something bad is driving them away. But immigration judges have preconceived notions and choose not to believe applicants. Otherwise, these folks would be able to meet their burden of proof."

Pierce circled back to his earlier point. "Like I said, a win in this case creates precedent for similarly situated migrants to rely on. We'll change the narrative."

Cynicism crept into Maggie's voice once again. "What makes you so confident that you can convince an immigration judge to rule in your favor?"

Pierce already considered that possibility. "If I can't, I'll appeal. Assuming you're right and the immigration judges are biased, we won't encounter the same prejudice in federal court. The cartel's abductions are well documented. Besides, I have a credible third-party witness who survived an actual attack and can provide a firsthand account of the cartel's abductions and murders of the camp's inhabitants."

Maggie's full lips curved into a frown. "I can certainly do that."

"Not quite as graphic as wheeling a bullet ridden corpse into the courtroom but still hard to ignore. Any other major concerns?"

Maggie fell back in her seat and folded her arms across her chest. "Unfortunately, yes." She felt her jaw tighten as she replayed the last time she represented a client in a withholding-only proceeding in her head. "Families that pursue withholding-only proceedings are separated and held in ICE detention throughout the entire process. They're not given the opportunity to ask a judge for release. . ." Maggie let her voice trail off, leaving an obvious "and" at the end of her sentence.

"And you're worried that if we file a petition, ICE will snatch Yamilet and Giovanny at the hearing."

Maggie gave a frustrated nod of her head as the image of Yamilet in a holding cell and Giovanny being placed in the custody of Health and Human Services flashed through her mind. "An appeal will take months, maybe a year."

Her remark elicited a flicker of a smile from Pierce. "Probably longer than a year." Then as if reading her mind, he added, "but Yamilet and Giovanny won't be incarcerated and separated during the process. They'll stay with Mo."

Maggie had the look of a serious skeptic. "According to ICE and the immigration courts, people in withholding-only proceedings are not eligible for bond. They're held in mandatory detention."

Pierce shrugged slightly. "That's been a contentious issue. The Second and Fourth Court of Appeals both recently ruled that immigrants in withholding-only proceedings may be released on bond."

"Interesting." Maggie actually smiled at that. "I assume you'll file the petition in one of those jurisdictions."

"Yes, and we will immediately petition the judge to release Yamilet and Giovanny on a bond."

"The judge could still deny the bond."

From where Pierce was sitting, it didn't make any sense for the court to deny the request. "The court gains nothing by refusing the bond. Because of the pandemic, all hearings are virtual. Yamilet can participate in the hearing without any threat of being taken into custody. So, granting her release in exchange for a bond is really form over substance."

Maggie drummed her fingers on the arm of the seat for a few moments, eyes locked on Pierce. She was rarely surprised and hid her awe behind a professional mask. She had to admit that his idea for handling Yamilet's petition was resourceful and sublime. However, ninety-nine percent of the immigration officers and judges she came across were career bureaucrats with no moral compass or empathy. "Looks like you got this all figured out. But I just don't know."

"Mags," Pierce finally said. "I don't mean to nitpick here, but we're teetering on the precipice, and I have a plan, and you don't."

* * *

An hour later, the jet started its descent into Miami, Florida. Yamilet was still white as a sheet. Pierce looked over and smiled reassuringly.

"We'll be landing soon. You're safe now," he comforted her in Spanish.

Yamilet blinked hard, took a deep breath, and willed herself to relax.

Chapter Twenty-One

Washington D.C.

At 4:30 p.m. on February 18, Governor Johnson spoke with the president. At 5pm the Texas governor held a press conference and announced that the U.S. Constitution authorizes Texas to exercise its "war powers" against an "invasion." Holding the twenty-page attorney general's opinion in his hand, the governor informed the press that an "invasion" includes the current surges of infected aliens crossing the border. The governor accused the president of failing to secure the border against the spread of the deadly virus in Texas.

With all the major news networks in attendance, the governor launched into a rhetorical flourish. "The federal government's failure to secure the border and protect Texas from invasion is dangerous and unprecedented. Texans are dying and our president offers sentimental hogwash instead of taking the necessary steps to contain the spread of this deadly disease. The Constitution offers states the ability to engage in war without the consent of Congress if they're 'actually invaded'. This 'invasion' need not be in the traditional sense of a military force. Immigrants are crossing our southern border illegally and spreading the virus." The governor's face projected only icy resolve. "Texas has the right to defend itself and protect its citizens," he declared.

* * *

Doctor Wild shivered from the cold and stood nervously on the curb just outside the Hampton Inn on H Street. She had been watching Governor Johnson's press conference on CNN when Colonel Cone called and told her that a car would pick her up outside of her hotel in thirty minutes. A gust of wind hit her square in the face, and she swore out loud. Sophia pulled the hood over her head and zipped the jacket all the way up to her chin.

An hour later, she was sitting in the Cabinet Room in the West Wing with a painting of the signing of the Declaration of Independence over her shoulder. Every chair except for the taller one at the center of the oval mahogany table was occupied by the National Security Team, which was assembled, waiting for the president to join them.

President Porter entered the room, and everyone immediately stood. Maria Flynn, his Chief of Staff, followed closely behind. The president stopped and shook Colonel Bernard Cone's hand. He had no doubt that the head of the U.S. Army Medical Research Institute of Infectious Diseases knew more about the virus than all his top advisors. He glanced at Sophia and tried to place her. Maria leaned in and whispered into the president's ear.

"Mr. President, may I introduce . . . ."

"Doctor Wild," the president smiled, finishing the colonel's sentence.

President Porter was tall, a bit over six feet in height. His dark brown hair was graying at the temples and his square chin had a deep notch in the center. Despite the great burden of the country placed squarely on his shoulders, he portrayed profound confidence and reassuring intelligence.

"Mr. President, Doctor Wild was the first doctor to discover and gather samples of the virus in Brazil. When it comes to combating this virus, she's the most experienced and talented doctor on the team. She has been on the frontline from the very beginning, a real asset," the colonel offered.

"Well, you have my gratitude," the president clasped her hand.

The colonel exaggerated a bit, but Sophia wasn't going to correct him. President Porter continued around the table and took his chair. Sitting across from the president, and next to the vice president, was the attorney general.

After President Porter announced the agenda for the meeting, he turned the meeting over to Attorney General Thomas Sullivan. Sullivan began on a somber note by saying, "Governor Johnson is relying on a legally flawed opinion to assume control of the National Guard and deploy them to the Texas/Mexico border."

Secretary of State, Robert Stephens, was more concerned with the state of the country than the ramifications of a Texas bureaucrat gone rogue. "The bigger threat is the skyrocketing mortality rate, and the economy grinding to a standstill. Even with the Quarantine Order in place our hospitals are on the brink of collapsing and our blood supplies are almost gone. Without a vaccine, ninety percent of the population will be dead in a year."

A morbid silence fell over the meeting as everyone wrapped their minds around the beckoning "end-of-days" scenario. The impact of the virus had shaken the country. Hundreds of thousands were fighting for their lives in hospitals.

The president took a breath and let it out slowly before speaking again. In the days and weeks ahead, he expected to see the number of deaths soar to an alarming level. Surviving the crisis was going to require strong intergovernmental coordination between the federal government and the states, as some regions had been harder hit than others. The country was weak and fractured, and images of the splintering effect Governor Johnson's actions would have if they went unchecked reeled through his mind.

"The governor is walking on a dangerous path. If we don't act quickly, this problem in Texas is going to fester," the president said, turning his attention back to the attorney general.

The attorney general flipped to the last page of the legal opinion and tossed it onto the table like an empty bag of potato chips. "Mr. President, this reads like back-of-the envelope rhetoric. It's an artificial construct. It'll be laughed out of court in half a second."

The president's fair complexion had grown flushed. "We both know it won't ever get that far."

Stephen's eyes narrowed suspiciously. "The governor is playing a high stakes game of chicken. He's banking on the idea that he can strong arm us into deploying more troops on the Texas border by threatening to do it himself."

Secretary of Homeland Security, Malcolm Grayson nodded uncomfortably. "I don't agree with the governor's tactics, but he does make a valid point about the infected immigrants and Texas becoming the epicenter if they continue to cross into the country."

Stephens looked at Grayson and said out loud what everyone in the room was thinking. "This is nothing more than shameful political gamesmanship. His approval ratings are plummeting. The more afraid the governor can make people, the easier it is for him to get re-elected."

Sullivan made a face that suggested that while he didn't condone the governor's motive, perhaps it was time to set political agendas aside. "Mr. President, this is a highly contagious virus. Every infected immigrant that crosses into the country puts the American public at great risk. Deploying troops to occupy the border and assist the Border Patrol with enforcement activities may be the most plausible solution."

"No," the president said with utter finality. "That train left the station the moment the governor decided to publicly shame the administration. We are not going to reward him."

The Chairman of the Joint Chiefs of Staff, General Mark P. Bronson, who had been quietly observing the proceedings, finally weighed in. "No matter how many troops we deploy, we can't stop every immigrant from crossing the border. One infected immigrant sneaking through is all it takes to infect thousands."

The strategy of deploying more troops to guard the border as the numbers of immigrants increased, resulting in the situation becoming even more desperate reminded Sophia of the vintage arcade game "Galaga" where the object was to kill all the enemy fighters diving towards you. As the game progressed, the number and speed of the enemy fighters increased until it was impossible to account for all of them. Eventually there were too many coming at once and they'd overwhelm the player, and it was "game over."

Stephens picked up on the president's tone and immediately felt a sense of dread. "What about sanctions? We can impose sanctions."

Frowning, the president shook his head. "This virus will continue to cause a great amount of suffering, fear, and death. We're not going to exacerbate it by punishing Americans for the actions of a sanctimonious blowhard. The pharmaceutical companies are working around the clock to develop a vaccine. Best case, we're two-to-three months away from having a vaccine we can fast track through the FDA approval process. In the meantime, food shortages will get worse, and millions of Americans are going to die," he said, sounding a little strangled as he reined in his distress.

Predictably horrified, Stephens grimaced. "Three months? If this goes unchecked, support for secession in the U.S. will grow as the situation continues to deteriorate, and the States become more polarized."

Grayson shrugged his shoulders, as if mystified by the state of the country. "Thirty-three percent of Americans already support the idea that it's time to split the country."

Sullivan did not share Grayson's sentiment. He sorted through his memory, almost as a law clerk would sort through legal citations, until he found the seminal case. "If there was any constitutional issue resolved by the Civil War, it is that there is no right to secede."

"The signs of dissension are everywhere. If we sit back and let the governor move the National Guard to the border, that could be a pivotal factor," Stephens said, shaking his head incredulously.

Grayson disagreed. "I don't believe that Governor Johnson would take it that far."

The president nodded thoughtfully but didn't immediately speak. He was pissed as hell but maintained a calm demeanor in the middle of the storm that made him so popular with Americans. "The governor is inciting sedition at the precise moment that we need to be pulling together. That's pushing free speech a little far. We need to respond to the Texas problem decisively."

Somewhat used to dealing with these scenarios strategically, Colonel Cone offered a different solution. "Mr. President, if I may?"

The president nodded, signaling the colonel to proceed.

"While I mean no disrespect to anyone, we should approach this as a simple physics problem. An indisputable law of physics is that water always finds the lowest level efficiently. It penetrates any crevice or path that will facilitate its flow. The immigrants attempting to cross into the U.S. are a lot like water. Some will find the crack in our defenses, no matter how many men we station at the border and get through. So instead of trying to stop the flow, we should guide it by focusing our efforts on funneling it to an area where we can test and treat everyone crossing the border."

The president's eyebrows arched in surprise. "You're proposing that we let the immigrants camped on the border cross into Texas?"

The colonel looked at the other attendees before answering. "Not just Texas, but Arizona and California. Mr. President, the only way to slow the spread of the virus is to isolate those that are infected."

The president looked at the secretary of state briefly and then back at the colonel. "Colonel, do you have a plan?"

"At this stage, its conceptual. Nothing concrete, Mr. President."

The president leaned back in his chair, considering what he'd just heard. "Lay out the big picture. If its plausible, we'll iron out the details later."

Cone nodded. "Yes sir. The first thing we'll need are several bases of operation close to the migrant camps on the U.S. side of the border. They'll need to be big enough to process and house large numbers. Like a funnel, we'll need to control the number of immigrants crossing at one time. With the combination of a buildup of troops and a safer alternative for entering the country, we can put a stop to people risking their lives to cross illegally."

Bronson assessed the logistical requirement. "Football's big in the Southwest, so there should be several large high school and college stadiums close to the border that would work for purposes of initially housing and testing the immigrants that are being processed."

"And what do we do with them once they are tested and processed?" Sullivan asked.

"We hang on to them and isolate the sick ones," Colonel Cone replied.

Grayson seemed confused. "We don't have enough blood and equipment as it is to treat our own sick."

"I'm not proposing that we treat them. We isolate everyone that tests positive and make them as comfortable as possible."

Grayson chewed his lower lip and nodded tentatively. "I guess that's still a lot more humane than their current conditions."

The chief of staff printed out a list of the stadiums and arenas in the border States and handed it to the president. His gaunt face and eyes had seen more than they wanted to in the past few weeks. The president studied the list and addressed the chairman of the joint chiefs of staff.

"How long before you can put this operation together?"

In his experience, an operation of this scale with so many moving parts would take time. "We'll need to coordinate with our Homeland Security, our medical team; prepare SOPs; set up testing sites –"

A hint of frustration crept into the president's voice. "How long?"

The general looked almost instantly uncomfortable. "At least forty to sixty days, Mr. President."

"We can't spend weeks talking about what we are going to do. We just need to do it. Make it thirty," the president said firmly.

There wasn't a clear consensus among the president's advisers. Several viewed the entire operation as rather hopeless. It was a plan fraught with risk. However, his advisors all agreed that one conclusion seemed inescapable. The president was heading towards a standoff with the governor of Texas and the state militia.

Chapter Twenty-Two

Miami, Florida

The virtual hearing before The Honorable Roberta Edwards on the cross motions for summary judgement lacked the venerated traditions, courtroom pomp and decorum that normally accompanied a hearing in U.S. District Court. Missing were the sights and sounds of the courtroom; lawyers shuffling back and forth, interested parties taking their seats, papers rustling, and the deputy commanding everyone in the courtroom to rise when the judge entered. The two-dimensional nature and limited field of vision of videoconferencing presented challenges for lawyers. Remote conferencing made it harder, if not virtually impossible, to make direct eye contact with the judge to emphasize a particular point and observe body language cues.

Pierce waited for a sign from the judge that he could begin.

Judge Edward's eyes darted across the screen as she confirmed that all parties were present. The judge's voice crackled into her microphone. "It appears that everyone that needs to be here is online."

"Good morning Your Honor. May it please the court, Pierce Evangelista on behalf of the Plaintiff. Appearing virtually with me today, are my co-counsels Moses Black and Ms. Maggie Malone."

The judge nodded. "Good morning."

"Good morning, Your Honor, Asher Tate representing the United States. Assisting is my co-counsel, Mr. Stephen Wong." She smiled, maintaining a look of casual confidence. Asher had all the credentials one would expect of one of the Department of Justice's fast rising stars. An Ivy League education, and a solid east coast pedigree. She spoke with forceful, clipped precision, coming off like an aristocratic dominatrix. She was smart and motivated but didn't seem interested in making a career out of working for the Department of Justice. Like a heat-seeking missile, she aimed herself towards the cases with the biggest likelihood of attracting the news and social media interest. She clearly loved the spotlight, performing for the media and they loved the sound bites she graciously volunteered. She played politics and relied on her family connections and good looks when necessary to land those assignments. She knew those were the cases that were her ticket to landing a lucrative private sector job after her civil service.

During their initial meeting, she came off as obsessive-compulsive and inflexible. When Maggie had disappeared and Mo asked for a short extension of time for the hearing date, she had refused, seeing it as an opportunity to cripple their case. Pierce told his mentor to let her have that small victory. It wasn't time to go to war yet.

Judge Edwards nodded. "You may proceed, Mr. Evangelista."

Pierce smiled. "Thank you. Your Honor, this case raises the issue whether a federal agency can promulgate a rule which fails to comply with the notice requirements of the *Administrative Procedures Act* when no exemption exists. As more fully laid out in our Memorandum of Law in Support of our Motion for Summary Judgment, the recent regulation closing the border and suspending asylum applications violates the APA's Section 553 Rulemaking Requirements. As a result, thousands of asylum seekers fleeing persecution are forced to stay in Mexico."

Judge Edwards cleared her throat and bristled. "Mr. Evangelista, I've read your legal argument in support of the issue here."

Asher Tate sat there with her best fake smile plastered on her face.

Pierce picked up on the Judge's tone. She was well versed in the legal arguments of both sides and the supporting case law. Like any great tactician, Pierce made a strategic adjustment and pivoted to the human element.

"Your Honor, the pervasive and systematic level of violence associated with the gangs in the Northern Triangle and Mexico has dramatically increased. The pandemic has set off the fastest mass migration in Central and South America in at least three decades."

Judge Edwards raised an eyebrow. "Yes, and as a result, the president has issued an Emergency Order," she interjected.

Pierce nodded. "That's correct. The context of the issue before the court, however, consists of the facts which were in existence at the time the Department of Homeland Security ("DHS") initiated the rulemaking process."

"Doesn't the president's Emergency Order render this case moot?" The judge asked in a doubting tone.

"We do not believe it does. The regulation shutting off asylum hearings will still be in effect after the Emergency Order expires; and plaintiffs have pled sufficient facts to show a widespread practice of denial of access to the asylum process existed even before the president's Emergency Order."

Judge Edwards tilted her head and regarded him. "Mr. Evangelista, then I take it that you have no issue with the Emergency Order closing the border?"

"Your Honor, plain and simple, DHS failed to follow the rules; and therefore, Customs and Border Patrol ("CBP") should be required to process asylum applications once the president's order is no longer in effect."

Pierce had the distinct impression that he was making a point that the judge had already considered.

"Now, if I could elaborate briefly on some facts?"

Judge Edwards managed a brief smile and nodded. "Please continue."

"Thank you. Ms. Yamilet Pereyra is a native of El Salvador. She is a 23-year-old mother of one child, Giovanny, age 10 months. In May, her husband disappeared after he refused to allow drug cartel members to use his home to hide drugs."

Pierce took a breath and sighed. "When she reported her husband's disappearance to governmental authorities, members of the drug cartel abducted her, held her at gunpoint, and threatened to kill both her and her child if she continued to investigate her husband's disappearance. One cartel member told Yamilet that she had to leave if she wanted to live."

Asher Tate unmuted her microphone and thought of making a hearsay objection but resisted the impulse.

"Fearing for her life, Yamilet fled and undertook the dangerous journey to the United States. It took her two months to travel from her village to Matamoros, Mexico. Yamilet has lived in Matamoros in what is commonly known as 'Tent City' for eight months. The worldwide shortage and demand for blood has also reached an unprecedented level; and the migrants forced to wait for asylum in Tent City are kidnapped, tortured, and killed for their blood by members of the drug trafficking cartel while we turn a blind eye to genocide."

The human suffering was hard to ignore, and Pierce thought he detected a hint of compassion in the judge's eyes. He paused, allowing his point to sink in before focusing on his next argument. Asher bided her time, sipping her tea and frowning at appropriate moments.

"Your Honor," Pierce continued. "The asylum provisions of the *Immigration and Nationality Act* ("INA"), reflect Congress's intent to "give statutory meaning to our national commitment to human rights and humanitarian concerns." Pierce raised his voice slightly. The inflection he gave the words *"human rights and humanitarian concerns"* was intended to give them greater weight.

Judge Edwards held up her hand, silencing Pierce. "In 1996, Congress tightened the asylum procedures. How is this any different given the dire state of the country because of the pandemic?"

Pierce nodded respectfully, taking a moment to consider the question. "There is a big difference, Your Honor. The 1996 Act was lawfully passed by an act of Congress and signed by the president. The DHS's rule, which is the subject of this complaint, violates the APA's rule making requirements. A federal *agency cannot* exceed the legal authority delegated to it by Congress, any more than other any branch of government can. Congress provides federal agencies with considerable power. However, failing to comply with the APA's rulemaking requirements is an abuse of that power."

The judge's reaction was a barely perceptible nod. "The APA does provide for exceptions to that rule."

Pierce acknowledged her point. "It does, Your Honor. But they don't apply in this case. Moreover, courts have uniformly held that an agency's failure to include a formal statement of reasons in the rule when bypassing Section 553's requirements is fatal."

Pierce sensed that the judge had come to roughly the same conclusion.

"If there are no more questions, I would like to defer the balance of my time for rebuttal."

"Thank you," Judge Edwards said, reaching for her water. "Ms. Tate, the court will hear from you now."

Asher Tate smiled. "Judge Edwards, may it please the court."

Asher cleared her throat gently before beginning. She raised several issues in her memorandum of law but decided to spend her thirty-minute allotment of time hammering away on the procedural point of law that without an actual controversy, the court does not have the ability to hear the case.

"When the Department of Justice looks at a complaint, we remember basic rules, basic things that we were supposed to be studying in law school, the approach to a case, the approach to resolving a conflict. In this instance, the court should grant the defendant's motion and dismiss this Complaint in its entirety because the case is moot and therefore must be dismissed under *Federal Rule of Civil Procedure* 12(b)(1)."

In a firm voice, Asher said, "First, the DHS has adopted a rule that comports with "officially sanctioned policy" of denying asylum seekers access to the asylum process. Therefore, the conduct alleged in the Complaint is lawful. Second, Section 553 specifically authorizes federal agencies to dispense with the APA's rule making requirements under certain circumstances."

Judge Edwards glanced over the top of the document in her hands. "Ms. Tate, let me cut to the chase. You're contending that this matter is moot, thereby depriving the court of subject matter jurisdiction. Correct?"

Asher nodded. "Yes, Your Honor. Federal courts lack jurisdiction to decide moot cases because their constitutional authority extends only to actual cases or controversies."

The judge gave Asher a skeptical look. "And you think this court should accept your contention that DHS properly invoked the good faith exception without conducting a fact-specific inquiry?"

"In this instance the rule comports with the president's directive which on its face establishes 'good cause'." She answered self-assuredly, with no sign of hedging.

Judge Edwards considered her answer and asked. "Even if the Emergency Order wasn't signed until after the DHS rule went into effect?"

Asher's response was skillfully noncommittal. "Your Honor, this court has the discretion to reconcile the officially sanctioned policy and DHS rule; and establish good cause after the fact. I don't think that the fact the rule was published before the Emergency Order defeats the regulatory objective here."

Judge Edwards gave Asher a doubtful look. "It may not be an automatic death sentence, but Courts have traditionally held that these exceptions are to be narrowly construed and reluctantly tolerated."

Asher glared at the judge with a silent challenge. "I don't believe that you can get to the merits of this case." Then she feigned deference toward the judge. "But assuming for argument's sake that you can find that this court has jurisdiction, your review is not limited to any single point in time and should weigh heavily in favor of the administration."

Pierce thought he noticed a flash of anger just beneath the surface. Judge Edwards quelled it and signaled to Ms. Tate to continue.

Asher spoke uninterrupted for the next twenty minutes. "In closing, the Constitution restricts the jurisdiction of federal courts to actual 'cases' and 'controversies.' To invoke federal court jurisdiction, plaintiffs must demonstrate that they possess a legal interest, or a personal stake, in the outcome of the action. That simply doesn't exist here."

Asher scanned the faces on her computer. She had one final point to make. "If an intervening circumstance deprives the plaintiff of a personal stake in the outcome of the lawsuit, at any point during litigation, the action can no longer proceed and must be dismissed as moot. The president's Emergency Order is an intervening factor. Therefore, this court lacks jurisdiction, and must dismiss this case."

The judge looked into her camera and robotically said, "Your time has expired, Ms. Tate."

"Mr. Evangelista, you have five minutes remaining."

"Your Honor, The D.C. circuit has made it clear that only one plaintiff is required to establish standing and enable review. Here, Ms. Pereyra is that plaintiff. She crossed the border three days ago and has a cognizable legal interest in pursuing her claims."

The judge looked at Pierce with an undisguised curiosity. "Do you have any substantive evidence that Ms. Pereyra is currently in this country?"

"Yes. We filed declarations signed by Ms. Pereyra, and my co-counsel Mr. Black with the court. The declarations were notarized by a Florida notary. We also provided copies to opposing counsel," Pierce said.

The confident smirk on Asher's face vanished as the table turned. Her co-counsel sat perched on the edge of his chair, searching furiously on his laptop for the documents.

Asher Tate's normally calm demeanor turned to one of overt irritation. "Objection, Your Honor, that fact is not supported by admissible evidence."

Judge Edwards pulled up the declarations on her computer and read them. "Hold on a moment."

Pierce adjusted the camera slightly so that it captured Yamilet and her son sitting on the sofa behind him.

The judge looked up. "Mr. Evangelista, is that Ms. Pereyra sitting behind you?"

"Yes, Your Honor. As previously stated, Ms. Pereyra only arrived in the country a few days ago. Her declaration is being proffered merely to dispute the defendant's contention that there is no viable plaintiff and therefore no genuine dispute."

The judge and Asher locked eyes. "Counselor, you'll be given reasonable time to respond to the declaration before I issue my ruling."

The frown lines deepened as frustration showed on Asher's face. Judge Edwards shifted her pensive gaze from Asher to Pierce and gave him a little nod.

Pierce proceeded in his typically calm and eloquent voice. "The defendant's mootness argument is flawed because the president's Emergency Order closing the border does not apply to Ms. Pereyra and her son. However, the DHS rule still denies her the right to asylum," Pierce said.

Pierce's phone beeped. He had programmed it to alert him when he had two minutes remaining. "In 1986, the coal mining industry turned to automation. An 'electric nose' took the place of the canary. Remembering the canary, though, represents an important opportunity as it relates to migrants denied entry into this country."

The judge shrugged and looked perplexed. "I'm not sure I understand your point."

"For decades, Your Honor, canaries detected and identified the toxic gases. Coal mine canaries never had a chance. They were always unable to breathe. Some of them just died a slow death. Some died quicker. It was always through choking, though. Always by saving someone else. Always ending up dead. Today, the pandemic has made poor people targets as a resource for blood so others stricken by the virus can receive treatment. The migrants camped on our border desperately seeking asylum are human canaries."

Asher rolled her eyes. A gesture intended to convey to the judge that Pierce's comments were extraneous. Judge Edwards remained absolutely unreadable as Pierce finished up his rebuttal.

"The cartels are killing poor people in Central and South America and selling their blood to companies like Lighthouse Blood Centers. The migrants are trapped facing a death sentence."

Judge Edwards eyed Pierce for a moment, her gaze tense. "You're out of time, Mr. Evangelista. Wrap it up."

"Yes, Your Honor. Albert Einstein said: 'The world is a dangerous place, not because of those who do evil, but because of those who look and do nothing.' We can do something today by overturning an illegally promulgated rule that violates U.S. law and exacerbates the humanitarian crisis by exposing asylum seekers to serious harm. DHS's rule denies people the protection of the United States and subjects them to the barbaric persecution of the cartels, essentially making them no different from canaries in the coal mines." Pierce paused for a brief moment and then said, "Thank you." His use of the pronoun *we*, was quite deliberate, and it had its intended effect.

Chapter Twenty-Three

Miami, Florida

Mo bounced into the room with youthful enthusiasm and plopped onto the long, blue leather couch next to Maggie. With a huge grin spreading across his face, he leaned back and clasped his hands behind his head. The more he thought about Asher's facial contortions when Pierce exposed the major crack in the government's seemingly perfect defense, the more satisfied he felt.

Mo's face broke into a genuine smile. "The look on Asher's face when she suddenly realized that she was up against one of the best lawyers in the country and he had a smoking gun was priceless."

Pierce narrowed his eyes because compliments from Mo were rare. Criticism was the norm.

"The canary analogy was a little long winded but effective," Mo mused. His tone was reminiscent of a time when Pierce was a wet behind the ears lawyer fresh out of law school.

"And there it is," Pierce said, closing the laptop.

Maggie's teeth flashed white in a content smile. "It surprised me as well. I did my homework on both of you when I found out that we'd be working together. I assumed that she would have done the same. And to make matters worse, not being prepared to deal with the declarations was careless."

Mo shook his head. "More like arrogant. I did a little research as well. Asher Tate hasn't lost a case in ten years. She probably figured it didn't matter who was on the other side."

Pierce peered at Mo. "You're getting ahead of yourself. We haven't won anything."

"Not yet," Mo shrugged. "But I've been doing this for fifty-plus years. I'd say we have a ninety percent chance the judge rules in our favor."

"Lucky for us that Yamilet was in the country," Maggie said. Her curiosity was piqued. "What would you have argued if she was still in Mexico?"

Pierce grappled with the implication. "I would have relied on the initial Declaration of Gabriella Nevarez. Gabriella crossed the border a few weeks before we filed the lawsuit. She was still in U.S. custody when the Department of Justice was served," he said, not the slightest bit deterred.

"Why didn't you go with Naverez's Declaration?" Maggie asked.

Pierce shrugged. "I considered it, but Gabriella was recently deported to Mexico. Most likely, Asher would have argued that we no longer had standing. Yamilet's Declaration made it possible for me to avoid having to charge and take that hill."

Mo's crinkled face had taken on a self-satisfied rosiness. "The Department of Justice predictably moves to dismiss cases. The facts in this case didn't favor the government, so we expected them to fight like hell to try to get rid of the case on procedural grounds."

Maggie looked a little stricken. "I wasn't aware that you were going to use Yamilet to prove standing. When was that decided?"

There was an awkward moment of silence and then Mo said, "It was a last-minute audible. When we filed Yamilet's Declaration, we expected the DOJ to move to postpone the hearing date under Rule 56 and demand that we produce her for deposition. If she showed up, they'd arrest her and deport her before the hearing date. If she didn't, they'd fight the admissibility of her declaration. They missed it."

Maggie squinted at Mo with suspicious eyes. "I get that. But why keep me in the dark?"

Mo smiled and said, "Plausible deniability. We thought it best to try to stay under everyone's radar. If your boss chastises you for not keeping him in the loop, you can honestly tell him it was a last-minute decision, and you didn't know."

Maggie sighed and sat back in her chair. "The DOJ can still demand to take Yamilet's deposition."

Pierce looked at Mo, who simply shrugged in a manner that said, at this point, what good would that do?

Maggie smiled warmly and squeezed Mo's arm. "That was the right call."

"And now we wait," Mo chimed in.

Pierce frowned with an analytical detachment. He thought to himself that even with a favorable ruling, nothing in the immediate future was going to change. The president's order would keep the border closed.

Almost as if he could read Pierce's mind, Mo said, "A Summary Judgment win is a step in the right direction. The Emergency Order will be rescinded in a few months at the most, and with no rule in place to keep the border closed, DHS will have to begin processing asylum applications."

Maggie agreed with Mo's point. 'It's not perfect by a long stretch, but it's a hell of a lot better than the present situation. Right now, the people over there are just waiting to die with no hope of a better future."

Mo glanced over at Maggie. He considered how she was doing. She'd been through a harrowing ordeal, narrowly escaping death in the camp and almost drowning in the Rio Grande.

"Maggie, how are you doing?" Mo asked quietly.

"Excuse me?" Maggie responded, surprised by the sudden change of subject.

Mo studied Maggie. "Just asking how you're doing? You've been through a lot recently."

Maggie made a noncommittal grunt. "I'm fine."

"Really? Because I'm here for you." Mo persisted.

"Mo!" Maggie groaned, tightening her grip on his arm. "I'm fine," she lied, more to herself than to him.

Mo sat there, watching Maggie sink into herself, trying to bury the flood of sensations washing over her. Her last visit to the camp had changed Maggie forever. Hiding from the cartel's men between rotting bodies felt like someone lifted a curtain and showed her another dimension to life. One where there was no hope, just misery and a sinister end for everyone.

"If you ever want to talk—"

Maggie looked at Mo and in a calculated voice said, "We talked the other day."

Mo couldn't speak at first. He sat there dumbfounded. Eventually he leaned over and whispered in Maggie's ear, "you, my dear, are an emotional dumpster fire."

Maggie grinned. "Don't I know it?"

Chapter Twenty-Four

Georgetown, Washington D.C.

The early morning sun hid behind the thick layer of gray stratus clouds that blanketed the skies above Washington. Senator Claude Littlefield munched on a piece of toast and sipped his morning coffee. With the quarantine order in effect, and with his wife staying in their home in Louisiana, he had to make his own breakfast. The senator enjoyed his early morning ritual. It was the only time of day when he could sit quietly and read the newspaper without interruption. In the background, the television in the kitchen was tuned into the Fox News Channel. The lead story was the president's recent deployment of 120,000 troops to the U.S.-Mexico border.

Littlefield had been in Washington for thirty-four years. He'd survived allegations of political kickbacks, marital infidelity and the #MeToo media firestorm that ensued when six women accused him of sexual misconduct. For Littlefield, qualities like integrity, honesty, and dedication to the laws of the country had little meaning. To him, being a senator was about holding on to power, no matter the cost. Lying, deceit, deal cutting, partisan politics and ruining the careers of anyone that got in the way was simply how business got done.

The doorbell sounded, and Littlefield looked up from his newspaper at the television. He could monitor the security camera from any television in the house. The television showed the senator a picture of Senator Amanda Cortez waiting by the front door. Littlefield walked to the front door and opened it.

"Amanda. Thank you for agreeing to meet in person."

"Good morning, Claude."

"Please come in. There's coffee in the kitchen if you'd like. With the help having to stay home, I'm afraid we're on our own."

"I think I can manage," Amanda said. She poured herself a cup of coffee and followed Littlefield to the study.

Inside the study, two armchairs were in front of the fireplace. Amanda sat directly across from Littlefield.

Littlefield set his cup down on the table between them. "Amanda, we have an important bill coming to the floor for a vote next week. My sources tell me that you and the votes you control are going to vote against it."

Amanda wore a stoic gaze. "Claude, I only control my vote. And yes, your people are correct. I can't support it."

Littlefield smiled sadly. "I'm sorry you feel that way. This is a very important piece of legislation."

Amanda sat back impassively, waiting for the senator to elaborate.

"This bill will pass even if you and the other senators aligned with you vote against it."

Her already narrow eyes grew more so as she studied the man. "If that's the case, why did you ask for this meeting?"

Littlefield avoided the question, sticking with the narrative that sounded a little bit over-rehearsed. "The country is reeling from this pandemic. This is precisely the time we should be sending a strong message to Americans that bi-partisan politics are not going to prevent the country's leaders from doing what's in the country's best interest."

Amanda nodded and said, "There we're in agreement. But this legislation eliminates transparency and accountability, putting companies' interests ahead of those of the rest of the country. I don't believe that's in the country's best interest."

Littlefield's mood seemed to darken. "Without blanket immunity, pharmaceutical companies will be reluctant to roll out the vaccine quickly. This legislation could save lives."

He reached across the table and handed Amanda a folder. "Here are the latest statistics and projections concerning the virus. Americans are getting infected and dying at an alarmingly high rate."

Littlefield sat back in his chair and let Amanda absorb the information.

Amanda studied the numbers prepared by the Johns Hopkins Pandemic Data Initiative. There were over 45 million confirmed cases and 39 million deaths. Hospitals were beyond capacity; and the death forecasts predicted the death rate to double weekly until it reached the projected plateau of 216 million in a year. When she was done, it took all the composure Amanda could marshal to continue to sit there.

"If these projections are correct, about two-thirds of our population will be dead within a year." Amanda started to reach for her cup, but her hand was trembling, so she placed it on her lap before Littlefield noticed.

That possibility brought a grimace to Littlefield's face. "Without a vaccine, that's probably somewhere between a best-and-worst-case scenario," he said.

"And where are we on the vaccine?"

"I'm advised that there have been very promising developments."

Amanda felt a lump in her throat. "Time frame?"

"Thanks to advances in genomic sequencing, PhRMA researchers successfully uncovered the viral sequence of the virus roughly 10 days after the first reported cases in Brazil. We're just now beginning human trials."

Littlefield noticed Amanda's slouched shoulders. "The bill granting companies immunity from any liability incentivizes them to move far more expeditiously . . ."

Amanda pursed her lips. "Saving lives isn't incentive enough?" She put her words in the form of a question, but it was obvious that it wasn't.

Littlefield straightened his posture and said, "Not if it could bankrupt your company. We're demanding that these companies speed through their standard operating protocols. We cannot hold them responsible for any mistakes."

Amanda hesitated to say what was on her mind, but a part of her wanted to take a stand. "The language in the bill is too broad." She looked for a sign that Littlefield was a man capable of reaching a compromise but didn't see one.

Senator Littlefield was used to getting his way. When people didn't bow to his whims, he became vindictive.

With a dismissive half smile, he said, "There's no wiggle room here, Amanda. Developing the vaccine and treating patients stricken by the virus is an all-encompassing undertaking. It would be extremely unfair to exclude companies that contributed to the effort."

There was a long sigh of frustration. "Claude, this bill is so broadly written that a company delivering paper products is immune from suit."

"We can tweak the language to exclude goods and services unrelated to medical treatment," he replied, tossing her a meaningless crumb.

Amanda stared at Claude with calculating eyes. She'd heard rumors that Lighthouse had contributed millions to Littlefield's political action committee. Protecting Lighthouse was the hill the senator would fight for and die on.

Amanda sighed. "Claude, I don't think I can support a bill that turns a blind eye to the questionable practices you're trying to sweep under the rug. Sure, right now there may be some support for the old adage that *the end justifies the means;* but once the vaccine is available, people's memories will fade, and they may not be so forgiving."

Littlefield kept his predatory gaze locked on Amanda as he was going over in his mind a list of possible ways to leverage her.

"Amanda, I've always preferred to cut through the crap, talk straight and to the point. Your Mental Health Justice Bill is currently stuck in the Appropriations Committee . . ."

Amanda grew tentative for a moment. "Claude, that bill would fund state and local governments so they could dispatch mental health professionals to respond to emergencies that involve people with behavioral health needs."

"I don't care what it does. If you believe in it, you'll . . ."

Amanda set her cup down, her mind rapidly filling in the blanks. "Vote for your bill as drafted," she said finishing his sentence.

Littlefield's caustic demeanor melted into a playful smile. "Smart girl."

Amanda frowned at his condescending gesture, then just shrugged. "I guess the Senate isn't above good old-fashioned extortion."

Littlefield waved a hand as if he was shooing a fly away from his face. He had no time for petty little laws, and he definitely had no time for someone else's morals. He intended to play the game by his own rules. "Grow up, Amanda. This is exactly how things are done in Washington."

Amanda was more than willing to match him toe-to-toe. She didn't respond immediately, trying to calculate a way to level the playing field, but finally resigned herself to the fact that Littlefield had the better hand. She stared at him for a long time and finally said, "I understand the big picture. The vote's in five days. I'll let you know my decision before then."

Chapter Twenty-Five

U.S. Army Medical Research and Development Command
Fort Detrick, Maryland

Doctor Sophia Wild was physically and emotionally drained. She'd been working non-stop since leaving the White House, setting up early identification and separation protocols for migrants at the border to prevent the transmission of the virus. Under normal circumstances, setting up an operation of this massive scale was difficult enough to manage, but in the wake of the governor's brazen attempt to undermine the president, the team was working under impossible conditions.

They were building seven refugee camps and seven clinics to conduct testing along the border in one month's time. Colonel Cone and his team quickly moved away from the initial idea of using existing sports stadiums and arenas and opted for modular membrane structures. Sprung structures were used in military facilities around the world. The high-tension fabric buildings took only days to customize and weeks to build. The added flexibility allowed them to locate the buildings in remote locations away from any population centers.

Troops were on the ground in Arizona, California, and Texas and took command of the border operations weeks before the medical teams were scheduled to arrive. The Texas governor was unaware of the president's plan and welcomed the buildup of armed forces on the border.

At half past midnight, there was a quiet knock on the door and Sophia Wild looked up to see one of her team members poke his head in.

"Major, Colonel Cone is on his way to see you."

Sophia leaned back in her chair and stretched the familiar kink in her neck. A souvenir of nine years of jiu jitsu training. "Thank you, lieutenant."

The cubicles smelled of unwashed bodies and were a beehive of activity. Team members stood at attention and saluted as the colonel walked past their workstations. The visit by the colonel had two purposes. First to raise the team's spirits and let them know that their country appreciated all their sacrifices. The second was to ratchet up the pressure.

The colonel rolled through the open door to Sophia's office. "Major Wild," he said as he entered, shutting the door behind him. Sophia stood and saluted the colonel.

A strand of Sophia's hair, which was normally tied and neatly pulled back, fell over her gaunt face and eyes. The operation was increasingly complex and demanded an exhaustive commitment from the team; and Sophia looked the part.

"At ease." Colonel Cone let out a bitter groan. "I can see that neither one of us is sleeping much, and it's too late in the day."

Sophia nodded, but her face was an empty mask. "It's been a few days since anyone here has had a hot shower and a change of clothes."

The colonel dropped into the chair in front of Sophia's desk.

"I have a briefing with the president and the joint chiefs of staff at zero-six-hundred. Give me a status update."

She glanced down at the printed agenda on her desk. "The SOPs for staff training are ready to be implemented. I sent your office the pilot registration program, and the Public Information Office is ready to launch the information campaign as soon as you cut them loose."

Cone nodded. "Where are we on housing shelters?"

"The Army Engineers and the private contractors have all the buildings up; and sanitation, wastewater and garbage disposal are finished.

We have sufficient latrines to accommodate five thousand at each site. Locating adequate sources of water, however, has been a challenge in Pima County."

The colonel's eyes narrowed into an analytical stare. As a man of action, nothing bothered him more than having to listen to excuses for failing to complete the assigned task. "We're out of time, Wild. Are you shipping in water until you find a viable solution?"

Sophia nodded. "Already done, sir. Just briefing you on a hiccup that needs attention."

The colonel gave a nod. "Where are we on medical staffing?"

"Just finished compiling the list," she said, handing him paperwork containing names and assignments.

The colonel read over the names. "Good! The president wants 500 migrants at each facility tested and processed per day," he said, still analyzing the list. He didn't look at Sophia or raise his voice, but she flinched just the same.

No matter how many times she tweaked and turned over the operations plan, she always came up well short of the 500 target.

Sophia looked the colonel in the eye and wondered if he had bothered to tell the president that processing and testing 500 migrants at each location was not possible. "Sir, we're equipped to test and process about 200 people per ten-hour shift." Her voice carried a hint of frustration.

The colonel shot Sophia an extremely dissatisfied look. "That's well short of the number in the president's speech."

"Excuse me, sir. I wasn't thinking. We certainly can't let facts get in the way of a good piece of political propaganda," she remarked in an openly disrespectful tone.

The colonel shot Sophia a watch-your-step sideways glance. "As far as the president's advisors are concerned, optics are almost as important as controlling the spread of the virus. People need to believe that this operation is the best way to keep them safe."

Sophia looked the colonel straight in the eye and said, "I understand, sir, but I can't stuff ten pounds of potatoes into a five-pound bag."

The colonel cocked his head to the side. "Excuse me?"

"There are safe distancing requirements that limit how many people I can have working at the clinic at one time. Ignoring them . . ." Sophia shook her head, "and cramming people into tight workspaces to get the numbers up . . . bad idea."

"I'm not trying to second-guess you. I'm only trying to figure out a way that we can get the numbers up."

Sophia's eyes narrowed into an analytical stare. "I told you there wasn't, and you keep persisting. I'd call that second-guessing."

The colonel tilted his head back and studied Sophia's face. After a long pause, he said, "You're probably right. But we have a directive from the president. I wouldn't be doing my job if I didn't push and second-guess you."

"I understand." Sophia took a breath and let it out slowly. "Then there's the protective clothing. The protective gear is hotter than hell. Workers won't be able to wear it for more than 30 or 40 minutes at a time."

The colonel had a look of intense concentration on his face just before he dropped the latest bomb. "There's been a change. The president doesn't just want the migrants tested for the virus, he wants them vaccinated."

"Vaccinated? Sir, it was my understanding that we've only begun Phase 1 trials."

"We're conducting Phase 2 and 3 of the clinical trials in the camps."

"I don't see how that's possible. We're not set up for this," Sophia protested.

The colonel raised one of his thick eyebrows in a manner that said the matter was not up for debate. "Have you seen the latest data, major? Thousands of Americans are dying every hour. We need to combine Phases 2 and 3, and test thousands of people as quickly as possible. The president wants us to be ready to roll out the vaccine in thirty days," he said in a stern voice.

Sophia was surprised. "To get data, we need to process the migrants and get negative tests results before administering the vaccine. Then we need to calculate the vaccine's efficacy. I don't see how . . ."

The colonel cut Sophia off. "You vaccinate everyone that tests negative for the virus and keep all the migrants, including those that test positive for the virus together in the same barracks. This virus spreads just by breathing or talking. Everybody does that. If we don't have an outbreak, you have your data."

The alarms in the back of Sophia's mind wanted to explode. They had only a superficial knowledge of the transmissibility of the virus. She felt her anxiety notch upward as she grappled with the ethical implications of unnecessary and questionable human experimentation. The idea of purposely exposing healthy men, women, and children to individuals infected by the virus was cruel and barbaric.

"No," Sophia shook her head. She looked at the colonel with a pleading expression. "We can't do this."

After watching Sophia with discerning eyes, the colonel nodded and in a very casual tone said, "We'll have consent forms for everyone to sign before having them vaccinated."

His last comment hit her like a slap to the face. "Consent forms?" Sophia exhaled. She tried to maintain an air of calm, but the pained expression said it all. "They're prisoners, colonel. Their consent is neither informed nor voluntarily given."

The colonel's jaw clenched at the insinuation of an impropriety, stood, and said, "They're given a choice."

"I beg to differ, sir. Anyone that doesn't sign faces expulsion. We're not giving them a choice. And as for informed consent, are they going to be told they are going to be crammed into chain-linked holding pens with people shedding the virus so we can see if they get sick after receiving the vaccine?"

Sophia's question brought a barely perceptible grimace to the colonel's face. "Major, the physical and psychological risks to subjects are reasonable. This operation will expedite our timeline for distributing the vaccine."

Sophia's eyes opened wide at the colonel's attempt to defend their actions. She could not hide her disapproval, no matter how hard she tried.

The colonel shrugged his shoulders and smiled kindly at the major. "The decision is above my pay grade. There's nothing I can do."

Such an open admission caught Sophia off-guard. She nodded and listened without showing an ounce of emotion. Inside, however, her stomach churned.

The colonel stopped with his hand on the doorknob and looked over his shoulder. "Relax, major," he said, remembering the other times when they worked together. "We weren't starting from scratch on this vaccine. Extensive research on previous viruses provided the necessary experimental experience and groundwork to develop this vaccine. When our backs are up against a wall, our people are a force to be reckoned with. This isn't our first rodeo."

Just before closing the door, the colonel snapped his head around and nodded. "Remember the Ebola outbreak in Sierra Leone?"

The question gave her a split second of pause, and she tilted her head and looked at him. "Yep. No matter how hard I try, it's impossible to forget," she said, her voice filled with disappointment.

"You had no resources, and yet you managed to bring the epidemic under control."

Sophia looked at him, or rather through him, with a kind of glazed over expression that the colonel had come to recognize as a sign of deep concentration. "What's your point?"

"This time you have a vaccine and the resources of the U.S. at your disposal. Compared to Sierra Leone, this should be a cakewalk for you," he said and closed the door.

Chapter Twenty-Six

Coahuila, Mexico

With the onslaught of the pandemic, Daniel Gonzalez, the hyperviolent and psychotic leader of the Zetas, recognized that he could make more money killing people than he could smuggling drugs. Gonzalez was tall, with olive-toned skin, brown hair, almond-shaped eyes that were unnaturally green, and a very quick mind. The forty-one-year-old had an appetite for violence and saw no difference between killing the migrants and the white-tailed deer that roamed across his ranch. Except for the desert bighorn rams that dwelled in steep terrain and required a longer shot, he enjoyed shooting human targets most. While the Sinaloa and Gulf Cartels were content with smuggling cocaine and crystal *methamphetamine*, when the virus sucked the world's blood supply dry, the Zetas expanded their operations to satisfy the booming billion-dollar demand. With blood transfusions serving as the only viable treatment for those stricken by the virus, the cost of blood exploded overnight from $350 to $20,000 dollars per liter. In a month, a single truck carrying between 1500 to 2000 liters of blood made the Zetas sixty million.

The cartel charged doctors, nurses, and lab technicians a tax called *servicio,* which could only be paid by working for the cartel. If they refused, their family members were kidnapped and killed. The Zetas were so feared that the medical industry referred to their conscription as *el servicio obligatorio* de *la ultima letra*, the obligatory service of the last letter.

The Zetas had a ravenous buyer in Lighthouse. Unlike drug transactions that required duffel bags full of American dollars and expensive fees for pumping dollars legally back into the international banking system, Lighthouse wired payment directly to the Zeta's front company.

Even with pictures of ashen husks piled on top of each other in mass graves flooding the internet, Lighthouse bought all the blood the cartel had to sell, no questions asked. The Zetas sold almost all the blood culled from migrants to Lighthouse.

Ben Bowman, the CEO of Lighthouse, recognized that the window of opportunity would rapidly close once a vaccine or cure for the virus was widely available. In his typical hard charging style, he pressed Ricardo Longoria, the head of one of the border's biggest banks in Texas and his connection to the Zetas, to triple the volume of blood shipped north on the I-35 corridor to his distribution facility in Dallas.

* * *

With Nuevo Laredo the epicenter of a war between the Zetas and the Gulf and Sinaloa Cartels, Daniel Gonzalez requested a meeting with the leaders of Juárez and the Tijuana Cartels at his ranch in Coahuila. They, along with the Beltrán-Leyva Cartel, a former arm of the Sinaloa Cartel aligned with the Zetas in the war with the Jalisco, Gulf and Sinaloa Cartels, agreed to meet.

Both Guillermo "Memo" Gallardo, the leader of the Tijuana Cartel, and Ismael Lozano, the head of the Beltrán-Leyva Cartel, nicknamed "Canelo" for his red hair, flew in on their private jets. Besides Daniel and his brother, Diego, waiting for them at the ranch, there was Ricardo Longoria and his business partner, Evan Greenfield.

When Ricardo got a call from Daniel ordering him to come to a meeting in Coahuila, he was afraid and surprised. Ricardo insisted on bringing his business partner along. If Daniel wanted to kill him, it wouldn't have mattered that he brought his business partner and Ricardo knew that, but he wanted him along just the same.

Rounding out the meeting and the last to arrive was Juan Pablo Guzmán, the patriarch of the Juárez Cartel.

Daniel had a plan for dramatically increasing the volume of blood shipped north. With migrants now heading west to avoid the Zetas, he wanted to cast a much wider net into the territories the other cartels controlled.

He spoke in English for Evan Greenfield's benefit. "I asked for this meeting because we have much to discuss. The virus is disrupting our drug production."

The men sitting around the table all nodded in agreement.

"In Colombia, our coca producers are suffering from a shortage of chemicals essential for cocaine production."

Memo puffed a frustrated breath. "Yes . . . yes . . . we all know that the closed borders in Bolivia and Venezuela are making it difficult to smuggle the chemicals to Colombia."

Canelo agreed. "The closing of the borders and the sickness itself is reducing the number of workers to harvest coca plants."

Ismael appeared to take the setback in stride. "The shortage will drive up the price, so we will charge more."

Memo shook his head. "Only temporarily. Virus or no virus, the plants continue to grow which will drive down the price of the coca leaf."

Canelo let out a long-frustrated breath. "Methamphetamine production has also slowed because of the shortage of fentanyl from China."

"So, we ride out the virus like everyone else," Ismael said.

Daniel had waited for the heads of the cartels to come to the pivotal moment before presenting them with an alternative. "Or we can recognize an opportunity right in front of our noses."

Juan Pablo looked like a disappointed father staring at an insolent child. "Yes, we've all heard about this new human slaughterhouse of yours."

Daniel laughed. "Juan Pablo, in your war with the Sinaloa Cartel, thirty-eight hundred died in just July and August alone. "So much blood flowed. No one mourned them; no women wore black for them."

Juan Pablo said, more with his face than with his words. "Half of those men were mine."

Daniel's voice took on a hint of resignation. "And the worst part, all that blood wasted." His gut churned. "Any idea how much the Americans would have paid us for that blood?"

The question coming from anyone other than Daniel would have had brutal consequences. But for a psychopath like Daniel, who appeared to lack the capacity for transgression, guilt or remorse, it wasn't meant to be disrespectful. Coming from him, it was a perfectly normal question and Juan Pablo knew it.

Given Juan Pablo's well-deserved reputation for ruthlessness, no one dared to answer.

The clatter of coffee cups on the serving tray when the server entered the room broke the tension.

Daniel waited for them to be alone before picking up where he left off. "Because of the sickness, blood is more valuable than any drug we sell to the Americans."

Juan Pablo eyed Daniel and took off his glasses, as if mystified by him. He cleaned them and put them back on, hoping with better clarity he would see Daniel in a different light.

Scanning the room, Daniel's eyes rested on Juan Pablo's ruddy face. "The blood of those killed in your war would have sold for $76 million," he said. His voice was devoid of any malice or compassion.

Ismael nodded profoundly. "$76 million is no joke."

"One kilo of cocaine costs us $10,000. Going rate in the U.S. is $27,000, so we have to move a lot of weight to make $76 million," Canelo said, as he began to warm up to Daniel's idea.

"An average adult has around five liters of blood in their body. At 20k per pint, each campesino is worth 212K," Diego interjected.

"And the best part, there is no cost to us for the blood. The blood is donated," Daniel said.

Everyone in the room except for Juan Pablo chuckled.

Diego flashed a sinister grin. "At $60 million per truck, the four of us can split a quarter of a billion a month."

"Clean money," Daniel nodded. "The money will be wired into each of your accounts."

Everyone was suddenly quiet and focused on the business opportunity.

"So, what you're asking is for us to kill people for you?" It was half statement, half question. But there was no mistaking the hint of judgment in Memo's voice.

Diego grunted, and with a scowl, he said, "You already kill people."

"Not civilians."

"Plenty of civilians die." Diego fired back.

Juan Pablo's eyes locked on Diego. His silence spoke volumes.

Daniel worried for his brother and waved his hand, signaling to him to be quiet. "Bring me the migrants alive. Pile them in buses, trucks, whatever you want; and have your people drive them to us. We'll take care of everything."

Canelo raised an eyebrow, already counting his money. "And what's our share?"

"Sixty/forty, less the expenses of testing, storing, and shipping the blood," Daniel said.

"Sixty/forty, which way?" Memo asked.

The question brought a deep sigh. Daniel looked long and hard at Memo, wanting him to believe he was sizing him up as he considered his options. After a deliberate pause, he said, "The only way the Zetas do business, my brother."

Diego flicked his fingers along the edge of the table as if playing a piano to rid himself of anxious energy. He was itching to tell them that all the other cartels had to do was load poor campesinos onto a bus at gunpoint and the Zetas would do all the work after that.

"So, we bring you a few buses a month full of migrants and you pay us each . . ." Canelo paused to do the math in his head.

Daniel nodded and tweaked out a grin. "Your share would be $25 million for every three hundred bodies."

Canelo frowned. "And you make thirty-eight."

Daniel was silent, disappointed that Canelo's first instinct was to focus on what the Zetas were making rather than the opportunity being presented.

Diego exploded at the inference that the Zetas were being pigs. "We have a team of medical personnel that safely and efficiently drain and then label the blood types. We transport the blood to the U.S. and get rid of the bodies. And we take most of the risk." He placed both palms on the table, readying himself to pounce. His eyes glazed over, daring Canelo to say something.

Memo laughed and switched to speaking Spanish. "Calmate hijo de puta. Le dije a tu papa un million de veces que te dejo chupar la teta de tu mama demasiado tiempo." Calm down, you little fucker. I told your dad a million times that he let you suck on your mom's tit for too long. "You have been a little firecracker since you were in diapers," he said in Spanish.

Ismael reached over and put his hand on Diego's shoulder. "This is business, *cabron*. Don't take it so personal."

Red-faced, Diego shoved his hand off.

Almost in slow motion, Daniel's green eyes flashed at Diego, as if to say, stick to the plan. Diego's mood instantly changed. He lowered his voice, apologized for his outburst, and sat back in his chair. It was like the brothers shared a secret communication.

Daniel knew that any allegiance between narco-traffickers was a treacherous one at best. The real purpose of the alliance had more to do with war than business. Together, they fought the other cartels for control of the valuable corridors. If the Juárez and Tijuana Cartels felt that the Zetas were growing too rich and powerful, they would turn on them; and it would be the beginning of the end. That was Daniel's second reason for bringing the other cartels in. He also knew they would balk at a sixty/forty split, but they would expect nothing less than that to be his opening salvo.

"We split it evenly—4 ways." Memo banged the conference table for effect, as if the decision was his to make.

Memo lifted an eyebrow, obviously waiting for the others to side with him.

Daniel leaned forward, setting his elbows on the table and folding his fingers together as if praying. He took a deep breath and slowly released it. "I can't agree with that."

Diego was tapping his foot on the marble floor.

Daniel stared at Memo, a man he had known his whole life. The brilliant green rings around his black pupils gave away nothing. "We cannot all share equally, if we all don't do the same amount of work."

Daniel must have clicked a switch in Ismael's head because he quickly sided with him. "If I bring in three truckloads and the others bring in one, I should get the largest share."

Juan Pablo sat back in his chair, folded his arms, and tipped his head silently. His vague response caused the two brothers to exchange a quick look. Satisfied that Juan Pablo agreed each cartel's share of the profits should be limited to the truckloads they delivered to the Zetas, Daniel cast his glance back at Memo.

His head shook with disapproval. "Not four ways. Fifty/fifty on whatever each of you brings."

Daniel noticed a glimpse of a smirk on his brother's face.

Canelo leaned in with a lifted eyebrow. "The split should be sixty/forty in our favor, and you keep one hundred percent of all the migrants your men capture."

Twenty long contentious minutes later, they all agreed to a fifty-five/forty-five split with the Zetas keeping one hundred percent of all the blood they accumulated without the help of the other cartels. They all also agreed that Ricardo's bank would act as the clearinghouse for the money. Ricardo wanted nothing to do with the cartel's new venture, but his business was already so intertwined with the Zetas that it would have been difficult to say no. He was also painfully aware that if he refused, Daniel wouldn't hesitate to kill a friend as swiftly as an enemy . . . so Ricardo was quickly amenable.

Chapter Twenty-Seven

Miami

At fifteen minutes after two on Saturday afternoon, six hours after her meeting with Senator Littlefield, Amanda Cortez put on a black N-95 mask and boarded a plane to Miami. Amanda was resolved not to let Littlefield's bill pass in its current form. It had been a frustrating meeting with Littlefield, neither one conceding in the ring. Littlefield's bill provided complete immunity for American companies connected to the virus, including even those that profited from the abductions and exterminations of innocent men, women, and children. With only five days left before the vote, Congresswoman Ana Marie Rodriguez and Amanda pressed for a face-to-face meeting with Pierce and his team in Florida.

Pierce scrambled his staff to make last-minute preparations for the spur-of-the-moment meeting. It was the first time anyone had been to the office since the virus invaded and the initiation of the government-mandated lockdown.

Amanda's plane landed just before six. J.C., Ana Marie's chief of staff was at the airport waiting to take the senator directly to Pierce's office. The law firm's offices were plush, well-appointed, with panoramic views of downtown Miami and Biscayne Bay.

Pierce was sitting in the large conference room with Ana Marie, Moses, and Maggie, waiting for the senator to arrive. They were watching the news reports on the rising death tolls. Across the world, reporters were revealing that thousands more were dying of the virus each day than the government's data was showing. A second story featured photographs of more than three thousand corpses lying in shallow graves. During one news segment, a reporter counted fifty dead bodies floating down the Rio Grande River. The news video captured dogs gnawing on human limbs and torsos a short distance from a crematorium in Nuevo Leon, Mexico. Every TV and radio channel was buzzing with similar stories.

The elevator chime rang, announcing that someone had just arrived on the fifty-second floor. Pierce left the conference room to let the senator and J.C. in. They waited in the lobby, basking in the fine Italian leather furniture, Persian rugs strewn across the marble floors, and ornamental millwork.

Out of habit, Pierce leaned in to hug the senator and caught himself. "Senator Cortez," he said, "it's good to see you again."

The senator smiled. "I wish it was under better circumstances."

Mo was about to stick a third cookie in his mouth when he saw the senator walk in.

She was barely over the threshold when Mo, in his typical cut-to-the-chase style, said, "senator, the congresswoman has been filling us in."

Amanda greeted him with her usual warm smile. "Hello, Mo." Mo's reputation as one of the best legal strategists was well known, if not legendary. Amanda's resolve to take the fight to the government over its immigration policies was energized when Congresswoman Rodriguez first informed her that Mo Black had been coaxed out of retirement and was part of the legal team.

"Nothing but old school politics," Mo sighed and gestured to a red leather chair at the head of the conference table that probably cost more than all the furniture in Maggie's apartment. "Senator, we saved that seat for you."

Amanda set her laptop on the table and handed her coat to J.C.

"Senator, can I get you anything to drink?" J.C. asked.

Amanda nodded. "Some tea would be lovely."

"Right away, senator," J.C. said, as he slipped out of the room.

Amanda greeted everyone and took her seat. Due to the hour, she decided to skip the small talk and launched into a detailed description of the events, including her meeting with Senator Littlefield.

"It started with the lobbyist, Lawrence Rinehart. We had a cordial meeting, but the tone changed when I told him that I would not support the bill sponsored by Senator Littlefield."

"Bush & Rinehart's minions have been lobbying pretty strenuously for the past few weeks for the bill's passage," Ana Marie interjected for everyone's benefit.

"Mr. Rinehart first offered to lend support for legislation that I was sponsoring," Amanda continued to lay out the facts. "When that went nowhere, he let me know that he could deliver a sizable check for my re-election effort. If I voted against the bill, he assured me that dark money groups would bankroll who ever runs against me for my Senate seat."

Mo wiped the corners of his mouth with a napkin. "Over the last ten years, dark money groups have spent roughly $1 billion—mainly on television and online ads, and mailers—to influence elections."

Maggie listened closely, then nodded. "They've been particularly effective in the southern states. People get bombarded with political messages paid for with money from undisclosed sources. Most folks don't question the message's credibility or the source. They just take it as gospel."

Mo agreed and turned back towards Amanda. "So, what happened next?"

"I told Mr. Reinhart that I ran for the senate seat to help people, not to hold on to it, and showed him the door."

Pierce studied Amanda's face for a moment. She looked at ease. Either she was very good at dealing with stress or she was a very good actress.

"A couple of days later, Senator Littlefield called and asked if we could meet to discuss the bill. When I told him that my mind was already made up, he insisted, so I agreed to meet him at his home on Saturday morning," she said, keeping her disdain for the Senate Majority Leader in check.

Amanda explained that the senator's insistence on a face-to-face meeting piqued her curiosity, and she looked into the list of donors for his political action committee.

"One donor immediately caught my attention," she said. "Lighthouse Blood Centers. They've contributed millions."

Maggie recognized the company. "They have a big presence in Texas."

Amanda gave a contemplative nod. "I've worked in the medical field in Texas my whole career and up until recently, they were a small player. In the past few months, they killed the competition, and took over the market."

"Unusual but not unheard of," Mo said, reaching for another cookie.

Maggie peered at Mo and made a sour face as she pulled the tray of cookies away.

Amanda defensively folded her arms across her chest and said, "Mo, if we're talking about technology, I could see it. A company bringing new AI technology forward can rapidly morph into a giant. But they're not a tech company. We're talking about a blood bank."

Mo nodded ever so slightly at the distinction.

"Lighthouse Blood Centers has become the largest supplier of blood overnight when the rest of the country is suffering from severe shortages,' Amanda continued. "My contact at the DEA identified a company linked to the Zeta Cartel that is selling blood to Lighthouse Blood Centers." Amanda found it difficult to say the name Lighthouse, without feeling revulsion.

Pierce traded a knowing look with Mo. Intuitively, each knew that this was no coincidence.

"Which brings me back to the senator," Amanda said. She had thought about her conversation with Senator Littlefield for much of the last nine hours since their meeting and come to a couple of disturbing conclusions: First, he could limit the immunity from all legal liability in the bill to only those companies performing research on the vaccine with a stroke of a pen. That realization was overshadowed by her second epiphany. She was sure he didn't want to.

Mo sipped his tea, which he liked to call "God's Brew." He believed that some men would sink to any depth if there was a pile of cold hard cash at the bottom of the deep, dark well.

Maggie made a habit of saying out loud what everyone was already thinking. "So, we have a powerful senator in the pocket of a company that is profiting big-time from the migrants that are being massacred in Mexico."

With a pained look on her face, Amanda looked at Maggie and said, "Exactly."

Mo tried to quell the sense of hopelessness that filled the room. "Senator, politics and the law are both a lot like a game of chess; and we'd like to think that we're usually three moves ahead."

Pierce was well acquainted with power politics and state-of-the-art tactics such as dirty political horse-trading, and gothic revenge used by the Senate and House leadership behind closed doors to secure votes. It had been the same story for hundreds of years. The political alliances forged, however, were often susceptible to crumbling under the right amount of pressure. What he needed was the right trigger point. Pierce's mind was busy at work thinking about how to create a propulsive narrative that would allow him to pull the ripcord and cause some of the senators to run for cover.

"Actually, in this instance, it's more like checkers," Pierce said. "The senators on both ends of this issue are firmly entrenched in their respective positions, it's those in the middle that are most likely to switch. To be successful, like in checkers, we need to control the middle of the board. There, we can find senators more likely to change their votes."

Amanda warmed her hands with her cup of tea. "How do you propose to do that? The majority in the Senate has been voting with their party on every piece of priority legislation."

Ana Marie nodded in agreement. "The Republicans hold fifty-one seats; the Democrats have forty-seven, and two senators are registered as Independent."

Maggie raised an eyebrow, an expression of dread coming over her face. "Assuming all the Democrats and the two senators registered as Independents vote against the bill, we're still two votes short."

Amanda was surprised by the genuine resentment she felt. The clarity in her eyes and wheels spinning behind them reminded Mo of his protégé. "This close to the vote most senators have made up their minds. Any strategy which primarily relies on face-to-face lobbying, hoping to convince two senators to change their minds won't work."

Mo could feel his cynicism grow. It was a feeling he usually got when he was caught in the middle of politicians entranced by their own agendas. "I'm afraid Amanda's right."

The normally stoic Ana Marie allowed a bit of irritation to creep into her voice. "So, what are our options?"

Pierce furrowed his brow a little deeper. He had spent a fair amount of time considering that very question. "The midterm election is later this year. A half dozen Republicans are expected to have very tight races . . . and there's a strong possibility that the Democrats will capture at least two of those seats."

"That's still four months away," Maggie said.

Pierce nodded thoughtfully. "Both liberals and conservatives are highly influenced by the opinion of the crowd, regardless of political partisanship. If senators believe that supporting the bill will cost them votes and possibly the election, they may vote differently."

Mo conjured a skeptical expression. "Not sure how we can do that. The media have been covering the death tolls to the point that people are becoming numb to them."

Maggie agreed. "People are dying left and right. Why would people suddenly care about a bill that is designed to encourage companies to work faster to find a cure?"

Pierce managed a vague smile. "We manipulate the narrative. The narrative that the Republicans are spinning is that the legislation adopts heightened legal protections for companies working on a cure for the virus."

"How do we combat that?" Maggie asked, prodding Pierce in the direction she knew he was heading.

Mo recognized the look in Pierce's eyes. It was the same look when he was about to make sashimi out of the opposing side's witness in a courtroom.

"Politicians consistently scramble for position, power, and survival. In this instance, we are going to focus purely on survival," Pierce said.

Amanda and Anna Marie sat up a little straighter in their chairs as Pierce laid out his plan.

"Littlefield is old school. He relies on powerful alliances and leverage to advance his political agenda. But his power-base can be neutralized by the internet, which relies on state-of-the-art tactics and spin."

Amanda's face twisted into a frown, having just borne the full brunt of Littlefield's arsenal.

"First, we introduce the carrot in the form of an amendment to the bill that limits the legislation to only companies actually conducting research and test trials," Pierce said.

Overcome by a sense of futility, J.C. chimed in. "Why would any senator support the amendment?"

"Because we're going to hit them in the gut with a two-by-four," Pierce replied. "The internet is a powerful weapon. Both liberals and conservatives are highly influenced by public opinion."

Amanda and Ana Marie nodded silently as Pierce continued to speak.

"The objective is to create enough of a stir on the internet that senators who expect tight races in November shift to survival mode and pivot to a safer and more socially acceptable option that still promotes research without rewarding the bad actors."

Amanda shrugged with a mix of dejection and hope in her voice. "It's going to be a heavy lift to convince them to vote against their party. However, if senators in close races believe that voting for the bill in its present form will cost them their elections, they could be persuaded to support the amendment."

Mo laced his fingers thoughtfully atop his head and adopted the pose of a wise and wily old man. "New York Mayor Fiorello La Guardia used to say, 'There is no Democratic or Republican way of taking out the garbage.'

Maggie sized up Mo with a befuddled look. "What exactly does that mean?"

"It means good government requires those elected to be pragmatic, and put the needs of their constituents first," Mo said.

Amanda nodded, adding, "It also means that when something directly affects the public or there is an issue that voters feel strongly about, political ideology takes a back seat."

"Up until now, the news reports focused on dead bodies. Eyewitness accounts aren't reflected in any of the news reports. So, the stories aren't as relatable as they would be if they included personal accounts of people that actually observed and survived the attacks. If we put Maggie and Yamilet's stories on the internet, they will give people an understanding of the genocidal violence experienced by the victims. Voters won't support legislation that sanctions murder when there is a humanitarian alternative," Pierce added.

Mo shook his head in agreement. "There is nothing partisan when it comes to saving human lives. Maggie's and Yamilet's stories will shine a different light on the atrocities committed by the cartel."

Amanda digested Pierce's plan and gave him a curt nod. "For this plan to work, Maggie's and Yami's statements will have to go viral, and public outrage will have to be intense."

Ana Marie pulled up the calendar on her phone. "The Senate is scheduled to vote on the bill this Thursday. We don't have much time to make all this happen," she announced anxiously.

Pierce sensed that she was a little frazzled, which for Ana Marie was a rarity. His mind was busy formulating a plan that would send a wave through the whole Senate and leave several senators running for cover. He'd done this dance before. "News on the internet goes viral in minutes, not days. We still have time."

Chapter Twenty-Eight

Thackerville, Oklahoma

Dorothy "Dode" Alexander had a master's degree in computer science from Georgia Tech and had spent the first fifteen years of her career working for the International Bank of Commerce. She was known in her circles as a 'white hat' hacker. Dode specialized in preventing computer-based fraud and cyber criminals from hacking into the bank's computer system and crippling its operations. True to the adage that the best way to catch criminals is to think like them, Dode possessed a rare skill set that rivaled those of the world's most notorious hackers; and was an expert at navigating the dark web and manipulating social media platforms.

She had grown up in the business. Both her parents worked in the research and development division of Lenovo. Spending time in computer engineering laboratories was part of her daily routine from the age of five. As a teenager, she broke into the computers of Fortune 100 companies but didn't destroy files or steal information. She slipped past their corporate firewalls and cyber security systems just for the challenge. Dode was not only proficient at finding where the corporate skeletons were hidden, she was one of the few hackers in the world capable of burying them so deep they could never be found. She was brilliant, obsessive, and driven by altruistic endeavors; and she was one of the most trustworthy people Pierce had ever worked with.

* * *

Dode was in the middle of a dream when her cell phone on her nightstand started to vibrate. Her eyelids flickered and then opened. She looked over at the bedside clock to see that it was 1:36 in the morning.

Slowly, like a bomb handler deciding which wire to cut, Dode reached out and pressed the green button instead of the red.

"If you're calling me at this late hour, you'd better be calling to ask me out on a date," she groaned into the phone.

Pierce laughed. Dode's flirtatious overtures always amused him. "You're never more than two feet away from your phone and it rang five times. That tells me you debated whether to answer."

"Or maybe I was asleep like most normal people," Dode snapped back. "You know I love you, but when you're calling at this late hour, it's never a good thing."

"We only have a few days to move the needle on this one, which is why it can't wait."

"And?" She growled before stifling a yawn. She'd always been there for Pierce . . . even when she should have run away screaming.

"I need your help," Pierce admitted and explained the situation. His plan was ambitious, but not without precedent. The MeToo movement started with an *exposé* detailing countless allegations against a Hollywood producer. Overnight the hashtag #MeToo became a rallying cry. Within 24 hours, Facebook had over 12 million posts, comments, and reactions. "We need to get the public pissed off and mobilized against a bill that's going to the Senate floor for a vote this week," Pierce said.

"Is that all?" She groaned sarcastically. Dode fancied herself a tough cookie, with little time for bullshit. Just give her the facts because she could damn sure handle them. Dode swung her legs from under the covers and sat up on the edge of the bed. "Let's hear it."

Pierce brought Dode up to speed on the Zeta Cartel and the brutal murders of innocent people in Mexico. She admitted to reading about the carnage and seeing the grisly photos of the growing sea of bodies. He explained that one company in particular, Lighthouse Blood Centers, was making a fortune buying blood from the cartel. Pierce also brought her up to speed on the backroom deals being made in Washington to keep companies like Lighthouse from being prosecuted.

"Thousands of people are being murdered by the cartels in Mexico," Pierce said.

Dode felt uncomfortable, her sense of foreboding deepening. Her thoughts returned to the first time they met, and she had agreed to help, even after learning that Pierce's plan included a game of chicken with the head of a murderous Venezuelan Cartel.

Dode let out a long sigh, mystified by Pierce's knack for getting mixed up in situations where he could easily end up dead and stuffed in a fifty-five-gallon drum. "What is it with you and drug cartels?" she scoffed with end-of-the-world angst in her voice.

"That was years ago."

"Feels like yesterday," she said anxiously. "Maybe it's all the sleepless nights I've had since."

"This is different. The man we need to go after is no criminal warlord in Latin America. He's a white Texan living in New Orleans . . ."

Dode knew that Pierce would not take "no" for an answer. She glanced at her pillow. If she was lucky, once she agreed to help, Pierce would let her go back to sleep. She blew out a breath in agitated surrender. "Okay."

"We can't slow down the murders and havoc on the Mexican side of the Rio Grande without holding the U.S. side of the equation accountable," Pierce said, continuing his pitch.

Dode sighed. "Didn't you hear me? I said that I'd do it."

Pierce sounded surprised. "This was a little easier than I thought."

Dode's already dour face twisted into a deeper frown. "Take the win, pizza man, and let me go back to sleep."

"We'll call you tomorrow morning at ten."

"Fine," Dode said, not hiding the irritation in her voice.

"I've missed you," Pierce said, teasing.

"Yeah? You think that by saying that you make everything better?"

"Did I?"

"You did," Dode said, smiling.

Chapter Twenty-Nine

West Texas

Sophia shielded her eyes from the West Texas sun as she looked at the rust-colored posts marking the invisible line between Mexico and the U.S. that stretched as far as the eye could see; on both sides, mile upon mile of bleak, flat, red-brown earth. Mexico was less than a half a mile from where she stood, but it felt a world away.

The distant sound of military vehicles grinding along the dirt road as they patrolled the border made her feel like she was in a dream suddenly gone sour.

Governor Johnson condemned the president's actions. "It's official. The president does not give a damn about us. The death toll is spiking in southern Texas, and he's importing the virus by opening the southern border. The president is not shutting down the virus, he's helping to spread it in our country. Every man, woman and child for themselves. Survive the best you can," Johnson said in a statement released by his staff to the media.

* * *

It was the night before they would begin transporting migrants from across the border to the camps for processing. Sophia didn't expect to get much sleep. It was late in the evening, and the temperature had barely gone down. Her mind kept relentlessly going over the details of the steps for testing and vaccinating the migrants. Exposing healthy men and women to people infected by the virus turned the camps into a petri dish designed to measure vaccinated migrants' antibiotic resistance to the virus. The do-or-die experiment, however, risked the lives of not just the migrants, but every person in the camps. If the vaccine was marginally effective or the virus mutated, the disease could spread and claim the lives of not only the migrants but also the lives of her medical staff and the troops. The concern Sophia felt was palpable as every one of the fifteen hundred soldiers and two hundred medical personnel involved in the seven refugee camps in Arizona, California, and Texas were under her care.

She turned thirty-nine in a month. A minor miracle but still not a complete surprise that an officer so young was placed in charge of an operation so important. Born in Samara, Russia, Sophia spent her early years in a Russian orphanage so dystopian that she still had nightmares. She was six years old when she was finally adopted by an American couple. Her father, Chuck Wild, sold insurance to farms and ranches, and her mother, Angie, bred Newfoundland puppies and Arabian horses on their farm in Missouri. In grade school, she became fascinated with science. It started with animal husbandry. Sophia spent endless hours working on the family farm, learning about and breeding horses. Her family worked closely with a geneticist, who specialized in developing genetic profiles and markers for horses. By the time Sophia was in high school, her Russian accent was only detectable by the most discerning ear; and her interest in genetics concentrated on virology and infectious diseases. With the regular outbreaks of influenza and noroviruses, as well as emerging and re-emerging viruses, Sophia became obsessed with understanding how viruses transmit, persist, and how they manage to evade the human immune system. After graduating from medical school, she joined the U.S. Army working for the Medical Research Institute of Infectious Diseases.

* * *

An automated horn sounded throughout the camp at 5:00 a.m. marking the start of what would be a long and busy day. An hour later, five buses followed by a military convoy pushed toward the border check point. Anyone awake would have thought that Texas was under siege. Sophia scrambled her medical team. She had a couple of hours before the first bus would arrive. While her personnel prepped the expansive medical tent, Sophia coordinated with the medical officers at the six other camps. The Texas camps were all scheduled to receive the first influx of migrants around the same time. Arizona and California were about one hour behind.

* * *

The sky was starting to brighten, and the still morning air provided little relief from the sweltering heat. Radios on the buses and military convoy squawked nonstop as personnel at the checkpoint checked in on their estimated time of arrival. The sheer volume of people desperately waiting at the border was staggering. Over 20,000 people began making their way in the same direction as soon as the buses came into view. The crowd surge trampled the X-shaped barricades placed there to break up the enormous crowd into smaller groups and funnel them to the checkpoint. As the route narrowed, the density of the crowd increased drastically as people pushed to get to the checkpoint. Individuals panicked and pushed in all directions, causing violent waves. The mob pressed into the perimeter fencing so hard that the faces of those in the front got disfigured by the steel fence panels. The crowd density continued to increase. People in the crowd were compressed, unable to move, their heads locked between arms and shoulders, their faces gasping in terror.

Some people had fallen, causing a pileup, and ultimately leading to the trampling of hundreds of migrants. The soldiers on the other side of the fence were powerless to do anything. The crowd was too large to push back the stampede in time to save those being crushed by the sheer motion of the crowd pressing forward. Two hundred and forty people died. Almost as many as the number that made it on to the buses that day.

Chapter Thirty

Miami

As the news anchor broke the story, "Two hundred and forty-three people have died and seven hundred injured at a U.S.-Mexico checkpoint in West Texas this morning," everyone sat around the conference room table without movement in stunned silence. The story included footage of U.S. soldiers wearing respirators helping the wounded and loading the dead into the back of vans.

Maggie did additional fact checking on her laptop. "The eyewitness accounts say that around seven this morning when the buses arrived, the crowd that had been camping outside ever since the news broke that the U.S. would begin letting migrants back into the country, started pushing forward and shoving when a spokesman on the loudspeaker announced that only the first 300 people in line would be permitted on the buses."

Mo's face squeezed into an irritated frown as he tried to make sense of this senseless tragedy.

The news anchor cut to a telephone interview with a medical expert. "In crowd collapse and crush incidents. the most common cause of death is asphyxiation, caused either by vertical stacking, as people fall on top of one another; or by horizontal stacking, where people are crushed together or against an unyielding barrier. Intense crowd pressures, exacerbated by anxiety, make it difficult to breathe. Victims can also exhibit fractures due to pressure or trampling injuries."

Amanda was visibly shaken by the news.

A quiet numbness was setting in. Ramifications of a tragedy like this weren't easy for anyone to wrap their mind around.

Maggie's mind flooded with recent memories, forcing her to relive her near-death experience at the camp. "What the fuck were they thinking? These people are being hunted. What else would you expect them to do when you announce that only the first ones in line are going to be saved?"

Ana Marie and J.C. looked at each other, neither quite sure of the answer.

"This was preventable," Amanda murmured to herself. Just then, the senator's phone chirped.

After several rings, the senator answered. "What do we know so far?" She asked her chief of staff.

"Not much. The crafted message we've received from the White House was deliberately vague."

"Not surprising," the senator remarked.

"The official word is that while the size of the crowd was the biggest factor in the deadly surge, they are still trying to figure out the catalyst that got everyone rushing in the same direction."

Amanda breathed a long, frustrated sigh. "The real question is why there weren't adequate safety protocols in place to spot the red flags and respond to the life-threatening situation."

"There was nothing in the preliminary briefing. Maybe in the follow-up briefing, but I doubt it. The White House is sharing only the most beneficial information."

The senator's eyebrows frowned at the observation. "The truth, but not the whole truth."

"Exactly. The press, however, doesn't seem to be falling for the White House's deceptive rhetoric."

"What about eyewitnesses? They have three hundred witnesses in the camp that were there when all this happened. Has anyone even bothered to question them?" The senator snapped.

There was a long pause while her chief of staff thought about the question. "We haven't received a briefing on any witness statements yet. My gut reaction . . . the administration is scrambling to put together a media strategy that will put the best possible spin on this situation," he replied.

"Call me as soon as you know something," the senator said and ended the call. Her tone smacked of blatant disapproval.

Pierce didn't need eyewitness accounts. He understood intuitively, as did Maggie, that an unbridled fear of infection and the unmitigated surge of brutal murders had caused the mass hysteria responsible for the deadly chain of events.

Maggie kept her eyes glued to the television and ruminated with a self-conscious intensity.

Pierce watched Maggie sink into herself, trying to untangle the flood of sensations washing over her. Her eyes dampened as she blinked away the tears.

Amanda's look of discomfort lessened but did not vanish. Mo turned away from the television and shook his head in disgust.

Pierce stared compassionately at Maggie and nodded solemnly. "Why don't we all take ten minutes?"

* * *

Dode was in her Georgia Tech sweatshirt and pajama pants, tapping away at her computer, waiting to be invited into the virtual meeting. A few minutes after 10:00 a.m., several faces sitting around a conference table appeared on her left monitor.

Pierce greeted her and introduced everyone seated around the table. Dode's smile widened when Pierce got to Mo.

"Mo Black! Finally, I get to put a face to the name." Dode had never met Mo, but she felt like she knew him from the stories Pierce shared with her over the years.

Still feeling the malaise that had taken hold of him after learning of the morning's tragic event, Mo couldn't bring himself to return the smile. He held up his hand and waved instead.

Pierce went over the plan for everyone's benefit. "For the message to go viral on the internet and get picked up by the news media, we need to make an emotional connection. Maggie's personal account of surviving the cartel's sicarios should strike an emotional chord. However, we need to do more than generate empathy. The message needs to make people so angry that they'll want to share it and make others angry. Dode is here to help us," Pierce said and turned the meeting over to Dode.

Dode cleared her throat and took center stage. She began by explaining that she uses algorithms to optimize viewer engagement by identifying the content for their online casino that is most likely to trigger positive reactions.

"The goal of our online casino is to develop and market to a worldwide audience. We utilize data-mining techniques to match names and home addresses with email addresses."

"That sounds like an enormous amount of work to get that done in a short period," Amanda said, with a note of skepticism in her voice.

Dode leaned back in her chair and nodded. "Normally, it would be. But like I said, we've already assembled most of the information we're going to use and have done most of the data mining for our online casino. All I had left to do was tweak the search optimization in the algorithm."

Mo took a deep breath and said, "Please elaborate."

By way of an answer, Dode shared her screen that displayed a long list of hyperlinks to news websites and political blogs.

"Well, for starters, I ran the top liberal and top conservative online news websites using Alexa traffic rank data this morning. From this initial pool of 10,660 headlines, I extracted the ones that were flagged by Claim Buster, leaving 899 headlines. I then randomly sampled 40 headlines from each news organization, manually excluding headlines that did not contain a claim or were not related to U.S. politics."

Dode paused for a moment to give everyone time to study the information on her computer. "The left panel shows how participants evaluated headlines that supported Democrat views. The right panel shows evaluations of news in favor of Republicans."

Mo looked confused. "I'm not sure what this all means." The quality and sheer volume of the data was astounding.

"That's understandable," Dode said as she nodded thoughtfully. "What it means is that we have identified the similarities and differences in the messages and can pinpoint those which are likely to be most effective regardless of the crowd's political makeup."

Mo frowned; unsure he understood what he'd just heard. Amanda came to the rescue.

"So, is the purpose of this exercise to use the information collected to create a script for Maggie that doesn't alienate anyone?" Amanda asked.

"Not exactly," Dode said. "Individuals tend to discard news claims that do not align with their political views. This exercise is just as much to find out about what doesn't work as what is likely to resonate with folks."

Mo shrugged. "And here I thought we were going to record Maggie's story and put it on the internet."

Dode chuckled. "We are, Mo. We're just going to take an informed approach designed to generate the reaction we want, as opposed to throwing stuff against a wall and seeing what sticks. Both approaches work, but we're talking the difference between a hand grenade and a megaton nuke."

The room fell into a deep silence. After a sip of water, Dode continued. "We already use social media services such as Facebook, for example. Facebook can match the email addresses to individual users to create a custom audience. This audience can then be sliced and diced into different demographic groups, right down to people's political and cultural preferences and biases."

"And?" Mo gave Dode a tightly screwed frown, as if he was disappointed. "Are you going through this exercise to only send messages to those people most likely to react?"

"To gain the traction that you want over this short period of time, we need to target specific voters with specific messages by studying their past behavior on Facebook. Then we deliver the messages that Facebook data confirms people want to hear, and we turn up the outrage and sensation factor to get attention."

"So, how do you do this with one message?" Maggie asked.

"We don't. We cut and splice the content and feed highly customized messages designed to push particular buttons so that the recipients will want to share them, and they go viral."

"A micro-targeted free-for-all," Maggie concluded.

Dode cracked a thin smile. "You could say that . . . Americans love a conspiracy. The secret sauce is presenting the message in the manner that resonates most."

Mo nodded his head, signaling a frustrated understanding. "Sounds more like manipulation than persuasion."

Dode shrugged her shoulders with indifference. "Nothing illegal about using algorithmic detection systems to manipulate the message."

Amanda's eyes squinted tight. "Not yet, but I'm hoping to change that."

Dode raised an eyebrow at the comment. Pierce picked up on her silent cue.

"Let's not take our eye off the ball. We're in a dirty street fight here, not a boxing match where the Marquis of Queensbury rules apply," Pierce reminded everyone. "We have three days to inflame public opinion and build solidarity to such levels that they scare a few senators into thinking that voting for the bill will cause them to lose their elections. Otherwise, the bill passes."

Dode focused on Maggie. "Outrage plays well on social media, and it works even better if you name your enemy. You should name Senator Littlefield and Lighthouse in your message. Studies show including names raises the odds that people would share the post by sixty-seven percent."

Maggie nodded. "Do you think it will work?"

Dode took a deep breath. "It can," and went back to the narrative she began a moment before. "Remember Maggie, it's not just about people clicking the link and sharing it even before they finish watching it. Going viral isn't the same as finding an audience. To have staying power, you need to keep people invested. Tying your personal experience to the deaths in the camps, and to Littlefield's attempt to sweep it all under the rug, will enrage people and rally them into issuing a call to action to kill the proposed bill."

Chapter Thirty-One

Miami

Maggie practiced her planned statement eight times. Each time, Dode meticulously analyzed every word, gesture and change of inflection in Maggie's voice, until she felt she had the desired performance. Mo loomed over Maggie's shoulder, blurting out last-minute reminders.

At 12:45 p.m., Dode announced that they were good to go.

Pierce connected a microphone to his smartphone to ensure that the video had crisp audio, and then secured it to a tripod mount.

"Ready," he said.

Maggie took several deep breaths. Then she nodded at Pierce, and he pressed the record button.

"Hello, my name is Maggie Malone, and I'm a genocide survivor. Medical doctors and scientific researchers have concluded that blood transfusions do not cure the virus. And yet, thousands of innocent people were slaughtered last month, and thousands more will die over the next couple of weeks. We can stop it. So . . . do I have your attention?" She asked.

"I was born in this country - New York City, to be exact. Not that it should matter, but I realize that it does for some of y'all. I'm 33-years-old and my home is in Houston, Texas; not far from the border and one of the migrant camps that everyone is talking about. Eight days ago, I was almost murdered in the camp in Matamoros so that they could sell my blood to American companies like Lighthouse."

Maggie described the haunting story of her night in the camp in painstaking detail, and how she barely escaped with her life.

"We are in the middle of a global crisis, a deadly pandemic, and the senseless murders of innocent human beings. Over the last few months, the massacre of poor people seeking asylum has spread like a cancer. They're murdered for their blood."

The images of her near-death experience began to surface again. The memories were still too fresh. Maggie became unsteady and overwhelmed by grief. She tilted her head back and exhaled, gaining control over her impulse to give in to her emotions. She looked over at Pierce and Mo, who were standing to the side. Pierce smiled reassuringly. Mo gestured like a stage director to keep going.

"Folks, I know most of you already know this and I have already said it, but in case you missed the beginning of my message . . . blood transfusions don't cure the virus."

Maggie fixed her watery eyes on the camera. Her dark look made it clear that she had suffered and feared for those left behind.

"Just this morning, two hundred and forty-three souls lost their lives. Trampled to death in their desperation to escape the violence at our border. Our government is more interested in passing a law to protect companies that are getting rich off the murders than stopping the systematic extermination."

Maggie paused and bowed her head as if in prayer.

Dode, watching on her computer, raised one eyebrow and shot Pierce a questioning look: mouthing the words, "What is she doing?"

Pierce nodded, implying to Dode that Maggie was doing fine.

Maggie looked up, her face drawn, staring into the camera and went off script. "I heard someone not too long ago refer to the migrants as human canaries. At first, it put me off. I thought the comparison marginalized the victims. However, when he explained our history and how coal miners sacrificed canaries in the mines to save human lives, I understood his meaning." Maggie's tone became assertive, but there was still a fragility in her voice. "This is much worse. The people being ruthlessly murdered are not saving lives . . . and they are not canaries. They are human beings!"

Maggie stared off into space, a mixture of resignation and sadness on her face. She thought about the men, women, and children in the camps, and felt her heart beat a little faster. Something about what she had seen or experienced in the camps made her think of the iconic line in the famous poem by Emma Lazarus on the bronze plaque at the Statue of Liberty: "*Give me your tired, your poor, your huddled masses yearning to breathe free . . .*" Maybe it was survivor's guilt, but the violent images of the mass killings were still with her, and she felt ashamed.

Her tears told her to finish. Maggie bit her lip. "This is our moment to do more than just talk about justice. Americans must punish those who commit these crimes. We cannot allow our leaders in Washington to turn a blind eye to the people that are profiting from these murders. We must choose to stand up for what is right—for our values. We need to send a strong message to Senator Littlefield, to every senator, and to every congressional representative that we *didn't* elect them to sanction murder. If they fail us and vote for this bill, we will elect leaders with a social conscience that represent our country's interests because that's how democracy works!"

Maggie was turning in an Oscar caliber performance. There was a long pause as she continued to stare into the camera and let the words she'd spoken hang. Maggie caught her breath, swallowed hard. Her mouth was suddenly dry but in closing she managed to say, "the Senate vote is in three days, it's now or never."

Maggie lowered her gaze, and Pierce pressed the button, ending the recording. She sat silently and felt the warmth of tears on her cheeks. While everyone seemed satisfied, there was an awkward silence.

Mo rocked back and forth on his heels. The last twenty-four hours had been non-stop commotion. He looked at the screen, and in a tired voice asked Dode, "What do you think?"

Dode took a sip from her water bottle, and a satisfied smile crossed her lips. "I think we got some contagious content," she said.

Chapter Thirty-Two

Oklahoma

Dode spent all evening editing and transforming Maggie's video into different versions of the message. While the differences were slight, each version of Maggie's message was nuanced to maximize appeal to that group or individual's political make-up. When she finished, Dode had to decide which version to send to each of the thousands of bloggers and media sites. She labored whether to include Maggie's improvised anecdote about the migrants being sacrificed like coal-mine canaries and finally kept it. Alternating between energy drinks and black coffee, Dode worked into the morning hours, methodically evaluating every influencer for purposes of determining which version to send. There was a pathological order to her process. She completed eight hundred fifty-three by 4:00 a.m. and realized that with each passing hour her ability to analyze tedious information was diminishing. Dode told herself she would work another hour and try to get a couple of hours' sleep before her scheduled teleconference with Pierce and the rest of the team.

For nearly an hour, Pierce had the conference room to himself. Slowly, the rest of the team trickled in one by one. They sat around the conference room table drinking coffee. The conversation centered around inconsequential small talk while they waited. At 8:00 a.m. sharp, Pierce double-clicked the icon on his computer and waited to be invited into the virtual meeting.

The high-resolution seventy-inch screen mounted on the wall opposite the conference table flickered from dark to light, as Dode's face appeared.

Dode peered over her glasses at each of the faces sitting around the table. "Good morning, everyone."

Pierce studied her face for a moment. Judging from her disheveled hair and red rims around her eyes, it was a safe assumption that she had not slept.

Mo took a gulp of coffee and asked from the far end of the table, "How are we looking?"

Dode stretched her hand over her head and yawned. "I've been up all night sending encrypted messages to my network of trusted influencers asking for them to cast as wide a net as possible."

Pierce nodded. "Senator Cortez and Congresswoman Rodriguez are heading back to Washington this morning. Is there anything that you need them to do?"

Dode shook her head. "No, just ask them to sit tight." She had a look of intense concentration on her face. "I still have more bloggers to contact. When I'm done with the initial rollout, we'll monitor the over-all response, analyze the video metrics, send out a second message and hopefully the dam breaks." Her tone was skillfully non-committal.

Mo looked almost instantly uncomfortable. "So, you're saying after all this effort, this might not work?"

Dode slowly peeled off her glasses with an air of exasperation. "There's no magic pill or 'can't miss' formula." Dode knew that hard work, educated guesses, and even a dose of good luck was no guarantee that the video would gain empathy and generate public outrage. "We can do everything right but, in the end, there is no guarantee that something will go viral."

Pierce turned to Mo, and with a hint of judicial neutrality in his voice, he made a point that Mo already knew. "This is no different from preparing for trial. We spend countless hours preparing and we can feel good about our chances, but in the end, we can never promise a client that we'll win. What Dode is saying is no different."

Mo made one slight nod in confirmation and let out an audible sigh. "Maybe, I'm just tired. I got the impression yesterday that all your algorithms and marketing strategies would ensure that Maggie's message reached a big audience."

"I believe it eventually will. I'm just not sure if we can get this fire started in our three-day timeframe. We can wait and see how it plays out, or we can throw some gasoline on the flames," Dode said nonchalantly. There was an additional avenue Dode could take. Dode was still trying to figure out whether she was going to play that card. It was an extreme measure. However, she had less than a week to turn the deep tides of public opinion. Establishing a collective mindset through which the public was likely to unite and take a stand required reaching a large audience. If she hacked into the Gmail, Yahoo, Microsoft, AOL and Zoho email servers, Dode could send Maggie's message to billions of people.

She'd cast the widest net possible and grab a few headlines in the process. As far as Dode was concerned, there was no such thing as bad publicity. A data breach and hack of the world's most used and popular email service providers would be the lead story in every newspaper, radio station, television network, and website. The stories would ultimately shine a spotlight on Maggie's message and Senator Littlefield's bill proposing to grant immunity to companies benefiting from the mass murders of migrants.

Dode glanced over her shoulder as if a non-existent person was listening to their conversation and said, "The only way to propagate the narrative and gain real meaningful traction in the time we have left is to hack into the largest email service providers and broadcast Maggie's message. I can't do this alone, but I know a team of hackers with the skills and tools to get past their firewalls and cybersecurity."

Mo grappled with the implications of what Dode had suggested. "So, you're proposing to deal with cyber terrorists. These are the same folks that are responsible for sabotaging governments and stealing corporate secrets."

Maggie shook her head gravely at Mo. "Ease up there, cowboy. Nobody's pissed in your Cheerios."

Mo exhaled an even, long breath. "Exerting political leverage is one thing. However, we're crossing the line by hacking into companies." He lowered his chin and peered disapprovingly at Dode. "Hackers are anarchists and criminals with no allegiances but to themselves, with no goals but to destroy and hold companies' hostage."

Dode shot Pierce an extremely dissatisfied look. Her face hinted that she was struggling between doing what came naturally, which was cutting Mo off at the knees, and trying a more diplomatic approach.

Pierce sighed and looked at Mo pensively. He could see that Mo was dug in on this issue. "Mo, considering the situation, I think it would be best to hear Dode out before snapping to judgment."

Mo shrugged his shoulders with indifference. "That ship already sailed."

Pierce squinted at his mentor, and with a big grin asked, "When did you become so virtuous?"

A look of annoyance rippled over Mo's face. "I've pushed the envelope, but in fifty years of practicing law, I never broke the law to win a case."

Maggie tapped her foot under the desk. Her nerves were shot from making the video the day before and too much coffee. For the first time in a while, she thought she might lose her temper. "It's not the same thing, Mo. You heard Amanda. These boys play dirty. We have to use every resource at our disposal."

Mo's face was drawn tight as the questions hammered inside. All ethical boundaries were being blurred beyond recognition. "I can't be a party to breaking the law."

Maggie didn't care for the remark, but when she reminded herself that it was just Mo being Mo, she shrugged and seemed to tolerate it. Her voice stayed even but gained a slight edge. "Then don't be a part of it."

Mo ignored Maggie and focused his attention on Dode. "Are you saying that you can legally hack into companies' servers?" Mo scoffed.

There was a moment of silence, then Dode answered, "No. I'm not saying that. The hackers that I would ask for help are technically skilled, politically conscious individuals. But I won't bullshit you and tell you they're good guys. They are dangerous, but they won't be attacking the sites. They're simply accessing email directories through backdoors and sending the same email containing Maggie's video to everyone. We won't break into the computer systems to shut down their networks or disrupt the companies' operations by installing malware."

Mo gave Dode a tightly screwed frown, as if he was offended.

Maggie tried to reason with him. "Mo, not all hacking is necessarily bad. It's something we live with every day."

Mo grunted and shook his head.

Pierce tried to read deeper into Mo's reaction. In a casual tone he said, "Why don't we look at this through a different lens?"

Mo raised his palms in a gesture indicating frustration. "This is a pretty black-and-white issue."

Cocking his head in a questioning manner, Pierce said, "You seem to be stuck on the word *hack* and all its negative connotations when Dode has already assured you that her people have no intention of taking any company's operating system hostage or engaging in corporate espionage. The primary objective is to have her people access email servers and disperse Maggie's video."

While Mo considered the point, Pierce added, "We all send emails every day. It's one of the principal ways we communicate."

Mo shifted uncomfortably. "I understand the whole 'we're just sending emails' rationalization. It's the shortcut we're taking by hacking into private servers that I have a problem with."

Pierce stared hard at Mo. "So, you're telling me you've never leaned over and glanced at opposing counsel's notes or used a confidential document mistakenly disclosed by opposing counsel in discovery to your advantage?"

Mo bit his lip and shook his head defensively. "That's completely different."

"Is it?" Pierce asked. "You took advantage of an opportunity for your benefit."

Mo shot Pierce a disbelieving look. "I didn't break any laws."

Pierce nodded while Maggie and Dode shook their heads. "No one has accused you of anything."

"All Dode is proposing," Maggie quickly added, "is to find a way to speed up the process of getting the message out."

Mo, once again, shrugged off Maggie's comment.

Pierce continued to talk in his smooth, even voice. "Like I said earlier, let's put this in a different context. Humans are natural hackers. We're constantly figuring out ways to game the system. It happens in all walks of life. For example, card counting in blackjack is a hack. Casinos do everything to make it difficult, if not impossible for players to count cards. And yet, there are still a few players with the skill set that do it."

"That's completely different," Mo snapped back.

Pierce shrugged. "Sports are hacked all the time. Your favorite sport, Formula One racing, is full of hacks. Racing teams work hard to figure out ways to modify car designs that are not specifically prohibited by the rulebook, but nonetheless subvert its intent."

Mo had serious doubts but could see that no matter what he said, their minds were made up. It bothered him that they were all so willing to bend the rules or color outside the lines. No matter how they spun it, or tried to justify their actions, gaining unauthorized access to a computer server was a crime. "There is a difference between breaking the law and gaming the system."

Maggie raised her eyebrows in a doubtful manner. "We're going up against powerful politicians that don't play by *any* rule book. These pricks write the fucking book. You can't expect us to jump into this brawl with one hand tied behind our backs." Maggie inhaled sharply. "I admit, we're taking a shortcut. But we're just sending emails. Companies collect and sell personal data, including email lists, all the time."

Pierce waited for further protest, but Mo was finally and sullenly silent. His eyes swept from Pierce to Maggie, and then to Dode; then he cast them down in defeat. Mo shook his head and finally, in a noticeably unenthusiastic tone, said. "We shouldn't do it. But I can see that I'm outnumbered."

* * *

Dode hoped Maggie's video would gain traction across the internet and attract the attention of hundreds of thousands of people in a matter of hours. What Dode didn't foresee was celebrities tweeting Maggie's video to millions of their followers. Instead of the message spreading online, what happened looked more like a tsunami—a string of celebrity tweets followed by a wall of powerful unforgiving comments felling anything and everyone in its path. Propaganda networks, some with Russian ties, clogged the social media sites and sent conspiracy theorists into a frenzy.

Once the world's richest billionaire and ultimate influencer re-tweeted a picture of a red circle with a line running through the silhouette of a bird with the words "No More Canaries," to his nearly ninety million followers, the slogan flooded media forums and became the rallying call to arms. The hashtag #NoMoreCanaries was downloaded 37,002 times in the first two hours, and 931,707 times before the end of the day.

The public outcry exceeded everyone's expectations. Within hours of the video being released, tensions mounted, demonstrators descended on Washington D.C.; and despite the shelter-at-home orders, protests were rapidly organized and erupted across the nation and around the globe.

<h1 style="text-align:center">Chapter Thirty-Three</h1>

New Orleans

Lighthouse's top executives hunkered down in Ben Bowman's private conference room, watching the bank of televisions that were all broadcasting images of protests and rallies opposing Senator Littlefield's bill. Bowman stormed into the room like a predator, his eyes taking inventory of everything around him. He had a full head of gray hair and a red bulbous nose that was the direct result of his heavy drinking.

Bowman looked at the TVs and barked at his assistant, Carol Hansen, "Turn that shit off."

Frank Collins, Lighthouse's chief legal counsel, was at the far end of the conference room, sleeves rolled up, engaged in a frantic conversation on his cell phone. Littlefield's bill was the biggest story of the morning. Maggie's message interrupted television and radio broadcasts every hour. The government's loss of control over the Emergency Alert System was the second most prominent story. To make matters worse, Lighthouse's reputed connection to the Zeta cartel tied the hacking of Google's and Yahoo's email servers for third.

With a look of utter frustration, Bowman asked, "Can anyone tell me how in the hell this happened?"

No one answered the question. The silence added to Bowman's frustration, and a rage started to consume him.

Collins ended his call and in a beaten voice said, "I just got off the phone with Rinehart. Two senators have withdrawn their support, and he's worried others in the Senate may jump ship."

Bowman's face twisted into an unhinged look. "We've spent the last twelve months and $16 million on lobbyists, campaign contributions, think-tanks and high-priced public relations firms on messaging. Now two fucking days before the bill goes to the floor for a vote, you're telling me we might not have enough senators to pass this bill?"

Collins nodded his head, signaling a frustrated understanding. "I've talked to every pollster from New York to L.A. over the last twenty-four hours, and they're all telling me the same thing. There's been a cataclysmic shift in public opinion overnight. Protests condemning the murders in Mexico are going viral, and Littlefield's bill has become toxic."

"Fuck them. They don't get to vote until November. What are Littlefield and Rinehart doing about this?"

"Littlefield is fighting an uphill battle to keep his coalition together." Collins exhaled as his shoulders drooped, and his face sagged. "Rinehart thinks pulling teeth without anesthesia might be easier."

Bowman emitted a strange guttural sound that could have passed for an expletive but wasn't a word at all.

Collins frowned and said, "Senators Anderson and Erickson are on the fence, and we need both their votes for the bill to pass."

"What's it going to take to keep them from breaking ranks?"

"Anderson isn't seeking re-election, so he isn't as worried about the public opinion polls, but he has some concern that supporting this bill will tarnish his legacy."

"Legacy?" Bowman chirped in an incredulous tone. His first impulse was to laugh, but he realized Collins was dead serious.

"So, what's it going to take to preserve the good senator from Ohio's legacy?" Bowman asked in a profoundly cynical tone.

"If we can secure the funding for a cultural center in his hometown, we'll hang on to his vote."

"How much?"

"$5.7 million is the number Rinehart tossed out."

Bowman absorbed it without a flinch. "What about Erickson?"

Collins shrugged his shoulders as if mystified by the duplicity of politicians. "That's a little more complicated. The senator is in a tight and contentious race for his Senate seat this November, so he's paying close attention to the public opinion polls and what's being said on social media."

There was a quiet exhaling in frustration, followed by a mumbling of obscenities. "He's been hanging on to that Senate seat for eighteen years like a screaming child clutching his favorite toy."

Collins nodded solemnly.

"How much have we contributed to that fucker's campaign?"

"A lot."

Bowman glared at Collins and growled. "I know it's a lot. How much exactly?"

"Four hundred and ninety thousand," Collins said sheepishly.

Bowman's fat jowls turned as red as his nose as he tried valiantly not to explode. "Tell Rinehart to pay him a visit and find out how much he wants!"

"I'm afraid it's not that simple."

"It's always that simple."

Collins wasn't so sure. "If Erickson thinks voting for the bill will cost him his re-election, he won't care about how much you're willing to contribute to his campaign because it won't matter."

"Politics," Bowman spewed, as if the word turned his stomach. He leaned back in his chair and glowered at Collins as if he would shoot the messenger if he delivered any more bad news.

"Rinehart has been working around the clock for the last three days trying to keep the votes needed to pass the bill," Collins said.

"Where do we stand on the vote count?"

"As of today, we still have fifty-three with a couple of undecideds."

Bowman mumbled something under his breath and then said, "Rinehart has got brains, and he's got balls, so tell him now's the time to use them both, preferably at the same time."

Collins shifted uncomfortably in his chair and finally asked, "What if Erickson passes on our offer?"

Bowman said nothing for a moment. He just stared at Collins as if the answer was obvious. "Well, shit, Frank. If the carrot doesn't work, then we'll use the stick . . . If Erickson pulls his support, then Petrovich will deliver the next message."

Collins' weather-beaten face twisted in a grimace of disbelief. "Sir, you can't threaten a United States senator."

Bowman frowned at Collins. "We're way past threats."

Collins' jaw went slack.

"If you think I'm going to walk away from half a million dollars, you're sadly mistaken. No one put a gun to Erickson's head and forced him to take the money," Bowman said, sounding like a man who wouldn't hesitate to green light Petrovich.

Collins knew of the infamous Alina Petrovich, but only by reputation. She spent her career slinking around the edges of every major political scandal. Petrovich was what was known as a black ops political fixer who operated from the shadows and on the sleazier side of a sleazy business. A kind of conspiracy-theory superstar.

One of the times that Bowman hired Petrovich, she used a trapdoor in a competitor's firewall to secretly monitor their financial transactions digitally and give Bowman private and sensitive information that he used to leverage his competitor and force him to sell. In online security circles, Petrovich was revered and feared among both criminals and security experts.

What Bowman had in mind for Erickson, however, was far more ominous. Using an illegitimate UPS shipping notice to gain access to

Erickson's computer, Petrovich downloaded a Trojan horse. Once she had access, she siphoned child pornography onto the senator's computer along with fabricated communications in which the senator appeared to solicit sex from underage children. If the senator didn't vote for the bill, Petrovich would arrange for an email soliciting sex from his IP address to be sent to one of the FBI's undercover operations.

By the time the FBI figured out that Erickson's computer had been hacked, the damage done would irremediably end Erickson's political career.

The cybertrail left by Petrovich would lead the FBI online cybersecurity investigators down various rabbit holes to two intelligence agencies, four senior intelligence officials, a tech company, and finally to a thirty-five-year-old Russian hacker who goes by the name *Boris Spassky*.

* * *

All the cell phones started blaring in unison. Bowman looked as if he wanted to choke someone as the Government Emergency Alert contained a manipulated image of Senator Littlefield standing next to a cartel hitman, each holding an automatic weapon in one hand and a bag of blood with the Lighthouse corporate logo in the other. Below the picture was the SMS-like message. *"Kill Littlefield's bill instead of Innocent People."*

Bowman glared at each person sitting around the conference table and lobbed harsh words and strings of profanity at everyone. No one dared to make eye contact. The rattled Lighthouse employees all fidgeted nervously, waiting for Bowman's tirade to end.

When he finished screaming obscenities, Bowman kept his predatory gaze on them while he considered how to turn the table on the group responsible for fanning the flames. His eyes eventually swept back to Collins.

"I want you to find who's responsible for hacking into the Emergency Alert System," Bowman snarled angrily.

"You want me to look for the hackers?" Collins' face contorted, genuinely confused.

"Use Petrovich if you need to."

Collins was not meek, but he wasn't a cold-blooded assassin. He hesitated while grimacing. "And what do you want me to do when I find them?"

Bowman picked up on Collins' apprehension. He was a capable lawyer, but he lacked a killer instinct. A black mark in Bowman's book. Bowman paused for a second and took on a decidedly more business-like tone. "I want you to hire them."

Chapter Thirty-Four

Miami Beach

The *New York Times* printed a poll the day of the Senate vote that said over seventy-four percent of the people surveyed opposed giving amnesty to any person or company profiting from the murders in Mexico.

Mo finished his morning coffee and announced he was heading back to his home on Hutchinson Island where he could detox from the frenetic pace of the last week. When Pierce asked Mo to stay so they could watch the Senate vote together, Mo shook his head no and smiled.

"There's nothing more for us to do. We've set everything in motion. Now we wait and see how it plays out later this afternoon."

Maggie set her coffee cup on the table and leaned back with a disappointed expression. "Aww stay Big Papi," her voice purred. "Who knows when we'll be able to hang out again?"

Mo smiled. He'd grown very fond of Maggie. Pierce was like a son to him, and Maggie was quickly becoming the granddaughter he never had.

Mo shook his head. "We can hang out when the light at the end of the tunnel isn't a train called Senator Littlefield." He sighed and said, "I've done what I came here to do, and now it's time for me to go back home."

Pierce nodded thoughtfully but didn't immediately speak. He knew by Mo's tone that his mind was already made up. He studied Mo for a moment and looked at Maggie.

"He's turned into a beach bum in his retirement. He can only stay away for so long."

Thick wrinkles broke out across Mo's forehead as he tried to remember the phrase his mother used to say when house guests stayed too long. The phrase came to him as he grabbed his bag. He smiled and said . . . "Guests, like fish, begin to smell after three days." He winked at Maggie and said, "So, I'm off like a prom dress."

Maggie rolled her eyes. "He's got jokes . . ." It suddenly occurred to her that she, Yami and Giovanny had been guests in Pierce's home almost as long as Mo. "Wait up, we've been here a week."

Pierce laughed. "Nobody smells, and I have plenty of room."

Mo offered to take Yamilet and Giovanny back to Hutchinson Island with him.

"They're pretty settled in here and she's more comfortable having Maggie around." Pierce replied.

* * *

Mo jumped into his sedan and waved goodbye. He turned right on Ocean Drive and followed signs for the MacArthur Causeway past the floating jewel known as Star Island with its impressive waterfront residences, and celebrated for the famous residents it attracts, then northbound on Interstate-95.

He'd grown accustomed to his semi-retired lifestyle on Hutchinson Island. The work was not over, by any means, but the heavy lifting had been done; and now it was time for him to go back home and spend time walking on the sandy beaches and protecting the sea turtle eggs from natural predators as well as tourists. The truth was that the case had the unmistakable feel of one too many. As much as he had relished the idea of going to trial with Pierce, his protégé and the most brilliant lawyer he'd ever worked with, he no longer had the unwavering focus his profession demanded. Nature's way of hinting that at eighty-three years old, he had given all he had, and it was someone else's turn to champion worthwhile causes.

Twenty weeks had passed since the virus forced the governor's de facto ban on non-essential travel as the state ramped up efforts to minimize the spread of the virus. Life had changed dramatically. One of the few bright spots of the pandemic, no more traffic jams. Mo stepped on the accelerator. The digital speedometer read 92 MPH. There were no Highway Patrol Officers around to write him a ticket. Mo sped along the desolate highway past a digital billboard displaying a message imploring people to oppose Littlefield's bill. The second billboard he passed displayed the silhouette of the bold and vibrant bird that Mo recognized as the now infamous canary, with the circle-backslash symbol.

"Those fuckers hacked everything," Mo cursed under his breath.

About thirty minutes later, up ahead, he noticed a car parked on the side of the road. Next to the car, a young girl was waving frantically. He looked around the highway. It was devoid of human existence. There were no cars, road crews, or emergency vehicles on the side of the road that could help her. People were terrified of catching the virus. All Mo knew was what he'd heard. The virus attacked a person's immune system and organs for a few days before claiming them.

Mo cursed quietly, trying to decide what to do. Continue driving home and be on the beach by noon or jump into something that had the clear potential of disrupting his plans for the day. Mo pulled off to the side of the road about fifty yards ahead and sat there for a few more seconds before putting the car in reverse. As he got closer, he heard the frantic screams of a young girl desperately shaking a woman slumped over the steering wheel.

As soon as Mo stepped out of the car and began walking towards her, she began pleading for him to help her. Mo placed a surgical mask over his nose and mouth.

"We're not sick. We're not sick. Please help my mom!" she shouted.

Mo kept his mask on just to be safe.

"Did you call the police or for an ambulance?"

The young girl managed to nod in between sobs. "No one's coming."

"What happened?"

"Drugs," she said, her eyes cutting in all directions, as if there was a long story behind their present predicament.

"What did she take?"

"Coke. She said she couldn't wait til we got home. Said all she needed was a little bump. A minute later she started having a seizure."

Mo held his cellphone in one hand and checked for a pulse with the other. She was hot to the touch. Blood and a pink drool flowed from her mouth with each convulsion. The emergency numbers Mo dialed were all ringing busy.

Mo turned to the young girl, who looked to be about fifteen years old. He asked, "What's your name?"

She choked back tears. "La . . . Lauren."

Mo nodded. "Okay Lauren. This is what we're going to do. I'm going to pull your mom out of the car. I want you to grab her feet and help me carry her to my car."

Lauren stood rigid. Her eyes didn't seem quite able to fix on anything. Mo twisted the woman's torso and curled his arms under hers. He took a step back and dragged her out by her shoulders. Her feet were the last part of her body to leave the car. The small woman was heavier than Mo expected. His back tightened. When her feet crashed on to the ground with a dull thud, Mo said, "Grab her ankles."

They trudged slowly toward Mo's car. The woman's body swayed as Lauren struggled clumsily with her mother's dead weight. They slid her on to the back seat and closed the car door.

Mo waited for Lauren to climb into the front seat and then gunned the engine. The black Mercedes sped towards the next exit.

"Use your cell phone to get us directions to the closest hospital," he told Lauren.

She sobbed quietly and typed unsteadily into her smartphone.

* * *

Mo took the exit ramp and sped down the road. A mile and a half down, the robotic sounding voice on the GPS directed him to take a right and announced that his destination was two miles ahead on his left. When Mo pulled up to the emergency room entrance, a security guard waved his arms while keeping his distance and shouted that they could not park there.

Before he could finish, Mo yelled, "Overdose."

The guard turned around and went back inside. Two hospital attendants dressed in hazmat suits pushing a gurney rushed past Mo towards the car and lifted the woman just in time for her to vomit all over the floor.

The attendant shouted at the security guard to clear the path as they raced the patient through the entrance.

Just before pointing to the two attendants and telling Lauren to follow them, they bumped elbows instead of shaking hands. Mo hated elbow bumps, but public health officials had been warning to switch to elbow bumps because touching elbows did not spread the infection the way touching hands did.

"They'll take care of your mom," Mo reassured her.

Behind her tears, Lauren drew a deep breath and said, "Thank you."

Mo got into his car and drove away.

<h1 style="text-align:center">Chapter Thirty-Five</h1>

Hutchinson Island, Florida

Mo's three-story house faced the water and was just inches from the sand. As part of his daily ritual, he brought out his chair, a small cooler and a novel; and settled in just out of reach of the incoming tide and the sanderlings skirting along the water's edge probing the wet sand for food. The usual cast of characters were all there. Beyond the rolling waves rising and falling and bringing the music of the beach, a squadron of brown pelicans circled overhead and dove into the ocean after their dinner. About a hundred yards away, a man, who Mo didn't know, and nicknamed Fisherman Bob, cast his line into the lush seagrass beds, hoping to hook a snook or mangrove snapper.

At 5:00 p.m., and right on schedule, Darcy appeared wearing metal detector headphones, steadily swinging the search coil from side to side. She and her husband Bill lived three houses down from Mo.

"Hey stranger, where have you been?" Darcy asked louder than normal.

Mo casually looked up from his book and smiled the way someone does when they don't want to be disturbed. He coughed before saying, "Miami."

Darcy frowned as if hit with irritable bowels. "Too much traffic," she said, and continued past him, moving in a methodical pattern down the beach looking for gold and silver.

"Not anymore," Mo mumbled under his breath.

The temperature had cooled to seventy from a high of eighty-five as the sun started its slow descent. Mo decided to read for another hour before heading back inside. Twenty minutes later, the cellphone in

Mo's pocket vibrated. He decided to let it ring. The phone eventually stopped vibrating. A few seconds later, the cellphone chirped. It was a text message from Pierce.

Good News. Senate failed to pass Littlefield's bill. Bill's dead.

It was almost time for a cocktail, so Mo reached in his cooler for a beer. He used his phone to search for articles on the internet reporting on the Senate vote. The search engine instantly identified links to pages covering the Senate vote. Mo clicked on the first one.

Amnesty Bill Fails to Pass Procedural Vote in U.S. Senate.

A bill to provide total immunity for medical companies died in the Senate on Friday after it failed to garner enough Republican support to pass a procedural vote.

The Health Protection Act sponsored by Senator Claude Littlefield was expected to pass. Republican leaders, however, recently came under enormous pressure from constituents to vote against the bill.

Human rights advocates characterized the bill as radical and said it would sanction genocide.

The vote was forty-seven to fifty-two. Four votes short of the fifty-one votes required for the legislation to pass. Protesters chanted and held signs that said, *"We believe Maggie Malone." Protesters cheered when news broke that several Republican senators broke ranks and would be voting no on the proposed bill.*

"It's extreme. It's an egregious violation of the most fundamental of all human rights, and that is the right to live without fear of being targeted and killed," Democratic Senator Amanda Cortez of Texas said of the bill in debate on Friday.

Mo scrolled through several more articles as he sipped his beer. When he finished surfing the internet, he got up out of his chair and walked to the edge of the ocean. He walked along the beach, drifting aimlessly like the waves, flabbergasted at how much the world had changed since he first started practicing law. The internet changed the paradigm of how power was wielded. Humankind was now almost entirely connected, and how information was dispersed and absorbed was dramatically different. People had moved away from traditional media sources for their news and had grown dependent on social media and social networking services for information. Gone were the days of people getting their news from a local TV station, their local newspaper, or the national newscast from one of the networks.

Painstaking hours dedicated to fundraising, lobbying, and developing relationships over years, sometimes decades, was no longer the recipe for success. The arrival of the World Wide Web made it possible for conspiracy theorists, radical thinkers, and groups advocating hatred and hostility to amplify disinformation, incite violence, and lower trust in the media and democratic institutions.

It took less than a week for a handful of twenty-and thirty-year-olds living on Hot Pockets and energy drinks to deploy computational propaganda, including the use of fake accounts–bots, humans, and hacked accounts to ideologically manipulate public opinion and change the course of history. For better or for worse, this cataclysmic swing made Mo deeply nervous about America's future.

* * *

The sunrise over the Atlantic Ocean the next morning looked like God had decided to light the day with a candle. It had only taken a couple of days on the island for him to transition back to his island life where his thoughts were uncluttered, and his only goal was to take in the radiant light stretching ever outward across the rich blue water. Mo stood at the water's edge, sipped his coffee and took a deep breath before heading back inside to start his morning routine.

Typically, Mo had a light breakfast before reading the online editions of the New York Times and the Washington Post and was surprised when his stomach flipped. He raced to the bathroom, where he vomited and retched until both his back and stomach ached. Moving around gingerly, Mo took two Extra Strength Tylenol, wrapped himself in blankets that he fetched from the linen closet and laid down on his sofa for a long time.

Early that afternoon, Mo's phone pinged with another text from Pierce. He had not returned Pierce's call. Unsteady as he felt, he just wanted to be left alone, but suspected Pierce would begin to worry, so he wrote back:

Sorry for not responding. Feeling a little under the weather, so resting up. How's everyone?

Everyone's good. Received an email from the Judge's Clerk advising that the Judge's order will be out on Monday.

Mo expected the court to rule in their favor. **It shouldn't have taken this long.**

Agreed. Do you want me to drive up and bring you something to eat or any medicine?

No. I have everything I need. Just need to get some rest.

Okay. Maggie and I will FaceTime with you tomorrow morning. Feel better.

* * *

It was the dead of night and Mo felt like his head was being split apart by a hammer and chisel. Sweat slicked his forehead. Mo padded along to the bathroom in search of more Tylenol. He'd been eating them every couple of hours to fight the headache. When he looked in the mirror, he began to worry. Now there were blotchy marks on his face, neck, and arms. He immediately felt an indescribable sense of dread. Mo ran through a string of screamed curses in his mind; and reached for the bottle of Xanax to settle his nerves.

At 5:45 a.m. Mo's temperature was 102. He reached into his shirt pocket and retrieved a few pills. Mo tossed them into his mouth, breaking them apart with his teeth and savoring the bitterness. He knew the pills would provide little relief against the virus, but he found something strangely comforting from the taste. He grabbed a Cuban Cohiba cigar he'd been saving, and walked unsteadily out to the beach, like a bleeding animal stumbling through the woods. Mo would not be robbed of the opportunity to witness one more beautiful sunrise.

Chapter Thirty-Six

Washington D.C.

The data from all seven camps confirmed that the vaccine was effective in helping the immune system target and fight the virus. Less than ten percent of fully vaccinated individuals when exposed to the virus developed symptoms. The vaccine decreased the transmission rates and disease severity.

The results, however, for mildly symptomatic and severely symptomatic patients were disappointing. Sophia concluded that part of the problem was that the replication process of the Kayapo virus was four times faster than what was thought possible. Once it is introduced to the host, the virus multiplied and spread so fast that the immune system was quickly overwhelmed.

A major limitation of the results was the size and length of the trial. Approximately three hundred migrants were tested and vaccinated daily in each of the seven camps. Sophia's medical team and the CDC had only twenty-nine days to observe the effects of the vaccine on just under 59,000 test subjects before the president decided to hold a press conference.

* * *

The president was wearing a dark suit, a red tie and a white shirt as a woman stood over him putting the finishing touches of concealer to cover up the dark circles under his eyes. Colonel Cone and Admiral Rachel B. Adler, MD, the Secretary of Health and Human Services, sat on either side of the president, waiting to be introduced by the president's press secretary to the White House Press Corps. Virtual press conferences made President Porter uncomfortable. It was much harder to read the room and work the crowd. The press corps no longer gave the president the benefit of the doubt. The honeymoon and the softball questions had ended a couple of months earlier after the Kayapo virus began claiming American lives with a vengeance.

Some in the press supported the president's efforts, recognizing that his administration was not to blame for the Kayapo pandemic and the economic crisis that followed. The hardened reporters saw the federal assistance checks and mortgage and rent abatement orders as unsustainable Band-Aids instead of remedies. The old guard of the press corps had been around too long to be fooled by an elaborate shell game designed to shift the focus from the fact that the country was in a free-fall.

"Good afternoon, Mr. President. Are you ready?"

With a slight smile, the president nodded and greeted everyone. "Good afternoon."

The president cleared his throat. "I've called this press conference to share some good news. It's been some journey for all of us. I am pleased to report that we now have a vaccine. We're grateful to be joined by Colonel Bernard Cone, the commander-in-charge of the U.S. Army Medical Research Institute of Infectious Diseases, and Admiral Rachel B. Adler. Colonel Cone and his team spearheaded the research effort; and they have done an absolutely incredible job. From the instant the Kayapo virus invaded our shores, we raced into action to develop a safe and effective vaccine at breakneck speed. Before the Coronavirus vaccine, a vaccine took four- to-five years to develop. While the Coronavirus vaccine took just over one year to develop, the Kayapo vaccine was developed in just under eight months."

Maggie and Pierce spent Saturday afternoon sitting in his living room watching the press conference on television.

President Porter took a sip of water before continuing. "To achieve this goal, we harnessed the full power of government, the genius of American scientists, and the might of the American industry, to save millions and millions of lives all over the world. We're just days away from FDA authorization, and we're pushing them hard, at which point we will immediately begin mass distribution. On behalf of the entire nation, I want to thank everyone here today who has been involved in this extraordinary American initiative."

The president looked on his monitor and spotted a friendly face. Tanya Robertson, the CBS White House correspondent.

Porter called her name.

Tanya smiled. "Mr. President, this vaccine has been developed very rapidly. You said the FDA will be approving it. But is it safe?"

Porter wasted no time responding. "The doctors assure me that it is safe. Medical researchers are no longer starting from square one. Thanks to advances in genomic sequencing, researchers successfully uncovered the viral sequence of the Kayapo virus-roughly ten days after the first reported pneumonia cases in Brazil. The ability to fast-track research was a direct result of this worldwide cooperation. Very shortly, the FDA is expected to issue an emergency use authorization for the vaccine."

"Follow-up question, Mr. President."

Porter nodded. "Just one."

"There is information on the internet contending that the vaccine infects people with a weakened form of the Kayapo virus."

The president chuckled. "Well, if it's on the internet then it must be true." The president's comment was followed by laughter.

"Nobody is getting infected with the Kayapo virus. Simply stated, the vaccine is an engineered protein that mimics the genetic material of the virus and trains the immune system to recognize and attack it."

More raised hands popped up across the president's monitor. This time the president called on Steven Mitchem from CNN.

"Mr. President, critics of the vaccine argue that you're rushing to the finish line. Too many corners have been cut."

Thick wrinkles broke out across the president's forehead. "Steve, I thought I already addressed that point. Tens of thousands participated in the trials. Our scientists meticulously adhered to rigorous guidelines. The last pandemic ushered in a new era of vaccine research. The combination of global collaboration by scientists and the ability to synthetically engineer vaccines that train our bodies to fight any virus is akin to the 'landing-on-the-moon' moment."

"Follow up. When will you start rolling out the vaccine?"

"We're spending billions to make the vaccine available in record time. Once we receive the emergency authorization next week, we will begin to roll it out."

The raised hand icon peppered the president's screen. Porter's eyes rested on another familiar face, Alex Bortz, the White House correspondent for the Washington Post.

"Mr. President, any comment on the Health Protection Act sponsored by Senator Littlefield falling short in the Senate?"

The president looked like he was tired of this line of questioning. He exhaled and shook his head. "The last few days leading up to the Senate vote marked a turning point in this nation's history. The truth of the matter is the American people spoke in one unified voice; and their elected representatives chose democracy over autocracy, light over shadow, justice over injustice."

"Follow up question, Mr. President?"

"Sorry Alex, you lost that opportunity with your last question."

"I have time for one more question."

The president's eyes rested on a new face. A young lady from United Press International. He assumed that her audience wouldn't care about the failed Senate vote that left a black eye on his administration, nor was she likely to care about the details for the plan for rolling out the vaccine to American cities. He decided that she was a safe choice.

"Katrina Jean-Pierre, UPI. Mr. President, Over the last several weeks, the numbers of migrants murdered in Mexico have more than tripled. Mass graves are littering the Sonoran Desert just south of the U.S. border. Mr. President, does your administration plan to take any action to respond to these crimes against humanity?"

Under the conference table, Porter clenched and flexed his hand in agitation. He lowered his head briefly, closed his eyes and appeared to be silently reflecting on the murders. A gesture designed to convey that he was deeply troubled by the mass executions in Mexico. Then he focused on giving the press perfect sound bites. The president cleared his throat gently. "Ms. Jean-Pierre, our national security is affected when masses of civilians are slaughtered, and murderers wreak havoc on regional stability and livelihoods. America's reputation suffers when we are perceived as idle in the face of mass atrocities and genocide occurring on our border, but it's not up to us to put a stop to the murders. It's up to the Mexican government to protect its people . . ."

Eyes started to roll. The cynical members of the press were getting sick of hearing political rhetoric.

Katrina talked over the president as he continued to try to justify the country's failure to take any action. His head shook and cheeks tensed as her voice overwhelmed his.

"This is much worse than sitting by idly. The U.S. is complicit in the atrocities that the cartel commits. The harsh reality is that this administration is not only failing to hold the perpetrators accountable, you're encouraging the mass murders by allowing American companies to buy the blood from the cartels."

The president removed his glasses. His expression had morphed into one of vague disapproval. He pushed back against the criticism, and defended his administration's efforts. "I've spoken with Mexico's president and insisted that his government take aggressive steps to stop the hostilities." He did not succumb to the press's expectation for details of the conversation. Porter glanced sideways at his press secretary, who pointed at her wristwatch. The president nodded. When Katrina raised her hand for a follow-up comment, he ignored it. He would not allow Katrina to have the last word. "The vaccine will all but eliminate the horrifying human rights abuses occurring just south of our border. The demand for the blood will soon cease to exist, and the carnage will stop. Even if the Mexican government fails to take any action." The president shook his head and said, "However, I want to be perfectly clear that the oath of office that I took is an oath of allegiance to Americans, and what matters most is saving American lives."

Unflappable as ever, the president flashed a grin. "This vaccine will not only save millions of American lives. but millions of lives around the world."

Pierce allowed the President's words to sink in. The president's remarks had a cloak of conspiracy draped over them. "The White House isn't an innocent bystander," Pierce said.

Maggie showed her displeasure with a furrowed brow. "It never is."

Chapter Thirty-Seven

Miami Beach

Sunday morning, Maggie sipped coffee and pecked away at her laptop preparing the asylum petitions for Yamilet and Giovanny. Pierce opened the window and inhaled the beautiful spring morning. It was far too glorious to stay indoors, so he decided a quick run seemed like an appropriate self-indulgence before checking in on Mo. When Pierce finished stretching, he tuned into NPR and launched into a four-mile run from South Pointe Park across the causeway. Senator Steve Erickson was being interviewed by NPR's Nancy Keith.

"Senator, you're in the middle of a close and contentious Senate race. Polling in Minnesota showed that the majority of registered voters in your state overwhelmingly opposed the Health Protection Act sponsored by Senator Littlefield. Why did you fight so hard for the passage of the bill, even after it appeared to be a lost cause in the Senate?"

"Because Littlefield owns your ass," Pierce said to himself. The footing on the hard-packed sands provided him with some cushion for his stride and some resistance for strength building.

"Nancy, my voters and their opinions are very important to me. But you have to ask yourself who conducted the poll? Did they manipulate the wording of the questions to get the answers they want? Even when people have strong views, a single polling question rarely captures those views," Erickson said.

Pierce picked up speed just as he hit the causeway. He never tired of the 360-degree views from the bridges connecting the man-made islands. The sights of the multimillion-dollar homes and the yachts made the miles fly by.

"Am I to understand that you believe that if the question was framed differently or, better yet, if the voters had a better understanding of the issues, they would feel differently?"

Erickson swatted away the question. *"This was a vital piece of legislation designed to protect the very companies that have just developed the vaccine for the Kayapo virus. We can't turn our backs on them by exposing them to lawsuits from people claiming to have suffered side effects from the vaccine."*

As Pierce reached the midpoint of his run and turned for home, it was obvious to him that Senator Erickson did not want to wade into any discussion where it could appear that he voted for Littlefield's bill rather than suffer the wrath of the pathological senator.

"Don't let him off the hook, Nancy," Pierce blurted out as he picked up his pace for the last mile.

"Senator, the legislation that failed to garner enough votes to pass would have done much more than grant immunity from lawsuits to Big Pharma. If that was the only objective, why not find a middle ground instead of trying to push through a law that critics of the legislation are saying protects companies and individuals that profited from the intentional acts that left thousands of innocent victims dead?"

"Nicely done," Pierce huffed as he lengthened his stride.

"An amendment to limit the broad immunity given by the bill was defeated on the floor."

"So, am I correct in thinking that you voted for a deeply flawed bill because that was better than no bill at all?"

Pierce had heard enough and switched off the interview as he cooled off on his walk back to his condo.

* * *

After trying to FaceTime with Mo all morning, he finally answered.

Maggie gawked at Mo's pale face. He managed to smile, but both Maggie and Pierce were too shocked to return it.

After retching for almost a minute, "Forgive me," Mo said calmly.

Pierce exhaled, as if somewhat overwhelmed.

Yamilet appeared and offered them coffee. She did not stay in the kitchen, but Pierce got the impression she was close by, trying to understand what was happening.

Maggie exhaled and kept nodding but struggled for words. "How . . . how Mo did you get sick?"

Mo grunted a response. "I hate the saying *no good deed goes unpunished*, but I'm afraid this time it may be true." He could hardly get the words through his dried, cracked lips.

There was a long pause as they struggled to make sense of it. Pierce gritted his teeth and said, "We need to get you to a hospital."

Mo coughed in his hand and checked it for blood. He thought about machines breathing for him and extending his life for a few extra days and decided death would be preferable. He growled as he tried to fill his lungs. "No hospital."

Maggie nodded her understanding as she wiped away tears.

Mo squeezed his eyes shut and let out a long, shaking breath. "I'm going to rest now. I'll speak to you soon," he said and ended the call.

Maggie cast an anxious look at Pierce.

A sense of fury and helplessness began to rise in Pierce. He paced to one end of the kitchen and back, tortured, and deep in thought. "I don't care what Mo said. We need to get him to the hospital."

Maggie nodded in absolute shock and struggled for words. Finally, she said, "I keep hearing hospitals are stretched beyond capacity; and doctors are playing God by deciding who should get treatment." She took a deep breath and sighed with frustration. "Let's be real. They aren't going to admit an eighty-three-year-old man who tested positive for the virus."

In Pierce's world there was always an appeal, technicality, loophole, a resource he could turn and finally a Hail Mary. He just had to find it. Over the years, Pierce, as a fixer, had done countless favors for elected officials and powerful people. Now it was time to ask for a favor in return. He looked at Maggie briefly and nodded, but he wasn't listening. His mind was focused on his cellphone. He walked around the kitchen scrolling through his contacts, trying to zero in on who he could call for help. He stopped on Hernan Mas, a close friend who also was the former Miami-Dade Police Chief. Hernan was a thirty-year veteran who served on numerous inter-agency task forces. If he didn't know the Martin County Sheriff personally, Pierce was confident that he would know someone who did. Hernan knew Mo as well and agreed to whatever was necessary to make sure that an ambulance would be dispatched to Mo's home.

Pierce's next call was to Congresswoman Rodriguez, who was stunned and emotional when she heard the news, and then rushed Pierce off the phone so that she could call her fellow congressional representative representing Martin, Palm Beach, and St. Lucie Counties. The congressmen twisted arms, and an hour later, the Cleveland Clinic in Martin County agreed to admit Mo.

On Sunday afternoon, a team of paramedics found Mo sprawled on a couch, semi-conscious and delirious from the fever. Pierce quizzed the paramedic when he received a call to inform him that Mo had been rushed to the hospital. The paramedic gave Pierce a windy summary of the frantic tussle that occurred when Mo's eyes locked onto the stretcher, and he realized what was happening.

"He took a swing at one of the medics and knocked his ventilator off his face and managed to kick one of my other guys in the ribs."

Pierce frowned and smiled at the same time. "Is everyone okay?"

"Yes, sir. That old man still has a lot of fight left. It took four men to load him into the ambulance," the paramedic replied.

Unsteady as she felt, Maggie managed to laugh out loud at the image of Mo fighting and cursing all the way to the hospital.

Chapter Thirty-Eight

Cleveland Clinic – Stuart, Florida

Mo had tubes in both arms and monitors above his head. The nurses came and went, sometimes tapping softly on the door as they pushed it open, and other times appearing at Mo's bedside without making a sound to warn him.

He was in an airborne infection isolation room required for patients with the Kayapo virus. The room was sealed and equipped with a HEPA filtration system specifically designed to reduce the risk of transmission of airborne droplets, and ultraviolet lights used for killing most viruses and bacteria.

A nurse wearing protective clothing stooped over him. "Good morning, Mr. Black. I'm here to check your vitals."

Mo nodded uncomfortably.

She studied his face for a moment. His discomfort was obvious. "On a scale of one-to-ten, how much pain are you in?"

Mo's face contorted. "Seven-to-eight."

The nurse frowned and made a notation on Mo's chart. "I'll speak with the doctor about increasing your pain medication." Redirecting her attention to his chart, the nurse went through it rapidly. Although not all the tests were back, those that were suggested kidney and liver malfunction.

At that moment, her cellphone buzzed. "Excuse me."

While on the call, she turned and looked at Mo in a manner that said she was intrigued. When she finished the call, she looked at her watch. In a voice tinged with surprise, she said, "You sir, must have some pretty influential friends. In about thirty minutes, we're going to bring in a laptop for you. There are some people that want to visit with you."

Mo felt a pang of guilt over what little he remembered of the altercation and the special accommodations. and nodded ever so subtly. Glancing at the clock on the wall, it surprised him to see it was almost eleven-thirty.

* * *

Predictably appalled, Mo peered disapprovingly at Pierce. "This was all your doing," he said in a scratchy voice.

Pierce shrugged off the accusation. It was obvious from his sunken eyes, haggard and unshaven face, that he hadn't slept. "The doctor told me they've been able to lower your fever."

Mo clutched the side rails on the bed and tried to sit up. He sat up as straight as his body would allow him to. His mind was swimming. The pain medication made it harder for him to focus. When his gaze settled on Maggie, his face broke into a genuine smile.

Maggie weakly returned a smile. His skin was a pasty yellow shade. The same color that Maggie saw in the camps on migrants that were near death or had recently died.

Deliberately, Mo switched the conversation. He didn't want to discuss his diagnosis that had no treatment. He asked, "Did the court rule in our case?"

Maggie glanced nervously at Pierce and in a subdued voice said, "Order was filed this morning. The judge ruled in our favor."

"The court found that the rule closing the border and refusing to process immigration petitions was enacted unlawfully and is now void," Pierce added.

Mo's mind grappled with the implications of the court's ruling, looking at it from every angle he could think of. "We should have the motion ready to file. As soon as the president lifts the state of emergency, we need to be ready to petition the court to order the release of the migrants in the camps."

That sounded like a good idea to Pierce.

Mo's face contorted again in pain. Mo's coal black intelligent eyes - eyes that had unnerved the most steadfast trial lawyers - were now red-rimmed, clouded, and wet. "What are your plans now that there is no amnesty for companies like Lighthouse?" Mo asked Pierce.

Pierce kept his emotions in check. The man lying in the hospital bed was not just a mentor to him. Mo was family. Pierce held no illusions about Mo's chances at surviving the virus. He would be gone in a few days. "We accomplished what we set out to do. The court declared the rule illegal, and the senator's bill died on the Senate floor. Once we get the migrants released from the camps and confirm that Immigration Services are processing applications for asylum and green cards, our work is done. Let someone else go after Lighthouse."

The nearness of death made Mo restless. Time had become his greatest adversary. He seemed like a man eager to settle one last account. His face contorted into anger, and he looked as if he wanted to spit. "There's still work to be done. Dode generated a media storm and widespread sympathy for the migrants. You need to finish this."

Maggie wiped her eyes, bit her lip, and said, "The ACLU won't help. A lawsuit against Lighthouse doesn't involve government policy or civil rights issues."

Mo's eyes closed as his mouth fell open slightly. A soft guttural sound, one from deep inside, came out. "Maybe it's time for you to leave the ACLU," he finally said.

With a dismissive half smile, Maggie said, "It's not that simple. Besides, we'll need a little luck if we're going to sue Lighthouse under the Alien Tort Statute (ATS). The Supreme Court cut back on the ability of victims to sue companies for acts that occur entirely in foreign countries."

Mo shooed away Maggie's point with a wave of his hand. "Federal courts have liberally interpreted the Supreme Court's ruling. If a company on U.S. soil "aided and abetted" a foreign group in committing abuses, they're fair game," Mo said. Without warning, he stopped talking and coughed violently into his hand. When he drew a few breaths to steady himself, Pierce heard a rattle in his chest. Mo needed to rest, but he was determined to make sure that Pierce finished what they had started.

Pierce looked at Mo and rubbed his temples. The knot in his stomach felt like a bowling ball. "If we can prove that Lighthouse wired funds to Mexico, that should be enough," he replied.

Mo managed a weary smile. "Exactly . . . Lighthouse's bank records should show that they purchased blood from companies connected to the murders. That's enough to withstand a Motion to Dismiss and make them liable."

Pierce suspected Lighthouse's lawyers would immediately move for a Protective Order and every procedural roadblock they could think of to prevent the disclosure of inculpatory financial information, but that was a conversation for another day.

Mo's breaths came in sudden gasps as he tried to finish his thought. "The Supreme Court ruling does not limit the ability of victims to bring lawsuits against individuals under the Torture Victim Protection Act."

Mo sounded like he was lecturing from a legal treatise, but his words were music to Pierce.

Maggie nodded and chimed in. "That would make Bowman as CEO of Lighthouse personally liable."

Mo lay back. The calculations were running behind his eyes, but the pain medication slowed his thought process and thickened his tongue. "The *Kobel* decision has no bearing on criminal prosecutions involving human rights violations committed abroad. The U.S. Attorney can criminally prosecute Bowman."

Maggie nodded in agreement. "We can ask Senator Cortez to pressure Justice to criminally prosecute him."

Pierce considered that for a moment and shook his head. Bowman had powerful allies in Congress. Forty-seven senators, to be exact. Notwithstanding their failure to pass the bill, Pierce suspected that Bowman still felt insulated. "If Senator Cortez convinces the U.S. Attorney to seek an indictment, Bowman would know about it before the ink was dry, move his assets offshore and disappear."

"What's keeping him from doing just that if we file a civil lawsuit?" Maggie asked.

"One of the fundamental weaknesses people like Bowman have is greed. Now that the vaccine is about to be made widely available to the public, his window to supply blood at fifty times the average price is rapidly closing. He'll do everything he can to squeeze every last drop out of what he's got," Pierce said. "As long as Bowman thinks he's safe from criminal prosecution, he won't run. He'll do what most do, hide behind an army of lawyers and try to wear us down. The secret to beating him is to make sure he *gets* that opportunity."

An older nurse pushed a cart around noisily. The clatter of medical equipment broke Mo's concentration. She leaned over and whispered into Mo's ear that she needed to take some blood. He knew there was nothing the doctors could do but ply him with pain medication to make him comfortable, but he played along.

His lips quivered just before telling Pierce and Maggie that he would call them after he got some rest.

Maggie struggled to control her emotions and conjured up the best fake smile she could. Pierce gave a distressed shake of the head.

Mo's breathing was labored, and every word was clearly painful. "There are only a handful of trial lawyers that companies don't want across the aisle . . . You, Pierce, are one of them," Mo said through badly blistered lips and dried blood on his front teeth. He took a deep breath and let it out slowly as the words, "but I'm just a little better," slipped past his lips.

The remark elicited a flicker of a smile from Pierce.

Mo gave them a thumbs up and tapped the red circle icon to end the call.

Chapter Thirty-Nine

New Orleans

At 8:30 on Tuesday morning, Frank Collins walked into Ben Bowman's office and announced that the feds were launching a vaccine campaign that was unprecedented in its speed and scope. "They're expecting to roll out a million doses of the vaccine a day . . . The Chief Medical Advisor to the president was on CNN this morning saying they're planning to have everyone vaccinated in less than a year."

Bowman rolled his eyes. "The feds are too bureaucratic and corrupt. Too many parasites sucking on the government's teat to get it done that fast."

Collins nodded solemnly. "Sixty-to-seventy percent of the population is probably more realistic."

Bowman grabbed a piece of paper and wrote the number ninety and slid it across the table towards Collins.

"Even if they vaccinate half of that number, we'll hit the herd immunity threshold in six months. The transmission of the virus will bottom out long before that." He locked his hands behind his head and reflected for a moment. Bowman's ample gut pressured the buttons of his shirt. "We have about thirty days left before we start to see a drop in the price of blood. After that, the price will steadily go down. In ninety days, it will be at or just above where it was before the pandemic."

Collins' eyes narrowed. That was a little quicker than he anticipated, but he trusted Bowman's instincts.

Bowman thought about the migrant camps, exterminations, corruption and all the payoffs that were necessary to making Lighthouse one of the most valuable privately held companies. He played by his own rules and saw no reason to change what had always worked for him. The heavily financed frontal assault, led by some of the most expensive lobbyists and legal talent money could buy, had failed. Now it was time for Bowman to take a different approach. "Call Littlefield and tell him I'm sending a jet to pick him up. We have several important matters to discuss as soon as possible, and it needs to be done in person."

"Will do."

"And tell Petrovich to get ready to turn the FBI loose on Senator Erickson."

Collins looked more than a little surprised. "I don't understand. Erickson not only voted for the bill. He fought hard to get it passed."

Bowman shot Collins a questioning look, raising an eyebrow and asked, "But it didn't pass now, did it?"

Collins considered the question for longer than it had taken Bowman to ask it, then reluctantly nodded. "No, sir. It didn't pass. But if you release that bogus information on Erickson, you'll kill any chance he has to get re-elected."

Bowman frowned at Collins's comment. It was clear to him that Frank's misplaced loyalty was clouding his judgement. "Frank, seven out of ten polls now have Erickson trailing by twenty points or more. He has no chance of winning."

Collins exhaled sharply. "So, we just turn our backs on him, and feed him to the wolves?"

A bitter smile spread across Bowman's face. He always operated in broad strategic terms—like a battlefield commander. Sacrificing Erickson was necessary to protect his flank. "Erickson still has some value. If he didn't, I wouldn't waste Petrovich's talents on him."

Collins nodded, trying to hide his displeasure.

Bowman was thinking about all the bad press connecting Lighthouse to the murders in Mexico and how to deal with it. "That fucking *Stop Killing Canaries* movement is still dominating every news and social media platform. Almost every news story that covers the murders in Mexico mentions Lighthouse." Bowman was thinking about how he could manipulate the media into focusing on a different issue. He was confident that a newsworthy story involving a U.S. Senator accused of being a sexual predator would trigger a feeding frenzy and shift the media's attention away from Lighthouse.

Collins nodded his head, signaling a frustrated understanding. "May I speak frankly?"

"Go ahead."

"It's clear that you have no misgivings about leaking fabricated evidence and destroying a man's career."

"None."

"He'll probably end up going to prison," Collins said, still processing the consequences.

Bowman looked sideways at him. "It's all circumstantial evidence—anyone with access to the senator's computer could have written those emails. There are no victims that can testify at a trial."

He gave a contrite nod. "But what if he does get convicted?"

"Then he picked the wrong lawyer," Bowman said with a slight smirk on his face.

Collins showed his displeasure with a furrowed brow. "You're really okay with all of this?"

Bowman ignored the question, sat forward, and said, "I need you on a plane to Mexico this morning."

"Mexico?"

"I want you to meet with the Zeta cartel. Tell them that the demand for blood is going to disappear rapidly, so they need to double or triple the volume of their shipments while the price is still high."

Collins' expression turned skeptical. He thought doing any more business with the cartel was a mistake. The narrative created by social media mobilized the public and shined a spotlight on the murders in Mexico. The silhouette of a canary had become the symbol of the public's outrage and the rallying point to a stop to the brutal slayings. Collins let out a long-frustrated sigh before advising Bowman to cut all ties with the Zetas, but Bowman wouldn't listen. His insatiable greed clouded his judgement.

* * *

Bowman had weathered trouble times before - wars, terrorist attacks, epidemics, market meltdowns and disastrous love affairs - and yet somehow, he had the uncanny ability to always manage ending up better off. The failure of the *Health Protection Act* to pass in the Senate was a setback for Lighthouse but not a deathblow.

Ben Bowman cancelled yet another dinner with wife number three. At 7.30 p.m., Senator Claude Littlefield and two assistants gathered around Lighthouse's long conference table.

Prior to his departure for Mexico, Frank Collins had briefed Littlefield, so there was no need to cover old territory. Bowman began with his nagging concern that without immunity protection, one day the Department of Justice could show up at his doorstep with a grand jury indictment and drag him off to jail.

Littlefield held up a hand. "Don't worry. I have a good relationship with the attorney general."

"Claude, that doesn't mean diddly to me. You have a good relationship with the majority of the Senate, and you didn't deliver a bill that I paid for with a shit ton of money in political contributions, exotic vacations and hunting trips to get passed."

Littlefield sipped his tea and wiped his mouth with a linen napkin. "A last-minute wave of propaganda, loose talk and gossip scared the shit out of a few of them." Then he added dubiously, "That was an aberration."

"Was it? I don't think so." Bowman shrugged. "The internet and social media are going to affect political outcomes from this day forward, and we'll have to account for them."

"Maybe so, but I don't need the Senate to keep you from being prosecuted."

Bowman nodded in agreement. "You need the attorney general on your side."

"Precisely."

Bowman marveled at how quickly the tide of public opinion had turned. "We just witnessed a mass movement ignited by social media that changed the political landscape overnight. In other words, Claude, nothing is solid. The attorney general isn't immune. I can't count on your relationship with the AG to keep me and my company safe."

Littlefield looked at Bowman pensively. He had a feeling that Bowman was up to something. Cocking his head in a suspicious manner, Littlefield asked, "What do you want?"

Bowman looked back at him and replied, "A bulletproof insurance policy." He moved his eyes to Littlefield's two aides and said, "Give us the room."

Neither man moved, unsure of what to do.

Littlefield was exhausted, having dropped everything to fly to New Orleans. He was in no mood for Bowman's schemes, or for the meeting to drag out any longer than it needed to. With a nod of the head, he said, "Wait for us outside."

Littlefield waited for the two men to leave. His eyes were locked in a stare with Bowman. "What do you want, Ben?"

"I want the AG to give me and my company an Immunity Agreement."

Littlefield let out a long-frustrated breath. "That's not how it works, Ben. The AG doesn't hand out pardons. You only get an Immunity Agreement if you can help the Department of Justice solve a case."

Bowman pulled a flash drive from his pocket and held it up for Littlefield to see. "This is what I'm offering," he said, and placed the thumb drive into his laptop. The laptop projected onto a large monitor hanging on the wall.

The file contained pictures and videos of children engaged in various sex acts with adults and other children. There was an email account with corresponding emails from Senator Erickson soliciting sex from children ranging in age from twelve years old to teenagers. Littlefield's face paled and his hands started to tremble.

"Senator Erickson is a close ally of yours," he said with a sigh.

Littlefield's eyelids tightened.

Bowman sat there solemnly. "Did you have any clue that Senator Erickson was a pedophile?"

Littlefield looked at the projected images and back at Bowman. For the first time in a long time, he thought he might lose his temper. "Of course not!" His penetrating gaze focused on Bowman as he asked, "How is it that you came to learn about Erickson's activities?"

Bowman shrugged his shoulders. "We take precautions when we make political contributions and support candidates. That means due diligence. We received a tip that a high-ranking member of the Senate was engaged in questionable activity, so I had my people do a deeper dive into the senator." His voice stayed even but gained a slight edge.

"I never expected them to find that he was soliciting sex from children." The disgust was openly visible on his face.

Littlefield gave him a tightly screwed frown. "I'm having a hard time believing this. I've known Steve for the better part of twenty years. If he was into some weird, deviant crap, he was good at keeping it hidden. Because I have never gotten a whiff of anything."

"The sicker the shit people do, the greater lengths they go to hide it."

Littlefield's expression became catatonic as he stared blankly at the screen.

Bowman leaned closer to Littlefield and in a low voice said, "We really have only one option."

Littlefield suddenly looked tired. He understood what was at stake. "And what would that be?" he asked miserably.

"You get the AG to give me an Immunity Agreement, and then together, we turn the evidence over. The only way for you to avoid being embroiled in this scandal and being grilled by the press is to create plausible deniability. If you're not part of the solution, the press will rush to judgement and accuse you of turning a blind eye to protect your slim majority in the Senate."

Littlefield took a sip of tea, and gingerly placed the cup on the saucer. Looking up with guilt in his eyes, he said, "Maybe I should have paid closer attention, but I didn't know."

"I believe you."

Bowman slid forward to the edge of his chair and placed his hands flat on the table.

"What's it going to be, Claude? Are we going to do this together, or is the flash drive going to find its way to the FBI without your help?"

Chapter Forty

Miami Beach

At 12:02 on Thursday afternoon, Pierce received a phone call from the hospital informing him that Moses Black had died.

"Thank you. I'll contact the hospital as soon as I can make the arrangements," he said and broke off the call because he was too stunned to say anything else. Pierce remained right where he stood, impassive, silent, and motionless.

Maggie looked up from her computer and studied Pierce, taking in his expression, and prepared herself for what she knew was coming.

"He's dead, isn't he?"

Pierce nodded gently. "Mo died this morning," he said in a bereft and empty voice.

Tears welled up and slid down Maggie's face. It didn't take long for Maggie to break down sobbing, loud, anguished, and uncontrolled. Knowing that Mo was going to die didn't lessen the pain when the news finally came. Mo's death was something Pierce could not prepare himself for, cliché be damned. He was like a father to Pierce. As for Maggie, Mo had walked right into her heart and made himself at home the very first time they met in Brownsville, Texas. During the long, bleak pandemic, Mo and Maggie grew very close. Neither with any actual family to speak of, so they adopted each other.

Pierce recalled with startling clarity the first time he had met Mo. He and Maggie spent the rest of the day sitting on the floor of his living room, reminiscing, sharing stories, laughing, and crying together. By the time they finished the third bottle of wine, they had both run out of tears.

* * *

Just before dawn on Saturday morning, Pierce sat at the kitchen table, sipping coffee and scratching out notes, lists, and questions on his legal pad. He had tried to stay in bed and sleep, but his mind wouldn't allow it. Work: that was the only way he could manage his terrible anguish. It was the same escape valve he used when his girlfriend was killed in an explosion triggered by the Carraboca Cartel, which had been meant to send him a message.

A dozen issues clamored for attention. At the top of his list, he'd written the name Maggie Malone, followed by a question mark. Mo had been lobbying Pierce to hire Maggie. Growing up on the streets of New York, Maggie honed her ability to quickly spot danger and see around corners. A skill set that served her well in the courtroom. She was a brawler, not some timid lawyer content to push papers around. That's what Mo liked most about her. Maggie had a quick mind and even quicker tongue. She had grown up an underdog, withstood all forms of bigotry, and succeeded against seemingly impossible odds. As a black woman, Maggie knew she couldn't settle for good; she had to be better than her peers. A mindset that Pierce liked.

But practicing law at an elite law firm such as Pierce's required more than a young hard charging lawyer with a gun slinger mentality. It required more than excelling at the hand-to-hand combat and trench warfare associated with going to trial. Sullivan & Swayze LLC, as an institution, was the holy grail. It was one of the most prestigious jobs a lawyer could get. The firm's lawyers predominantly hailed from five law schools: Harvard, Yale, Chicago, Stanford, and Columbia. Every lawyer possessed the ability to deftly navigate metaphysical impracticalities and turn complex legal challenges into successful results.

As the former chair of the litigation section at Sullivan & Swayze, Mo still had some clout and cut a swath for Maggie. The firm's hiring committee had reacted like a palm tree facing the strongest of winds from the most brutal of storms and bent but did not completely capitulate. Instead, they had decided to leave the decision in Pierce's hands.

Pierce took another sip of coffee as he tried to decide whether Sullivan & Swayze was a good fit for Maggie. He imagined Mo's voice as if he were alive, telling him to cut the crap. His words rattled noisily in Pierce's brain. *"Talent and ability can come from anywhere, but the opportunity to maximize it is closed to most. I brought you into the firm to change its antiquated ideologies, and help it evolve and adapt to a changing world."*

The rich aroma of the coffee drew Maggie to the kitchen. She appeared clad in a borrowed sweatshirt.

"Morning."

Pierce quickly dried his eyes with the back of his right hand. "Good morning."

Maggie poured herself a cup and took a sip as if she needed fuel.

She pulled up a chair and sat at the table next to Pierce; and speaking in a hushed tone so as not to wake Yamilet and Giovanny.

"We're going to be heading back to Houston just as soon as I can book us a flight," she said.

"You're welcome to stay as long as you like," he said softly. "It's nice to have the company."

With a noticeably unenthusiastic tone, Maggie shrugged. "No sense putting it off any longer."

Pierce shrugged as he replayed in his mind their last conversation with Mo. "We still have some unfinished business."

Maggie took a deep breath. "I don't think the ACLU will join a lawsuit against Lighthouse."

Pierce didn't care about the ACLU. Before he died, Mo asked them both to finish what they had started. His FBI contact, Special Agent

Nick Russo, confirmed that Lighthouse was using the cartel to do the wet work in Mexico and buying blood from one of their shell companies to keep its hands clean. That made Lighthouse a loose end that needed to be tied.

Pierce assessed her with penetrating eyes. "So, what about you? Are you on board?"

Maggie gave Pierce a curious look. "On board, how?"

"Mo and I had several conversations . . ." He heard his voice crack suddenly, feeling burdened with memories. He kept his tears at bay, but he could feel them teetering just beneath his eyelids.

"We talked about making you an offer to join my firm."

The subject caught her off guard, so she nodded, unsure of how to respond.

"I've given this a lot of thought, because I wanted to make sure that Sullivan & Swayze was a place where you could thrive long after this lawsuit is over," Pierce said.

Maggie raised a skeptical brow and took another sip. "What did you decide?"

Pierce wanted to honor Mo's wishes. "I think you can succeed anywhere," he said.

She thought about Pierce's answer and shook her head as if trying to free an irksome thought. "But would I be happy there? I became a lawyer to make a difference, not to help rich people get richer."

Pierce almost smiled. "We've represented poor Indian tribes, charitable organizations, poor communities, and championed many philanthropic causes." He took a breath and exhaled slowly. "But truth be told, we also represent oligarchs; and public and privately held companies."

"And make rich people richer."

Pierce walked Maggie through the firm's culture and commitment to its strong pro bono program. "Sullivan & Swayze gives me a wide berth to take on several cases every year and advocate on behalf of disadvantaged groups. Doing pro bono work is not only good for the firm's image but in some cases, it also enhances the firm's exposure."

"Other than winning a crystal or gold-plated trophy, I'm not sure why that really matters much."

"It's a good business development tool."

"Interesting," Maggie mumbled as she came to dwell on the tactic before taking another sip.

Pierce decided to explain further how pro bono work helped the firm. "Do you know how many oral arguments are held in the United States Supreme Court each term?"

Maggie shook her head. "Not a clue but gun to my head, I'd guess less than one hundred."

He nodded. "On average, there are only thirty-five."

"So let me ask you this," he continued. "If I'm arguing before the U.S. Supreme Court, and prospective clients are looking to hire a lawyer, what do you think matters most?"

Maggie thought about it for a moment. "I'd say that they probably wouldn't care much about who you're representing, or the legal issue being argued, unless it directly affects them. The fact that you're arguing before the Supreme Court would probably be most important."

"Precisely," Pierce nodded. "Our firm typically donates hundreds of hours each year on appellate cases with the trade-off being if the case goes up to the Supreme Court, we get to argue it."

Maggie understood perfectly. "I got it. Clients looking to hire the best-of-the-best use the Supreme Court as a measuring stick."

Pierce nodded slightly. "Most cases don't get to the Supreme Court, but they are still important cases just the same and many of them involve vulnerable and marginalized groups that are treated unfairly."

"Killing two birds with one stone," Maggie quipped.

"In a manner of speaking, yes."

Yamilet rubbed the sleep from her eyes as she walked into the kitchen and headed straight for the coffeepot. She topped off their cups as part of the routine. "*Buenos dias*," she whispered.

Pierce smiled. "*Buenos dias,* Yami."

"*Buenas*." Maggie nodded and stared at Pierce in a trance-like state, still processing what he had just told her.

Pierce tore a page from his legal pad, wrote a number, and handed it to Maggie.

"What's this?"

"Your starting salary."

Maggie stared at the number on the piece of paper and looked up at Pierce with questioning eyes, trying to make sure he hadn't mistakenly reversed two digits or included an extra zero. The number Pierce had written on the piece of paper was almost triple what she was making at the ACLU. Maggie was aware that her jaw had dropped slightly so that her mouth was wide open.

Pierce's assurances that the firm's commitment to service for the public good by providing free legal services to the poor and organizations that serve the poor helped to minimize most of the concerns she had expressed a few minutes before. A bit stunned, Maggie responded by saying, "I'm in," as if Pierce had invited her to a movie or a happy hour.

Chapter Forty-One

Chihuahuan Desert, Mexico

On the sweltering spring evening, ninety-three people were jammed inside of a sealed tractor-trailer as the truck lumbered to Nuevo Leon. There was no light inside the trailer. It was so dark that those inside couldn't even see their own hands. The only light the panicked group had to penetrate the thick cover of the night was the faint glow of the Mexican moon.

The trailer was purposed to transport food items and not cramped human cargo. The heat held steady throughout the night and lack of air circulation turned the trailer into a sauna. Everyone in the trailer was sweating furiously. Some people remained on their feet, leaning against walls, while others squatted, and yet others sat with their legs pressed against their chests.

Spanish pop music played on the radio in the truck's cab while Enrique Nava, a member of the Zeta Cartel, steered the eighteen-wheeler. An hour into the two-hundred-kilometer drive, Enrique heard faint noises coming from the trailer, and knew something was wrong. The noise grew louder as desperate passengers banged to get the driver's attention while others clawed holes for air.

The thermostat reading on his dashboard read one hundred forty-seven degrees Fahrenheit. He had a bad feeling and snarled in Spanish at Raul, a seventeen-year-old boy recently recruited to work for the Zetas.

"I told you to turn on the air conditioning unit before we left, *puto*."

Raul shot Enrique a defensive look. He didn't understand why he was so angry.

"*Tranquilo, jefe*! We're dropping them somewhere so they can be killed, so who cares if they're uncomfortable?"

Enrique glanced again at the temperature reading on the dashboard with concern and moved his eyes back to the road. "Uncomfortable is one thing, dead is another. Their blood is only good if they're alive, *pendejo*. If we drop off a shipment of dead peasants, we'll have to answer to the *Padron*." Enrique's fear was borne out of knowledge that the only apology Daniel would accept was their brains splattered on the floor.

Raul answered, a bit nervous at the thought of having to account for the dead peasants. "We're going to lose a few when we're packing them in tight like sardines."

Enrique kept his eyes on the road. "One hundred and forty degrees is going to kill more than a few," he snapped back, slowing the truck down and pulling to a stop on the roadside.

Enrique mopped his glistening brow and neck with his bandana. He could scarcely believe Raul's lack of urgency. He made no effort to move, instead, he was too busy texting and smiling at the screen. Enrique found his behavior downright irritating.

"What are you waiting for, *cabron*?"

The young man waved him off. "One minute," he said in a dismissive tone. "They're not going anywhere."

Enrique's face twisted into a disgusted scowl. He had no intention of going down for this colossal fuck up. He pulled out his pistol and pointed it at Raul's crotch.

"I'm going to count to five. Unless you want to spend the rest of your life without a dick, you better jump out and turn on the air conditioning."

Raul thought about telling Enrique to go fuck himself but remembered his reputation for having a quick temper and an even quicker trigger finger. Instead, he climbed down to hit the start-stop continuous button and waited for the green light to turn on before climbing back into the cab.

Thirty minutes later, the passengers felt the air-conditioning kick in. The temperature began to decrease, making breathing easier. However, for some, it was too late.

* * *

At 1:35 a.m., the truck pulled into the parking lot of HemaMex. Despite the early hour, the facility was buzzing with activity. The stadium lighting illuminated the main building and parking lot, which provided a stark contrast to the vast darkness of the surrounding desert. There were a half dozen trucks bearing the red, white, and green colors of the HemaMex logo waiting in the loading dock.

The loud clang of the latch being lifted and the squeaky hinges of the doors swinging open ushered in a wave of fresh air that wafted across the overheated bodies. Those closest to the door fell to the ground with tears in their eyes, gasping for air. The migrants that were situated farther back in the trailer walked like zombies towards the open doors, sloshing through the puddles of urine on the floor. Most were too weak to lower themselves down the three steps that separated the truck from the ground. HemaMex personnel helped them out of the truck and handed out water bottles. The cartel's men, armed with automatic weapons, stood nearby waiting to march them into the facility.

Twenty-two bodies remained strewn across the floor inside the trailer. A couple were unconscious, but most were either dead or on the brink of death.

Enrique turned on his flashlight and stared at several people in a fetal position. A woman cried out, *"Estan Muerto!"*

Raul grew increasingly anxious. He realized with a discomforting level of certainty that he would be held accountable for the deaths.

One of the cartel's men climbed into the trailer to get a closer look. A mixture of saliva and blood trickled from the mouths of most of the still bodies.

Enrique clicked on the radio and relayed the latest development.

Raul rambled on and on, trying to explain to the cartel's soldiers that he hadn't killed them.

It was obvious from the look on the men's faces that it didn't matter. The dead bodies represented $2.1 million in lost revenue. The head of the Zetas would demand that someone be held responsible. Otherwise, Daniel would unleash his wrath on everyone involved.

Enrique walked over to Raul. He looked at him grim-faced and shook his head. "You disappointed the *Padron*."

Raul shifted nervously and pleaded with Enrique. "Call him back and tell him that the temperature controls malfunctioned."

Enrique subtly made a gesture to one of the cartel's sicarios and took a half step away. "*Dios te bendiga*."

Raul didn't understand why Enrique had blessed him until it was too late. The assassin plunged a hunting knife into the side of Raul's neck and sliced open his carotid artery. He fell to his knees, clutching desperately at his neck, unsuccessfully trying to stop the strong spray of bright red blood.

Chapter Forty-Two

Miami

There is an African proverb: "If you want to go fast, go alone; but if you want to go far, go together." Pierce assembled a team to work on the lawsuit against Lighthouse. First, he needed someone to find valuable nuggets of information that would allow him to develop a novel theory; a creative argument that Lighthouse's defense attorneys didn't prepare for. He asked Dode to look for financial records that tied Lighthouse to HemaMex. If any records existed that proved Lighthouse was complicit in the murders, Lighthouse's lawyers would file motions for protective orders to keep any records that weren't already destroyed from being produced. Dode needed to find them before Pierce filed the Complaint.

Congresswoman Rodriguez volunteered her chief of staff, J.C., to be part of the team. As a Washington insider, he was tucked away behind the scenes and privy to all the gossip regarding the backroom deals and moves lobbyists, stakeholders, elected representatives, and other Washington officials made. In a high-stakes lawsuit, nothing was off limits. The only rule was don't get caught. Once the lawsuit was filed, the case would quickly turn into a bare knuckles brawl. Lighthouse would use every weapon in its arsenal to bludgeon Pierce into submission, hoping to derail him before a settlement became an unavoidable reality. Pierce knew they would throw everything at him they could think of. He just wanted to see them coming.

Maggie Malone was Pierce's co-counsel. She had accepted Sullivan and Swayze's job offer and was determined to see Mo's dying wish to bring Lighthouse to ruin through to the end. Pierce's law firm would give him all the professional support he required to sue Lighthouse. The firm had some of the very best investigators and jury consultants at its disposal. Pierce, however, had one specific person in mind to round out his team, Hernan Mas, the former Miami-Dade Chief of Police.

When Hernan had retired after thirty-five years on the force, he kept a promise to join Navitas Tech, his family's renewable energy business.

Maggie gave Pierce a disbelieving look when he mentioned he wanted Hernan to lead the investigation into HemaMex.

"What is it?"

"Just thinking is all," she said. "He's been out of police work for a minute."

Pierce made a show of pondering Maggie's point of view, then shook his head. "He has, but no one has better instincts than H. His first year on the force, he worked the Miami River Cops case that led to over one hundred crooked cops being arrested, fired, or suspended." Pierce nodded, as he tried to get Maggie to realize that his skills and experience put him on a higher plane than other investigators they could use.

Maggie shrugged. "Like I said, that was a long time ago."

"It was," Pierce quickly added, "but Hernan was also one of the lead investigators in the Jack Abramoff lobbying scandal."

Maggie frowned. A memory was coming back to her. "Wasn't that the case where a lobbyist cheated an Indian casino out of millions in fees?"

"Yes," Pierce said. "A couple of months after the court sentenced Abramoff, Hernan's team followed the money and tied it to the murder of Konstantinos Gus Boulis, the owner of SunCruz Casinos . . . He's got a real nose for detective work."

Maggie gave him a wary look. "We crossed paths at the airport after we landed in Miami . . . He's a strong flavor."

The right corner of Pierce's mouth turned upwards, showing the slightest hint of a smile. Maggie was more spit than polish and didn't hold anything back. "Your point?"

Maggie's face soured. "He's a misogynist, for one."

"Pierce grinned. "You're only half right."

"Meaning?"

"Meaning, he doesn't have anything against women. H doesn't like or trust anyone, men included. But that's part of what makes him a great investigator."

Maggie regarded Pierce with a skeptical squint of her dark brown eyes. "Let's be realistic. I googled the dude, and he's got a high-paying, cushy job. Unless I'm missing something, I just think you're setting yourself up for a big fat 'No,' when there are other perfectly good investigators we could use."

Pierce turned that possibility over in his mind. What Maggie had yet to understand was that Hernan's skills and experience surpassed their other options. He looked at Maggie pensively. He understood her reservations with the man. His eyes narrowed, and he took a breath. "I'll tell you what, if you're going to be in a foxhole, you want Hernan in there with you. Besides, Mo and Hernan share a lot of history," Pierce said in a reflective tone.

Maggie could tell by the tenor in Pierce's voice that he was digging in, which got her wondering. She started to say something but held back as she noticed the look on Pierce's face. It looked like he was reliving a memory, and she didn't want to intrude.

"It was Mo who introduced us," Pierce finally said. "We have nothing to lose and much to gain by asking for his help."

* * *

The country was set to emerge from the Kayapo virus that infected ten percent of the world's population and took the lives of thirty-four million Americans. The Florida governor unveiled a plan to lift the state's shelter-at-home orders amid the Kayapo virus that he titled *"Safe, Smart and Step-by-Step."* Under Phase One, retail stores and restaurants could reopen to people that had been vaccinated - but only at fifty percent capacity. Eateries were allowed to seat people, but they had to maintain six feet of social distancing between tables.

Hernan and Pierce agreed to meet at *Bachour's* restaurant in *Coral Gables.* Pierce walked over to the table in the back. Hernan tracked him and those milling around the restaurant with his eyes. The habits he developed from his years on the force were hard to break. He sized up every person he met within the first minute and noticed the smallest details, as if every situation or person was part of a crime scene. His years on the force and family's wealth opened doors and gave him extraordinary contacts and access. He was connected in some way to just about everyone who mattered. His reach extended to Fortune 100 CEOs, celebrities, and high-ranking government officials. His inner circle of friends, however, was very small. A couple of classmates from Columbus High School, his former Deputy Chief of Police and Pierce, were the only people outside of his family that Hernan trusted.

A young woman wearing a black mask covering the lower half of her face approached the table and asked if they were ready to order.

Hernan nodded and ordered scrambled egg whites and a side of avocado.

Pierce shot him a surprised look. "What . . . no guava pancakes?"

Hernan scowled. "Olga says I've put on too much weight since I retired from the force. I need to cut down on sugar and carbs."

Pierce ordered just coffee.

Hernan gave Pierce a sideways glance. "That's it? You don't have to hold back on my account."

"I haven't had much of an appetite lately." Pierce's steady demeanor made his pained expression all the more obvious.

Hernan took a breath, trying not to let the look of utter sadness cross his face. Finally, he said the only words he could think of. "Yeah, I'm sorry about Mo."

Pierce grimaced. "Me too."

After a few minutes, Pierce changed the somber mood by jumping into a summary of the lawsuit he was preparing to file against Lighthouse.

Hernan's face seemed to grow darker as Pierce reached the part of the conversation when it was obvious that he was about to ask for his help.

Pierce put his words in the form of a statement of facts, but his tone sounded more like a plea for help. "Getting proof that HemaMex is responsible for the mass murders taking place in Mexico is going to be a challenge. They have a facility outside Nuevo Leon, but it's surrounded by miles of desert. There's no way to get close without being seen."

Hernan gave him a slight smile that could not be mistaken for anything other than confidence. "There's always a way. You just need to find it."

Pierce started his approach. "Well, that's why I'm here."

Hernan's eyes tightened. "I let you use the company jet a couple of weeks ago to rescue some folks. I've already helped."

"Agreed," Pierce conceded, just before baiting the hook. "I won't press. Just tell me how you would do it and I'll be on my way."

Hernan pulled his iPad from his bag and googled the name HemaMex. Once he found their address in Nuevo Leon, he typed it into Google Earth. He studied the topography on the map and satellite imagery. Pierce was right. There was only one road cutting through the rugged terrain. They'd have a clear view of anyone approaching before they reached a hide site.

"It will be tough to get close to this place without them seeing you … I'll study the area and see if there is anyplace where we can get close enough to conduct surveillance without being spotted," Hernan said.

Pierce liked that Hernan had said *we*. *Baby steps*, he thought to himself. "I appreciate your help, H."

Hernan nodded. "No problem." He recognized the look in Pierce's eyes and understood it. This case was personal. A mission. He'd been there himself. The murder and decapitation of nine-year-old Jimmy Ryce in Redlands, Florida got under the skin of every officer in the county's South Operations Division. Hernan was part of a task force that worked closely with the FBI, following every lead until a tip led them to a trailer where they found Jimmy Ryce's bookbag. After a fifty-five-hour-long interrogation, Juan Carlos Chavez openly admitted to abducting, raping, and murdering Jimmy.

Chavez led police to the boy's body, which was cut into pieces and hidden in concrete in three plastic planters. Images of Jimmy's dismembered body haunted Hernan's waking thoughts and offered him no respite or rest by invading his dreams.

On February 12, 2014, Chavez died by lethal injection. Seeing Chavez pay for his crime didn't give Hernan the feeling he had hoped for. Hernan thought with Chavez's execution and knowing that he would never hurt another child, he'd close the book on what had been an emotionally gut-wrenching case. But this case left a permanent stain on his psyche. The nightmares continued and plagued him for months after finally prompting him to enroll in the Department's mental health and wellness program.

Hernan pushed the memory from his mind and solely focused on a ridgeline about forty miles east of the facility. "I'll need to study some more detailed aerial photos."

He lifted his coffee cup and tilted it towards the server. She nodded and returned carrying a full pot of coffee and refilled it.

Pierce held up the palm of his hand, letting her know that he was good.

"How much time will you need?" Pierce asked.

Pierce watched as Hernan considered his question.

Hernan shook his head and continued to study the map. He knew Pierce's expectations. Finally, he said, "Give me a few days, and I'll have something for you."

Chapter Forty-Three

New Orleans

There was a knock on the door and Ben Bowman's assistant, Carol Hansen, poked her head in.

"Louis Gaines would like to see you, sir. He says it's urgent."

Bowman felt his eyebrows rise involuntarily. Gaines was the Chief Information Officer for Lighthouse.

"Can it wait? I have a full morning."

Hanson shook her head. "I realize that sir, but he says it's important."

Bowman nodded slowly. "Tell him to come up."

"Actually, he's waiting in the lobby."

"Really?" Bowman said, a little surprised. "Tell him to come in."

Gaines entered, looking a bit haggard.

"What is it, Louis?"

"There's been an infiltration of our system," he said, wearing a vaguely stunned expression.

Bowman's face turned sour. "How extensive?"

"They seemed to be after one specific thing. Our financial transactions with HemaMex."

"HemaMex," Bowman said, reflecting for a long moment on his recent Immunity Agreement with the Department of Justice. His lawyers assured him it was airtight. He couldn't be criminally prosecuted for any of his business dealings with HemaMex, and at that moment, that had been his primary concern.

Louis nodded. "They were after purchase orders, records of delivery, and payments to HemaMex. Nothing critical or terribly confidential."

Bowman let out a long-frustrated sigh. "Did they get anything else?"

"I don't think so . . . But I can't say for sure," replied Louis after a moment's hesitation.

Bowman inched forward and looked at Louis suspiciously. "If they didn't get any sensitive information, why do you look so worried?"

"It's not what the person was after that worries me. It's how they did it. Whoever hacked us is exceptionally skilled. They got past our security wall undetected. Our system treated them like they were an authorized user with the highest security clearance."

Bowman thought about his answer for a second. "Well, sounds like you discovered the breach before they inflicted any real damage like holding our data hostage."

Louis didn't respond, looking more concerned.

"Louis?"

Louis was slightly embarrassed. "The only reason I discovered it was because I was running a diagnostic when a query came in. It was dumb luck. They had full access to all our databases. If I hadn't been running it at that exact moment, I would never have known."

Bowman held up his hand, silencing him.

"Are you sure they didn't get anything else?"

"Can't say for sure, but I disconnected the hardware and took the system offline. We don't have sufficient safety protocols to stop this hacker, so I had no other option."

Bowman frowned at Louis. "So, we're offline?"

Louis grimaced. "Very offline. I actually disconnected some hard-ware. You would have to have physical access to the server to get to our files."

"Shit." Bowman leaned back and clasped his hands behind his neck. "Can't you put in more firewalls or whatever it is you people do to make sure it doesn't happen again? Or better yet, now that we know what happened, can we track the person if they try it again?"

Louis shook his head with a pained face. "The way the system is designed—"

Again, Bowman cut him off with a wave of a hand. He didn't want a lengthy explanation on security protocols and encryption algorithms.

"Yes, or no?"

"Both actually. I can reprogram the system with a major security update to shut whatever door the hacker used, but that means everyone in the company will get locked out and have to redo their logins . . . But I don't know if I can track the hacker."

"Why is that?"

"Because the query came from inside our office," he said uncom-fortably. "But I don't think it did."

"How can you be sure?"

"I'm sure, sir."

"Why is that?"

"Because the hacker used *your* user ID and clearance, and the trail ends there."

Bowman looked like he wanted to choke someone. "If you transfer all the confidential information offsite and purge our system, will that do it?"

"Louis thought about it for a second and nodded anxiously. "It should, but . . ."

"But what?"

"The only way we can be sure is to store the sensitive files offsite and switch out the hard drives. Even if we erase the hard drives, they can retrieve deleted material."

* * *

Dode converted her dining room table to a home office during the pandemic. The surface of her solid oak dining room table was covered with four computer monitors, multiple mice, keyboards, scanners, and other hardware essential for riding the wild waves of cyberspace.

She was shoveling Raisin Bran into her mouth and intermittently pounding away on her keyboard when a window popped up on one of the monitors, alerting her to an incoming virtual call.

She tapped on the green button.

A drop of milk ran down her chin. "Hey, Pierce."

"Your text said you dug up some intel and it couldn't wait. Were you able to get the financial information we discussed connecting the Lighthouse's purchases of blood from HemaMex?"

Her nod was followed by a chortle. "I got all the evidence you asked for, but there's more."

"Meaning?"

Dode grinned; her mouth full of bran cereal. After she swallowed, she said, "I also found evidence of bank fraud."

Maggie overheard Dode's comment as she walked into Pierce's kitchen. "J.C. heard through the grapevine that Bowman and Lighthouse have Immunity Agreements so they can't be prosecuted for anything having to do with the activity in Mexico."

"Yeah, but this is different. This happened before the pandemic. The Immunity Agreement wouldn't shield him from prosecution for this because the DOJ doesn't know anything about it, and if they did, they couldn't give him a pass . . . not on this. Not without looking like complete asses." Dode shoved another spoonful into her mouth.

"What did you find?" Pierce asked.

Dode's face lit up. "Bowman defrauded the U.S. government out of $35 million in forgivable loans through the Paycheck Protection Program."

"Give me a minute," Dode said, and padded over to the kitchen next to the dining room to drop her bowl in the sink. A moment later, she plopped back in her chair and continued to share the information she had uncovered.

"$35 million is a lot of money for one company's payroll," Maggie said.

Dode shook her head. "Not one company. Bowman leased several storefronts and incorporated forty-two companies. He falsified documents and applications, including bank statements and counterfeit IRS payroll tax forms. He used nearly identical versions of the same fabricated bank statements, recycled in the PPP applications for multiple companies with minor changes."

Pierce raised one of his eyebrows that said he was intrigued.

Maggie's voice was filled with doubt. "I don't see how he could get away with it?"

"The Paycheck Protection Program was a brand-new program with no real safeguards. It was quickly cobbled together to help small businesses severely impacted by the COVID-19 pandemic to keep their workforce employed. Without any real guidelines, it was susceptible to fraud," Pierce answered.

Dode tried to paint a practical picture for Maggie. "The SBA's personnel and the bank personnel responsible for processing the PPP applications were all working remotely. It was difficult for them to confirm that the information submitted was accurate."

Pierce took a second to recall the specifics of the program. "All that the PPP loan applications required for a small business were average monthly payroll expenses, and number of employees."

Dode nodded in agreement. "Banks were facilitators, not the lenders. Wasn't their money. If a PPP loan application was complete, it was approved and the participating lender funded the PPP loan using its own monies, which were 100% guaranteed by the Small Business Administration."

"Add that to that the fact that the banks were being pressured to process, approve, and get money out quickly to struggling businesses, and you had the perfect storm," Pierce said.

Maggie seemed to soak the words in for a second and then said, "This is unbelievable."

Dode shot Maggie and *I totally get it* look. "I did a little research on PPP loans after I found Bowman's files. What I learned was that out of a total of $813 billion in loans that were made, more than seventy thousand totaling over $4.6 billion are suspected to be fraudulent."

Maggie shook her head sadly. "So, Bowman got away with it?"

Dode nodded. "Looks like it."

Pierce frowned as he tried to figure out where this latest piece of the puzzle fit. "What do you have?"

"I downloaded all the files. I even downloaded all Bowman's deleted emails to his accountant in Columbus, Ohio, about setting up multiple businesses to obtain Coronavirus-relief loans for all of them."

Pierce didn't bother to ask how. He stopped wondering years ago how Dode was able to hack into files and get her information.

"The interesting part . . ." Dode's voice took on a more animated tone, ". . . is that Bowman used the names of relatives and their social security numbers and gave them a fifty-one percent interest in the different companies. Their signatures appear on the loan applications and the falsified quarterly federal tax returns."

Maggie thought about Bowman's scam for a second. "I guess having different owners for the companies helped keep him off SBA's radar?"

"Oh, I think you'll like this one," replied Dode with a smile. "The bank accounts for all the companies that applied for loans were opened online, and Bowman was an authorized signatory on all the accounts."

"Meaning he had access to all the money." Maggie frowned. "Hell of a scheme," she said sarcastically.

"One huge flaw," Dode interjected. "I did a little digging, and Bowman's relatives were all dead at the time the bank accounts were opened."

The last comment brought a smile to Maggie's face. "So, when do we take him down?"

"We don't," Pierce said. "We need to keep our powder dry on this and not spook him. The lawsuit against Lighthouse has to be our first priority." Pierce paused for a moment, then looked at Dode like a troubled father. "I hope you were careful."

Dode acted slightly offended. "After all these years and you still doubt me . . . Relax, I didn't leave a trail for anyone to follow."

Chapter Forty-Four

Chihuahua City Airport, Mexico

When the jet finally started to descend, Hernan picked up his satellite phone and called Pierce. It had been nearly a week since their meeting. Hernan had studied a detailed map of the area and identified a location just below a ridgeline about fifty miles west of the HemaMex facility. Having learned as a young police officer that complexity is the enemy of execution, Hernan liked to keep things simple. His plan was entirely predicated on stealth and the best escape option. Navitas Tech assigned one of its drone pilots out of Presidio, Texas, to meet Hernan in front of the Plaza Hotel in downtown Chihuahua City. From there, they'd travel back roads through the rugged desert grasslands.

"What are you doing in Mexico?" Pierce asked.

Hernan grunted. "There's a limit to what you can let slide even these days. What you're looking for can't be found on a hard drive. Like we discussed, the only way to get the physical evidence you want is boots on the ground."

Pierce agreed. "I know, but you were supposed to give me some ideas on how to get the evidence. Not pull a Harry Bosch and conduct the stakeout yourself," Pierce teased him.

"I call bullshit," Hernan said. "I've known you for twenty years, and I've seen all your moves. You were working me from the moment you sat down at the restaurant."

Pierce laughed. "You're wrong. You haven't seen all my moves. Seriously, though, thanks for the help."

"Don't mention it. We're not dealing with gangbangers or street thugs. These guys are organized, well-armed, and connected down here. Trying to do surveillance without serious tech would be a waste of time and could get someone hurt. Knowing you, you'd probably fuck it up . . . and I'd have to come out and do it, anyway."

"Once a cop, always a cop," Pierce replied mischievously.

"Nah brother, I'm just cutting to the chase," Hernan said, though he was nonetheless happy to be doing something that resembled police work.

* * *

Mr. Kenny Kirkley was one of Navitas Tech's more experienced drone pilots. Kenny performed remote inspections of the company's natural gas pipelines covering vast areas that extended through diverse terrains and hazardous environments. He jumped at the opportunity to work out in the field. Most of the time, Kenny piloted the drones from his cubicle, remotely gathering, reporting, and analyzing data.

The white van with a large Navitas Tech logo was parked directly across from the hotel's entrance. Inside the van was a Fixed Wing VTOL hybrid drone that, when fully assembled, looked like a giant robotic flying bug with a four-foot wingspan.

Emerging into the blazing Mexican sun, Hernan squinted his eyes and shielded them. Ten yards away, he spotted a man in a golf shirt and cargo pants holding a Starbucks cup and smoking a cigarette.

"You must be Kenny," Hernan said, extending his arm for a handshake.

The bearded man's face turned into a smile behind a pair of aviator sunglasses.

"Yes, sir."

"Thanks for agreeing to help out."

"No problem. Corporate called and told me to drive down to Mexico and do whatever you asked . . ." Kenny took a drag of the cigarette and exhaled a puff of smoke. "I'm not going to lie. I'm happy to get out of the office."

"We've got a long drive ahead, so we better get going," Hernan said, as he opened the door and slid into the front passenger seat. He watched as Kenny flicked his cigarette onto the ground and stepped on it.

Not one to keep his opinions to himself, Hernan waited for Kenny to jump into the driver's seat next to him and said, "You really should think about quitting."

Kenny put the van in gear. "Nobody likes a quitter, sir." Kenny smiled and maneuvered the van out of the parking lot and onto the road.

Hernan studied the map on his laptop to guide Kenny to the area where they would launch the drone.

"We're going to have to turn left in about a mile," Hernan said.

The turn appeared. "A left?" Kenny's voice betrayed his confusion.

"Yep. Take a left here."

Kenny exited the main road in favor of a dirt track that was more of a trail carved into the terrain for hikers than a road meant for cars.

The van's suspension took a beating, rattling, and shaking as it headed southeast on an unsigned, unmaintained road. Kenny kept a news satellite radio program on and had the uncanny ability to engage in conversation while keeping an ear on the radio and from time to time sharing his opinion on the news. The lead story was the success of the nationwide vaccination campaign. More than fifty percent of the country's population was vaccinated. On the heels of reaching the vaccination milestone, the president continued to ease the Kayapo restrictions. At the press conference the president said, *"The statistics in terms of hospitalizations have dropped considerably and we can already say that our health system is no longer compromised; that the level of infections is controlled; and our vaccination level continues to be the best in the world."*

At 11:35 a.m., the radio station broke the news that Minnesota Senator Steve Erickson resigned in disgrace two days after he was arrested on child sex abuse charges. The St. Paul Republican was accused of soliciting sex from boys ranging in ages from eleven-to-fifteen. Although he resigned, Erickson maintained his innocence, claiming he only stepped down to devote more time to his criminal defense. The journalist reported that lawmakers on both sides of the aisle, led by Republican Senator Claude Littlefield, had demanded Erickson's resignation.

Hernan let out a long breath that spoke volumes.

* * *

An hour later, Hernan's laptop froze and stopped working.

Kenny made a show of deliberation. "Not surprising . . . Strange things happen in this area. There's some kind of energy vortex out here. People call it *Zona del Silencio,* that means, *the Zone of Silence.*"

"I know what it means," Hernan said skeptically.

"Cell phones don't work here." Kenny gestured at Hernan's laptop. "And there's no internet."

Hernan peered at his computer and grimaced as the hourglass icon spun round and round.

"Fun fact, this Zone of Silence is located in the same parallel as the Bermuda Triangle, and the Pyramids of Giza in Egypt," Kenny continued.

Hernan frowned and put the laptop away. He could do without the explanation that sounded like one a tour guide might give.

"This region has also been a magnet for meteorites. In fact, a US Athena Rocket was launched in July 1970 from Utah. The rocket shot past its programmed destination and crash-landed hundreds of miles south of its destination. Care to guess where?"

Thick wrinkles broke out across Hernan's head.

Kenny didn't wait for an answer. "Yep . . . *Zona del Silencio*."

Hernan maintained a sphinx-like silence, with his thick arms folded across his wrestler's chest and an inscrutable expression on his face for the remainder of the trip.

Near the end of the secluded canyon, the dirt track turned steep enough that the van was struggling to hold traction.

"Stop here," Hernan said.

Mountain crags made of large sedimentary rocks with scattered junipers framed the ravine on both sides. They were about fifty to sixty miles east of the HemaMex facility. Hernan cast his seasoned eye around the area. The ascending ridgeline gave them adequate cover from the cartel's men. However, if their location was discovered, he wasn't sure, given the condition of the road, that they could make it to the border before the cartel's men ambushed them.

Kenny opened the doors to the back of the van and began assembling the drone. He secured the wings to the airframe in less than fifteen minutes. The rotors attached to the wings allowed it to hover, take off, and land vertically.

"How long can we fly over the target area?" Hernan asked.

Kenny stood and stretched his back. "With the installed pay-load about eight hours, give or take."

Kenny then engaged in a long practiced preflight checklist, that obviously was second nature. "This baby is equipped with a full HD 30x optical zoom Yandga camera, with anti-fog and video enhancement features," he pointed out like a proud father.

"Will it work at night?"

Kenny nodded. "The camera is equipped with night-vision. Some of our pipeline inspections run into the night. With the installed software on my controls, we'll also be able to simultaneously view and transfer the pictures and video footage to an external source."

Hernan accepted his explanation with a crisp nod.

By the time Kenny finished, it was approaching three o'clock.

Hernan tramped up the steep peak and scanned the vast desert. The dry air was barely moving. He always loved the calm before a mission. It was those moments that got his heart pumping and were impossible to reproduce in civilian life.

Hernan inched back down the rocky slope. He barked last-minute instructions at Kenny.

"Keep the drone as high of an altitude as possible without compromising the accuracy of the video footage . . . I can't stress enough that these are bad people. If the cartel's men see the drone and track it to us, we won't make it back to the States alive . . . Capeesh?" Hernan said, with practiced indifference.

Hernan could see it on Kenny's face: the crazed excitement, the fear, the rush. Kenny mumbled incoherently, as if trying to hide words, but he understood perfectly. His wide-eyed expression and jittery hands fumbling over the controls suggested that he might cut and run at any second, but so far, he was staying put and following orders.

At 4:20 p.m., the drone that Kenny fondly called Alex climbed to twenty thousand feet and banked to the east, crossing over undulating dunes and arid grasslands towards the HemaMex facility. Kenny piloted Alex from the back of the van while Hernan sat next to him, monitoring the mission.

The drone circled at high altitude for two hours. HemaMex was oddly quiet. Alex zoomed in and took pictures of the license plates of the HemaMex trucks parked in the loading docks. After one more pass,

Hernan directed Kenny to fly the drone back and told him they would send it out again at night.

* * *

At 8:52 p.m., Kenny saw something on his screen.

"There's a group of men moving around. Looks like they're getting ready for something."

Ten minutes later, Hernan spotted a convoy of three trucks turning into the complex. He picked up his satellite phone and called Pierce.

"You might want to watch the live feed we're streaming to your computer," he said.

Men carrying automatic weapons waited just outside the trucks' doors. When they opened them, men, women, and children withered down to human shells were forced out of the trucks at gunpoint and marched into the HemaMex facility.

After that, trucks arrived at twenty-minute intervals. The hostages were dispatched and marched into the building at gunpoint with assembly line efficiency.

At 11:46 p.m., the expression on Kenny's face abruptly turned from grave concern to complete terror when men in blood and sweat stained clothes took turns dragging and loading hundreds of lifeless bodies back into the truck trailers.

"Are you guys seeing this?" Hernan asked, speaking into the phone.

A flash of anger crossed Pierce's face, but he remained silent. Maggie found herself unable to respond. She let out a long, slow breath as her eyes misted over with emotion.

"Yes, we're watching." Pierce's voice faltered.

Cold, hard to stomach, and gruesome images dominated the video footage as Alex scanned the grounds.

"Stay on the trucks," Hernan told Kenny.

Kenny nodded, looking queasy. Field ops weren't his thing, but there was no denying his skills as a drone pilot. Alex hovered above the trucks, zooming in on the grisly scene.

The sheer mass of bodies made the hair on the back of Hernan's neck stand up. Despite all his years doing police work, seeing lifeless forms was something Hernan never got used to.

One of the cartel's men heard a faint buzz and began shining a flashlight into the darkness above him. Seconds later, Hernan noticed a few more flashlights aimed at the sky as men were trying to locate the source of the buzzing sound. A sliver of light flashed. One minute later, violent flashes from the ground appeared on the screen.

An ominous premonition hijacked Pierce's thought. "What's going on?" He asked.

"Shit," Hernan said under his breath. He felt an involuntary shudder crawl up his back. Pierce stared at the screen. "From here it looks like . . ."

"They're shooting at us!" Hernan snapped.

Chapter Forty-Five

Chihuahuan Desert, Mexico

Hernan remained outwardly serene, but his heart rate notched higher.

"Make sure you save all the video footage on your computer," Hernan told Pierce just before the call went dead.

The sound of gunfire brought more armed men, who immediately started firing into the darkness above them.

Kenny's expression was a mix of fear and resignation, nostrils slightly flared, eyes fixed on the screen. "What do we do?"

Hernan pushed him down with a firm, but kind, hand on his shoulder. "Get the hell out of there and keep flying east for a few miles. We don't want to tip off our location."

Kenny climbed out of range of any potential small arms fire and tilted the controls forward, pushing the drone to its limit.

"How much juice do you have left?"

"Two and a half, maybe three hours."

"Start flying back towards Chihuahua. We'll pick up Alex on the road back."

Kenny was panting, struggling to catch his breath, his eyes as wide as saucers.

"Do what I tell you, and you'll be all right," Hernan said, with the unshakable confidence of someone who had years of experience of getting out of tight spots.

Hernan made a three-point turn and gunned the van. He kept the van's headlights turned off, using only the moonlight to navigate the road in front of him. He couldn't risk the van's lights reflecting off the rocks or casting shadows the cartel's men that by now were looking for them, might see.

* * *

The van clattered along the dirt road for the better part of four hours before Hernan made it back to a paved highway.

"Where's Alex?"

A glint of fear remained in Kenny's eyes as he pinpointed the blue light on his screen.

"About thirty miles north of us."

The drive on the highway made them feel halfway safe until Hernan spotted the glow of headlamps in the distance resembling eyes of a predatory animal closing in on its prey. The headlights behind him spread like sunrise across the deserted roadway as a truck sped up behind them. For a brief moment, Kenny could not breathe or feel any part of his body.

Hernan reached for his Glock and slid it out of his holster. He realized his skill with a handgun wouldn't be enough against a gang of heavily armed sicarios. But Hernan wouldn't make it easy. He'd take as many out as he could before they killed him. He glanced again at the rear-view mirror and took a breath. The truck was closing fast.

Kenny looked through the windows in the back of the van. "They're hauling ass!" He shouted, *"Go! Go! Go!"*

Hernan was already pushing the van as fast as it could go.

When he realized he couldn't outrun them, Hernan pumped the brakes and turned the wheel, the tires skidding off the road and stopping just short of the ditch. His heart was racing.

He snapped his head around and glared at Kenny. "Get down on the floor. Stay down, no matter what you hear."

Kenny blinked several times before nodding his understanding and curling up in a fetal position.

Hernan jumped out and crouched behind the van, leveling his weapon. His finger on the trigger, he stole a quick look. He expected the truck to stop just behind the van and the cartel's men to spray them with overwhelming firepower. The thumping and vibration grew stronger as the truck now was only a few feet away. A gust of wind caused the van to rock slightly when the truck cruised by them at full speed.

Hernan waited a second before looking up and seeing the red tail-lights disappear into the darkness before cursing himself. Ordinarily he would not have overreacted, but the sudden turn of events made him paranoid.

"*I'm too old for this shit.*" The thought hit him like a lightning bolt. Getting back in the game one last time was what he needed to fully retire and transition to his corporate office. Any desire to jump back into police work was gone. Hernan took a wobbly step and called out to Kenny.

"It's over. You can come out."

Kenny jumped out of the van and vomited what little food his stomach had contained.

* * *

The rest of the drive was uneventful except for one stop to pick up Alex. It took them forty-five minutes to dismantle the drone and load it into the van. The engine hesitated, then fired. Then the van was on the move again, speeding through the darkness on the deserted roadway towards the Chihuahua City Airport.

Hernan called ahead to the pilots and told them to be ready to take off in an hour.

"We're going to fly you and Alex back to Texas. For all I know, the cartel could have people on the border waiting for you."

Kenny nodded vigorously. "What about the van?"

"We'll park it at the airport and send a team to retrieve it in a few days, after all the excitement dies down."

Chapter Forty-Six

Miami

At 4:45 on Friday afternoon, Pierce put the finishing touches on the ninety-two-page Complaint against Lighthouse Blood Centers. Mo liked to call it "adding venom." His secretary and paralegal were bustling with the frantic, nervous energy one might expect just prior to filing a Complaint in federal court demanding $2.5 billion in damages.

The Center of Human Rights and Constitutional Law helped by interviewing immigrants in all seven camps and documenting the atrocities suffered by those individuals that were part of the class action lawsuit.

Maggie had encountered a few speed bumps with her transition to working in a corporate environment but clung rigidly to the belief that Lighthouse had to pay for its crimes against the innocent victims and their families. That was all she needed to make it work.

Just before the Complaint was ready to file in the United States District Court for the Southern District of Florida, Pierce called Maggie into his office.

"You wanted to see me?"

"I just emailed you the Complaint. It's ready."

The news brought a smile to Maggie's face.

"Would you like to do the honors of transmitting the Complaint to the court?" Pierce asked, though his tone suggested the question was just a formality. Of course she would.

Maggie felt a surge of adrenaline. This was one of those rare moments where she had the opportunity to give a voice to thousands of invisible victims. Maggie smiled. "With pleasure."

She pulled out her tablet and silently scrolled down to the bottom of the last page. Maggie noticed that Pierce included her name as co-counsel on the signature block. She looked up at Pierce and said, "Thanks for that," as her eyes returned to the Complaint.

"Couldn't have done it without you."

"I'd like to believe that, but I know better," Maggie said, still focused on the document. By the time Maggie looked over the revised version of the Complaint, it was approaching 5:30. "I have to say," she murmured approvingly, "I can't think of a better way to start the weekend and ruin Lighthouse's."

The Complaint against Lighthouse represented a well-aimed opening salvo. Conventional wisdom dictated that Lighthouse would hit back with its entire arsenal designed to intimidate and frighten them into settling for a much lower-than-necessary amount. Pierce expected Lighthouse's lawyers to use the rules to hide evidence and tilt the game in their favor. It was all a part of the legal maneuvering and tactical dance they were ready for.

Maggie swelled with pride over the finished product and clamored to get the lawsuit started. She was determined and ready to cross the psychological Rubicon, which had come to symbolize a point of no return, when the time for deliberation was over and the time for action was at hand. Maggie logged on to the website of the United States District Court for the Southern District of Florida. "I'm ready," she said. "Shall I file it?"

Pierce made a slight nod in confirmation. Maggie smiled and hit the send button, and away it went.

* * *

The lawsuit against Lighthouse Blood Centers was assigned to John G. Dimitrouleas, a senior judge that had been on the federal bench almost thirty years. He had been an assistant public defender for the 17th Judicial Circuit of Florida for two years, and then an assistant state attorney of the same circuit for another twelve. The district judge had a reputation as a tough but fair jurist. Having worked both as a public defender and a state attorney, he threw his pitches right down the middle.

Dimitrouleas was incredulous when he saw the Certificate of Service. The law firms and lawyers on both sides were real heavyweights. Lighthouse assembled a dream team of high-powered lawyers reminiscent of the talented legal team that got O.J. Simpson acquitted. He emailed his clerk: "This reads like a 'Who's Who' of the top lawyers."

The clerk responded: "It does. It looks like Lighthouse shopped for the best legal talent money could buy."

Judge Dimitrouleas: "I assume Evan Dunn will be lead attorney for the Defendant."

The clerk: "I will confirm."

Judge Dimitrouleas: "Pierce and Evan have both appeared in my courtroom, but with the recent social media frenzy and the stakes so high, schedule a discovery conference with counsel to discuss the case and lay out the ground rules to make sure that this doesn't turn into a circus."

The clerk: "I'll check the magistrate's schedule and contact counsel."

Judge Dimitrouleas: "Put it on my calendar. I'll handle it."

The clerk: "Will do."

Chapter Forty-Seven

Wilkie D. Ferguson Jr. U.S. Courthouse
Miami

Judge Dimitrouleas continued to dispense with procedural motions by video conference. However, once the president had relaxed the restrictions and the courts reopened, the judge required that all criminal and civil trials take place in his courthouse in person. During the health crisis, the judge had no choice but to rely on technology. Dimitrouleas, however, was extremely uncomfortable with permitting jurors to receive evidence and deliberate remotely. In physical courthouses, distractions and the availability of extrajudicial evidence were limited. In the comfort of their homes, jurors could surf the internet, watch television, or take care of children rather than listen thoughtfully to the evidence.

* * *

The lawyers agreed to appear in person for the discovery conference, which was typically a brief meeting of lawyers to discuss the initial stages of the lawsuit. The CDC cautioned that social distancing should be continued for gatherings of six people or more, so the judge's clerk scheduled the conference to take place in the judge's courtroom in the Wilkie D. Ferguson Jr. Courthouse.

The design of the United States courthouse in downtown Miami was modern in spirit, featuring two glazed towers that appeared to be engaging each other in dialogue. The courthouse towers were also magnificent examples of the classic principles of federal architecture such as processional steps, slate floors, and grand public spaces to create a strong sense of civic identity.

On the right side, and to the judge's left, was the plaintiff's team of Pierce Evangelista and Maggie Malone. On the left side, and to the judge's right, was the team of nine lawyers representing Lighthouse. Their lead counsel was Evan Dunn.

The Judge knew both lawyers well. Pierce Evangelista was a virtuoso at taking the facts of a case, pulling them apart and putting them back together into a winning argument. The other side of the equation was Evan Dunn, a dominant force in the courtroom. Dunn was a man without ideology or politics; a mercenary for hire who used his razor-sharp skills and strategic mind to represent the highest bidder. Evan Dunn was a force who spent almost as much time cultivating his hefty image as he did representing important clients.

Dunn, a slight man of wiry build and soft features, was the mirror opposite of Pierce's chiseled features and physically imposing physique. However, what Dunn lacked in physical stature, he more than made up for in brainpower.

Pierce stood and introduced himself, and his co-counsel, Maggie Malone.

The judge then looked at the defense and said, "Good morning, Mr. Dunn."

Evan Dunn stood and introduced himself with a deep, ominous voice. "Good morning, Your Honor. Evan Dunn on behalf of Lighthouse and sitting next to me is my co-counsel, Michael McGuire."

The judge's eyes swept across the other lawyers also sitting at the defense table. "And the rest, I assume, is Lighthouse's legal team."

"Yes, Your Honor."

"You've assembled a lot of legal talent for a simple discovery conference?"

Dunn turned and looked at the faces of his legal team. "We have indeed, Your Honor, but this isn't a typical discovery conference. We have a pending Motion for a Protective Order; and the Plaintiff has a Motion to Compel. Since the court has set aside sixty minutes this morning, I assume that the court intends to address the pending motions."

Judge Dimitrouleas adjusted his reading glasses and gestured to Pierce to proceed.

Pierce stood up. "Your honor, the Plaintiffs respectfully request that the court start with the pending motions, as they are both related to discovery."

"Very well. Which one would you like to deal with first?"

Before Pierce could respond, Dunn took the initiative and stepped towards the lectern. "May it please the court. The Plaintiffs initiated this action by filing a nine-count Complaint. As explained fully in the Motion for the Protective Order, the Plaintiffs have made wild unsubstantiated allegations without a shred of evidence to support them. Mr. Evangelista is taking a buckshot approach, hoping to find a magic bullet in its overly broad discovery requests. He has an obligation to provide the grounds of entitlement to relief that requires more than threadbare recitals and conclusory statements. A formulaic recitation of the elements of a cause of action will not do."

Judge Dimitrouleas leaned forward and calmly said, "Mr. Dunn, we're here on a Motion for a Protective Order, not a Motion to Dismiss."

Dunn smiled uncomfortably. "Unfortunately, in this instance it is impossible to separate the wheat from the chaff; as the Complaint is nothing more than a well-crafted work of fiction and the Plaintiffs want highly confidential documents hoping to build a case."

Dimitrouleas shot Dunn a look that said he was pushing a chain uphill. "Counselor, bank records documenting wire transfers are hardly considered proprietary."

Dunn responded with one of his sly grins. "In most cases, I'd agree with you, Your Honor, but the nature and functionality of Lighthouse's business operations makes the bank transactions confidential."

Dimitrouleas twirled a pen in his right hand while Dunn droned on.

"All of Lighthouse's business transactions are done through bank wire. If Lighthouse turns over its bank records, it's essentially turning over its customer list, which is proprietary."

Pierce was not surprised by the Motion for a Protective Order. It was a predictable maneuver. In fact, he expected it. Dunn was running the plays from the defense attorney's playbook. Challenge every request for documents and contest the admissibility of everything proffered by the Plaintiff.

Pierce stood up and waited for the judge to signal to him that he could begin. Unlike in state court proceedings where lawyers acted like rabid dogs scrapping for the last piece of meat, the rules of decorum in federal court were followed and Dimitrouleas in particular had a short fuse.

The judge looked at Pierce Evangelista and said, "And your response?"

Pierce smiled and slowly nodded. "Your Honor, we're no longer requesting Lighthouse's financial records."

The look on the Judge's face was one of intense curiosity. "Interesting, and why not?"

"Because we have them."

Dunn's normally calm demeanor turned to one of overt irritation. "Your Honor, my client's computer network was recently targeted and hacked. The hacker seized the same information that the Plaintiffs now claim to have. This information was illegally obtained and should, therefore, be inadmissible." Dunn turned and gave Pierce an extremely dissatisfied look.

"Judge, counsel's hyperbole is unfounded," Pierce said, trying to sound reasonable.

"The U.S. Supreme Court and Florida courts have only applied the exclusionary rule to criminal prosecutions . . . This isn't a criminal proceeding." He paused, allowing the point to sink in before continuing. "Moreover, under common law there is a strong policy that all logically relevant evidence should be admissible . . ."

Dunn cut Pierce off. "This court cannot reward a criminal act."

Pierce could sense the anger in Dunn's voice. "Your Honor, applying the rule in a civil case, especially when there is no proof that the evidence was obtained by unreasonable methods, is inequitable."

Dimitrouleas stopped and glanced above his reading glasses halfway down his nose. "Let me stop the two of you there," the Judge said with a note of impatience. "Mr. Dunn, that's a serious accusation you just made. Do you have any proof that the plaintiffs were responsible?"

With a dismissive half smile, Dunn said, "How else would the plaintiffs come by confidential records? If it walks like a duck and quacks like a duck . . ."

"A quacking duck? Really?" Pierce said, vaguely amused.

The judge's face seemed to grow darker. He was growing weary of the constant crossfire between the lawyers.

Dimitrouleas held up his hand before Dunn could respond and looked at Pierce. "I know the Supreme Court gives courts a wide berth to consider evidence obtained under colorable circumstances, but I won't tolerate corporate espionage in my courtroom."

"Nor would I expect you to, Your Honor," Pierce replied. "Lighthouse's records are on three different whistle blower websites. The

'Stop Killing Canaries' movement targeted companies believed to be involved in the atrocities committed in Mexico. If you believe the postings on social media, Lighthouse is one of them . . . May I approach?"

The judge nodded. Pierce approached the bench and handed the judge a folder containing copies of pages from the websites. Maggie handed an identical set to Mr. Dunn.

"Your Honor, the financial records in the folder were all downloaded from websites and are in the public domain. The links to the websites are on top of the pages. To exclude this evidence when it is readily available to the public would prejudice my client."

The Judge reviewed the documents for a few moments and handed the pages to his clerk.

"Check the websites," he ordered.

The clerk typed the links into her computer. Five minutes later, she informed the judge that the websites all existed, and Lighthouse's financial documents were on them.

Dunn stood up. "Your Honor, I'd like to respond."

Dimitrouleas frowned with deep judicial deliberation. "That won't be necessary, Mr. Dunn," he said. "Your motion is denied."

The Judge turned back to Pierce. "Let's move on to the next motion. Mr. Evangelista, you have a Motion to Compel before the court."

"Yes, Your Honor. I have reviewed the case files on two other lawsuits involving Lighthouse. In those cases, Lighthouse was sanctioned by the court several times for failing to turn over documents and produce witnesses."

"Your Honor," Evan Dunn jumped out of his chair and glared at Pierce. "This gross mischaracterization is offensive."

Pierce had laid the groundwork. "No disrespect intended. Neither Mr. Dunn nor the lawyers before the court today except for Lighthouse's General Counsel, Mr. Collins, were attorneys for Lighthouse in those cases. However, there is one striking similarity: we have repeatedly sought dates for Mr. Bowman's deposition. Lighthouse is intentionally playing keep away with Mr. Bowman, a key witness who substantially participated in the events that give rise to this litigation; and who has unique personal knowledge of the facts and circumstances involved in this case."

Dunn stood at his table. "Objection. Mr. Bowman is the Chief Executive Officer. However, he lacks unique personal knowledge of the issues being litigated."

Pierce knew this was another textbook move by Dunn to attempt to tilt the board. "Your Honor, Lighthouse has had ample time to move for a Protective Order. Under the "Apex Doctrine," they have the burden of persuading this court that the Mr. Bowman lacks unique personal knowledge of the issues which are the subject of this litigation. They have not done so, nor can they, because Mr. Bowman cannot submit the required affidavit without committing perjury." With that parting shot, Pierce took his seat.

Maggie almost smiled. "Shots fired," she whispered to Pierce under her breath.

Dunn immediately stood up and objected. The Judge looked confused.

"Mr. Dunn, do you have a Motion for a Protective Order?"

"No, Your Honor."

"Then your objection is denied."

Dunn remained standing.

"Mr. Dunn, I see you're still standing. Is there anything else?" The judge asked.

"Your Honor, we are prepared to make Mr. Bowman available for deposition. We request, however, that the deposition be conducted virtually. Mr. Bowman's wife has a compromised immune system, and since we're still not completely out of the woods with the pandemic, he would like to avoid unnecessary risks."

The judge swiveled in his chair and looked at Pierce for a response. Pierce wanted to sit across from Bowman. In a virtual deposition, it would be much harder for him to spot a nervous tick or catch a slip that would allow him a glimpse behind the curtain. Like any good litigator, Dunn would continue to place obstacles in Pierce's path. Something Pierce expected and planned for.

As with a great poker player, the name of the game was to keep a straight face whether you were holding a Royal flush or nothing but a high card. Under Mo's tutelage, Pierce had mastered the skill. He picked up a manila folder marked "New Orleans," and asked, "May I approach?"

The judge waved Pierce forward. Pierce handed the judge a folder containing pictures of Ben Bowman eating inside three different restaurants. The first showed Ben Bowman eating with his wife inside the Red Fresh Grill, a popular bistro in the French Quarter. The second picture showed Ben Bowman and five other men in business suits having lunch at GW Fins on Bienville Street. The third picture was taken late at night. Ben Bowman was shown having an intimate dinner with an unidentified woman at Commander's Palace. All three were date stamped and taken within the last ten days.

Dimitrouleas studied the pictures before continuing.

Dunn leafed through the three pictures. If he was surprised, Pierce thought he hid it well. He objected to the pictures. He stood but did not move to the lectern. A sign that he did not expect to succeed but wanted to state his protest to preserve his opposition on the record. "Your Honor, this is a Motion to Compel discovery; and Mr. Evangelista is sandbagging me by introducing pictures that I am now only seeing for the first time." Dunn glared at Pierce. "The origin of these documents is unconfirmed and questionable. For all we know, the pictures may have been altered."

Pierce returned the glare. "Your Honor, the three pictures are only being proffered for rebuttal purposes. All three pictures were taken by my investigator, Mr. Hernan Mas, a decorated police officer and former police chief for Miami-Dade County . . ."

Pierce brilliantly neutralized Dunn. "What's really happening here is the defense is running out of excuses. Mr. Mas is here in the courtroom and prepared to testify to authenticate the pictures."

"Mr. Dunn," the judge intoned, the first note of annoyance in his voice. "Would you like to question Mr. Mas?"

Dunn stood in silence for a moment, brooding. Finally, he raised both hands in a sign of frustration and said, "That won't be necessary."

Judge Dimitrouleas digested the arguments presented for a few moments before responding. The air momentarily left the courtroom while he deliberated. "Mr. Evangelista, your Motion to Compel is granted. Mr. Dunn, you will make Mr. Bowman available for deposition in person. The deposition will take place in New Orleans since Mr. Bowman appears to be comfortable going out in public in his city."

The Judge studied his calendar and looked up at Pierce and Dunn. He cleared his throat and said, "You have sixty days to complete discovery."

Chapter Forty-Eight

Miami

Maggie was sipping a double latte from Starbucks to get rid of the morning cobwebs. The temperature on the digital clock read sixty-eight degrees, which was not uncommon for 6:30 a.m. in early January. Maggie crossed the street and walked to the edge of Bayfront Park. She checked her watch. It was still an hour before the morning staff meeting. Maggie wandered along the palm and oak-lined sidewalk, abutting the water, taking in the early morning sunlight. The view of the sun peeking out over the bay helped soothe away the stress that came with sixteen-hour days that were becoming more frequent as the trial date grew closer.

The trial team had grown to include two more paralegals and two junior level lawyers. One paralegal and lawyer were scrambling on many fronts, organizing, and preparing trial exhibits. The other two plowed through the myriad of details in the deposition transcripts. On board was also a jury consultant, part human behavior expert, part magician whose job it was to research the jurors' backgrounds and develop trial strategies to help shape juror perceptions.

Each morning over bagels and coffee, Maggie herself would hand out the daily assignments and then spend hours preparing outlines, strategic goals, and questions for each witness that they expected to call and cross-examine at trial.

* * *

At 7:30 sharp, J.C. and Dode joined the meeting from remote locations. Maggie started off the meeting by informing the trial team that the subpoenas for the bank officers responsible for managing Lighthouse's accounts and overseeing bank wires had been served.

"What's the status on Special Agent Russo?" Pierce asked as he walked into the conference room.

Maggie peered over her shoulder at the sound of Pierce's voice. "He's scheduled in at the end of the week."

Pierce acknowledged the faces seated around the conference room table before turning his attention back to Maggie. "After you meet with Nick, serve the subpoena on the FBI. While Nick has agreed to testify in a limited capacity, the bureau will only let him cooperate if they are served with a subpoena from a federal judge." Pierce reminded Maggie.

"Got it. Already prepared, and we'll ask the judge to sign it right after the meeting."

Pierce nodded. "We'll need Nick's testimony to further establish the fact that it was common knowledge that HemaMex was a front for the cartel and behind the murders."

She let out a long, skeptical sigh. "Do you really think that Lighthouse is going to expect a jury to believe that they didn't know how HemaMex was able to supply them with so much blood when no one else had any?"

Pierce raised an eyebrow. "So far, based on the depositions, that appears to be the angle they're taking. They want to lull us into thinking that they're only going to rely on plausible deniability as their defense."

Maggie had thought through that argument thoroughly. "Nick is the Special Agent responsible for operations in Mexico. I don't see how they rebut his testimony?"

"They may not have to. Nick's testimony only establishes that HemaMex was a front for the cartel," Pierce said.

Maggie looked at Pierce suspiciously, like she was looking for a trap. "If the jury believes Nick's testimony that it was common knowledge that HemaMex was a cartel operation, then Lighthouse would have to be deaf, dumb, and blind not to know."

"Maybe," Pierce nodded thoughtfully. "But without a witness that can corroborate that Lighthouse had actual knowledge, Dunn doesn't have to poke too many holes in Nick's testimony . . . Common knowledge of HemaMex's connection to the cartel certainly creates the inference that Lighthouse should have known but does not by itself lead to the inescapable conclusion that Lighthouse knew."

Maggie nodded in agreement. She understood that they couldn't rely on the jury to apply common sense. They needed to do a better job of connecting the dots for them.

"Evan Dunn hasn't played his hand yet," Pierce said confidently. "We'll get a closer look at his trial strategy next week when we attend mediation."

Maggie looked at him, barely able to conceal her impatience. "We still don't have a date for Bowman's deposition. Every time we agree on a date and time, they call us a couple of days later asking to reschedule, claiming they have a conflict," Maggie said acidly.

Pierce seemed to soak the words in for a second and then said, "Dunn will stall us until after the mediation. He'll want one chance of settling this case before exposing Bowman to any formal questioning."

Maggie made a show of deliberation. "In that case, I'll stop working on the questions for Bowman and finish up the opening statement for the mediator."

Something flashed behind Pierce's blue eyes, a revelation, a memory. "Let's keep the opening short. Dunn likes to use mediation to figure out the opposing side's strategy so he can throw a wrench in it at trial."

Maggie allowed herself a moment of self-congratulation. "We've put together a strong case. It just needs a little fine tuning."

Pierce's eyes narrowed. "Don't underestimate Evan Dunn."

Pierce had been busy plotting another angle he wanted to pursue. He looked at the monitor on the wall. "J.C., did you get an answer from Senator Cortez?"

J.C. nodded. "Yes, the senator said she's willing to ask the DEA for help."

Pierce suspected that by this time, Lighthouse and Evan Dunn were keeping a close watch on his team. The senator's meeting with Lloyd Hogan, the chief of intelligence for the Drug Enforcement Agency so close to the trial was bound to set off alarms in Lighthouse's camp. Mediation was a week away. Plenty of time for Lighthouse's Washington contacts to report back that Senator Cortez, a known ally, met with a senior DEA official.

Over the years, Pierce had made powerful friends, and Lloyd Hogan was one of them. Lloyd and Pierce didn't start off on good terms. They were on different sides of the same problem. Lloyd headed up a DEA task force in charge of extraditing Mr. Juan La Porte, an important witness whose firsthand knowledge of the operations could help the DEA cripple a powerful drug cartel. Pierce represented Mr. La Porte and his wife, Alexis. The cartel desperately tried to keep Juan from co-operating until they could kill him and tried to kidnap his wife. Pierce risked much to protect Juan and Alexis. and ultimately paid a high price. However, with Pierce's help, Lloyd Hogan and the DEA dismantled the Venezuela-based Cartel's operations and extradited its leader, Dario Carraboca, to the United States.

Pierce asked Lloyd to keep his meeting with the senator confidential regardless of who did the probing. After the mediation conference in New Orleans, Pierce would devise a way to leverage his DEA card.

"I also got a look at Lighthouse's Immunity Agreement," J.C. added. "It appears that they provided information on Senator Steve

Erickson that led to his arrest in exchange for immunity from criminal prosecution for any actions relating to the blood they purchased from HemaMex."

"How would Lighthouse come by dirt on the senator?" Maggie skeptically asked.

J.C. referred to pages of scribbled notes. "Lighthouse allegedly did background investigations on every candidate that it supported. When they did a deep dive into Erickson, some questionable information came to light. What exactly, I don't know," J.C. said. "But it was something that was serious enough for the FBI to get a subpoena to search his computer."

Dode shrugged as if it wasn't true. "I'm sorry, guys. If you tell me that the senator got caught exchanging emails with an FBI agent posing as a juvenile, I'd buy that. But unless the senator recklessly sent a copy of an email thread to Lighthouse, I don't see how they could have intel on his pedophile activity when the emails only existed on his laptop . . ."

Dode frowned first in disbelief, then great disappointment. "Sorry J.C., but as we say in Oklahoma, that dog don't hunt."

Then Dode hit upon another possibility. "Call me a conspiracy theory junkie, but maybe Lighthouse framed the senator."

Maggie was bewildered. "Wouldn't be surprised if Bowman made the senator the fall guy just so he could cut himself a deal." Then she added dubiously, "I agree with Dode. This smells like a setup."

"Let's keep our eyes on the prize, people," Pierce said as he finished scratching out some notes.

Pierce lifted his eyes from his legal pad and looked at the faces silently staring at him. Each wearing an expression of reflective curiosity. It was a new idea hatched within the past few minutes. "J.C., can you get me the names of the DOJ lawyers that worked on the Immunity Agreement?"

J.C. drew an imaginary line in the sand. "They won't talk to you. The Immunity Agreement is confidential. The DOJ lawyers won't discuss its contents. I had to pull a lot of strings just to get a glimpse of it."

"I realize they won't talk to me," Pierce admitted.

Maggie's brow furrowed as she pondered Pierce's next move.

J.C. was overcome with curiosity. "So why do you want their names?"

Pierce, for a reason he was about to lay out for everyone, said simply, "So, I can serve them with subpoenas and list them as witnesses."

Maggie shrugged as if to say, why bother? "They can't testify about the agreement. They'll assert that the document is privileged and confidential."

"I don't need them to tell me what's in it. I just want the jury to hear directly from the DOJ under oath that the Immunity Agreement exists."

Maggie and Dode looked at each other with uncertainty.

"They won't confirm its existence." Maggie insisted.

"Maybe not," said Pierce. "But if there was no Immunity Agreement, the feds would simply deny its existence. The fact that they can't speaks volumes . . . and we'll make sure the jury understands that."

Maggie raised an eyebrow.

J.C. chewed his nails for a moment and then asked. "But what good is that if they won't testify as to its contents?"

"They won't have to. We'll do it for them." Pierce laid out a sequence of questions designed to put the feds in a corner where they would 'neither confirm nor deny,' - the standard answer that Pierce counted on. He also hoped the court would give him sufficient leeway, in the face of Dunn's withering objections, for him to spin enough of a narrative for the jury to conclude that Bowman's reason for entering into an Immunity Agreement was to shield himself and Lighthouse from prosecution for their involvement with HemaMex.

Maggie's features settled into an expression of recognition, followed by profound approval. "There was only one reason for Bowman to cut a deal with the feds. He knew what HemaMex and the cartels were doing and realized that he could be criminally prosecuted."

Pierce smiled, and his eyes lit up. "That's the seed we'll plant with the jury."

Chapter Forty-Nine

New Orleans

Thirteen high-back chairs stood around a long table. All but two were occupied. One on one end was C. Edward Pettigrew, an accomplished mediator. On the other end, Ben Bowman was seated like the godfather in a gangster flick. To his right, Evan Dunn, his wartime consigliere. Next to him was Frank Collins. The other seven chairs around the table were his team of grim-faced legal assassins, his *capos*.

Bowman instantly recognized Maggie from her video and stared at her through contemptuous eyes. Pierce and Maggie took the two open seats closest to Pettigrew. Pettigrew gave a few opening remarks before turning to Pierce as counsel for the plaintiffs. He had no set formula for how to conduct his mediations. Pettigrew permitted the parties to determine the course.

Pierce attempted a brief introductory statement. Bowman made it his mission to rattle him and get on his nerves. Each time Pierce spoke, Bowman interrupted him. It was his way of sending a message that he was the one with real power. His money, his rules. How much he spent to settle the case, if he decided to settle, would be completely up to him and not the ivy league penguins sitting around the table.

Pettigrew was predictably appalled. In his long career, he'd come across a few bombastic clients hell-bent on hijacking the mediation, but nothing like Ben Bowman.

"This is a fucking witch hunt," Bowman growled, pointing a menacing finger at Pierce from across the room. "You should be disbarred. The dead people whose blood you claim I bought from HemaMex were Mexican peasants, not Americans. That blood helped keep Americans alive. Otherwise, thousands more hard-working people in this US of A would have died. All I asked HemaMex to do was to run standard tests on all the blood, like blood type and screening for the Rh antigen. I never asked them to kill people."

Pierce almost smiled. His gaze was steady, though behind his eyes he was sliding the puzzle pieces into place. He had gotten his measure of the man. He was mean, conniving, and had no conscience. Traits that Pierce planned to expose at trial. Pierce continued to make mental notes of what buttons he could push to provoke Bowman to spiral out of control. The more Bowman criticized and attacked, the more Pierce liked what he saw - an extremely volatile witness that Dunn couldn't control.

Dunn's eyes closed slowly. Then they opened again, and he looked at his client with great disappointment. "You've said enough, Ben," he growled in a rare display of anger.

The mediator tried in vain to maintain some semblance of order and move the settlement negotiations along. To Bowman, his entire narrative was nothing but babble. The sole purpose of the mediation, as far as he was concerned, was to send a message that it would be years before Pierce saw a penny. Pettigrew finally gave up, turned to Dunn, and asked sarcastically if he had anything to add to Mr. Bowman's colorful tirade.

It was 11:20 a.m. Dunn frowned, clearly annoyed by his client's transgressions. "We'd like to take a break."

The mediator seemed particularly edgy. "We could all benefit from a long lunch. Let's reconvene at one."

* * *

Ninety-five minutes later, Ben Bowman and his legal entourage returned. Bowman took his seat quietly as though he had been slapped across the face. Pettigrew made a couple of opening remarks about maintaining civility in the afternoon session while looking directly at Bowman. "I expect you to behave yourself. If you can't or won't, I'm going to terminate this mediation." The outrage was clear in his voice.

Collins assured the mediator that Mr. Bowman and the rest of the Lighthouse team would proceed in good faith.

Pettigrew raised one of his eyebrows, showing what he thought of Collins' assurance, and gestured towards Dunn. "Mr. Dunn. The floor is yours."

Dunn cleared his throat and took center stage. He started by insisting that his client was innocent of any wrongdoing. He explained that the only thing the financial wires to HemaMex represented was that Lighthouse paid its bills. Nothing more. Dunn didn't dispute that Lighthouse purchased blood from blood banks and supplied hospitals around the country. He argued that during the pandemic, the blood shortage made the United States extremely vulnerable and resulted in a wave of deaths.

"Lighthouse's ability to pivot quickly towards additional sources when its trusted suppliers could not meet the surging demand stemming from the Kayapo pandemic was both critical and necessary for the nation's healthcare workers to treat hospital patients." Dunn insisted that American lives were at stake.

"Lighthouse was responsible for saving American lives. We should be thanking Ben Bowman, not persecuting him." Dunn paused to underline the empathic statement and then rattled off statistics of how many Americans were treated by the blood supplied by Lighthouse.

Pierce had gotten a glimpse of Dunn's trial strategy. In the Midwest or in the deep South, like Mississippi, Alabama, Tennessee, Georgia and parts of Florida, Dunn's compelling narrative might be able to convince a jury that the end justified the means and return a verdict for the defendant. But this case was going to be tried in Miami, where seventy percent of the population consisted of Cubans, Colombians, Puerto Ricans, and immigrants from the other Central and South American countries. Given Miami's multilingual and multicultural makeup, it was likely that most juries would look to make an example of an individual or company that preyed on innocent Latinos. A possibility that Evan Dunn unfortunately could not ignore.

When Dunn was finished, Pierce's eyes turned from serious to ice. "Mr. Bowman," Pierce addressed him directly. "I don't plan on being here all afternoon, so I'm going to cut to the chase. First of all, whether you realize it or not, you're in a war you can't win. That's no reflection on your lawyers. You have a great legal team. I have tremendous respect and admiration for Mr. Dunn. But not even he can turn water into wine or perform miracles . . . and that's what it will take for you to win this case. It's going to take a miracle."

Bowman seethed but said nothing.

Pierce continued to talk in his smooth, even voice, diverting everyone's attention away from the volatile Bowman. "Here are the undisputed facts. 1) The Mexican cartels murdered thousands of innocent people to harvest their blood; and 2) HemaMex is a front for the cartel."

Dunn skeptically shook his head. "I object to your characterization that these facts are not in dispute."

"Evan," Pierce snapped in a stern voice. "We're not in court. There's no one here to rule on your objection. I have the floor. I'll remind you that you made your argument without any interruption from my side. I'd appreciate the same courtesy."

The unprecedented rebuke immediately silenced Dunn, and he sat back in his chair.

Pierce nodded at Maggie, who distributed a set of pictures of the video footage captured by Alex. Several pictures captured the migrants being marched by men carrying automatic weapons into the HemaMex facility. Other pictures showed dead bodies loaded onto the trucks. There were also pictures of the mass graves. The last picture showed the license plates of the trucks photographed at HemaMex parked at the Lighthouse facility. "These pictures were taken by a drone that our investigator flew over the HemaMex and Lighthouse buildings two weeks ago."

Dunn couldn't keep from frowning. "This may show that HemaMex engaged in questionable acts. But there's no proof Lighthouse had any knowledge."

"Then why push so hard to be included in the legislation?"

Bowman's eyes narrowed. "Why not? The pharmaceutical companies were pushing for it, so why not jump on the bandwagon? Seemed like a prudent thing to do." Bowman's words were suddenly short and dripping with sarcasm.

Pierce continued the ambush. "Except, when that didn't work out, you negotiated an Immunity Agreement with the Department of Justice."

Dunn's face twisted with anger. "That is a confidential document. The Judge will never let it in."

"There's more than one way to cook an egg." Pierce replied sardonically. He decided to give Dunn a little peek at one of his cards and slid his witness list with an abbreviated summary of what each witness would testify to across the table towards him. "My revised witness list," he said. "I plan on adding a few more names by the end of the week."

Dunn glanced at the list and saw the names of the Department of Justice lawyers that worked on Lighthouse's Immunity Agreement. The look on his face was one of deep thought. It suddenly clicked. Pierce didn't need to enter the Immunity Agreement into evidence. All he was after was a confirmation from the DOJ lawyers that an agreement existed. He'd leave the rest to the jury's imagination.

"This is thin," snapped Dunn, pretending not to be overly concerned. "An Immunity Agreement doesn't prove anything. There's no evidence or testimony that even remotely suggests that Lighthouse knew about HemaMex's activities."

With a nod, Pierce said, "Special Agent Nick Russo will testify that HemaMex's ties to the cartel were widely known."

Dunn shook his head. "Still doesn't prove that Lighthouse had actual knowledge."

"We don't have to prove Lighthouse knew, although we will. Conscious avoidance or willful blindness is all we need to prove. I'm sure you're familiar with the U.S. Supreme Court decision in *Global-Tech Appliances, Inc. v. SEB S.A.* where the court imposed a responsibility on the company to investigate questionable or suspicious circumstances . . . Most would agree that the CNN reports of thousands of bodies in mass graves qualifies as suspicious circumstances."

Maggie turned in her seat and gave Pierce a look that said he was revealing more than he should. Pierce's instincts told him he had arrived at the key moment in the mediation.

Turning to Bowman, he said, "The only remaining question is whether you're smart enough to settle and save your company."

Dunn nodded at his client, and in a noticeably unenthusiastic tone asked Pierce, "What number do you have in mind to settle the case?"

Pierce shared the number he had in mind for quite some time. "$500 million. Not one dollar less is what it will take to settle this case."

Bowman's first reaction was suppressing a laugh. "You must be kidding."

Dunn responded with a doubtful look.

"The offer is off the table once we start jury selection," Pierce said with a detached calmness. "Now if you'll excuse me, I'm going to take advantage of my visit to New Orleans and treat myself to a beignet.

Café Du Monde is great, but for anyone interested, I found an absolutely delightful spot just down the street from the Hotel Monteleone. Wonderful." Pierce slowly pushed his chair out and walked to the door.

"Gentlemen." Pierce smiled and left the room. He was gone in an instant, with the door closing behind him. The trap had been sprung; Bowman had been caught. He just didn't know it.

Bowman exhaled an even long breath. "What the fuck just happened?" Bowman looked bewildered and turned to Dunn. "Is he coming back?"

Dunn shrugged and managed a feeble, "I don't think he is."

Pettigrew frowned and smiled at the same time.

Maggie stared unflinchingly at the group of pompous little bastards around the table in their dark suits as they sat in stunned silence. Bowman stood and walked around the room rubbing his hair, scratching his chin, and trying to clear his head. Finally, he gawked at Maggie. "I thought this was supposed to be a settlement negotiation. He didn't even bother to stick around for my counteroffer."

Maggie did her best to hide her contempt. "There's where you're mistaken. This was never a negotiation," she said, managing a smile. "We came to New Orleans to deliver our terms. Nothing about the settlement terms is negotiable."

Maggie let the idea sink in for a moment, while she closed her laptop and readied herself to leave.

Bowman scoffed. "You're bluffing."

Maggie was more spit than polish and had an irritating habit of speaking the truth regardless of her audience. When she finished packing, her eyes locked on Ben Bowman, and she shook her head sorrowfully. "Mr. Bowman, you are a very naïve man . . . Pierce Evangelista doesn't bluff." She picked up her bag and said with a slight smirk on her face. "If you'll excuse me, I have to go see a man about a beignet."

Bowman showed his displeasure with a furrowed brow. As Maggie was about to close the door behind her, he yelled, "Tell Mr. Evangelista that he's going to have to do better than that."

She briefly considered his last statement and glanced over her shoulder. A devilish smile creased her lips. "You still don't get it, do you? Pierce Evangelista isn't a boy crying wolf . . . he *is* the wolf."

* * *

Pierce waited for Maggie at Café Beignet on Royal Street, a street filled with happy tourists in the heart of the French Quarter. He was sitting in the café's garden with its view of the street, watching men and women ambling by arm-in arm, celebrating, and descending onto the crowds of revelers, live music, and street performers on Bourbon Street. Pierce was in the middle of feasting on an Andouille sausage and crawfish omelet, when Maggie arrived at the restaurant floating on adrenaline.

Pierce lowered his sunglasses a bit and looked over them. "What took you so long?"

Maggie demonstrably shook her head. "You left me with a bloody mess back there that needed tidying up."

He responded with a rapacious grin. "I've ordered us some beignets. You should try the café au lait. It's the best in the city."

Maggie looked at Pierce pensively. "Feels like Bowman is close to rolling over."

Pierce nodded and sipped his café au lait.

"So, what's our next move?" Maggie asked, still feeling the high from rattling swords with the bad guys.

Pierce took a bite of a beignet and washed it down with another sip. His blue eyes glinted like ice in the sunlight. "Now, we back him up to the edge of the cliff."

Chapter Fifty

Miami

For two long, hard-fought months, Pierce Evangelista and Evan Dunn had gone head-to-head, toe-to-toe. Both sides pushed themselves with sixteen-hour days, mock trials, and relentless research.

Pierce had been meticulous in his planning, and decided it was time to play his Lloyd Hogan card.

"Where are we on the subpoena and motion requesting protective measures for the undercover DEA agent?" Pierce asked.

"We've requested that the testimony be video linked, to avoid any prolonged absence or anyone seeing the agent entering a federal courthouse. We've also asked the court for image and voice altering devices to protect against the witness being recognized." Maggie pursed her lips. "The only cases where I've seen the judge approve such extraordinary measures have been in criminal cases."

Pierce nodded. "File the motion under seal along with the memorandum setting forth the facts and *legal* basis for the protective measures."

"Honestly, I can't see a judge granting this motion," Maggie said, almost in a mumble.

"File the motion and let Dunn and his team fight it."

Maggie had a slightly troubled look on her face. "What about the *Touhy* regulations? I know we were able to persuade the judge to issue the subpoenas for the DOJ lawyers because you convinced him that they could testify without divulging any confidential information. But an undercover DEA agent is a different ball of wax."

Pierce agreed. "It's a heavy lift. Most judges won't compromise an ongoing investigation or put an agent at risk. I don't think the judge will agree to the subpoena of the undercover agent."

"So why pursue it?" asked Maggie with a raised eyebrow.

"Because it makes a statement that Lighthouse is guilty, and we're closing in on the evidence."

"I'm curious. How did you even know about the undercover agent?"

"I didn't," Pierce said. "But the DEA always has agents infiltrating the drug cartels. Call it an educated guess."

Maggie didn't like the sound of that bluff. "This could blow up in our faces."

Pierce had thought this through thoroughly. "It could, but it's not likely. When we pivot and ask the court to issue a subpoena for Agent Hogan, our request will appear much more reasonable."

"You would still be asking the agency to divulge confidential information."

"We'll make the same argument that we did to get the court to issue the subpoena for the DOJ lawyers."

Maggie shook her head. "Apples and oranges. The Immunity Agreement was already signed. Hogan would be testifying to an ongoing investigation."

"Bowman isn't the person of interest and not part of any investigation. All we're after is confirmation from Hogan that, based on his personal knowledge, Lighthouse was more involved in HemaMex's operations than they're admitting to . . . If the judge agrees that Hogan can testify without divulging confidential information, he'll issue the subpoena and give the government an opportunity to challenge it."

"I know that you and Lloyd Hogan are friends. Did he ever confirm this to you?"

"Confirm what?"

"That Lighthouse is more than just an innocent bystander."

"He didn't have to . . . Besides, Lloyd would never reveal any confidential information. Let's just say, sometimes you learn more from what a person doesn't say than what he actually says."

"So, do you really think he'll testify?"

All scenarios were on the table. Pierce suggested, for the sake of argument, that they shouldn't plan on Hogan giving them anything that they could use. "Hogan is old school. He'll most likely testify that his opinions and impressions are based on official information and refuse to say anything more."

"Then why are we going through this exercise?"

Pierce looked at Maggie with calculating eyes. "Because he'll show up."

"What's the benefit of that? And why would he do it?"

"Agreeing to honor the subpoena helps our case . . . and he owes me."

"I'm listening."

Pierce contemplated the tactical moves that had already taken place. "By now Dunn knows about the meeting between Agent Hogan and Senator Cortez. So, he'll assume that Hogan showing up to court means he's prepared to testify about Lighthouse's connection to the cartel."

Maggie leaned back even deeper in her chair, smiled, and savored Pierce's shrewdness. "Dunn will have no choice but to expend all his resources trying to keep Hogan's testimony out."

"It's a big distraction from their trial plan."

"I have a request."

"Okay. Let's hear it."

"Let me argue the motion," Maggie asked, her voice a shade more excited.

* * *

Maggie Malone came to court with a plan to tip the scales permanently on the plaintiffs' side. She scripted her argument down to when to pause to allow the judge more time to consider a particular point that she believed was important. She planned on convincing the judge that the witness, along with his family, would be harmed if his identity was discovered. However, the witness' testimony was critical to the Plaintiffs' case because he could directly tie Lighthouse to the murders committed by the Zeta Cartel. If the judge denied her motion, she was ready to ask the court to sign a subpoena for the Chief of Intelligence for the Drug Enforcement Agency, Mr. Lloyd Hogan.

Judge Dimitrouleas stepped through the door and moved quickly up the steps to the bench.

"We have the plaintiffs' Motion Requesting Protective Measures for a Witness at Trial." Maggie stood and moved towards the lectern. This provoked a curious look from the Judge.

"Who will be arguing for the plaintiffs?"

"I will, Your Honor."

"Very well, Miss Malone," the judge said. "I have the motion and the memorandum in support before me. Do you have further argument before we hear from the defense?"

Maggie glanced down at her legal pad filled with notes. "Yes, Your Honor. While most of the cases where Motions for Protective Measures are granted by the court, are criminal cases, the reasoning for allowing for protective measures is to provide for the witness's safety. The rules do not prohibit the extension of these safeguards to civil cases. The overall objective here is to protect a witness critical to the litigants while ensuring his well-being."

"Your Honor," Dunn cut in loudly. "Am I missing something? Last I checked, this is a civil trial. The relief requested is reserved for criminal cases and even then, only under extraordinary circumstances. There is no legal precedent for granting this motion, and the court should refrain from making up the rules as it goes along. It will interfere with the rights of my client to a full defense and a fair trial."

Dunn's last comment drew a harsh glare from the judge. He cut off Dunn. "Mr. Dunn. There's no press, cameras, or a jury in my courtroom. You can dispense with the theatrics."

Dunn looked up at the judge. "Your Honor. The Rules of Criminal Procedure address protective measures for witnesses to ensure that cases are successfully prosecuted, and the trial process is not compromised. There is no equivalent in the Rules of Civil Procedure."

The judge frowned. "I don't need a lecture on the Rules of Procedure."

"Nor would I presume to lecture you. The growing trend in civil proceedings is to require the disclosure of identities of confidential witnesses. To that end, the court in *Marsh & McLennan* interpreted Federal Rule of Civil Procedure 26(b)(1) to require the disclosure of the identities of all individuals who have knowledge of any discoverable matter, whether or not the individual will be called as a witness."

"Your Honor," Maggie pressed. "This evidence is crucial to our case. And there are special circumstances, the DEA agent's identity—"

"Thank you, Ms. Malone," the judge cut in. "I've heard enough. I'm going to deny your motion."

"Your Honor," Maggie persisted. "The DEA will not produce the witness if we cannot protect his anonymity. How am I supposed to get this evidence in?"

"You're a smart lawyer, Ms. Malone. You'll find a way."

Dunn smiled.

Maggie kept a perfectly composed veneer.

"I think we're finished here," Dimitrouleas said.

"Actually, Your Honor," Maggie chimed in. "In light of the court's ruling, I'd like you to order Lloyd Hogan, the Chief of Intelligence for the Drug Enforcement Agency, to appear in court to testify."

Dunn stood and objected. "Judge, under *Touhy*, this court cannot force Director Hogan to testify."

"Judge, Mr. Dunn doesn't represent the government. If the feds object to Director Hogan testifying at the trial, then they'll file an appearance . . ."

"Your Honor," Dunn roared. "Director Hogan works out of the DEA headquarters in Springfield, Virginia and has no firsthand knowledge regarding the cartel or Lighthouse."

"Judge," Maggie shot back. "Mr. Dunn has no idea what Director Hogan knows."

"Hold on," the judge said.

Dunn cut in loudly. "Your Honor, this is incredible. Miss Malone is attempting to parade a federal agent in front of the jury and railroad them into thinking that if Lighthouse was on the DEA's radar, they must be guilty of something. They want to con the jury to buy into their big conspiracies and high drama B.S. Nothing more!"

Maggie kept her eyes on the prize and pushed back. "You'll get your chance to cross-examine the witness."

The skin around the judge's eyes tightened. "That's enough from the two of you." His voice had an irritated tone to it.

The judge rubbed his face and brooded over the issue. He had denied the plaintiffs' motion to introduce evidence through a protected proceeding. If he refused to subpoena the chief of intelligence for the

DEA, his ruling could prevent the plaintiffs from introducing important evidence.

Dunn's instincts told him the judge was leaning towards signing the subpoena and retooled his approach. He couldn't let the jury hear testimony from the DEA chief that his client was caught in a wide net cast by DEA when investigating the cartel's operations in Mexico. With Hogan's testimony in evidence, any doubt whether Lighthouse knew about HemaMex and the Zeta Cartel's connection, as well as the murders, would be erased.

"Your Honor, don't tell me you're falling for this well-orchestrated con! You're smarter than that."

The two men locked eyes for a tense moment. Dunn hoped his emotional outburst might get the judge to take a second look at the issue before ruling. It was a risky move that rarely worked with Dimitrouleas, but Dunn was out of options. He continued his charade by apologizing for his uncharacteristic lapse in judgment. Humbling himself before the judge, Dunn pushed the words through gritted teeth. "Your Honor, I apologize to the court." His act of contrition hung in the air for a second.

The judge glared at Dunn through squinted eyes as he wrestled with the idea of holding Dunn in contempt, then let it pass. "Apology accepted," he said coldly.

Dunn took a deep breath. He had not only dodged a night in jail, but he was also confident his outburst had the intended effect of nudging the judge towards reconsidering both arguments before making a final decision. "If I may, Your Honor. We're being blindsided here. This is the first I've heard about this witness."

"Your Honor, our initial motion requested that the undercover agent in the field under Director Hogan be allowed to testify under protective measures. You told me to find another way," Maggie said.

The judge swiveled towards Dunn. "Do you have a response?"

"As far as I see it, we still have to contend with *Touhy*. I think we're getting ahead of ourselves here. Federal court subpoenas require the consideration of *Touhy*-related issues. If the court issues a subpoena, Director Hogan will also have to make himself available for deposition. Otherwise, my client would be severely prejudiced if we cannot depose Director Hogan before he's allowed to testify."

"Judge, Mr. Dunn doesn't represent the government," Maggie jumped back in. "We have already provided the deputy attorney general with a summary of the testimony we are seeking as required under the DOJ regulations. If the feds object to Director Hogan testifying, they'll move to quash the subpoena."

The judge raised an eyebrow. "Counsel makes a good point, Mr Dunn. The Department of Justice could file an objection to the subpoena under *Touhy*."

"I don't think they will," Maggie added smugly, as if she was privy to some dark, dirty secret. She paused, allowing the words to settle, then said, "Director Hogan recently met with Senator Cortez, and agreed to appear if served with a subpoena." A deliberate slip of the tongue that Maggie intended for Dunn to chew on.

Dunn smirked and shrugged his shoulders as if vindicated. "Your Honor. I trust that you can see through this charade. This was always about getting Hogan on the stand."

Maggie shook her head in dismay, appearing to be mildly offended. "Full disclosure judge, Director Hogan was our contingency plan."

Before Dunn could respond, Judge Dimitrouleas put up his hand like a traffic cop to cut off further debate. "Both of you are bringing more heat than light. I'm going to continue this motion. Mr. Dunn, I want your memorandum supporting your position to my clerk by 5 p.m. Monday. You will copy Ms. Malone . . . Ms. Malone, I have your memo. Should you wish to rebut any of the points in Mr. Dunn's memo, you will have until the close of business on Tuesday to do so. I will provide you with my decision once I have reviewed all the material."

Chapter Fifty-One

Miami

The hallways in Edgar Dunn's office were choked with secretaries and legal assistants, all running back and forth as the promise of a nasty trial was just around the corner.

After the hearing, Dunn had worked the phones, tapping into his extensive network of Washington gossipmongers and reliable contacts at the Department of Justice and the DEA. A high-ranking career prosecutor from the DOJ finally confirmed that his office had been instructed to stand down. Nothing official, there was no formal memo or direction given in an email. It was strictly off the books, but it was obvious that strings had been pulled at a very high level, and it was understood that the DOJ would not be fighting the subpoena if Judge Dimitrouleas issued it. Dunn thought this through and decided that the lack of official communications between the DEA and the DOJ on this could only mean that the Chief of Intelligence for the Drug Enforcement Agency had agreed to play ball, and he wanted no interference.

Evan Dunn was tense; more tense than he'd been in several years. He glanced over at the engraved paperweight on his desk bearing the inscription, *"The only inexcusable offense for a trial lawyer is to be surprised."* By the time Pierce was finished questioning Director Hogan on the witness stand, Ben Bowman would be the most famous white-collar criminal in America. Most people would want to see him pay. He saw Lloyd Hogan as a stoic witness on the stand, sitting confidently as a representative of the U.S. government in front of the jury, thoroughly convinced that he would not bend or break, regardless of the barrage of cross-examination. Dunn could not allow Pierce to put Hogan on the witness stand.

He fought the urge to lock the door and open the bottle of Scotch in the bottom drawer. But Dunn couldn't put off discussions concerning settlement any longer and prepared himself for Bowman's withering and belligerent tactics. He reminded himself to keep his eye on the bigger picture. A decision had to be made. Time was running out if they were going to settle the case. Any further delays would cost the company millions. It was time for Dunn to raise the red flag, mark the minefield that lay ahead and talk some sense into his client. Bowman was used to getting his way. So much so that when people didn't bend to his whims, he became an insufferable bastard. He would regard a settlement as capitulation, rather than a strategic decision to minimize losses that could potentially be catastrophic and impossible to recover from. The thought of going toe-to-toe with Ben Bowman to get him to settle the case was something Dunn didn't look forward to.

His assistant's voice came on the intercom.

"Sir, Mr. Bowman and Mr. Collins are waiting for you to join the Teams meeting."

Dunn gritted his teeth. "They're twenty minutes early," he answered in a voice full of tension. Dunn thought about letting them wait. For Bowman, it was a control thing. He liked to dictate when things happened. Twenty minutes early or ten minutes late, the time wasn't important.

When Dunn entered the meeting, the first thing he saw was Bowman and Collins sitting on the same side of an enormous conference room table, chewing their lunch.

"Gentlemen," Dunn greeted them.

"I understand the hearing this morning was a total shit show." It was classic Bowman. No greetings, no niceties, no small talk.

Dunn didn't mind skipping the social pleasantries and launched right into his reason for asking for the meeting. "It's time to revisit the idea of settling this case," he started.

The chewing stopped. There was a long pause. Bowman was bewildered, and not certain where to start. He had made his intentions clear to Dunn when he hired him: No settlement. Take the case to trial. If a jury rendered a verdict against Lighthouse, appeal it.

"I can't believe I'm hearing this bullshit," Bowman said, launching into an expletive filled tirade with no attempt whatsoever to conceal his disgust.

Dunn absorbed the roar without paying much attention to the words. He looked at Bowman and said, "Ben, you have hundreds of people working for you that tell you what you want to hear. You didn't hire me to do that."

Bowman grunted with disdain and shook his head. "I hired you to represent me in a lawsuit. Not bend over and take it up the ass the minute things got dicey."

The game was on—a flood of colorful words crossed his mind. Instead, Dunn looked at them with the same judgmental eyes that his dad would shoot him when he failed to get a hit in his high school baseball games. "You hired me to protect Lighthouse, not exercise poor judgment."

Bowman continued to glare at him. His composure was sending Bowman's blood pressure north. Dunn realized that he needed to quickly lay out the facts before his knuckle dragging moron of a client worked himself into a lather and refused to listen to reason.

Collins read his boss's expression and quickly asked, "What are the chances that the judge will issue the subpoena?"

Red faced, Bowman yelled over Collins. "The judge has given them everything they've asked for. Why should this be any different?"

Dunn calmly responded. "He denied the Plaintiffs' Motion For Protective Measures to allow an undercover agent to testify. I don't think the judge will want to completely keep out evidence that the plaintiffs contend is critical to their case, and risk reversal on appeal."

Bowman mumbled something under his breath. Collins' eyes told Dunn to ignore the comment and keep going.

Dunn obliged him. "I'd say the chances are pretty good that Dimitrouleas will subpoena Director Hogan and let the feds sort it out."

"If he does testify, do we know what he's going to say?" Collins asked.

Dunn shrugged at the obvious and assumed that working for Bowman for the last few years must have flattened all of Collins' edges. "I imagine he'll have something to say about Lighthouse's connection to the cartel. We'll know more after we depose him."

"Once you know what he's going to say, you can punch holes in his testimony," Collins said.

"That really depends on what he says." Dunn's face was as vague as his answer. He wasn't as confident as Lighthouse's General Counsel.

Bowman scoffed. "He doesn't know anything."

Dunn looked down his nose like a schoolteacher addressing a student. "Ben, this is not a criminal case. Plaintiffs do not have to establish facts beyond a reasonable doubt. In civil cases, they just need to show that a particular fact or event is more likely than not to have occurred. They're building their case block by block. Coincidence by coincidence. If you string together enough coincidences, it stops looking like one."

Dunn held up a bottle of water.

Bowman rolled his eyes and growled. "Spare me the half empty/half full speech."

Dunn had an easy smile that he used to defuse confrontational situations. "Fine, but it applies to some extent here. What I want to point out to you, however, is the product's label. Whether a juror sees the bottle as half empty or half full, the one thing they will all agree on is that the product labelling says 'Fiji.'"

"And why do I care?"

"Because whether the jury believes us may not be what ultimately influences them to award damages. The verdict may not turn on whether the jury can agree that you knew, didn't know, or should have known where your blood was coming from. We could split the jury on that issue and still lose. Like the Fiji label, there won't be any disagreement that the cartel murdered millions of people, and you profited from their deaths. No matter how you look at it, those facts are indisputable."

Dunn let the tension grow before he continued, "So, you may want to reconsider and accept Mr. Evangelista's settlement offer."

Bowman cocked his head to one side and was angry again. He wanted to lash out at Dunn but for the moment he decided to show restraint. "Are you saying you can't win this trial?"

Dunn shook his head. "I'm saying that the only way for you to control the outcome is to settle." He waited for the tension to ease, then explained that if Hogan's testimony revealed that Lighthouse was involved, it was 'game over.' There would be no way to come back from that.

Dissatisfied, Bowman snapped, "We'll know more after you depose him."

"If the court issues the subpoena, there's a good chance that Pierce will pull the settlement offer."

"Pierce said we had until jury selection to accept the offer. Why would he pull it?" Bowman grumbled bitterly.

Throughout the litigation, Dunn developed a good feel for Pierce's tactics and countermeasures. "If the judge lets Hogan testify, Pierce will believe he can get you to pay more."

Bowman clenched his jaw. "You're giving this Hogan character too much credit."

Dunn shook his head defiantly. "If the chief of intelligence for the Drug Enforcement Agency testifies and does nothing more than confirm that Lighthouse's name is in the DEA's investigation report, it's a problem. If Lighthouse is mentioned in the report, it's not because they're playing mahjong with the cartel."

Bowman rolled his eyes in frustration. "That's not really saying we're guilty of anything."

"Again, Ben, this isn't a criminal proceeding," Dunn frowned, trying to pound common sense into his client. "When you add to the equation the makeup of Miami-Dade's population, half of the jury could be made up of Latinos who'll identify more with the victims that were murdered by the cartel than with those that received the treatments. The half a billion to settle now will seem like a bargain compared to the trainload of money the jury could award the plaintiffs."

Dunn could see another expletive-ridden tirade coming. Bowman just shook his head. His eyes were narrow, his eyebrows pinched together. Much to his credit, he shrugged and said, "If that happens, we'll declare bankruptcy."

Dunn shook his head at the two men on his flat screen monitor. "Same result from a different angle. The bankruptcy court will liquidate your assets to satisfy the judgement." He did a quick calculation. "I get it. $500 million is a fortune. It will sting, but with your assets and reserves, the company will manage. It beats the hell out of the alternative. If the jury renders a verdict for the plaintiffs in the billions, Lighthouse will have to shut down."

Collins appeared rattled, took a deep breath, and let it out slowly. "We can appeal."

"That will only buy you an additional eighteen months."

That led to a lengthy internal tirade as Bowman grappled with the implications.

They had finally arrived at the pivotal fork in the road. "The big question you want to ask yourself is . . ." Dunn shrugged and said with an air of melancholy. "For something so unprecedented and fraught with risk, wouldn't you want to control the outcome, as opposed to putting your company's future in the hands of twelve people who weren't smart enough to think of an excuse to get out of jury duty?"

Chapter Fifty-Two

Oklahoma

Once Dode learned that Ben Bowman received an Immunity Agreement from the U.S. Attorney in exchange for his cooperation, she closely chronicled the media reports of the FBI's investigation into former U.S. Senator Steve Erickson.

Ten days prior to the federal arraignment, the FBI reported that it received startling and unexpected information from a fifteen-year-old hacker named Timothy Hearn, alias Swaggerboy15.

Swaggerboy15 hacked the internet with the ferociousness of a starving Cuban slashing away at stalks of sugar cane. For an upfront payment of $10,000, the enterprising teenager guaranteed a high school senior admission to his or her college of choice. Swaggerboy15 changed grades, test scores and in one case changed a rejection to an acceptance letter in Harvard's Office of Admissions.

Swaggerboy15 installed malware in a browser extension for Chrome and Edge browsers. The extension couldn't be detected since the university's authentication and security measures had already authenticated the browser. Once the malware was downloaded, Swaggerboy15 could read and alter admissions files. One major flaw in a seemingly flawless plan was that Swaggerboy15 never accounted for the bragging and audacious selfies his clients posted wearing brand new university sweatshirts on social media publicizing their acceptances. The blowback from incensed parents who challenged the college's admissions decisions, when *their* children with higher grade point averages, more extracurricular activities and overall stronger applications were denied admission, was palpable. An investigation by university officials led to the discovery of discrepancies between the test scores in the College Board's records and those on file. An experienced professional would have hacked into the College Board's servers to make sure the test scores were the same and the subterfuge could not be so easily discovered. It wasn't long before the FBI picked up the scent of the admissions scandal. A few days after conducting initial interviews, Special Agents Alvarez and Monroe were sitting in Timothy Hearn's living room across from his parents and a very terrified and cooperative Swaggerboy15.

In desperation and to avoid spending time in jail, Timothy became willing to share secrets. Timothy claimed that Senator Erickson was framed, and he could prove it. Special Agent Alvarez nodded and sent a text. Thirty minutes later, Assistant U.S. Attorney Alan Taft was on the phone.

Timothy couldn't identify who was responsible, but the chatter in a particular private chat room on the dark web was that over one thousand four hundred images and thirty-one videos of child sexual abuse material had been downloaded from a site on the dark web dedicated to child pornography, and remotely uploaded onto the former senator's computer. The hacker remotely controlled Erickson's computer and fabricated fictitious email exchanges between Erickson and minors, where he discussed his sexual fantasies about children and solicited sex. Erickson's computer was infected with "bots"—software programs that directed his computer to search the web for child pornography sites.

Timothy provided the special agents with numerous details, such as the existence of the thirty-one child porn videos on Erickson's computer. The mention of the specific number made Taft flinch. That particular piece of information was known only to the FBI investigators and the Assistant U.S. Attorney in charge of prosecuting Erickson. Timothy gave the FBI the IP address to the host of the private chat room as well as his explicit username to allow them to pose as Swaggerboy15, and gain access.

The information provided by Timothy sped up the investigation, and a few weeks later, the digital forensics team at the FBI confirmed that the senator's computer had been breached. The U.S. Attorney's Office dismissed all charges against Steve Erickson and reported that the FBI traced the cyber-attack to Russia.

* * *

Dode's mind ran through the gamut, processing the facts she knew and separating the partial truths from the outright lies that the FBI fed the press. She no longer wondered if Senator Erickson's arrest and indictment was a setup perpetrated by Bowman. She could smell it from a mile away. The lead story in Sunday morning's paper was the U.S. Attorney's announcement that she was dismissing all charges against former U.S. Senator Steve Erickson. The article reported that the digital forensics team at the FBI concluded that Erickson's computer had been hacked. Buried in the local section of the Boston Herald was a story about specious standardized test scores and doctored transcripts that resulted in nine students inadvertently admitted to Harvard. The story proved rather interesting. Dode read it twice before she connected it to Erickson. Someone with less experience would have missed it.

* * *

Pierce was sitting at his kitchen counter, sipping a cup of coffee. At 6:23 a.m. the chirping of an incoming call played on his computer. Pierce noticed the time before he answered the call.

"Good morning."

"Did you read my email?" Dode asked.

"Read it a few minutes ago."

"According to the rumor mill on the dark web, Alina Petrovich was the hacker responsible for Erickson."

"The news reports are saying that the FBI suspects someone else."

"Yeah, I know. They're saying a thirty-five-year-old Russian hacker who goes by the name *Boris Spassky* was responsible."

"You don't think that he did it?"

Dode shrugged elaborately. "It doesn't fit . . . Most hackers operate anonymously. They don't leave a trail for law enforcement to follow. A few have huge egos and want the world to know that they were responsible. Alina Petrovich falls into that category. She's known as the Houdini of *Hackers*. Leaving a trail that leads to someone else's IP address is Alina's calling card."

"What makes you so sure it wasn't Spassky?"

"If it was him, they wouldn't have found him so easily." Dode's tone was grudging.

Pierce slid his forefinger and thumb down over his stubble, pinching his chin while he made a mental note.

"Besides, Boris hasn't fucked with U.S. politics since the Clinton-Trump election. At least that's what I hear," she added.

Pierce brought the cup to his lips and took a sip of coffee as he thought. Dode was a brilliant strategist who had, over the years, cultivated reliable sources among white and black hat hackers. When it came to collecting information and filling in the blanks, there were very few who could match her skills.

"This reeks of a hatchet job," Dode said.

Pierce frowned. "You could be right. Not that it makes a difference, but why Petrovich and not Spassky?"

"This type of work is more up Alina's alley. She sells her services as a cyber assassin to the highest bidder. Boris is more of a cyber-terrorist. He works on a much more prolific scale. His last botnet, for example, reached millions of computers around the globe, infected them with ransomware, and stole all the data, resulting in over $100 million in damages. It took the FBI nearly eight years before they figured it out and finally pinned it on Spassky . . ."

Dode kept talking. "The deeper question is who benefited most from the former senator's arrest?"

A few names quickly came to mind. If Pierce penciled out a list, Ben Bowman's name would be on it. "And you suspect Ben Bowman?"

Dode shook her head. "This goes *beyond* simple suspicion. This has got Bowman's DNA all over it."

"Any proof, or is this just your gut?" His tone suggested that he wasn't entirely convinced.

Dode paused for a moment to light a cigarette, a cheap Native American brand she had been smoking ever since she was twelve and fished them out of her grandfather's front shirt pocket when he was sleeping. "Bowman got immunity from criminal prosecution for the shit that went down in Mexico. Nobody else benefited like that. This deal reeks of desperation. Only one dot to connect here, pizza man," she said, pleased with herself.

Pierce once again rubbed his stubble thoughtfully and shook his head. "Why Erickson? He was one of the biggest supporters of Littlefield's bill."

With a slight cock of the head, Dode said, "Now we're in your wheelhouse, but my guess is that he became expendable when the bill didn't pass."

Pierce had a hunch and started typing on the keyboard of his laptop. "His Senate race was too close to call this past summer." He started tapping again. "Erickson came out in support of Littlefield's bill before the vote, and it cost him a couple of points."

"What about after the vote?" Dode asked.

Pierce frowned as he studied the screen. "A couple of weeks after the vote, a poll showed him eighteen points behind and losing ground."

"Like I said, he became expendable," Dode interjected. She paused to take a long pull on her cigarette and exhale a cloud of smoke. "Bowman is one tactical S.O.B. To manipulate the FBI, he needed to flip on someone that he had a relationship with to make it believable. Bowman was a supporter of Erickson's re-election campaign."

Pierce settled back in his chair and sipped his coffee. "He clearly had motive. One way or another, Bowman was determined to get immunity for what happened in Mexico."

"Exactly." Her dark eyes gave off a no-nonsense intensity. "The last nail in the coffin. Now, he won't have any choice but to settle."

Pierce instinctively frowned, then said, "I can't use this to force Bowman to settle. Even if I could, it still might not be enough." He fell back into his thoughts, the pictures of the mass graves indelibly burned in his mind. His eyes turned distant as he imagined all the faces of the brothers, sisters, fathers, and mothers. Entire families massacred and forever forgotten.

Dode looked at him, clearly wanting him to say more, and regarded Pierce with a skeptical squint. "What is it that you're not telling me?"

His expression was somber, perhaps even grave. Despite his best efforts to put Bowman into a no-win situation, Pierce hadn't been able to get him to settle. There were moments when Bowman seemed close to pulling the trigger; and most other times, he appeared to be digging a foxhole to hide in and ride out the storm. The consequence was clear, and it gave Pierce a combination of adrenaline and satisfaction.

She recognized the familiar glint in his eyes. Pierce was dialed in, focused solely on convincing a jury to make Lighthouse and Bowman pay for their sins. Everything else was just noise to him.

Chapter Fifty-Three

New Orleans

With the day shot to hell, Bowman buzzed his secretary and asked her to hold his calls. He stretched out on the sofa, massaging his temples, and trying to think the situation through. Bowman could feel his time running out, and as it did, his rage intensified. He felt like he had a stone lodged in his throat. He was having a hard time swallowing that he'd been outgunned by an ambulance chaser. When Pierce filed the lawsuit, Bowman pressed his lawyers to shotgun counter claims and put them on their heels. There would be no settlement. When Bowman was finished with them, Pierce Evangelista would be lucky to still have his law license.

But nothing turned out like Bowman expected. He never got the chance to go on the offensive and hadn't had a good night's sleep in weeks. What kept him awake were the questions. How would the company survive if it had to pay $500 million to settle the lawsuit? As the hours passed, Bowman moved from worry to panic.

One plan was to run. If the jury did award the victims billions in punitive damages, how quickly would he be able to turn the company's assets into cash and disappear? If Pierce was as good as Dunn said, he would surely try to freeze his accounts the moment he liquidated assets and before he could move the money offshore, where it would be beyond the reach of a U.S. court. His reaction to his options was mixed. Paying the settlement amount would force him to sell assets and downsize his operations. It was a heavy cost, but he would avoid the impending disaster that Dunn had predicted.

Bowman walked over to the bar in his office and poured himself a drink. He stopped for a moment, catching his reflection in the mirror. He didn't recognize himself. His nose creased in a faint scowl. Long gone were the smirk and arrogance. All that stared back at him were fleshy jowls and puffy, dark eyes. He stopped at the window and stared out at the Mississippi River. A cargo ship pushed upstream against the current. He sucked down two ounces of Scotch while he watched it for several minutes.

What Bowman needed was more time. He would compromise by agreeing to settle for $500 million, if he could pay it over ten years. If the plaintiffs agreed, he'd have a year before the second installment was due. That would stretch things out and give him the time he needed to move his money and slowly liquidate his assets without raising too much suspicion. By the time Bowman failed to make the second installment payment, and the hammer dropped, his fortune would be parked in Zurich, safely out of reach. He walked back to the bar and refilled his glass. He wasn't exactly gaming the system. Bowman imagined the look on Pierce Evangelista's face when he realized that he would never see the remaining balance of $450 million; and deep down it gave him a small measure of pleasure even though it had a $50 million price tag attached to it. After draining his glass of another toxic dose, Bowman felt like himself again.

* * *

At 4 p.m., Dunn and his legal team were busy reviewing and putting together the exhibits in support of their memorandum to prevent Lloyd Hogan from testifying when Bowman called and instructed him to schedule a meeting with the plaintiffs' legal counsel to discuss settlement.

"We have too much to do to get ready for trial to be playing games."

Bowman took a long draw on his scotch before he answered. "Set up the meeting and let's get rid of this case. My assistant booked a suite at the Biltmore Hotel. Let's meet there tomorrow morning at ten," Bowman said.

"If you're not willing to pay the $500 million, there's no point in meeting," Dunn said without hesitation. He didn't want to waste time.

"I understand the amount is not negotiable. He's a shrewd lawyer and he's got us backed into a corner," Bowman grudgingly admitted a little admiration. "But we still have things to discuss like terms for the payment."

"What do you have in mind?"

Bowman decided to lay it on thick. Make the request for terms about avoiding collateral damage. "I'll pay the $500 million, but I need to pay it out over time. A lump sum is not something I can do without having to lay off employees and putting families out of their homes and onto the streets."

"How much time are you looking for?" Dunn asked, his tone was suspicious.

Bowman needed Dunn firmly on board if he was going to have any chance of pulling it off. Pierce was damn good, and if Dunn wasn't completely invested, Pierce would see through the attempted subterfuge.

"Ten years."

"I'm not sure Pierce will agree to that."

Bowman painted a "throwing the baby out with the bathwater" scenario and ended with, "The virus caused the economy to go into a freefall. The last thing I want to do is to put people out of work."

There was a gap in the conversation. Dunn was naturally puzzled by his client's sudden concern for his employees' welfare.

Bowman drained his glass, slurping it loudly while Dunn continued to weigh the issues.

"The capital markets are shit right now. They've suffered historic declines, and no one knows when they'll come out of it. Banks are paying less than two percent. They'll get a better return by giving us terms," Bowman added, laying it all on the table.

Dunn pondered this for a few more seconds, then asked, "What interest rate are you thinking about?"

"What's the highest permissible interest rate?"

"That depends. Eighteen percent, but on loans that exceed $500,000, the maximum legal rate of interest is 25 percent."

Bowman didn't want to appear too eager. If he agreed to the highest interest rate allowed, that might raise a red flag. Finally, he said, "I think ten percent is more than fair."

Dunn worked his calculator. "That's $263 million in interest. That's a big number, Ben."

Bowman agreed. "It's not chump change." He didn't care about the number because he was never going to pay it. He just needed to sell it.

"We've calculated the principal and interest payments. It comes to 71 million a year over ten years. It won't be a walk in the park, but we can swing it without having to lay off workers."

Dunn had spent too much time with Ben Bowman to fall for his Mother Teresa act. He assumed he was working an angle. However, spreading out the liability in the form of a structured settlement made financial sense for both parties. He thought for a second, cleared his throat and said, "It sounds like a reasonable counteroffer. I'll call Pierce and set up the meeting."

Chapter Fifty-Four

Biltmore Hotel, Coral Gables, Florida

Unlike many buildings that superstitiously omit the 13th floor, the Biltmore Hotel doesn't. Bowman insisted on booking the lavish Everglades Suite that occupied two entire floors of the hotel's copper clad tower. The suite featured a vaulted, chandelier-mounted, hand painted frescoed ceiling depicting scenes from Florida's Everglades. The living room was big enough for two sitting areas, a desk, grand piano, and a dining table—all on a terrazzo floor and hand knotted area rugs. Antique furniture decorated each of the rooms and featured intricately ornate pieces that were particularly popular during the Victorian era, when too much was never enough. The two balconies on the second-floor mezzanine encircled the suite, offering a three hundred sixty degree panoramic view of Coral Gables.

The secret staircase and private elevator were some of the suite's unique offerings. Dubbed 'The Al Capone Suite,' it was widely believed that the back staircase led to a speakeasy and an illicit gambling den that was operated by Al Capone during Prohibition. Bullet holes on the fireplace and walls were further proof of Capone's notorious encounters. The stories of the infamous guests and luminaries who, in one way or another, left their mark on the landmark hotel were of little importance to Bowman. The only thing he insisted on was that his secretary book the most expensive suite. The Everglades Suite went for $20,000 a night.

Pierce couldn't help but smile at the irony of meeting Ben Bowman in the very place that served as Al Capone's residence when he was in Miami, and where the mobster & hit man, Thomas "Fatty" Walsh, was shot dead. When Pierce and Maggie arrived at the suite, Evan Dunn was waiting by the powerful oak door to greet them. They shook hands properly, but not like friends. They all understood their roles in this transaction, and there was no point in pretending otherwise.

As soon as Pierce and Maggie stepped inside, they came face-to-face with the devil himself. But the devil was quite pleasant, remarkably gracious, a different man than the one they had encountered in New Orleans.

"Good morning, Pierce. Maggie, nice to see you again. Thank you both for coming," Bowman said warmly, and extended his hand. Maggie glanced over at Pierce and gave him a look that said, *What the hell is going on?*

Next to the massive stone fireplace, the dining table featured coffee, juices, and an assortment of pastries and fruit.

"Please help yourselves to coffee or something to eat before we start," Bowman offered.

Four chairs had been pulled around in a loose circle on the mezzanine.

Bowman was all smiles. "Another perfect winter day in Miami. It's still pleasant enough so I thought we could sit outside," he said and sat back in his chair, casually crossing his legs.

Bowman cleared his throat and launched into a lengthy overview of his company's current operations and financial condition. He presented the advantages to both sides of a structured settlement. His thirty-minute overture ended without a single interruption.

Pierce glanced to his right at Maggie. Her face conveyed the obvious—she wasn't drinking the Kool-Aid.

At the end of Bowman's proposal, Dunn added, "The structured payout schedule and interest payments are going to yield a better return than you could realize from a lump sum payment."

Maggie's nose wrinkled as if their proposal had a foul odor. She trusted Evan Dunn even less than she did Bowman. She could see Bowman coming from a mile away. Evan Dunn was polished and much better at hiding his true intentions.

Bowman stood up. "Would anyone like a glass of champagne?"

Pierce couldn't help but glance at his watch. It seemed a little early to start with the booze.

"No, thank you," he said.

"Maggie?"

"Maggie frowned. "No, I'm good."

"I'm good too," Dunn said, even though Bowman never offered.

Pierce appeared to be weighing the proposal. "Frankly, there's also much more risk associated with the structured settlement," he said.

Bowman shoved a raspberry macaroon in his mouth and washed it down with champagne. "Risk? What risk? You have a settlement agreement that you could enforce in court if we're one day late on the payment."

"I'd rather not have to chase you for a payment."

"Chase me?" Bowman shrugged. "I'm not going anywhere, except to get another glass of champagne."

"Pierce, this is a good faith offer," Dunn interjected. "We could simply file a petition with the bankruptcy court to extend payment terms."

"Exactly." Bowman nodded, followed by another raspberry macaroon and another slurp of champagne to wash it down.

Maggie scrunched her mouth to the side and posed like she was actually considering Dunn's point. "Under a bankruptcy scenario, you'll wind up owing a lot more than $500 million."

Bowman's eyebrows arched in great doubt. "How do you figure?"

Maggie was trying to get under Bowman's skin and get him to slip up to reveal his true intention. "Because if we leave here today without an agreement, we hit the gas and move on to the main event. At trial you can bet your ass that the jury is going to award us more than $500 million."

Bowman was too cagey and looked smugly at Maggie. "If we go to trial, I could wind up owing nothing."

Maggie took the defensive answer for what it was. "If there was any chance of that happening, you wouldn't be so willing to fork over $500 million. Bankruptcy isn't a walk in the park. You're going to have to contend with a creditors' committee and bankruptcy trustee looking over your shoulder, watching your every move, and reporting back to the court. That's not an ideal situation for you, Ben."

Bowman looked at Maggie sideways and waved his hand dismissively.

Maggie looked at his face. She didn't get the reaction she was hoping for, so she took on a decidedly less business-like tone. "You have to realize by now that yours is a suicide run. Sometimes, you have a shot. It might be a long shot, but it's a shot, nonetheless. So, you take it. That's not the case here. You've got no chance of winning. Free piece of advice, Ben . . . put your dick away. This isn't a measuring contest you can win."

Bowman's eyes widened, and he thrust his chin out, "Excuse me?"

"Sorry. Slip of the tongue, but you get my drift," she said dismissively.

Pierce leaned back in his chair, watching Maggie's little dance.

Dunn frowned at the verbal sparring. "We're not anxious. We're simply exploring the possibility of a settlement that could work for both sides."

Pierce held no illusions that Bowman and Dunn were there in good faith to hammer out a fair settlement. Their change of heart and sense of urgency was something to consider. It clearly sent a message. There was, however, a famous saying among trial lawyers, "A bad settlement is better than a good trial." Just because they were suddenly disinclined to roll the dice on a jury verdict didn't mean that $700 million paid out over ten years wasn't a good offer. It was too much money to walk away from.

Pierce nodded, projecting his lower lip in a manner that suggested he might have a solution. "I think I have a middle ground," he said. "One that lets you spread out the payments over ten years; *and* addresses our concerns regarding having to take on additional risk."

Bowman's ears perked up. "I'm listening."

"We can accept your terms, provided you back it with a letter of credit," Pierce said. "If you default on any of the payments, we can present the letter of credit to the bank, and we're paid in full. You become the bank's problem, not ours."

A letter of credit to secure the balance of the settlement amount would cost Bowman an additional $45 million in cash. Bowman stood up and paced around the mezzanine. He alternated between muttering to himself and thinking out loud.

"If we have to come out of pocket $95 million, I'm going to have to lay off some employees," Bowman complained bitterly.

Pierce let him twist for a moment before giving him the final push that he needed. "It'll be a lot fewer employees than if you have to come up with $500 million all at once."

It only took Bowman five more seconds to blow a gasket. With all his real estate holdings and assets, the thought that Pierce would insist on a letter of credit never crossed his mind. $95 million was more than Bowman wanted to spend or ever thought he would have to pay, but it was still much less than $500 million. He continued to pace along the mezzanine. His eyes were squinted, his forehead wrinkled in a deep frown. The letter of credit presented another obstacle beyond its significant cost. The bank would then be on the hook for the balance of the payment owed if he defaulted. They would undoubtedly keep a close watch on his deposits and monitor all his transactions. Any attempt by Bowman to move money out of the country would raise warning flags. He suspected that one of the conditions for the credit instrument would be that he agrees to always maintain a sufficient amount of money on deposit to cover the bank's exposure. He would have to scrap part of his original plan that called for moving his cash deposits out of the country slowly to avoid notice. This new wrinkle would require a change in tactics. He would still transfer his real estate holdings to an irrevocable trust to shield them from creditors. However, he would need help to move his cash. Someone on the inside of the bank would have to be paid off to manage the wire of $2.74 billion before anyone noticed that Bowman had emptied his accounts. Since international wires could take a few days to complete, as a precautionary measure Bowman would need to first wire his entire fortune to a friendly bank in the U.S. before sending it on to Zurich. Once the wire was accepted, there was nothing the bank could do to reverse it. By the time the bank got a court order freezing his account, Bowman's funds would be in a Swiss bank.

Bowman looked at Dunn, who up to that point had done nothing to back Pierce off his latest demand. His weak, passive-aggressive posturing only fortified what Pierce and Maggie already suspected. They had no appetite for a full-blown trial.

Bowman turned his back and took a step to walk away, giving the impression that they'd reached an impasse, and the meeting was over. Pierce locked eyes with Maggie and silently told her to sit tight, they had him. Maggie gave Pierce a nod. She had picked up on Bowman's classic tells as well. He had one obvious weakness. Money. He loved it too much to risk losing more of it on a bad jury verdict. The Texas jury verdict that had ordered a cable company to pay $7 billion in punitive damages to the family of an eighty-three-year-old woman murdered in her home by one of their cable technicians had him running scared. Pierce would undoubtedly use that as a measuring stick for the jury. If a cable company's gross negligence resulted in a verdict of $7 billion in punitive damages for one eighty-three-year-old woman, Bowman didn't want to gamble on a jury award, *especially* if it decided that Lighthouse was negligent and liable for thousands of murdered victims.

Bowman stopped and swore quietly under his breath. He turned, glaring at Pierce, moving towards him as he spoke. "Never in a million years did I ever think I would be in a position where someone could bend me over and fuck me like this."

"Don't get it twisted, Ben," Maggie snapped, still baiting him. "If you settle, you'll still have a hell of a lot of money left when this is over."

Bowman was fuming. Pierce could see the fire in his eyes.

"This is a bunch of bullshit, Evangelista, and you know it. You represented that $500 million would get it done."

Pierce maintained a calm demeanor, even when Bowman pointed his finger inches from his chest.

"Like I said earlier, your counteroffer substantially increases our risk. You changed the terms, not me. I could have simply refused to consider your counter, but instead I offered you a solomonic solution."

"Another $45 million isn't exactly splitting the baby."

Maggie turned to Pierce. "He seems pretty trustworthy to me."

Bowman nodded, distracted, not picking up on the sarcasm in Maggie's voice. He was deep in thought as he looked out over the hotel's world-famous pool below, and out over the golf course in the distance.

Pierce and Maggie didn't say another word. It was Bowman's move.

After a few minutes, he blew out a breath in frustrated surrender. "Fuck it."

Maggie arched an eyebrow. "Fuck it?"

"Yeah, fuck it," he repeated, before reluctantly turning to Dunn. "Write up the settlement."

Bowman turned to Pierce and Maggie and spit out the words like they were poison. "We have a deal."

Chapter Fifty-Five

Coral Gables, Florida

A small group of friends were waiting inside Fleming's Prime Steakhouse & Wine Bar to celebrate. When Pierce pulled up to the valet, he saw Hernan Mas standing outside the restaurant's door by himself smoking a cigar. Even from twenty feet away, he could see the displeased look on his face. After turning over the keys, Pierce walked over.

"You coming inside?" Pierce asked.

"In a minute," he said. "Everyone is inside waiting for you."

Pierce looked at Hernan's body language and could see that he was unhappy. "What's up? It seems like there's something on your mind?"

Hernan was aware that he had almost no control over his temper, so it was his habit to keep things brief when he was upset and talking to someone he liked. He flicked the ashes from his cigar and squinted up at the moon. "Nothing really. . ."

The chill in his mood was obvious. Normally, Hernan would have greeted him with a hug or a slap on the back.

Pierce tilted his head to the side. "Let's cut to the chase, brother. Something is clearly bothering you. You're out here instead of inside, so there's obviously something you want to get off your chest."

Hernan had never quit anything in his life and was having difficulty understanding why Pierce agreed to settle and let Bowman off the hook. "*Whyyyy*!" Hernan drew out the word as he shook his head. "You had everything you needed to bury this guy, if you had taken this all the way to trial."

Pierce offered him a tight smile. He could see that his friend needed to unload.

The expression on Hernan's face changed from mild curiosity to great disappointment. "You might have gotten ten times what you wound up settling for." Hernan took a puff from his cigar. "We risked a lot by going down to Mexico and spying on the cartel's operation," he snapped, his tone dripping with disapproval.

Pierce gave Hernan a curious look. Over their twenty-year friendship, Pierce had never known him to fixate on money. There was something else behind this. "We considered that possibility before agreeing to settle. There's no denying that we might have walked away with a jury verdict in the billions."

Hernan stared at Pierce for an uncomfortably long moment. "In all the years we've known each other, I've never known you to back away from a fight. You had this guy."

Pierce was surprised by Hernan's genuine resentment. "Give me more credit. I didn't exactly let him go. He's $700 million poorer."

Hernan let out a long-frustrated sigh. "You could have gotten more."

Pierce felt a twinge of guilt. "I could have gotten a bigger jury verdict, and still walked away with less."

"How do you figure?"

"He would have appealed a jury verdict, for starters."

Hernan shrugged his shoulders and gave him a nod to go on.

Pierce ticked off several reasons. His logic was sound, and he finished with the simple fact that the appeal would buy Bowman the time he needed to liquidate assets, move his money offshore, and run to the bankruptcy courts for protection to shield whatever assets that remained in the country.

"Then why didn't he do that?"

"I'm sure he considered it," Pierce said. "But my guess is that he preferred to have this matter settled, and behind him, same as us. He would have spent the next few years fighting to keep his money and looking over his shoulder."

Pierce patted Hernan on the back. "$700 million is going to make a world of difference; and help fund a lot of programs for immigrant families."

The faces like pictures in an album of the men, women, and children as they were marched into the HemaMex facility at gunpoint sliced through the curtains of Hernan's mind. Then followed the contorted dead bodies as they were loaded onto trucks. Never had so much blood flowed with so little accountability. The sound of a car revving its engine as it drove by broke his concentration. He glared at nothing in particular and murmured, "He gets to walk away with a few bumps and bruises. No one should be able to operate with impunity. He got off easy."

Pierce nodded in agreement, mystified by the flaws in the criminal justice system. "There's no denying that. He won't be criminally prosecuted for what happened in Mexico." Pierce looked at his watch. It was 7:36 p.m. "Why don't we go inside?"

Hernan hesitated before answering. "I'm not in much of a mood to celebrate."

"No one is saying you have to celebrate. Let's just go inside and share a meal with our friends and loved ones, and all raise a glass to Mo."

Hernan wrestled with his thoughts for a moment, then put them away. The horrible images wouldn't go far, and they were sure to return to visit him later in his dreams like they always did. He waved his cigar in a manner that said all sins are forgiven. As he put it out in the ashtray, he caught a glimpse of his fractured reflection in the window. After thirty years on the force, he thought that by now, he would have developed a thicker skin, or better coping strategies and responses for dealing with emotional wounds resulting from senseless deaths. Hernan nodded to himself and took a deep breath before going inside.

* * *

The hostess was dressed in a black dress that flattered her sinuous curves. She smiled and cast an admiring glance at Pierce as her eyes swept up and down.

"Hello," Pierce said. "Evangelista. We have a reservation."

She briefly glanced down at her monitor, then raised her pair of perfectly shaped brows. "Yes, you're in the private room in the back," she said warmly. "Please follow me."

The smell of food on the tables as she led Pierce and Hernan to their party was almost overpowering. Hernan turned and craned his neck to see what some of the other patrons had ordered.

With the turn of the door handle, she gestured them inside with a sweep of her arm. The hostess gave Pierce the look most women did, like she wanted to have *him* for dinner. "Please let me know if you need anything at all." This time, her smile was filled with promise.

Pierce glanced at her name tag. "Thank you, Petra. I'll be sure to do that." He smiled back. After months of quarantine, he couldn't remember the last time he flirted with someone.

Everyone was already there. Senator Amanda Cortez and Ana Rodriguez were seated in the corner, cheeks flashing pink, laughing, and sipping wine. Dode had flown in that morning to join the celebration. She was seated between J.C. and Yamilet.

Maggie waved at the server, who filled glasses of champagne. Pierce held up his glass. "Let's raise a glass to our beloved friend, Mo, who improved our lives in many ways."

When every glass was lifted, he continued. "I'm reminded of something Mo used to say. I don't think he came up with it. In fact, I'm almost sure he borrowed it from one of his favorite TV shows."

Everyone chuckled.

"To our collective wounds of war, long may they remind us of the cost of everything we've won. Mo, we will remember you always. Death ends a life . . . not a relationship."

Pierce took a sip, then closed his eyes.

They spent the rest of the evening drinking, laughing, and taking turns telling stories about the great lawyer, mentor, and friend, Moses Black. The stories continued until 1:00 a.m., three hours past the restaurant's normal closing time.

* * *

The next morning, red-eyed, unshaven, and with steam flowing from a paper coffee cup, Pierce settled into the two-hour drive to Hutchinson Island. Maggie sat next to him in the passenger seat, drifting in and out while nursing a nasty hangover.

"Wake up. We're almost there." Pierce nudged Maggie.

Maggie frowned theatrically. "I don't see why this couldn't have waited until tomorrow."

Pierce flashed a smug *I told you so* grin. "I warned you to ease up on the champagne."

After six months of fourteen-hour days and seven-day work weeks, once the wire for the first $50 million hit their trust account and the letter of credit was delivered, Maggie wanted to blow off some steam. She glanced out the window to her right and noticed a marquee sign that featured their law firm's name - Sullivan & Swayze LLC.

"Does the firm have an office here?" Maggie asked.

Pierce nodded. "We opened a small satellite office in Jensen Beach when one of our partners decided to semi-retire and move up here."

"How far are we away from Mo's place?"

"About fifteen minutes. Hutchinson Island is just over the two causeways up ahead."

Moments later, a security guard waved them through a large and impressive archway. The entrance to the exclusive community resembled a smaller version of the famous Arc de Triomphe de l' Étoile at the west end of the Champs-Élysées in Paris.

Mo's three-story home in South Hutchinson was nestled between the Atlantic Ocean and the Indian River. Maggie gawked at the splendor of the mansion with unmatched views of the crashing surf to the east, and the Indian River across Florida State Road A1A on the west.

Pierce carried the urn containing Mo's ashes as they walked past the infinity pool that seemed to melt into the Atlantic Ocean, down the private boardwalk to the secluded beach directly from the lower terrace. The air carried a salt whiff of the high tide.

They traipsed across the expanse of white sand beach that ended at the ocean's edge thirty yards away. The sky was clear, except for a few scattered clouds. The breeze coming off the ocean rustled the sea oats on the dunes.

When they arrived at the shoreline, Pierce sobbed and laughed at the same time as he told stories of when he and Mo had first met, and of their subsequent adventures and mishaps together. Maggie's tears streamed down her anguished face as they scattered Mo's ashes. It was a somber moment. When it was done, they spent the rest of the afternoon sitting on the beach in quiet reflection until the sun sank into the western sky.

* * *

The last glimmers of red sunlight illuminated the terrace. Maggie sat in a settee watching the cluster of boats rocking gently in the river. Pierce joined her, holding a large white cardboard box and a bottle of wine.

"Are you hungry? I ordered us a pizza," he said, opening the box.

Maggie reached for a slice. "Thanks."

Pierce uncorked the bottle and took two wineglasses from the small bar.

They ate their pizza and sipped the wine in reflective silence until it became awkward.

Maggie poured more white wine into both glasses, and broke the ice by asking, "So what time tomorrow are we heading back?"

"After breakfast," Pierce said. "There's something I'd like to talk to you about."

He looked exhausted, sad, and troubled. Maggie could tell by his tone and expression that something in addition to Mo's passing was occupying his thoughts. "Okay." she nodded. "What is it?"

Pierce cleared his throat and said, "You know Mo had no family."

She shook her head. "I didn't know, but I suspected. He never mentioned having anyone."

"He was very fond of you."

Maggie dabbed at her eyes with a paper napkin. "It was mutual."

Pierce stood and walked to the edge of the terrace. The moon floated over the Indian River, casting a shimmering wake that danced across the current. Pierce got stiff, and his legs suddenly felt rubbery. "Mo left this house to me in his will."

"It's more of a palace than a house," Maggie remarked.

Pierce nodded in agreement. "Mo really loved this place. It was his sanctuary . . . I'd hate to sell it."

Maggie stared out at the horizon, then back at the water. In the distance, she heard the surf as the tide rolled in. "I'm sure you'll have no trouble renting it. If you decide to hold on to it." Her eyes swept over floating staircases connecting all three floors, the chef's kitchen, the tasteful furnishings in the great room and settled on the exquisite painting hanging just above the marble fireplace. "It's really a beautiful place. Who knows, you may want to move up here in the future."

Pierce smiled and replied, "I was thinking that you could work in our Jensen Beach office and live here."

Maggie looked at Pierce to see if he was serious. There was a long pause before she responded, "I can't afford this place."

"The house is paid for. All you'd have to cover are the utilities."

"What about our cases?"

"You're working remotely half the time, anyway. On days when you have hearings in Miami, you can drive down."

She stood up, holding her wine, and considered the offer. "I was planning on letting Yami and Giovanny stay with me until she could get on her feet."

Pierce smiled and made a sweeping motion across the house with his arm. "There's plenty of room here."

"You'd be okay with that?"

"Mo would have been more than okay with it. He would have insisted on it if he was still with us."

They clinked glasses and Maggie said, "Mo will always be with us."

Epilogue

Lowry Hill, Minneapolis, One Week Later

Steve Erickson sat in the office he kept in his Minneapolis home. After the U.S. Attorney indicted him on five counts of crimes related to child pornography, child sex trafficking and soliciting sex with minors, the news of Erickson's alleged exploits broke; and the senator could no longer safely travel to his downtown office.

His colleagues on both sides of the aisle acted *ever so shocked.* "The Steve I served with worked hard on behalf of his constituents and the country. I'm shocked and saddened to learn of these reports," said Senate Majority Leader Claude Littlefield in an interview.

"It seems so out of character for Steve. I just never could imagine that he'd be involved in anything like this," said Democratic California Senator Maria Elena Rubio.

Erickson had no idea where the allegations came from or how the fabricated evidence that he was engaged in sexually molesting four boys had wound up on his computer.

News of an FBI investigation was the final blow that put his Senate seat permanently out of reach. It seemed surreal how one false story instantly put an end to a once promising political career. No amount of campaign damage control strategy or political spin could put out this raging dumpster fire. The support of the party disappeared overnight. Even his good friend, Senator Littlefield, had stopped returning his calls.

Erickson had barely slept. Even after the FBI tracked the incriminating evidence to a notorious hacker in Russia and dropped all charges against him, he could never get back what had been taken from him. His reputation was forever stained. His political career was over.

Steve Erickson was no longer running for political office. His new objective was about survival.

* * *

Steve's body tensed when he heard a knock on the door. He swallowed and finally managed to say, "Come in."

Pierce opened the door and walked through it. "Good morning, senator. Your wife was kind enough to let me in. I appreciate you taking the time to see me."

"Steve, please. I'm no longer a senator." Erickson had a curious expression. "Senator Cortez called and insisted that I take this meeting. She was one of only a handful of my colleagues that bothered to call me after the U.S. Attorney dismissed the charges. The senator spoke highly of you."

"I'm happy to hear that."

"So, tell me what is it that you want to meet about?" Erickson's tone radiated an air of edginess.

"May I sit?"

Erickson nodded towards the chair.

After some awkward chitchat, Pierce said, "I know who was responsible and why you were set up."

Erickson was surprised. His face was ashen. Pierce's declaration was met with a grimace and a question, "Why would anyone want to set me up?"

"We recently settled a lawsuit against Lighthouse. Investigators working with my firm came across some information when we were looking into Mr. Bowman."

Erickson shook his head sadly.

"Bowman used you to negotiate an Immunity Agreement," Pierce said with a nod. "He gave you up in exchange for immunity from prosecution for his involvement in the massacres in Mexico."

Erickson's face was flushed, and his fists were clenched tight. "Ben couldn't have been involved in that."

Pierce didn't answer right away. After a long pause, he said, "The cartel was behind the murders. But they sold the blood exclusively to Lighthouse."

Erickson took a moment to process what he had learned. With a sour, confused look on his face, he said, "It doesn't make sense. I supported the amnesty bill."

Pierce nodded in agreement. "I'll give you the short version. When the bill didn't pass and with you trailing in the polls, you became expendable."

Erickson gave Pierce a hard stare. "You don't have any proof of that."

He was right. Pierce didn't have any proof, but he *had* given an explanation of sorts that Bowman needed to sacrifice someone close to him to appear believable. Then he continued to connect all the dots that led to one logical conclusion. "Only one person benefited from your indictment, and that was Ben Bowman. He used a specialist to hack your computer."

Erickson was caught completely off-guard. "How can you possibly know this?"

Pierce looked at Erickson with an unwavering stare. "I have a very reliable source."

"If I had a nickel for every time . . ." Erickson smiled but in a way that was devoid of humor.

Pierce reached into his jacket pocket and handed him a flash drive.

Erickson took it and stared at it. His eyebrows arched with great suspicion. "What's this?"

"All the proof you'll need to make Ben Bowman pay for setting you up," Pierce said.

"You just finished telling me he has an Immunity Agreement."

Pierce shook his head. "The Agreement only covers what happened in Mexico. It doesn't protect him from what's on the drive."

Erickson held up the drive and inspected it closely, as if he could see what was on it without loading it onto his computer. "What's on it?"

"Only one way to find out."

Erickson let out a tired sigh and closed his eyes. "I've already been burned for having shit on my computer that didn't belong to me."

Pierce shrugged. "Either way, this information is getting into the U.S. Attorney's hands. I wanted to give you an opportunity to play a small role in bringing Bowman to justice, since he was responsible for ruining your life."

Erickson took a deep breath and plugged the flash drive into the computer. He scrolled through countless federal loan documents. "What exactly does this all mean?"

Pierce detected some tension in Erickson's voice. He was facing a very tough but ultimately easy decision. "The documents prove that Ben Bowman defrauded the U.S. government out of millions of dollars."

Erickson glanced at the dates and frowned. "These loans happened years ago."

"The statute of limitation begins to run when the government discovers the fraud. Mr. Bowman can still be prosecuted, and he's looking at twenty years in prison."

Pierce slid a card across Erickson's desk. "This is the number of an eager U.S. Attorney clamoring to take this case to a grand jury."

Now Erickson looked really uncomfortable. "What if I want to stay out of it?"

"Ben Bowman will still stand trial. You can stand on the sideline if you prefer. No judgement," Pierce assured him.

Erickson shot him a dubious look. "I find that hard to believe. You came all this way."

Pierce smiled at him, didn't speak right away, and then finally said, "Growing up, my mom wanted me to learn that there often was more than one way to solve a problem or react to a particular situation. People could have different opinions. They could see the world through different lenses, and they could all be right. It was simply a matter of different perspectives and preferences. She would use the ice-cream parlor Baskin Robbins to illustrate her point."

Erickson nodded. "Please continue."

"When I was a kid, Baskin Robbins would advertise a wide selection of flavors. Thirty-one, to be exact. Baskin Robbins claimed to always have thirty-one flavors to choose from. So, whenever my family members argued, my mom looked at both sides and settled things by saying 'that's why Baskin Robbins has thirty-one flavors'."

Erickson's shoulders sagged. He had no fight left in him. Finally, he managed a feeble, "So, if I sit on the sidelines and do nothing . . . I guess that would make me vanilla."

Pierce considered how he was handling all this and smiled. "Nothing wrong with vanilla." He looked at his watch and stood up. "If I leave now, I can still catch my flight." He went to the door and paused with his hand on the knob. "Thank you for agreeing to see me. The flash drive is a gift. Feel free to do with it as you please."

Erickson gave him an analytical look, then cocked his head to the side. "I'm curious Pierce, if you were in my shoes, what flavor would you choose?"

There was a twinkle in his eye. The right corner of Pierce's mouth curved upward, showing the slightest hint of a mischievous smile. "I've always been partial to Rocky Road."

And then he was gone.

Erickson stared at the card that Pierce had given him for a long time. Finally, he picked up the phone and dialed the number.

About the Author

Luis Figueredo was born and raised in the Bronx, New York. He completed his undergraduate degree in History from Brandeis University in Massachusetts and earned his law degree from Harvard Law School.

During his legal profession, Luis developed a nationwide practice representing a diverse group of clients that include municipalities, national trade associations, corporations, real estate developers, and Indian Tribes.

www.ingramcontent.com/pod-product-compliance
Lightning Source LLC
Chambersburg PA
CBHW031523150726
47990CB00001B/42